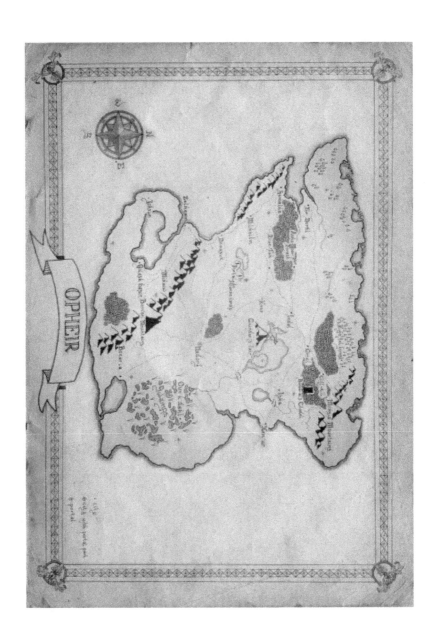

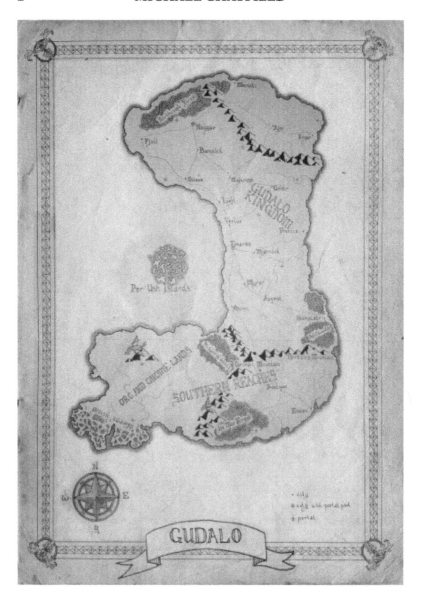

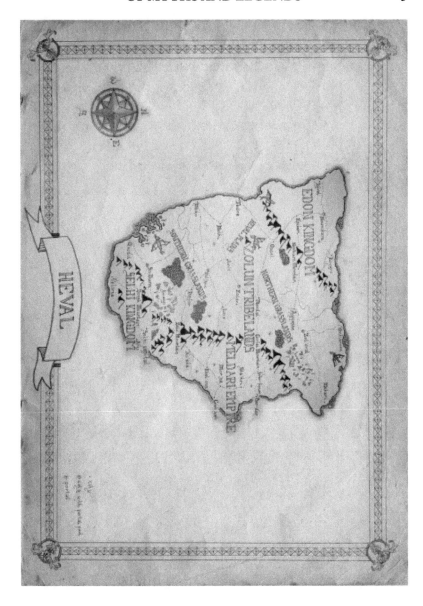

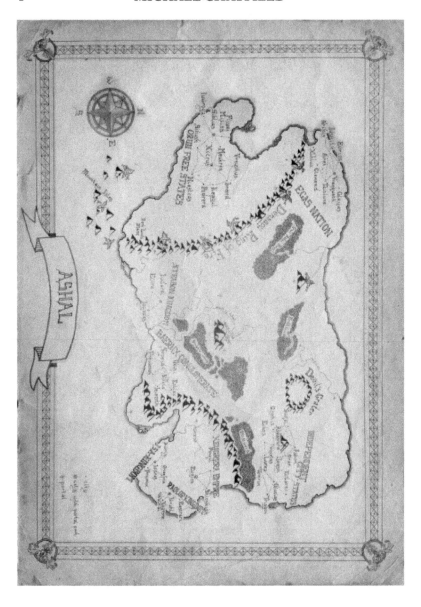

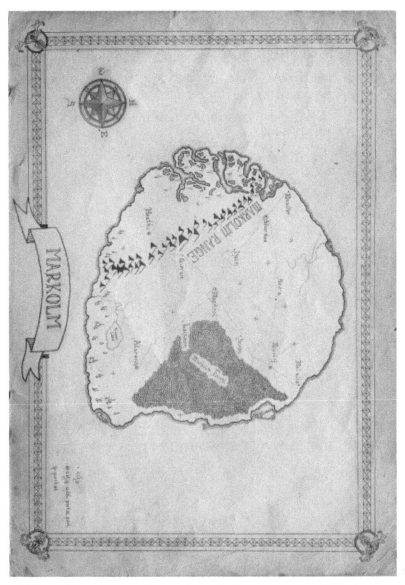

Want a bigger map of Emerilia and the continents? Check out
http://theeternalwriter.deviantart.com/
Character Sheet is located in the back of the book for reference.

Emerilia

Of Myths and Legends

Chapter 1: Welcome to Emerilia

Dave's Mirror of Communication activated, receiving a message being broadcasted from Emerilia.

"All Stone Raiders are to immediately return to Terra. All members of the Terra Alliance are to move into readiness positions, ready for immediate deployment. This is not a drill!" Josh's voice cut through the silence that had descended over Party Zero as they stopped, looking out over the asteroid and the heavens above.

"You heard the man!" Deia yelled. All of Party Zero turned and rushed toward the portal to the ice planet, their bodies mere blurs.

None of them talked as they rushed from the asteroid to the ice planet, and then through Nal to Pandora's Box through the power facility and into Terra. Bob had taken a separate portal in Pandora's Box to reach the *Datskun*.

Automatons and carts were the only things in the sky. Massive barges carrying troops from across Emerilia were moved to and from the teleport pads. The city streets had quickly been cleared by Shard. The businesses and people of Terra, as well as their visitors, looked in shock as the military units that had been stuck in training or were being called up rushed into Terra.

No one was allowed in the sky; Shard took over the automatons to move everyone without having any accidents.

People who had been relaxing in the taverns now rushed through the city in squads, their eyes hard as they moved toward their barracks.

Party Zero called up their armor. Everyone was in a state of shock with all the movements going on.

"Party Zero, there is a cart outside waiting for you. Please board it. Steve, I could use your help in organizing the movements of the city." Shard's voice came from overhead Party Zero.

"Linking in," Steve said as Party Zero moved toward the waiting carts. As soon as they were secured, the carts took off toward Stone Raider towers.

Dave found Deia's hand, holding it as they rushed forward.

***

Across Emerilia, the same scene took place. With the interfaces and party chat, information passed at an alarming rate.

The message was simple and terrifying.

The portals had opened and creatures from the other planes were now descending. With them were creatures that were part of the Myths and Legends event.

People checked their weapons. City guard and military units were put on full readiness as the city's defenses were checked. The horns of the elves were heard across Markolm as the military units within their beautiful towers marched out to the city walls in crisp, orderly lines. Old Alliance agreements were checked over and units were sent to Terra as per the Terra Alliance agreement.

Tribes checked their defenses and reached out to one another in aid.

The ground around the dwarven mountains shook with the sound of drumbeats, the dwarven warbands called to service.

Within those mountains, bellows worked harder as weapons were checked and armor was fitted. Dwarves donned their armor, moving into their warbands and War Clans. Artillery was checked and tested.

In the north of Opheir, War Clans that had been based out of the Mithsia Mountains, training behind their massive defensive wall, now moved out of the mountains and to preset positions.

War drums filled the Kufo'tel forest rolling down from the Mithsia Mountains as horns from the Kufo'tel elves called the people back to their city in the forest. Retired and reserve rangers donned their armor and moved to full readiness.

Several War Clans and supporting Kufo'tel elves gathered themselves together, marching out of the defended land and toward Cliff-Hill.

Cliff-Hill had grown into a massive city now, larger than even Omal. Their defenses were checked as they manned their walls and watched for danger.

Bob watched this all, a solemn look on his face as he checked the action logs that showed what the empire had done.

"Those mother fuckers," Bob said with a cold voice. "They opened almost all of the portals that hadn't been discovered and random ones that have to link Emerilia to the other systems containing aggressive species. Twelve races in total, even races that were closed off due to having low numbers or because they unbalanced Emerilia before. They also spammed the damn spawn points. Do they just not care anymore?"

Bob went through the information and frowned. He typed out a quick message with all that he knew, sending it on to Party Zero, Fire, and Water. He stood up from his chair and headed back toward the portal that connected to Pandora's Box.

"I might not be able to do anything on the main stage of Emerilia yet, but I can support them from the rear with what we're doing in the Nal system and Moonbase," Bob said, his voice hard and his eyes cold. He would take over the various projects that were ongoing to take some of the pressure off Party Zero and the others.

***

Josh looked at the message he had received from Bob. His lined face grew darker and he quickly shared it with the other leaders in the Alliance and Lucy, who would share it outward to everyone.

"Okay, well, it looks like nearly everyone is here." Josh looked to everyone in the room. A few were missing but they would be there shortly.

"All of the undiscovered portals across Emerilia, as well as a number of spawn points, have become active. We've got creatures from all of the different realms and planes now on Emerilia. Most of them are around cities. I was going to call a meeting later today anyway to address something else. It seems that there were a number of sub-quests connected to the event of Myths and Legends. Most of the disruptions and quests that have been given out in the last couple of months dealt with creatures and people who were released for the event. Thankfully, with our people being out in the world, a number of these quests were dealt with. However, now it looks like it will be hard to focus on just these quests as we have to deal with this new threat. I suggest to everyone that they should first secure their cities. The lands of Emerilia might not be safe in the near future to roam around in."

"If we lock ourselves up in our cities, how will we support ourselves? This isn't a long-term solution," one of the leaders said.

"It is not, but with all these creatures and people that are now roaming Emerilia. We don't know enough about them or what is going to happen. It is best if people hole up, train to their limit and be ready for what's about to come, whatever that might be," Josh said.

"Do we have a plan to deal with this?" another asked.

"We first need to find out where these portals are. This is something that the various scouting elements of the Alliance are looking into. Once we know their locations, our aim is to move from portal to portal, set up bases that will stand in the way of the portal and its exit, stopping anything from exiting," Josh said.

How I wish we could use that shield that Dave has come up with for the portals. If we were to show it off, it would show that we know how to use portal technology and the Jukal might not take too kindly to that. And if we blatantly destroy the portals, then we will get penalized heavily.

Barring the use of Dave's technology, they would have to do it the hard way: fight whatever came through those portals and hold them off as Emerilia dealt with their own issues before they could even think about heading through these portals to try to secure the locations on the other side.

"If they are invading, have the defensive castles like the ones surrounding Goblin Mountain appeared?" another asked.

"We have had sightings of the castles. We have teams ready to move to these locations in order to take over these castles before others get there," Lucy said.

"We only have a dozen onos at our disposal right now. We need more from the Aleph before we can put one at every castle location so we can support the people who are capturing these places. We're working with the Aleph to increase the production of onos at this time," Florence said, having rushed over from Verlun.

"Make sure that your forces are ready. We will hold thirty percent of our forces here. The rest will be capturing castles, or they will be assisting in clearing up any quests that have been left open in the cities as part of this alliance. If we get all those quests sorted out, we should flush out some more creatures from the event, securing our towns and quickly gaining experience to level up people." It was clear that Josh's words weren't a request but an order.

***

Party Zero all heard a similar briefing from Esa, who stood in front of a number of groups that had been picked out from the fighting forces—Stone Raiders and other guilds that had joined the Alliance.

"You are all to act as capture parties. This means that you will be moved across Emerilia in order to move to castles that have been located around various active portals. You will move in, place a drop pad and begin capturing the area. An ono will be shifted to your location to allow reinforcements in to support you. We need these castles. If the forces exiting the portals take these castles, they will have a firm beachhead into Emerilia, making it easier for them to launch attacks and move in more forces to Emerilia.

"Each of you has been sent a location. All fees are waived from the onos with these tokens." Esa threw out the tokens, her hand blurring as they arrived in front of the different parties. "We don't have time to wait, so move out! Party Zero, come and see me!" Esa yelled as people charged out.

A space was made for Party Zero as they moved to the front. Esa invited them to a private chat.

"Malsour, Induca—talk to your family, see if they can put down some drop pads for us. Dave, whatever plans you have to make those castles mobile, I want it sorted out and soon. Take whatever resources you need from the guild to make it a reality. We need them mobile yesterday," Esa said.

Dave nodded and looked to Steve and Malsour.

"Deia, I know that Party Zero is the strongest group that we have; you decide which locations you want to take, I'm sharing with you a map that will update with where people are being sent. I want you to go for the locations that are the farthest from an ono," Esa said.

"We can split up if needed to put down the drop pads." Deia looked to Party Zero, who nodded.

"Good. Then I don't think that there's anything else I need to tell you. Good luck." Esa turned and left.

"Dave, what are you going to need?" Deia asked. "Anna, find us a portal to go to."

"Just Steve and Malsour since we've pretty much got everything sorted out; we just need people to build the components. I'm going to send the list of things to the Aleph, dwarves, and the smithies under the Grahslagg Corporation. With the Stone Raiders' resources, we can speed this up so we can get the first castle ready in a few weeks. If I was willing to pull apart one of the first version destroyers, then I could get another two in a week." Dave sounded as though he was seriously considering it.

"Do you need to work on it or will you be coming with us?" Deia asked.

"I will be with you lot. We've gamed out the project—now it's just getting the prototype and working it out. Steve, get with Shard and Bob and start to run those simulations. Get Bob to contact Sato if he needs more assistance," Dave said.

"Done," Steve said.

"Okay, let's move. Anna, you find any potential locations?" Deia moved to the carts that were waiting for the remaining parties that were about to depart for the teleport pads.

"We've got two between the Gorlei Mountains and Aygasse on the Heval continent," Anna said.

"Steve," Deia said.

"Planning our route for the cart. It's going to be a hairy ride," Steve said.

Party Zero reached the carts. Already tens of them filled the skies, filled with other parties headed out.

"Carts my ass, these babies are strait up shattlecrafts right here!" Steve chortled before letting out a whoop of excitement.

Their carts took off, flying through the air at speeds that pushed them back into their chairs. Faint blurs and whirs went past as they missed other carts by mere inches. With the AIs controlling traffic, there wasn't a chance of collision but that didn't mean they weren't flying a hundred things through the sky at one time.

To any other sentient, it would have been complete madness and led to countless accidents.

They shot down toward a teleport pad. All traffic between teleport pads had been locked down for the use of the Terra Alliance. As one party rushed through, another location was immediately dialed up and another group would pass through.

The carts stopped just outside the teleport pad area. Party Zero rushed off, the portal changing locations. "Aygasse, Heval!" the controller yelled out.

Party Zero turned into streaks as they rushed through the area and into the teleport pad. They came out of an ono in Aygasse. Turning upward and charging into the sky, two way points appeared in the distance.

"Lox, Dave, Induca, Lucy, and Anna—move toward the second portal. The rest of you with me to the first portal," Deia said.

"Watch out." Induca's body changed as she extended into her Dragon form as they flew toward the second portal. Malsour also changed.

Two Dragons appeared in midair, Party Zero on top of them.

Induca and Malsour roared into the sky, stretching their wings as they pushed forward toward their way points.

Deia ignited the air behind Malsour to increase his speed. Jung Lee cast enhancing spells and pulled out Affinity spirits that moved around Malsour, aiding him. Malsour's speed surged, breaking through the wind with thunderclaps.

Deia glanced to Induca. Around her, Lucy's creations were supporting, as was Anna, whose sword whistled, guiding the air around Induca while a spell formation around Dave passed around Induca's body.

Induca's speed was even greater than Malsour's. Deia let out a breath of relief. The second location was farther away and she was hoping that Lox and his group would be the faster of the two. It seemed that her guess had been right.

She focused ahead as the wind howled. They left Aygasse behind as they passed over fields and forest, and rushed toward the south.

It wasn't long until Malsour spoke up. "I see the castles. They're around a ruin. The portal must be underneath it. Wait a minute—something is coming out." Malsour paused, taking a moment. "They look like Xelur soldiers to me."

"Shit, this one must be connected to the Xelur realm," Deia hissed between her teeth. She hadn't forgotten her fight with the reincarnated Xelur Demon Lord at Cliff-Hill.

"There are four castles around the ruins," Malsour continued.

"Jung Lee, you're the fastest of us—you get to the southern castle. Malsour and I will go to the east and western castles respectively. The rest of you take the northern castle," Deia said.

All of the party nodded in agreement.

It took them nearly twenty tense minutes before they reached the portal from Aygasse, a speed that would have made most people look at them in shock.

"Ready?" Gurren said to everyone as they prepared themselves.

"Go!" Deia yelled.

A red and gray streak shot off toward the south and west. Malsour banked toward the west while the remaining members of Party Zero jumped off and dove toward the northern castle that was below.

Fire Mana surged around Deia. She didn't even take the time to look back as she was wholly focused on the oncoming castle. The Xelur soldiers on the ground cried out at Deia. All of them looked different from the other; however, all of them seemed to be crying out in pain. Once they saw Deia, their pained cries turned to excitement and madness. These creatures survived off eating people's souls. Or the nanites that made up their bodies and the power that sustained them.

They had been a once powerful techno race; however, they had turned to fighting and in their decline, they had lost a great number of their power supplies. All of them naturally possessed nanites in their bodies. When they killed and consumed other's nanites, they would have great gains in power. They would attack and kill anyone not of their tribe for their nanites. All the races within the Jukal Empire used nanites in their bodies and were natural prey for the Xelur race.

When a portal opened to Emerilia, they quickly rushed through. However, the tribes that had been around the portal on the other side, upon seeing the portal open, had engaged in fighting one another, not willing to split up the spoils of Emerilia with any other.

Even those who had made it through the portal were fighting one another. This gave Party Zero the time they needed to rush toward the castles.

"We've secured the eastern tower," Lox said from the second group.

Deia's eyes widened before she nodded. She had thought that the speed Malsour displayed had been great but Induca had clearly defeated them in speed.

Deia slowed her progress as she reached the castle, using the full force of her Mana to slow herself. She cut down on her speed, quickly passing over the large walls, and headed into the inner castle. She flew through the halls and entered the area underneath the large tower that rose above the inner castle.

A status bar appeared, telling her that she was capturing the castle.

"Drop pad down in the north. Ono is here." Gurren sounded a bit shocked.

She pulled out a drop pad, quickly clicking it together and placing it on the ground in the middle of the area underneath the castle and right on the capture point in the center of the castle.

She stepped backward as the capture continued. "Drop pad down." A flash of light filled Deia's vision. An ono appeared in the place of the drop pad. A moment later, the ono's runes started to light up as a teleport pad connected to it.

"Drop pad down," Malsour said.

"Here as well," Jung Lee said.

The ono in Deia's castle connected to the teleport pad. It seemed that the moment it did, people flowed outward.

A man at the front looked around, locking eyes on Deia before he jogged over. "Esa told me to tell you to move to the next location."

"Thank you," Deia said. She switched back to the party chat. "Once you have people coming out of your onos, then go back to Terra. We'll regroup and head to the next location."

"Got it. We've got Ooinfa coming out of our portal. What you got over there?" Lox asked.

"Xelur," Gurren spat.

"Lovely," Lox said in a dark tone.

Deia passed through the ono and entered Terra once again. The rest of Party Zero did the same, quickly meeting up. It didn't take them long to find a new location to head toward as they repeated the process over again.

Chapter 2: A Change Overnight

Josh hadn't slept in hours. Thankfully he didn't need much of it with his high Endurance. However, the matters that had gone on in the last couple of hours weighed heavily on him.

There were a total of nearly thirty portals that had opened up across Emerilia. For twenty of them, the Terra Alliance had been fast enough to get a command of the surrounding citadels. Two of the portals had two of the invaders holding two citadels and the Alliance or people from Emerilia holding the other two. There were five with the invaders controlling three and one where the invading species had taken all of the citadels around the portal.

Nearly all of these citadels were under attack in some form or would be shortly.

The people of the Terra Alliance had come together. A few kingdoms had opted out at this time; it was expected that there would be a number that would leave as soon as things got tough. However, the great majority stayed, seeing that the Alliance would make them stronger when dealing with these threats.

Soldiers had swarmed through Terra and into these citadels that appeared all across Emerilia.

The various citadels fought against the forces in the areas around the portals, or fought other citadels that were quickly becoming strongholds for the invaders.

The invaders didn't just stay in the area around the portal. A great number of them, like the Galis, a race that lived in the air, only used the citadels to rest before they sped off across Emerilia.

People who had stayed outside of the defendable cities were now in a rush to create their own defenses or move toward the overpopulated cities. Anything that wasn't a city or town with defenses in place was being left behind.

He looked around the room there was the Stone Raider leadership as well as leaders from all of the major powers in the Terra Alliance.

Everyone was too tired to stand on much ceremony as they took their seats, looking to Lucy she started talking as the last person entered the room.

"It's clear that this is just starting. We've got nearly a dozen aggressive species pouring through those portals, and we're finding more and more creatures and sub-quests from the Myths and Legends event that are undermining our strength in various cities. We've got to build up Terra to feed, clothe, and house more people," Lucy said.

Koza cleared his throat. Everyone in the room looked to him with a questioning glance.

"The Aleph have many areas that we can't fully man. We have hired people in the past to work with us and seeing as we have this room and need more people, we will open up these opportunities to more people. We are also willing to help with the design and building of more places," Koza said.

There were relieved and agreeable murmurs from around the table.

"Thank you, Koza," Josh said, with a slight smile.

Koza simply nodded, as if it were nothing.

"We have also hired a new group of Dark mages who will be able to increase our ability to expand Terra and any other facilities that we make. I had other Dark mages work to place down drop pads in different locations around Terra. We need resources, crops—all those kinds of things to keep us going," Lucy said.

"It looks like this is going to turn into a battle of attrition more than anything," Dwayne said.

The other people in the room had bitter looks on their faces. If their people had to hide in cities to survive, then resources were going to get a lot scarcer. The production from farms would greatly decrease. They had plans in place but they hadn't thought that something on this scale would happen.

"The dwarves will also open their mountains," the dwarf from the dwarven war council said.

This was more shocking than the Aleph. Although the Aleph hadn't had really anyone new go into their cities, they weren't as well known as the dwarves.

They rarely let people into their cities other than for the dwarven tournament that was held in specially made arenas; the stores and various places around the tournament had been built by them. Few actually passed into the mountain.

"We also have a list of people we would like to meet and talk to." The dwarf shared a list to them all. There were names across the paper: famed blacksmiths, Dark mages, Earth mages, warriors, and battle mages.

"What do you want them for?" Josh asked.

"The blacksmiths we want to train higher if at all possible and give them a place to work that allows them to push their limits. Same for the Earth and Dark mages. We have an even deeper understanding of these two magics than the mage's college and guild." The dwarf looked to the representatives of these institutions. Both of them nodded in agreement. "The warriors and various other mages, we have many Weapons of Power—now is the time to use them. If the weapons agree with them, then they will be gifted a Weapon of Power to defend Emerilia and its people."

There had been rumors and talk that people in the dwarven tournament were pulled aside and given Weapons of Power. A great number of people, upon returning from the tournament, had greatly increased in their strength. Not many were willing to declare that they were holding Weapons of Power. Jealousy and greed were deadly sins. If someone who wanted these items heard that a weaker person had a Weapon of Power, they might kill them off to gain it.

A few had said they had Weapons of Power but out of respect for the dwarves they hadn't said where it had come from.

Now the dwarves were confirming these rumors. All of those around the table were a little stunned at the turn of events.

Josh secretly looked to them all. There seemed to be a sense of unity, of drive in the room. That they were in this together. After the dwarven war council leader spoke up, some other groups started to talk about their ultimate weapons. Instead of holding onto these trump cards that they might use at a later date to get greater standing in the Alliance, they were using them now to show their dedication to see this through.

Looks like this Alliance might work out.

***

"Get those cannons mounted!" a Beast Kin yelled over the roar of battle. People from all races ran around. Dwarves with their artillery cannons to the top of the inner citadel, getting mages to assist them in taking them to the roof of the central tower.

The walls had mages and warriors on them, unleashing their attacks on the writhing mass of green caterpillar-looking creatures.

These creatures were from the Erach race. Their nickname in the Jukal Empire was world devourers. These creatures had eaten everything that was on their home planet, from planet matter to other creatures and then once they had eaten everything on their planet, many went into hibernation and underwent a metamorphosis to absorb sunlight and various energies to support themselves.

They were about as large as a baseball and a foot long. They spat out a numbing and stunning agent, and they could burrow through the hardest of materials with enough time. They were currently coating the walls of the citadel that the Terra Alliance held, eating their way through as the defenders tried to lay down as many area of effect spells as possible.

There were hundreds of thousands of the creatures that had come through the portal like a flood, but they had been so focused on eating everything around the portal that the Alliance had been able to make a decent foothold in the surrounding citadels.

With all of the stored energy within them, the more mature Erach were able to unleash a green beam of light that could burrow through shields, barriers, and materials that lay in their path.

However, this energy, once burned up, would take days or weeks to regenerate; by killing these creatures with explosion spells, their power would actually erupt, destroying a large area. Otherwise, the soul-capturing runes across the walls would light up, capturing this potent power. With the death of every Erach, their power was unleashed on the world.

This, in turn, was drawn in by the hastily made runes, powering the few vault soul gems that the people of the Alliance held.

There weren't many soul gem constructs made by the Pandora's Box team. Their resources and time requirements for the constructs weren't small. However, it was clear that they couldn't let the Erach spread across Emerilia. The soul gem constructs at every citadel were growing faster and faster with all of this power being drawn into them.

Artillery spells howled overhead, raining death onto the Erach or creating spells that trapped the creatures for other spells to wipe them out.

It was chaos looking out upon the green caterpillars that charged toward the citadels. They fed off a person's energy—eating plants was good, but eating a Level 200 person? There was nothing that could compare to this treat.

Bob watched this and countless other battles even as he was within the moonbase, working on his own Altar of Rebirth. The other projects were all automated. He had even set up the asteroid mining facilities, shipping drills that had been used to create Terra through the portals and to the ice planet and the asteroids. There were factories and repair bots that would help to create the bases on both of those planets, as well as Jeeves, who was managing it all and moving resources between all the various locations to keep them running at optimal conditions.

"How did it come to this?" Bob asked himself. He had hoped to keep humanity alive, maybe to sneak them away and allow them another chance. With Emerilia becoming the entertainment of the Jukal Empire, it had become impossible. Now he had put all his hopes and dreams into Party Zero and the people he had come to know in order to overthrow the Jukal Empire. There was just no other option. However, with this goal in mind, all of these hardships had come up, from the event to the opening of portals across Emerilia.

This wasn't a game; it was genocide.

Just as it looked as though the citadel besieged by the Erach would fall, a rain of fiery arrows came from the sky, killing thousands of the tightly packed Erach.

Runes along the walls were changed, the stone and metal moving into the new formations. The Erach let out pained shrieks as the walls became cursed and acidic, burning and weakening the Erach.

Party Zero had arrived just in time; Gurren and Lox flew out of the inner citadel, rushing to the walls to help the defenders who had come face-to-face with the Erach that had made it inside the citadel.

With all of this killing, the power to the soul gem construct increased as it grew out of the inner citadel and spread to the walls.

Induca formed a massive fire wall that covered the worst fifty-meter-long stretch of the outer wall. Anna called down a storm spell that formed multiple tornadoes that covered a hundred-meter square area, moving across the battlefield, pulling Erach from the ground and cutting them apart with the sharp blades of air.

The other mages within the citadel unleashed their spells. The Erach's attack was held off and actually pushed back under this combined pressure.

It gave the dwarven artillery enough time to get into place. Their guns bellowed as they unleashed area of effect spells that would clear a fifty-meter area of Erach.

Bob was powerless in this battle, but he felt a bit of hope after seeing the Terra Alliance working together to save Emerilia.

***

Dave, Malsour, and Steve were all at the first southern citadel around Goblin Mountain. They were in the central castle underneath the main tower that extended into the sky.

None of them were talking as they worked. The rest of Party Zero was off acting as a reactive force: they would rush through teleport pads and onos, laying down massive damage to give the defenders or the attackers trying to take citadels some relief and hopefully allow them to hold on or enter the citadels to capture them.

It was madness, with the dozens of battlefields changing constantly. The Alliance had lost some citadels and gained others. Some were simply watching to see what the enemy would do, or were stuck in a chaotic battle for survival.

The Pandora's Box crew didn't pay attention to the outside world. A number of craftspeople stood around them, ready and waiting to get whatever they needed.

Dave once again went into the Mirror of Communication. He quickly shared out his problem to his class of coders. Creating a coding think tank focused on the problem. Nearly three hundred people were here, from all across Emerilia. Some were part of the Alliance; others worked in Grahslagg Corporation and others were simply helping out. Among those helping out there were hidden figures of people from the Deq'ual system.

Dave would simply go in, share a problem he was getting stuck on and leave once again, or pass out a simulation to run. He'd also drop off Malsour and Steve's questions and work.

This sped up the process of working on the citadels' new systems immensely. They never stopped working, always turning from one roadblock to another question that they could solve.

Malsour turned from their work and looked to the forty or so Blood Kin that were off to the side and back to Dave. They might need blood in order to display their power, but they weren't bad people. With a large supply of blood crystals coming in, they were stronger than ever, allowing them to become a small but incredibly powerful building force.

"It's time." Dave nodded, seeing the question in Malsour's eyes.

Malsour stood, cleared his throat and moved to the Blood Kin. "All right, listen up because time is of the essence. We're going to form the basis of the new system that will be running through this citadel. Here are the plans," Malsour said as a person ran up with a bag to the Blood Kin.

The haughty Blood Kin glanced over the plans. Their normally indifferent faces turned alarmed at the plans while one of them took the bag and opened the top.

"These..." the one who had taken the bag said, looking into the bag.

"There should be a few hundred blood essence crystals in there. I have someone who is working on making something more Mana-potent than these simple crystals. Now get them in you and let's get to work!" Malsour said.

The Blood Kin pulled on their masks and their hoods. Blood essence crystals were distributed to them all as they moved out into the citadel. They quickly moved to the various cardinal points.

The citadel that they were in was no longer a simple Level 1 citadel. As it had been under the Terra Alliance's control for so long, it had actually progressed to a Level 3 citadel and was about a week away from making it to Level 4.

Level 2 had taken the simple outer wall and inner citadel with a large town in the middle of it and expanded everything. The wall had expanded outward, becoming taller and thicker. The inner citadel had risen up as well, its walls becoming thicker and adding two new floors so that it looked out over the outer walls. Four small towers at the cardinal points had grown from the inner citadel and reached upward. In the center, the main tower had doubled in size and also grown four more stories. A second outer wall had risen around the first, increasing the depth of the defenses.

With the third change, the second outer wall became as thick and strong as the first wall in the second stage and moved outward. From it, eight small towers had appeared at the eight combined cardinal and inter-cardinal points.

The biggest change was the original castle and walls. The walls became thicker as the ground rose up, creating a hill underneath the walls and the castle.

Now, instead of being flat, the different layers of defense were stacked. The inner castle didn't grow outward but instead in places the stone was covered in sections of metal to defend against possible attack and shore up weak positions.

The towers became more refined and actually held their own Mana barriers instead of just the Mana barriers created by the soul gem construct.

Soul gem constructs were still growing. The area was so large and power was at a premium that the Alliance hadn't wanted to spend much of it on the citadel to begin with.

Now they needed something to help turn these battles.

Pandora's Box had been secretly supplementing the power needed for the project, running their reactors to charge vault soul gems.

Bob was overlooking the soul gem factories while he worked on his own projects. There simply weren't enough vault soul gems to keep everything powered continuously. They had to be dumped into the soul gem construct and whisked back to a recharge point.

Still, the growth had been immense.

Within the inner castle, there were multiple storage crates that had been dropped off by the automated carts for the next part of what was needed for the citadel.

Malsour stayed in a hidden room within the center of the citadel, trying to clear his mind of all distractions. He changed into his Dragon form as much as possible. Power surged through him as he sensed the ground underneath him, overlaying the ground with the plan that Pandora's Box and their coding helpers had come up with.

"This is going to be difficult," Malsour said to himself, feeling the Blood Kin reach the various positions across the citadel and its defenses.

They all took a few moments to get into a comfortable position, consume their blood essences and submerge themselves into the ground under their feet.

"Open the resource chests," Malsour said across the support party chat.

Around the citadel, resource chests were tipped. Mounds of resources fell out of them as automatons and people started to let the resources out.

"Begin," Malsour said as he gained control over these resources.

The material piles seemed to melt, disappearing from sight. They were being pulled on by the Blood Kin and Malsour into the ground.

Malsour pulled down tons of resources. As they moved through the ground, he formed them into various threads. They encompassed the foundations of the citadel and spread out over the surrounding area. The Blood Kin also made their own metal plates.

These metal plates came together to form a single sheet underneath the citadel. From this, metal supports twisted down from the edge of the metal sheet, creating a cone that pointed down into the ground.

As the Blood Kin made these different strands, working together so that their magic was impossible to tell apart, Malsour formed a massive magical coded formation on the underside of the massive metal sheet. Thick, coded lines moved from the formation to the supports, following them downward.

From these supports, it seemed as if metallic roots sprouted from them and spread out through the surrounding dirt and rock.

A thick column from the center of the steel plate started to form, covered in the geometric lines of magical code that was being formed on this ten-meter-wide pillar that extended all the way down to where the other one hundred or so supports met up in a point.

Time lost meaning as this work went on.

The Blood Kin would constantly consume their blood essence crystals. They were in awe of the power and control that Malsour showed with his work, increasing their own depth of knowledge and abilities in manipulating Dark Mana.

The main supports were finally finished as the roots continued to spread out through the rock that lay within the supporting beams and around them.

To someone who knew the human body, it might look like the circulatory system. The main beams were the arteries; the roots were the capillaries that stretched out to reach into the surrounding material, becoming thinner and thinner as it reached out to all of the ground around.

Malsour breathed heavily, his body covered in sweat and his head woozy from the power expenditure. It had taken nearly nine days for them to work together and bring this about. To the Blood Kin and Malsour, it felt as if it had been as short as hours but as long as years.

Malsour turned his attention to the metal plate. The roots had not simply grown down but they had also spread up and into the citadel, its towers and surrounding walls.

The soul gem construct that covered the citadel welcomed these roots and actually spread them throughout the Citadel.

If only we could hook up a fusion reactor to the citadel, we could change this all in a matter of days instead of weeks. Malsour sighed to himself.

Malsour finally opened his eyes, his face pale, a coughed his entire body shaking as he continued to cough, his original paleness turning a fierce red as he tried to fight the coughing. He got some water from his bag of holding, quickly drinking it to relieve his parched throat. He was hungry and tired as hell but instead of resting, he slowly got to his feet. His half-draconic form disappeared as he returned to his human state. He drank Stamina potions, although they didn't have much effect as he'd been using them nearly constantly for a week and a half straight. He didn't even touch the Mana regeneration potions; they had little effect on him now. He had used them so many times in a row that they barely helped to regenerate his Mana any more.

What he needed was rest to recover his Mana and get back to his peak condition.

With his senses, he looked out over the city. While he and the Blood Kin had been making changes underground and through the city walls, Dave and Steve had been making a lot of changes to the soul gem construct that was spread out over the massive defensive works.

Dave looked up from where he had been working. It didn't look as if he had taken a break either. "Looks like you're just in time for the fourth change," Dave said.

"I hope that the metal plate is enough," Malsour said.

"Just reached one hundred percent," Steve said. The ground shook as a faint glow of power spread out over the citadel and its defensive walls.

The citadel shook as stone changed to metal in places, condensing and giving greater support. It grew higher and the curtain wall gained strength. Casting balconies and archery positions appeared; positions for ballistae and trebuchets formed on the roof of the citadel.

The towers didn't move but instead gained more metal reinforcement. The outer wall became eight meters thick and twenty high; the ground behind it also rose. The eight towers dotted around it also grew in size and prominence, overlooking those pristine, smooth gray walls.

The secondary inner walls started to gain metal sections in places as the ground inside also reached higher, with the inner castle on top.

The defenses looked much like a birthday cake instead of being on top of a hill now. Instead of the gentle elevations, the defenses were laid out with painstaking detail, altering the world around it to give greater defensive abilities.

This was a castle with defensive walls no more—this was a true citadel.

On the roof of the central tower, a large magical formation could be seen forming in the air before it slammed down into the stone and metal of the rooftop.

A blast of magical power rippled outward as magical formations appeared on the roofs of the already large towers around the main castle. As they finished, four smaller pulses spread outward. On the eight towers around the outer wall, more magical formations appeared.

As these finished, a magical pulse went out; as it touched upon the inner magical formations, they lit up the formations once again. A phantom image appeared above the outer towers, then the inner towers and finally the central tower.

Mana poured out of these formations in a stream, creating a cone shaped Mana Barrier around the citadel.

"You ready with that power coding?" Dave asked.

Malsour sent his senses downward through the structures below his feet. "Yeah."

"Good." Dave stood. The central area under the tower was still massive, with the first two floors open for anyone to look at; above, large lights illuminated the space in the center of the floor with the ono in it.

"Could you bury the construct and Mana well?" Dave moved toward one of the towers that was a part of the inner citadel.

"Can do." Malsour looked to the soul gem pillar that held the Mana well. Power descended through the thick coded lines that surrounded the Mana well.

A hole appeared under the Mana well that disappeared underground. The floor sealed up as the soul gem around expanded over where the Mana well had been. He watched the Mana well and the core of the soul gem construct descend until it was right above the massive metal plate under the citadel, above the metal pillar that stretched down to the base of the support cone.

Threads spread out from the soul gem construct, across the metal plate and reaching up and into the citadel, connecting to the soul gem that pervaded the structure above the ground. The threads came up and connected to the soul gem constructs that had spread over the towers around the inner castle.

Malsour was tired but he wanted to see what Dave did next. This was the culmination of all their work over the last couple of weeks.

Dave made it into a tower; around the inner castle, instead of going upward, he went downward. Steve and Malsour followed him. They went to an inconspicuous-looking doorway. Dave opened it up and they found themselves in a closet.

"I'm not as powerful as you, but I can do this," Dave said. Dark Mana surged around him as the floor beneath them started to drop down and then moved on a slant.

They reached a point directly underneath the center of the tower in the citadel and above the center of the metal plate where the soul gem construct and Mana well were.

Dave pushed his hands outward. The open area they were in expanded into a horseshoe.

"Looks a bit *Enterprise*-y," Steve commented, looking at the different consoles that formed the horseshoe.

"The *Enterprise* has the open side of the horseshoe pointed at the screens—we've got the closed end," Dave said.

"By Fire, can we stop talking about your damn television and just see if this all works?" Malsour asked.

"Someone's grumpy." Steve chuckled, his eyes flashed for a moment. "I'm connecting to the soul gem construct and sending a thread back up to us to connect into the consoles."

"Good." Dave commanded the ground to create chairs and areas where consoles would be, as he smoothed out the floor and walls. He threw out mage lights, illuminating the space fully so that not only people with a mastery of night vision could see.

A sprout of soul gem cracked through the floor, forming into a console at the rear of the command room, which was raised a bit higher to see the other consoles. It was clear that the commander of this room would sit here.

The soul gem construct finished forming the console and spread across the room to create the floors and reach out to where the other consoles would be before it stopped.

"We're going to need a hell of a lot more power. That's all I can do right now without more juice," Steve said.

Dave closed his eyes and checked his senses. He opened a nearby chat, encompassing all of the modified citadel. "Do not step outside the walls of the citadel, or come within five kilometers of the citadel. If you are leaving, please do so through the ono. Tell everyone who enters these rules. If not, you or they could die," Dave said.

"Nice. Really uplifting. You should do speeches for your day job," Steve said.

"Ass," Dave said, unable to fully suppress the smile that rose to his lips.

"Well, I hope this new power system of yours works," Malsour said.

"You and me both." Dave pressed different controls on the console as well as using his own interface to change settings and prime a program.

Runic lines across the citadel walls and the supports, pillar, and the roots that came off them, running deep into the ground, all lit up.

At first nothing happened, and then Dave started to feel that the area around the citadel was cooling. In his senses, he could feel all of the heat energy around the city being pulled inward by the various runs, converted into Mana and poured into the soul gem construct that started to slowly grow more.

The temperature outside started to drop, faster and faster, going from a hot, sunny day to a crisp autumn day.

"Okay, so the heat exchangers are working." Malsour used his own senses and feeds to the Aleph automatons to see what was going on outside of the city.

"I just hope the cold exchangers do as well," Steve said.

The soul gem construct that weaved through this massive structure both underground and above it grew faster and faster, strengthening its ties to the different parts of the citadel and connecting to more and more of the supports. The more supports they attached themselves to, the faster power was pulled into the citadel as it wasn't lost in transferring it through the supports' runes.

The metal supports were good with the runes but the soul gem construct was many times more powerful. Because they gathered power faster, they were also a better material to code. As they seeped into the metal runes, they had the effect of making them much more powerful, making the temperature around the citadel drop faster and faster.

"Welcome to a winter wilderness." Dave sensed that the ground around the citadel was actually freezing over.

"Readying the cold exchanger," Steve said.

The ground temperature around the citadel reached minus five centigrade before the power they were getting was diminishing returns.

"Switch," Dave said.

"Cold exchangers are active," Steve said. This was one of the projects that had been giving the three of them and the other coders a headache for a while. Turning heat into power was pretty easy, and spells could be made from Mana to create something cold. So if there were runes that could convert heat into Mana, then there had to be runes that could convert cold into Mana. At least, that was their running theory and hope. If they could have two of these systems that collected this ambient cold or hot energy, as long as they were in atmosphere or a place that could be heated and cooled, then they could get power.

The runic lines for the heat exchangers dimmed as runic lines for the cold exchangers spun up. The heat exchangers didn't turn off but seemed to dial down.

The ground around the citadel started to melt rapidly.

A notification appeared next to Dave's screen as power started to seep into the citadel.

Dave, Malsour, and Steve let out excited cheers.

"It works! It fucking works!" Dave yelled, high-fiving Malsour and hitting Steve's hand. "Fuck, that's hard!" Dave yelled, his hand numb from high-fiving Steve.

"Sorry—that's what she said?" Steve laughed.

Dave let out a frustrated sigh and threw a wrench at Steve who was nearly falling over, the satisfying noise of crystal hitting metal not stopping him in the slightest.

"This—this is huge. With this, we can power this citadel indefinatly. It could take off relying on just the vault soul gems," Malsour said, his face filled with joy.

"Seriously you guys gotta stop I'm going to break something!" Steve continued laughing, if he was physically capable of it, there would have been tears streaming down his cheeks.

Dave and Malsour continued to ignore him.

"It's going to take a hell of a long time to get this system to try to power up all of the citadel's soul gem constructs that are running all over the place, but at least we can do it!" Dave said, joy on his face. They hadn't had a proper meal in a week; they were tired and needed to have a long shower but now that fatigue seemed to fall away in the face of their excitement.

This wasn't going to another planet or seeing the beauty of the universe laid out before them. Those things inspired and made one's heart beat with passion. This was created for one reason: to survive. Their laughs reflected their crazy idea coming together, of the hope and worries that had plagued them but coming to a realization that they would work—that their idea, as audacious as it might be, could work!

Dave opened up his notifications, finding three screens waiting for him.

Quest Completed: Librarian Level 6

Use research to prove a theory (2/2)

Rewards: Unlock Level 7 Quest

+10 to all stats

600,000 Experience

Class: Librarian

Status: Level 6

　　　　+60 to all stats

Effects: Read 5% faster

　　　　Understand 10% more of the information that you read

Quest: Librarian Level 7

Use research to prove a theory (2/3)

Rewards: Unlock Level 8 Quest

Increase to stats

Dave quickly opened his character sheet to check it.

Character Sheet

Name:	David Grahslagg	Gender:	Male
Level:	240	Class:	Dwarven Master Smith, Friend of the Grey God, Bleeder, Librarian, Aleph Engineer, Weapons Master, Champion Slayer, Skill Creator, Mine Manager, Master of Space and Time, Master of Gravitational Anomalies
Race:	Human/ Dwarf	Alignment:	Chaotic Neutral

Unspent points: 0

Health:	49,100	Regen:	24.42 /s
Mana:	15,930	Regen:	58.95 /s
Stamina:	5,420	Regen:	51.40 /s
Vitality:	501	Endurance:	1,221
Intelligence:	1,603	Willpower:	1,179
Strength:	552	Agility:	1,028

"Balancing out the cold and heat exchangers," Steve said, distracted for a moment.

Dave and Malsour held their breath in anticipation. If the two exchangers could be balanced out, then they would be getting power from both as they pulled in the cold and heat energy around them. By creating a balance, they would get a continuous stream of incoming energy that was higher than just one or the other exchanger working.

"We've just hit balance." Steve smiled to the two others.

Malsour checked the power numbers. They weren't as high as the Mana well, and nowhere close to a fusion plant, but it was more energy than they were getting before. As the soul gem construct filled in the runes along the supports, then the rate of power they would gain would only increase, allowing them to get three or four times the energy from their exchangers compared to the Mana well.

"As soon as we get all of the different components of the exchangers covered in soul gem construct, I want to halt all progress and focus on holding energy and creating vault soul gems," Dave said.

"The resources we used to make this citadel weren't inconsiderable. We can only make one or two others," Malsour said. Their plan worked but having just one working citadel would only provide limited help.

"It's time I went back to Earth," Dave said.

Chapter 3: Descend into Chaos

While Dave, Malsour, and Steve worked on the citadel, Emerilia had gone through some major changes.

The wilderness was once again no longer safe to venture out into. Cities were quickly improving their defenses and being largely overpopulated. People were put to work, being trained or taught some kind of skill by the major Emerilian guilds, like the mages, traders and adventurers.

The mages and adventurers weren't teaching them all the mysteries of their arts but instead making them capable of defending themselves and being of use to the city guard and armies. The trader's guild was no longer focused on pushing goods; instead, they were turning toward becoming efficient quartermasters. All three of these groups had become part of the Terra Alliance and saw that they couldn't be at every city in order to help them, but they could do everything in their power so that those within the city could defend their homes.

The Mirrors of Communication that were connected to the colleges proved their worth as people from the most remote communities were able to learn from true masters of different arts.

The people of Emerilia lived in a world of danger. Now that the threat of more violence had arrived, they were desperate to learn anything or do anything in order to protect their lives and survive this latest tragedy.

Player groups were still moving around Emerilia. They called the guilds and the people who were holed up in cities weaklings and made fun of them across the forums, until they started to run into more and more of the creatures from the event or the portals.

The portals had opened, unleashing thousands of creatures upon Emerilia. Not all of them were contained and even if they held all of the castles, the Terra Alliance and other militaries weren't always able to stop the different creatures from leaking through their lines.

As for the creatures that were part of the event, they were so scattered that finding them had been hard at first, now they were emerging from where they had spawned and setting out to attack Emerilia once again.

As they swarmed, the towns became islands of peace in a world at war.

Even they were not without conflict. Having so many people in the cities and with resources already starting to get scarce, people were panicking and crime was rising. Even some of the cities were being attacked in such numbers that they had to call in reinforcements from the Alliance or their governments.

Josh looked to Lucy, Cassie, and Florence; Kim, Dwayne, Esa, and Jules were all out in Emerilia, commanding the forces of the Alliance and trying to fight the unending tide that seemed to be coming from the portals.

"It's already clear that the thing that's going to mess up this alliance is the people panicking," Cassie said.

"Well, we need more resources and we need them soon," Florence said.

"We don't have anywhere else to go to get the necessary resources." Josh hadn't slept since this event started and he felt like hell.

"That isn't necessarily true," Lucy said.

The others looked to her.

"That Blood Kin family—they've nearly completed the third section of Terra already, so we can help take some of the pressure off the various towns and cities that way. However, I feel that the person we should be talking to the most is Suzy. She's running an errand for Dave then coming here. I just sent her a message and she should be here in a few seconds," Lucy said.

"Excellent," Josh said, sitting up in his chair. Since Party Zero had told him what was going on with the Earth simulation, Emerilia, and the real history of the human race, he had started to see them all in a different light. He knew that they were up to something—what else would explain the long absences by Dave, Malsour, Steve, and the man they called Bob, the creator of Emerilia and its original inhabitants? He had never asked what they were doing, trusting in them as they had trusted him with the truth.

Lucy sent a message again, telling her what room they were in. A moment later, Suzy walked into the room. She looked to them all with a somber expression on her face. She shut the door behind her, making sure that it was secured and the runes that stopped anyone from listening in or trying to spy were active.

Then she threw out necklaces to everyone and invited them to a party chat. She indicated for them to put on the necklaces. They were nothing more than a simple chain with a five-centimeter wide, ten-centimeter long piece of metal that had runic lines carved into its surface.

"Those necklaces you're wearing are called Band-Aids. They're meant to detect the kill signal from the Jukal and stop it. They decrease the effectiveness of Jukal signals as well as magical attacks. We're running these things off like crazy as an aid for everyone on Emerilia. We already have a batch to start passing around. I'll have them to you within the day. I'm going to make this short as the rest of Party Zero is deep in their work or their fighting. Austin Zane has been putting away a bit of his funds over the last year or two while Emerilia has been going on. It's been rather hard to divert the money to make sure that there's no paper trail. It's legal and it just seems that Austin is trying to keep more money to fill his hobbies. Now he's built up a rather considerable wealth. A wealth that he can use to buy items within Emerilia without it seeming too much. Actually, this event will be perfect to funnel a great amount of money from Austin into Emerilia. Being from so many different accounts, it will be hard to trace. And even if the AI pick it up, they will see it as a gamer wanting to boost his guild." Suzy looked to them all.

"So he's going to use his assets within the Earth simulation to buy items for the game?" Josh said.

"I was wondering why he didn't do it earlier." Cassie looked to Suzy.

"Few reasons. One, because if he did it at a time that his avatar on Earth was doing something else, then alarm bells would be going off; he needs to go back to Earth in order to complete the transaction. Second, if he had just simply taken his money and dumped it into video games, it would have raised red flags. Sure he could have done a few thousand here and there but it wouldn't have had a real impact.. Now he can do more in one go and has the streams set up to funnel more money into the game in a more continuous manner while making it look like he just has a gaming addiction and the event has pulled him in. The AI will still see it, but it will look like Austin is trying to cover it up. Now this will also relieve some of the pressure on the Grahslagg Corporation. We own the rights to the green towers built in Terra. Devil's Crater and the Aleph are both interested in this stuff but it was at a high price before. We can give them packages to get them started and growing. Combined with soul gem constructs, and enough power, they will at least double or triple their current outputs of fresh food," Suzy said.

"Why didn't you give this out before?" Lucy asked.

"Grahslagg Corporation has a lot of different projects and expenses over a vast area. The costs of running these different ventures are astronomically high," Suzy said.

Josh could tell that there was more to her words but Suzy had been a senior executive for so long that there was no way even he could read her.

"In about two to three weeks, we will also be increasing our soul gem output, to try to reach necessary numbers required by this war and consumption. Dave also suggests placing two more ley line power plants down," Suzy said.

"Can we expect any more aid from other areas?" Josh tried to sound as vague as possible.

Suzy tapped her chin in thought before she shook her head. "You might see some hints of it in different projects but this is too early to start pulling out the real guns."

Josh's right eyebrow rose. His interest increased several times by this confirmation that there was something being worked on and it was powerful.

"These Band-Aids are impressive," Florence said.

"We will be selling them to you at one gold, which is at a loss for us. However, everyone needs one, not only to stop the Jukal from using their kill switch but they will decrease attacks against those wearing them," Suzy said.

Josh looked to the Band-Aid. His own appraisal skill was low but it allowed him to still see the Band-Aid's abilities. It wasn't particularly impressive, but in the middle of a fight it would help out.

"I have also been told to inform you that the Dragons are moving to help," Suzy said.

Everyone forgot about the Band-Aids and looked to Suzy. They'd seen the power of Induca and Malsour before, but there were tens of Dragons who stayed within the Densaou Ring of Fire, their power unknown.

Already the Dragons have come out to assist us, Josh thought. They were quickly running out of trump cards to pull out and use against the forces arrayed against them.

***

Deia and Party Zero were around the Erach portal that was located in the Northeast corner of Gudalo. The worst fighting of the Event had happened at this portal. The ground was a mess of impact craters and dead Erach. The walls were under constant repair by the Dark and Earth mages as the Erach tried to eat and burrow their way through.

Magical spells and artillery fired throughout the day and night, illuminating the wasteland around what had been a large cove reaching out toward the sea. Now the cove had been hit by so many attacks that the ground opened up to reveal the cover underneath that was filled with raging water.

The Erach were a big pain in the ass but they couldn't swim. Any that went into the water and couldn't find a wall to pull themselves up with died.

Which only served to funnel them out of the cove and toward the various castles.

Deia wiped her sweat-covered brow as she panted. She had been calling down flame arrow storms for the last couple of days and still, it had only slowed the Erach instead of stopping them.

The Erach had thankfully just attacked the castles around the portal instead of trying to go on and attack the settlements that were farther inside the Gudalo continent.

Deia raised her bow to the sky once again. The runes activated on her bow. She fired upward, altering her aim slightly and then firing upward in another direction. Once again the sky was filled with a heavy rain of Fire arrows.

These tore through the Erach with ease, killing off thousands. But their numbers couldn't be counted: they writhed and moved over one another, some ten or twenty thick as they all tried to attack the walls.

Deia continued to fire arrow after arrow as the dwarves unleashed grand workings that created lightning storms that hovered in the air, killing anything that lay below, or unleashed ice rain from above or tornadoes.

The ground was chaos, with every manner of large-scale area of effect spell and round being fired and used.

A shadow passed over Deia. She looked toward the shadow. Her eyes widened as she saw three Dragons overlooking the battle-field. They wheeled around the portal and the castles, heading out to the ocean. They banked over the ocean, coming so low that the water underneath them deformed and shot outward like a jet flying over a body of water.

The three Dragons formed a triangle as the water around them raged with increased ferocity. Their speed increased until three sonic booms made everyone nearby wince from the noise.

A line of water ten meters wide and growing followed them, rising out of the ocean in their wake. The Dragons flew toward the cove. The ground shook violently as the trail of water behind them formed a point and started to spin.

It broke through the cove's different natural rocks and the inlets that it was formed from. The ground exploded outward with the pressure of the massive Water spear that was as large as an aircraft from Earth.

A clear path was drilled through the ground.

A sound of metal hitting metal rang out as the open portal shook with the impact of the Dragons' attack, which was forced through the portal.

Two of the Dragons who made the base of the flying formation turned back around toward the castles. One unleashed a green-colored flame; the other unleashed a white breath. Their respective flames left lines in the ground, killing anything in their path. Behind the green Dragon, the ground seemed to rise up and attack the Erach.

From the wings of the white Dragon, Air blades shot out, cutting apart anything in their path.

The blue Dragon came into a hover; magical formations appeared around it before solidifying.

Water from the ocean was swirled up in a tempest, as if it were alive. From it, a water snake seemed to appear. It shot forward through what had been the cove, cutting past the rocks and debris, throwing them outward as the water covered the interior of the cove and washed away any Erach. It hit the portal, going right through.

The Water Dragon let out a roar; the Earth Dragon replied with a roar as well and dove into the water stream. The Earth Dragon collapsed their wings and headed through the portal.

The portal on Emerilia's side distorted slightly as the Earth Dragon reappeared out of the other side of the portal. Water continued to pour through as the Earth Dragon rose into the sky, letting out a roar of victory.

The ground around the Emerilia portal seemed to shake before it dropped downward in the center of a large crater. Water filling it to the top. Any Erach that came through now found themselves in a large pond, the ocean filling it up rapidly.

Ragged cheers rose up from the surrounding castles. The Erach couldn't swim and with the water in the way, it was easy to see that the portal had been effectively cut off from the Erach's planet.

The Water Dragon moved, flapping her wings as she unleashed her attacks with her wind brother.

The Earth Dragon moved to one of the castles, digging his claws into the castle walls to hold themselves as a magical formation appeared around them. A pulse of massive magical power shot out from the Earth Dragon, covering all of the castles and a few kilometers beyond. The pulse ended and the ground started to rumble. Erach were shot out of the ground, as if the ground refused their entrance. They were tossed out of the ground. The Water and Air Dragons moved to kill all of the ones that had made it past the castle and were now being tossed into the air.

"Kill the Erach that are past the castles!" Deia yelled out across the command channel. If the castles fell, that was one thing; if the Erach were able to move past the castles and start to spread across Emerilia, then they would turn the planet into hell as they consumed anything that was living.

The Terra Alliance changed their aim as Deia unleashed more and more Fire arrows that multiplied before hurtling back toward the ground. The Dragons systematically moved with the Terra Alliance's help, killing off the Erach that had made it past the castles and forcing them backward. It was a slow process but it was working.

They finally reached the castles, The Dragons were massive and powerful beasts but they had burned up a lot of Mana. They landed on different castles, adding their support to the defenders.

"Aunty Deia, it is good to see you," the large Water Dragon said. "My name is Liera. My siblings and I live in the mountain range to the south. Ilas is using his Earth magic to make sure that none of the Erach escape into Emerilia. He was able to make a crater around the portal on the Erach side, like the one here. Basically, if any Erach want to come here, they're going to have to go through two very large ponds in order to do so."

Deia nodded. It was a smart idea, and it effectively cut off the Erach. "Thank you for your help," Deia said, relieved.

"It is my honor. My sister Rela and I are both tired from our Mana expenditure so we can help a little but we aren't as effective as we would have been with all of our power," Liera said.

"Rest and help out as much as you can. Now that we don't have to worry about more Erach coming through the portal, we can focus on wiping these bastards out," Deia said, a grim look on her face.

Anna, Jung Lee, Lox, and Gurren were all fighting down along the main walls.

While the Earth and Dark mages were doing everything that they could to try to deal with the burrowing Erach, in some locations there were simply too many of the creatures and they had been able to enter the castle. The members of Party Zero rushed from breach to breach, helping to push back the Erach and try to contain them.

Their experience rose as a result and while they gained levels here and there they needed a truly insane amount of experience to level up now.

Induca and Deia were focused on long-range spells and thinning down the Erach in the distance. Now, with no more Erach reinforcements, they could change their tactics.

"I vote for killing off the Erach that are on our castle walls and in the nearby area, now that they can't escape. We can defeat them in close, repair our walls and hit them at range," Deia said to the castle commanders.

"I agree. It would be good if we could get some DCA fliers to drops some Mana bombs on these bastards," one said.

"No harm in asking the higher-ups," another added.

All across Emerilia, similar battles were happening, not all of them as successful.

***

"Pull back!" Esa yelled, waving her sword at her people as a Xelur Grand Demon Lord that was fifteen meters tall slammed his war axe the size of a small boat into the walls of the defending castle. Rocks exploded outward with the impact of the axe.

It's skin was purple in color and as tough as a beasts, their bodies were covered in complex Xelur tattoos to channel their soul energy these symbols were marred by battle scars and piercings. Their eyes glowed with a yellow light and twin horns that looked similar to a rams curled around their heads.

Their hands were sharpened into claws while they wore simple shorts around their waist.

Those with less power were smaller their tattoos less profound and their horns shorter.

The demon soldiers made up most of the forces but the Xelur, by using souls, were able to increase their size and their ability to store more souls and more power. The larger they were, the stronger they were. Minor Demon Lords could be up to three meters tall; Demon Lords were up to ten meters tall; Grand Demon Lords were ten to fifteen meters tall. They didn't get taller than fifteen meters, but they had different capabilities. A young Grand Demon Lord wouldn't be as close to an ancient Grand Demon Lord that had come to understand their power to a higher degree, creating more power augmentation for its own attacks and reducing the power it needed to draw from its souls.

Rocks from the castle walls crushed people as they ran, players and POE alike.

Esa couldn't do anything but grit her teeth, dodging rocks and hitting others aside with her shield. The impacts were so powerful even from the small rocks that she saw her hit points falling slightly.

Motes of light covered the Grand Demon Lord's weapon, looking similar to the light that one would see within a powered soul gem.

The Xelur Demon hit the wall again. The wall exploded outward.

Esa was hit by a slab of rock that slammed her through a wall. She lay there broken, her Health points falling down as she looked through the hole in the castle that she had come through.

The Xelur soldiers and various Demon Lords charged into the castle. Any wounded they killed with their enchanted weapons; motes of light floated up the carved lines in their weapons, passing through ports in their hands. The Xelur's strength increased with each kill and soul they absorbed.

Finally, darkness surrounded Esa until it started to get brighter again. Esa looked around at the room she was in. It took her a moment to realize what it was as a screen appeared in front of her.

This is my game lobby. Esa felt cold fear as she read her screen.

You have died in Emerilia

You have been returned home.

You have 5:59 hours (game time) until you can re-spawn at (Nadorf, Opheir)

Or

1:59 hours in real life

Would you like to play a different game while you wait?

Dismissing the screen, she let out a shaky breath, her face pale and her hands clammy. Since coming to know the truth of Emerilia and Earth, she knew that every time she saw this screen, she had actually died.

It took a force of will for her to calm down. Quickly, she accessed her settings on her interface and moved to the shared lobby of the Stone Raiders.

There were tens of Stone Raiders hanging about, talking about their battles, how they'd died and replaying the death cam footage to the others. They greeted Esa as she took a seat, looking at the information that was being passed to those in the lobby. It allowed them to know what was going on with the guild across Emerilia.

"It doesn't look too good," Esa said to herself. The Xelur had come out of a few different locations. She had been based at the portal on Opheir between the Donasuk and Zelheam cities, near the Benvari Mountain Range.

The Xelur were powerful, able to create powerful Mana shields but unable to create Mana barriers, which meant that they used a lot of power.

Being fueled by souls, the Xelur were akin to walking, talking soul gems. Some might be even as powerful as a vault soul gem, but these were leaders of the Xelur race and rarely ventured out into battle, instead taking a tithe of soul power from those beneath them, which continued to keep them as the highest power of their planet.

Esa's castle had been the second to fall, though the others were holding on still. The ono at Esa's castle had been removed and placed in one of these other castles. Right now, with the lack of onos, they were being constantly switched between different locations so that people could move quickly. It was a stopgap measure as it took time for an ono to connect to the teleport pad and reconfigure itself before it could be used.

Time they didn't have.

"Yes!" Esa stood and pumped her fists into the air as shells exploded over the portal that was hidden within an old ruin that had been camouflaged into the forest. Remaining trees were shattered, turning into splinters that tore apart the Xelur forces.

"Where did that come from?" one of the Stone Raiders asked.

"That was from Benvari Mountain. The dwarves' artillery, when combined with grand workings and enough power, can reach out and barely touch the portal's location," Esa said excitedly, slumping back into her chair in relief.

"I didn't think that the dwarves' artillery could go that far," another commented.

"Remember when we were dealing with the Elsoom spores? Those artillery cannons were massive and they were using reduced charges so that they wouldn't overshoot where the Elsoom were," the first Stone Raider said.

"Damn. Maybe we can get more of that support in other places," the second said.

"It is powerful, but it wouldn't take much for them to miss a portal and hit a castle nearby. That's why they're using grand workings, as the spells will affect the enemy and can be directed after it goes off to not hit allies. We would need to be having our battles a lot closer to the mountains if we wanted to use their normal rounds." Esa's voice trailed off as a notification appeared.

She went to it. Finding a message, she quickly read it and frowned at the words within. "What the hell is she up to?" Esa muttered under her breath.

***

Markolm might be a small country compared to the others but it was no less populated and it had a lot of undiscovered portals. One had opened on the shores between the Markolm forest and the ocean; another was in the swamps on the opposite side of the island nation. One opened between Mel'alla and Hovulof. One opened north of the capital Maphrol and another south of the city Ataraxis.

This meant that the island nation was dealing with five different portals. They had only known about the one to the north of Maphrol and the one between Mel'alla and Hovulof, calling on the Terra Alliance to assist them.

However, when creatures started coming from the southeast and west, the elves were shocked. They locked down their cities and were put under siege. There were Alturarans, Ooinfa, and Jera Root. However, the Jera Root didn't come from the portal; instead, it had been released by the event near the swamps, though it had been so powerful that it killed off the Jakan forces. The Alturarans came from the south; the Ooinfa came from the eastern forests while the Jera Root spread from the western swamps.

Alturarans were creatures of limited intelligence and were created from inorganic materials. They manipulated their own inorganic bodies into weapons and lived to destroy life around them. The Ooinfa were beings of illusions; they could hypnotize people with a weak Willpower into a lull before killing them. They saw the portals as a desecration of their land. They, just wanting to be left alone. Thinking that it was the people of Emerilia placing these portals down they attacked again and again trying to shut down these entrances into their homeworld.

While this behaviours had been understood, there was simply no known way to communicate with the Ooinfa.

No one even knew what an Ooinfa looked like.

The Jera Root was the most terrifying of them all. The root wasn't sentient nor could it create slaves of others like the Elsoom spores. Instead, they were a plant of poison. They were created by a chemist in the midst of a blood war on Ashal in ancient times past.

The Jera Root spread across an area, creating different poisons. The Jera Root naturally mutated the poisons it created in its body every time a new Jera Root grew. They spread across a large area in just a few days, growing at a speed visible to a person's eye. They would look like a colorful field, inviting and pleasant, with a slight haze over it. If someone were to get close, they would fall victim to the multiple kinds of poison, falling down and dying from exposure and feeding the Jera Root.

Incredibly hot temperatures were needed to burn away the Jera Root and its spores. And it had to be done at the same time because the Jera Root would mutate so that it would become harder and harder to burn them.

So far, they were having a hard time crossing the mountain range that went through Markolm, and were being funneled down toward Heatho.

There was an ono evacuating the city but it was slow progress. The fields continued to grow, day by day—even in the night—as they moved south.

The Lady of Light looked over Markolm, a calculating look in her eyes.

Markolm was the center of her power, an island that had once dominated the skies of Emerilia, an untouchable city of light, called home by angels, divine beasts, and warriors of Emerilia. People would look up at this floating nation with awe and respect in their eyes.

Such times were in the ancient past for the people of Emerilia, where the world changed every week.

For Light, it had never been far away from her mind. Every time she thought about those days, her anger was ignited to the boiling point. However, she never let this show on her face, only a slight twitch at the corner of her eye or a light tapping. She had kept her anger and her power hidden.

As the nation of Light had landed in the sea, war was waged over her nation. She used the lives of those who died to fill her divine well, seeing an oncoming storm and waiting to reveal her power.

Markolm was conquered by the elves, who then raised edifices to the Lady of Light. Their devotion had diminished over the years but they were still believers that Markolm was a holy land, their true homeland.

They think too much of their bloodline. The Lady of Light looked down at these noble houses and their powerful and pure bloodlines.

The Lady of Light sat in her hall; her attendants and her people were gathered around. All of them focused on the orb that floated in the center of the hall. Khanundra was to the Lady of Light's right, midway up the stairs that climbed to her throne. Along the base of her throne were several men and women, all wearing the golden armor of a warrior of the Light. Light had gathered these people who escaped from their bonds as Khanundra did. These were the eight generals of Light. On their backs, two wings glowed with brilliant radiance. Their eyes had a golden light to them as they watched the sights through the orb impassively.

Through it they could see the city Heatho.

They could hear the screaming and crying as people tried to move faster and through the single ono within the city. The fields of Jera Root had spread across the fields outside the city and were encroaching on the city. The walls were already sprouting with deadly flowers. Every minute, more and more of the flowers creeped through the city and toward the fleeing residents.

The Lady of Light watched, hiding her pleasure as she saw the looks of despair within the eyes of those elves. *This is power, to watch those last moments and decide their fate.*

Light waited a few moments and composed herself. It had been so long since she had the power that she now commanded that it was intoxicating.

"Go and save them, that they might learn the error of their ways and live with new life," Light said, her words for her followers and angels as she waved an imperious hand. Golden light wrapped around the generals and Khanundra.

Light zoomed out seeing as the eight generals made a semi-circle in front of Khanundra, who stood above the Ono in the middle of the city.

People looked upward at the gold-covered angels with their pure white outstretched wings.

"With me!" Khanundra yelled out, pulling her weapon free as she charged forward. The eight heavenly generals yelled out as their weapons appeared in their hands, blazing with golden light that forced many to look away as they charged valiantly toward the Jera Root!

Golden spell formations appeared around them. Their speed made them seem like golden lights as their attacks lashed outward. The Light attacks were made to destroy the Jera, not the buildings or anything else. The precision needed was immense, but after making all of her generals also her champions, their power had doubled.

They passed over Heatho. People looked up in wonder and awe.

Light was unable to hide a hungry smile. Her eyes flickered in lust as she watched those expressions with glee. *The time for Light to return to Emerilia has begun!*

The angels pushed forward; in their path, there was no sign of the Jera Root. It was as if they were cleansing Emerilia of poison.

Cheers rang out of the elven people's throats. Some dropped to their knees in prayer and devotion.

Light let out a sigh as power from the devotions made by the elves poured in, filling Light's divine well. She looked to her left side. In the shadows, away from everyone else, there was a woman who looked nearly identical to Khanundra. Instead of the golden armor that the angels wore, this person wore simple clothes.

This was Daeundra, Khanundra's sister. She was a fallen angel, part of Light's forces that worked in the dark.

Although the angels were the public display of Light's power, her control over her followers came from these fallen angels. Few of them had been released across Emerilia and many were making their way back to Light, working to undermine the other members of the Pantheon and inspire panic within different locations.

Daeundra, seeing Light's look, bowed her head and moved away from the hall.

Light wanted to win the people of Markolm over to her side. They would act as a constant and empowering force for her and her divine well.

To do this, she needed them to believe and follow her. She had removed the people who would have been in her way, destabilizing the government of the elves. It had been bad when Khanundra was seen killing the first leader of the elves, and she had killed off others who weren't too popular with the people.

Daeundra and her people had removed those who were well liked and gave the governments stability through blackmail or killing. They would do anything to succeed in their tasks.

Now this siege provided Light with the perfect opportunity. The elves were shattered; besieged on all sides and looking for aid from anyone able to save them s. The Terra Alliance was helping out but in limited areas. They didn't have the forces to be everywhere at once.

Then here came the angels of the Light, pushing back the enemies of Markolm, snatching them from the jaws of destruction. It was enough to sway the hearts of these people who had already given up on life itself.

Now their plans were starting to come to fruition.

Daeundra and her fallen angels were placed in every city that had an ono, drop pad, or teleport pad. Their job was to disrupt these different teleportation devices, making the only way on or off Markolm via ships. With no outside aid coming in, the elves would start to panic.

I will play off their fears and prejudices. As they have sealed themselves here, not accepting many people coming to their island, it won't be hard for them to start to think that the other people of Emerilia don't care for them. That is when I will strike—offering them aid, re-

minding them of all I have done to assist them in this struggle. Then they will freely deliver themselves to me, becoming the soldiers of the Light. While the rest of Emerilia burns, we will gather strength and once again rise to the skies of Emerilia, to spread my domain to all of those who call Emerilia their land.

While the rest of the world seemed to not care about the elves, she would support them, groom them and manipulate them into becoming her faithful and devoted followers.

She grabbed a glass of golden-looking wine to the side of her throne; she sipped it, hiding her hungry smile.

Chapter 4: Entering a Dream

"What the hell is going on with the teleportation network in Markolm?" Lucy asked Dave, who was checking the runing on a console within the command room of what he was calling Citadel One.

"Someone is disrupting the location where the different teleports are, accelerating particles through the event horizons whenever they're open—which takes up a hell of a lot of power to transmit all of that really fast matter. The teleportation networks are all being drained of power. The method is simple and it has to be done nearly all the time but it effectively reduces the time that the teleport pads and onos can work for." Dave's brow furrowed as he worked on the runic lines under the console.

"So, someone is sabotaging them?" Lucy tapped her chin in thought. "It has to be the Lady of Light, but why the hell is she trying to keep people on her island? Wouldn't she want to kick them off?"

"Well, how does the Lady of Light or any of the Pantheon get their power?" Dave asked.

"From devotions, given by the masses... Shit, she's using them as a devotion farm, an entire nation under her command. It explains the angels who swept away the Jera Root and then started to push back the other forces. I thought that they were kind of milking it. With their power, it should be easy for them to fight back the enemy forces on Markolm. However, the more time that they fight beside the POE and the elves of Markolm, the more ingrained their actions will be. Already there are stories coming out of Markolm of miracles. These might be events that the Lady of Light has come up with in order to get more people interested in supporting her. The churches of Light have also become louder in their preaching, not only in Markolm but in other places. They're using Markolm as propaganda: look, the Lady of Light will save us! The Terra Alliance can't even help us!" Lucy said, growing more and more alarmed.

"It's crazy, and impossible, but it could work. If it could work..." Lucy's voice trailed away, her eyes unfocused as images and possibilities played out behind her eyes.

Dave continued to work on the runes, making sure that they and the ones throughout the citadel's structure were good. It was a lot of checking but there was a ton of runes; if just one of them was out of place, then everything would come apart.

"When will the citadel be ready?" Lucy asked.

"That's the eight-million-dollar question," Dave said. "We just need power, at this point. We've got Shard, Jeeves, and Steve all combing through the magical coding as well as a number of servers in Deq'ual Sato has allowed us access to. They should be done soon, but to power this thing up and have something in reserves—that will take awhile."

"You've given us a basic idea of what it will be able to do, but I looked at the plans and there's a lot more that you've done to this place than we expected," Lucy said.

"And there's more to come," Dave said as an alarm went off on his interface. "Okay, looks like it's time to go and see how Earth is doing." Dave stood.

"Nervous?" Lucy asked as Dave moved to the commander's chair in the command room.

"A little bit." Dave laughed awkwardly as he sat and opened up his interface. "See you in a bit." He pressed the logout button. The room around him slowly faded. The lighting strips of the room and the consoles disappeared.

Dave found himself lying down, he quickly sat up in his bed and looked around. *Well, this isn't my house,* Dave, now in the body of Austin, thought to himself as he looked around.

It was dark in the room. Without his dwarven abilities and his night vision, he was back to the same blinding darkness that humans on Earth experienced. He slowly got up, finding a desk next to him. He nearly knocked the lamp on the nightstand right off. He caught it, his heart racing as if he were on some thieving mission and had nearly been caught.

He turned the lamp on, light filling the unfamiliar room. Spotting the door, he walked towards it.

There was a murmur from the side from someone else in his bed.

Deia is going to kill me! Dave thought, his eyes going wide and icy fear running through him as if he knew Deia could see him this very moment.

"Babe, is there something wrong?" Suzy, wearing pajamas, looked to Dave through sleepy eyes.

"Uh." *Why the hell is Suzy in my bed?* "Yeah, I'm fine. Just going to get some water. Had a bad dream."

"Okay," Suzy said sleepily. Then her body froze for a split second before a confused look appeared in her eyes. She looked to the side, to Dave.

"D—Austin," Suzy, the real Suzy who had logged off Emerilia and was taking over Suzy's body, said. Dave was now in Austin's avatar.

"Hey, Suzy, I was wondering if you had that information on those accounts?" Dave asked. He knew that the Earth simulation AIs were extremely powerful and they could watch any part of the simulation. If Dave or Suzy were to do something too far outside of their normative parameters, then they might look back on this conversation and start looking to see whether something odd happened. Like, if Suzy called Austin Dave.

"Yes, I can do that." Suzy frowned slightly as she raised her hand, a piece of silver metal on her hand with a black band inside.

Dave felt his own ring finger, finding an identical wedding band here.

Their eyes locked onto each other with odd expressions.

We're married! The two of them thought in alarm.

"If you can find out about those accounts, I'm going to get a glass of water," Dave said.

"Okay," Suzy said, still a little stunned.

Dave moved out of the bedroom down a long hallway that opened up into an open-plan living area with a balcony above the hallway. He passed the living room and entered the kitchen, as he went, he saw pictures of him and Suzy—their different achievements, their wedding photos as well as them on vacation thrown in with abstract art that some interior designer had filled the large modern mansion with.

So we're married, okay.. They were good friends but living together and marrying? That was a little extreme! *Seems that the AI that took over our avatars as we became bleeders was a little liberal with their actions.*

As Dave started to get over the shock, it started to make a certain sense: if Suzy and Dave had romantic feelings for each other, then they would make a powerful couple who could stabilize each other and the entity known as the Rock Breakers Corporation.

Dave tapped on the kitchen countertop. The black marble changed to a screen. He quickly looked up the news about him and Suzy.

Seemed that they had got close on their Tokyo transfer and now the entire company was based in countries outside of the US. After their departure, a number of other businesses were also looking to move overseas even as the US government threatened them with penalties.

Dave shook his head and grabbed a glass and filled it up with water as he read on about Suzy and Austin having a surprise kiss when they once again started dropping materials from orbital holding stations into the Pacific.

From there, they had dated, traveled and within a few short months, they had a very quiet wedding ceremony.

They were called the power couple of the business world.

"Austin!" Suzy's voice carried through the house from the office.

"Coming!" Dave moved from the kitchen to the office. He found two large desks facing a large single-pane window that looked out over a carefully manicured garden lit with subtle lights.

Suzy sat at one desk, a holographic display lit up at the other computer. "Okay, so the accounts are here." Suzy grabbed a screen and held it up so Dave could see it. Dave scratched Austin's face, only finding a light stubble instead of his usual beard. *Weird.*

"What did you want to do with it?" Suzy looked to Austin.

Now time to act our damn asses off for the cameras.

"Well, you know how there's that event going on in Emerilia. It seems like the gamers are getting just run over. I was thinking of maybe sponsoring a few of them so that they can keep playing and get more items." Austin shrugged.

"You woke me up to look at these accounts for that? You really are a gaming nerd." Suzy sighed.

She should get a damn Grammy—or is that music? A Golden Globe? Whatever that one is for acting. Oscar! That's it!

"Okay, well, what do you want to do?" Suzy sighed.

"Well, I was thinking a sponsorship for the Stone Raiders and the Alliance, with the stipulation that they have to use the money to build stuff or get materials. They can't use it for just straight gold unless that gold is to get resources. That would be cooler than just using the money for more money," Austin said. "Also, building all these things on Emerilia, I need some coin to keep up with it all.

Can you get me a whole bunch of vault soul gems? That's possible, right?"

"Yes, you can buy soul gems from Jukal Enterprises. Though they only come in the grand size and smaller."

"Okay, that'll work, get as many as you can with those after all of the sponsorships and that," Austin said.

"Aiming on being a general or something, coordinate their fighting by their resources?" Suzy joked.

"No, just, well, got a ton of money and I want to see the people of Emerilia win. Anyway, what is a few million to us when spread over like twenty different guilds?" Austin snorted.

"I don't know why you want to use these hidden accounts for that," Suzy asked.

"Well, as much as I love gaming, people would lose their minds if they found out I was spending anything like this kind of money on nothing but a video game. I really hope that Jukal Enterprises comes out with a new game." Austin sighed.

Yeah, a game called Alien Blasters, where I can kick their froggy asses back to the primordial goop they came out of. Not like I have a grudge against them or anything.

"Okay, I'll get it done, but you owe me." Suzy tapped away on the keyboard in front of her. Even with all of the touch and holographic interfaces, Suzy liked a good old-fashioned keyboard.

"You in for a late night Emerilia sesh?" Austin asked.

Suzy rolled her eyes as she worked on the multiple holographic screens around her.

"Fine. You're addicted to playing Emerilia now that this event is going on."

"Got to have some fun!" Austin smiled. He headed out of the office. He had seen a room filled with gaming equipment as he'd walked from the kitchen. He went back to the room, pulling out one of the immersion helmets, and put it on his head as the large server tower in the corner booted up.

Time to leave this nightmare.

He left Earth behind and stepped into his lobby. With a smile, he used his interface to open Emerilia before a screen popped up.

System Message

Would you like to begin your game?

Y/N

Dave logged back in. He reappeared in his command center and quickly opened up his in-game interface and connected to his bank.

He watched his bank's inventory as more and more charged soul gems started to appear, as well as rare materials. Their price wasn't low in the Earth simulation, but he had millions of dollars to play with—the resources he gained could be immense!

A party chat invite from Suzy came a few minutes later.

"Happy yet?" Suzy asked.

"Yep, wife in an alternate universe." Dave laughed.

"Gross." Suzy huffed. "Anyway, all of your resources are now accessible from any of the banking terminals or locations on Emerilia. So you're going to need to go to a bank in order to get them all, or you can send them to the corporation and I can get the resources loaded up onto carts and shifted to Terra for distribution."

"I'll transfer them. If we can get them on the automated carts, then we can start juicing this citadel up and make good progress on our projects in Nal as well as modify the rest of the citadels around Goblin Mountain," Dave said.

"Okay, I'll look after things on my end," Suzy promised.

"And I'll get back to work on this damn citadel," Dave said.

Dave turned to Lucy, relief evident in his tone. "We just got a whole lot of resources and the Stone Raiders are now sponsored by Austin Zane—well, unofficially."

"Good. I'll check things on my end to see that everything goes smoothly," Lucy said.

***

Bob took a deep breath as he looked inside the capsule in front of him. He was in the moonbase. Usually there would be myriad screens around him to work off of and keep updated on all the projects that were going on at the various bases.

Now all of them had been moved away as he looked at a single capsule.

All around the capsule and linked into it, there were coded machines with tubes and runic lines carved through the soul gem construct in the ground and along the walls. There were containers of all manner of liquids and materials around.

Bob took a deep breath as he pressed a button on the console in front of him. Power surged through the runic lines as machines started to come to life.

The interior of the capsule was lined with runic lines and holes at certain points. Now these runic lines started to glow brighter and brighter. They glowed with all the colors of the affinities, red, blue, white, black, gold, and green. These lights spread outward, combining and melding into a gray miasma that shone like a light in the middle of the night, illuminating the capsule and the room that Bob was in.

Bob turned his attention from the capsule to the console, checking the readings and the different information that was being pumped out. His hands moved across dials. His breath was short and fast, his heart feeling as if it would come out of his chest at any moment as sweat covered his body. Even with his nerves at their end, his hands moved with careful grace, not making the slightest mistake as his eyes followed the information on the screens.

Different liquids flowed from their holding tanks and into the capsule, whatever was happening in there hidden away.

More and more power was consumed as from the gray miasma that covered the inside of the capsule motes of light started to flit about.

For several nerve-racking hours, Bob didn't dare to look away, watching everything that happened like a hawk.

Then, without preamble, the machines stopped pumping materials into the capsule. Still, other runic lines were lighting up, doing different things as Bob continued to watch.

"And that was just the first part." Bob laughed dryly to himself.

Hours slipped by as the tension within Bob's mind and body only seemed to increase. Finally the runes along the capsule stopped surging with energy and slowly started to stabilize. They started to glow softly, pulsing rhythmically, much like a person's heart would beat.

Bob braced himself, letting his hands fall away from the console. His body, mind, and spirit were all drained. He had a hopeful but solemn look on his face.

He took slow steps forward, moving around the console and to the capsule. His feet came to a stop as he was just a foot away from it.

With a deep breath, he pressed a button on the side of the capsule. The gray smoke pulled back deeper into the capsule revealing a completely hairless human male, naked as the day he was born was resting within.

Bob watched the man's chest slowly rise and fall. It would have been hard to know whether the man within was truly alive or dead unless someone was looking for it.

"Well, happy birthday." Bob smiled as he looked down on the human body. It had taken nearly three days but he'd done it!

"Shouldn't have left me on Emerilia, you Jukal assholes." Bob laughed and a smile split his face as he let out a laughing cheer of victory. He looked to the racks of capsules that were within the moonbase. "Well, once we get this all set up on the ice planet in the Nal system, we'll be good to go. I never thought this day would come." Bob smiled.

The ice planet wasn't under observation and was far safer than the Emerilian system. There, Bob could freely create the bodies of the players who were being stored within Emerilia.

"Soon, they'll wake from their dream." Bob had a complicated look on his face as he wondered what those who woke up from the Earth simulation would think and do.

He patted his pocket and pulled out a thin crystal.

"With this uploaded, we'll be able to start pulling people from the simulation without anyone knowing about it." Bob had Jeeves working on the program for months, using all of the *Datskun*'s servers in order to complete the complex code that would trick the AI watching over the players.

"Those AI controllers might be able to see everything that's going on in the players' lives when in the simulation, but they're weak to outside attacks. Just change their orders and they'll broadcast whatever." Bob tucked the crystal away and watched as a cart moved into the moonbase, taking a rack of capsules and putting it into its storage. In other areas, soul gem constructs were being "grown" from the original soul gem construct of the moonbase.

The fusion plant hummed and customized repair bots worked on the massive greenhouses that had been erected to fulfill Bob's needs for organic materials.

It was the sign of progress and a sign that they were indeed succeeding.

Bob frowned. "Even with all of this, it will be useless if the people of Emerilia are killed off in this event." Even though he was tired and fatigued in the extreme, instead of heading to rest, he pulled out some jerky and water, consuming them as he checked the moonbase and headed off to Pandora's Box.

They were all holding back their power. Although Bob couldn't fight, he would do his best to be prepared for when they were truly backed into a corner and had to use their full strength.

Chapter 5: Onto a New Dawn

Dave held little Koi as he looked out over the modified citadel Steve, Malsour, and he had worked on tirelessly.

The wind around Dave was cut down by a Mana shield, keeping Koi warm as she looked around in interest at the goings-on of the citadel.

With every minute, the soul gem construct that acted as the veins and arteries of the citadel grew. Since Dave had visited Earth, the resources had been coming in.

Soul gems by the ton were being poured into the citadel's soul gem construct. The exchanger system was complete, pulling in more power from the surrounding area every hour.

The metal roots within the ground were being quickly covered by the soul gem construct that now permeated the ground, converting the rock around the roots into a soul gem.

The walls of the castle seemed to have been brought to a polished finish, cold and hard. Now soul gem weaved through these walls, keeping that same polished finish but adding to it veins that glowed with power.

Dave looked from the citadel to Koi. He could feel the power that filled the citadel, the domineering force that would be at his fingertips when the modifications were complete. The Blood Kin, with their mother Yemi, worked tirelessly to modify the other citadels around Goblin Mountain and expand Terra and its supporting facilities. Supplied with as many blood essence crystals as they could need, their power was even greater than Malsour's when backed up by these kinds of resources.

Dave smiled at his daughter. He had come to this world to escape Earth; he had found friends and started a family. He had fought in the name of friendship and according to his own beliefs. At first, it was to fight against the injustice, to regain the freedom that humanity had been denied for so long. A thought rooted in defending his friends, his family.

Now, he not only fought to regain that freedom, he fought to gain it for his daughter, so that she didn't have to see the violence of the world, to be scared of the what-ifs and maybes that plagued the people of Emerilia.

In Dave's heart, she and Deia were the most precious people to him. He would not let the Jukal continue to lord over them. He wanted to spend his time with them without the pressures and uncertainties of tomorrow. For that—for his family, for their future and their freedom—he would go to war with the galaxy if he had to.

He smiled into those innocent eyes. Koi smiled as she reached out for her dad with excited hands.

This is what I'm protecting. Dave couldn't help but smile as he looked down at that face.

"Dave, Citadel Three's root systems have been completed and the soul gem construct is already growing according to plan." Malsour walked up behind Dave.

"It looks like we'll be ready to start using this thing soon enough." Dave kissed Koi's head and then once again looked over the city. "There's not much for us to do here. Shall we go meet up with the rest of the party?"

"I think it's time," Malsour said.

Dave took a big breath and looked at Koi once again, unable to not smile. "Okay, little one. Going to have to leave you with your grandmother for a bit. You and Desmond will have a lot of fun. Daddy is going to help Mommy kick the bad guys' butts," Dave said in the exaggerated tones that people used with dogs and small children throughout time.

Koi made a happy noise as Dave stepped off the tower, descending slowly. Malsour followed, his hand sticking in the wall as the wall moved to allow him to descend with Dave.

***

With the Erach being cleared out, Party Zero had been shifted to the castles surrounding a portal within the Densaou Ring of Fire, south of Egas Nation.

These were the same series of castles that Esa and her forces had been holding. Esa was alive once again, feeling her loss of stats as she had returned to command of the castles. At the beginning, the Xelur had only controlled two of the castles, with the Terra Alliance taking control of the six remaining castles.

Thinking that these Xelur were like the ones coming out of the portal on the Heval continent south of the city Aygasse turned out to be incorrect, instead of working together they were at one another's throats fighting among themselves.

With their forces divided, the Terra Alliance found it much easier to fight the pockets of uncoordintated Xelur.

In Ashal, the portal had been within one clan's controlled area. As such, they were much more coordinated and they didn't have any troubles advancing into Ashal. They had consolidated their strength and only when they were confident did they start sending out lightning-fast raids that would hit the other surrounding castles.

They had taken two more castles: one within the inner circle and one in the second ring. With this development, more people were moved to the castles in order to stop the Xelur.

This had turned from a defensive operation into a castle capture.

Now the final castle within the inner ring was fighting off the combined attacks of three other castles.

The Terra Alliance was firing on these Xelur-controlled castles with all that they had, but they were unable to grind the Xelur defenses down. Fighting at long range was not working so they were going to have to get in close.

The atmosphere within the command room was tense. The sounds of spells and artillery could be heard through the large walls as Esa stood at the front of the room.

"With this, we've got to play the objectives. We take out the Xelur—they can just hide in their castles and recover. We need to get into those castles before they improve upon their defenses or get more capture points and take them. Once we control the castles, we give the Xelur less options to work with," she said. "Party Zero, I want you to spearhead this. This is going to be a player guild-only attack. We can't drop Onos in areas that we don't have a drop pad placed. We don't care about killing off all the Xelur. As long as we can capture those castles then the mission will have been a success."

"Dragon!" someone yelled as a shadow passed over the castle.

"They're on our side!" Esa yelled over the command channel, not wanting to have an incident on her hands.

"So we've got Dragons for support?" Lox asked.

"Well, they do call the Densaou Ring of Fire their home—it wasn't hard to ask them to help clear out the Xelur." Esa smiled. She was clearly tired but there was a tenacity and unwavering energy that came from being the leader of all that was going on.

"When do we leave?" Deia asked.

"We're going to get the dwarven artillery, Dragons, and DCA aerial forces to soften up the target some, get them scared. You will move under the cover of this bombardment to the eastern inner castle from the secondary eastern inner castle. The northern inner castle will provide close support. As you get to the eastern castle walls, the other outer castles will shift their fire to the other Xelur-controlled inner castles so that they don't mess with you. At that time, it will be up to you and the other players to gain entry into the outer castle walls, then force your way into the central castle and the capture point," Esa said.

"Sounds almost easy." Gurren snorted.

"I'm glad you think so. The assault will begin in the morning, when most of the players are online." Esa tapped the desk with her hand, announcing the end of the meeting.

Party Zero and the others left the room and headed out toward the walls once again. There was a long night ahead of them before they could put Esa's plan into action.

"Let's go take over a castle," Lox said.

"Not even going to send us an invite?" a familiar voice said.

Deia looked down a hallway where a massive man with glowing eyes, a half-dwarf, and a human walked toward them.

"Well, they've got no chance now with all of us here." Gurren laughed.

"How did the citadel go?" Anna asked as Deia and Dave greeted each other with a hug.

"It's nearly ready—just needs more power. We should have three more ready soon," Malsour said.

Dave and Deia kissed quickly, the two of them in their own world.

"Miss me?" Dave said with a cocky grin.

Deia hit his chest and rolled her eyes. "I missed Koi. You're simply a side benefit."

"Why, thank you." Dave shook his head, his grip on Deia not lessening in the slightest. "Before you ask, Koi is fine. I left her with your mom and dad. Seems that she and Desmond are having a lot of fun within the mountain. Your mother also told me to tell you that Koi already has a high Affinity toward Fire and will be quite the little mage when she grows up."

"Someone's a proud dad," Deia said. Dave's face looked as though it would split apart with his wide smile and the glow in his eyes.

Dave picked Deia up and whirled her around. She let out a surprised and adorable shriek at his actions.

"Just a little!" Dave laughed.

"Big oaf." Deia hit his shoulder but she, too, was smiling with him, happy and excited for their daughter.

The rest of Party Zero had been talking among themselves, getting up to date on what everyone was doing.

An alarm rang through the castle.

"Looks like the Xelur are leading an assault," Jung Lee said, his senses better than Dave's as he had come to understand and control his Free Affinity spirits.

"Check your gear and let's go see if we can't help out. The more we weaken the Xelur now, the less we have to fight tomorrow," Deia said.

Dave released her.

She would cherish the moment that they had but they were still within a battlefield and they couldn't let themselves be too distracted from what was going on around them.

"Grand Demon Lords!" someone yelled out. Beams of light that looked like the light contained within a soul gem tore through the night sky and slammed against the Mana barrier of the castle.

The entire barrier shook with this impact.

"They must be some of the more powerful Xelur Demon Lords!" Induca yelled as Party Zero exited the castle. Looking up, they saw as another pillar of light formed from the souls of the Xelur Grand Demon Lord's victims tore through the night sky, making Party Zero shield their eyes at the sudden brightness as the Mana barrier was once again shaken with the impact.

These twin beams didn't fade but continued to burn away the castle's barrier.

Smaller, less powerful beams started to add to the two initial attacks, filling the sky with light.

"Get to cover! The barrier can't take much more of this!" a commander of the outer wall's defenses called out.

"Artillery, get me those Grand Demon Lords! Just need to disrupt them!" Esa yelled out over the command chat.

"We've got incoming!" someone on the wall called out on the information chat.

Deia's ears perked up as over the sounds of hundreds of people moving, a rumbling noise built within the air. There was no way to see outside of the castle as the Mana barriers and attacking soul-formed beams fought against the mana barriers. Even though they couldn't see anything, the defenders could still hear what was happening on the other side of the wall.

"Xelur forces!" someone yelled out on the chat as the rumbling noise of thousands of people charging across the open ground around the castle was overtaken by the bloody war cries of the Xelur as they charged.

"It's like a tide of darkness. I...I don't know how many there are. There has to be thousands—maybe twenty or thirty thousand!" A scout at another castle sounded as if they were in a state of disbelief at what they were seeing approach the last remaining inner castle controlled by the Stone Raiders.

"They're coming from the eastern and western castles!" the scout continued.

Without a clear line of sight, the defenders of the northern castle could only hold their positions, looking up at the Mana barrier that was being burned away and listen to the unseen enemy and the reports coming in from the other castles.

An angered roar filled the air as one of the two strongest beams was cut off.

A Dragon's roar came from the sky as golden light filled the sky. A spell formation appeared in front of the Dragon. Their mouth opened as golden spears of light appeared from the center of the overlaid spell formations.

The golden light was overbearing as the spears shot through the air in a blur. It was only because of Deia's high understanding of magic and high stats that she was able to see the spear and the buffing spell placed upon it.

A massive fifteen-meter tall Xelur Grand Demon Lord leapt from the castle where he had been, stepping upon the air as if it were a stair, and launched himself toward the Dragon.

His progress was slowed by the Dragon's attacks hitting him, making him defend and be pushed back down toward Emerilia.

The Grand Demon Lord deflected the attacks, letting them pass by. Where they hit the ground, ten-meter-wide craters would appear. The wall of the castle would crack where it was strong, and explode outward where it was weak.

The attacking beams reduced in numbers as the Xelur had to now focus on defense. As the beams dimmed, the artillery on the northern castle and the ranged attackers were able to see some of the enemy approaching.

Spells and artillery were unleashed on the oncoming Xelur soldiers and their more powerful masters. Even through these attacks, the spears of light from the Dragon continued to cut through the pitch-black night sky.

Xelur that were in the path of these light spears were nearly all wiped out.

Xelur Demon Lords of the lower ranks and even two Grand Demon Lords by the power stored within their bodies and overall height chased after the first Grand Demon Lord, who was just getting into range with the golden Dragon in the sky, wielding a massive war hammer with savage blood-red runes on his weapon that would draw out one's Willpower and pull on the soul energy of whatever creature it hit.

Soul-fueled beams shot out from those following the Grand Demon Lord, hitting a dazzling Mana barrier.

Just as the Grand Demon Lord was about to hit the Golden Dragon it let out a cry of pain as a ranged spell from the Golden Dragon hit it in the back. In a flash the Dragon moved out of the way, unleashing golden flames from its mouth and the Grand Demon Lord was hurled across the sky. He stopped after being thrown nearly two hundred meters, golden flames across his body.

Soul energy grew around the Grand Demon Lord. His aura increased in power as he charged forward to meet the Dragon again. The golden flames around his body died off as the soul energy defeated them.

"Looks like the Grand Demon Lord is burning his soul energy to enhance his attributes," Deia said to the others as they stood in the open area between the wall and the castle, ready to react to any breaches or where the worst attacks came from.

The golden Dragon and Grand Demon Lord clashed in the sky. Spell formations appeared on both sides as they came together in massive clashes, the impacts of which resounded through the sky.

The aides to the Grand Demon Lord, seeing the power displayed, paused in their advance. The battle had reached a level at which they could no longer help their leader.

With roars of anger, the Demon Lords quickly moved to catch up with the assaulting Xelur army.

Four more Dragons roared as they cleared the mountain range that made up the Densaou Ring of Fire. They were part of the force that would help the players retake the inner eastern castle.

They were supposed to arrive during the night so that they could surprise the Xelur, but with the ongoing battle, they had increased their speed in order to help repel the oncoming assault.

Grand Demon Lords unleashed attacks at the Dragons, some were as strong as the one that was fighting the golden Dragon in the air. Most weren't and were only distract the Dragons, many of them perishing in the act.

The Dragons were proud and powerful creatures. These four combined their power into spell formations that appeared over the Xelur-controlled areas. When combining Mana and having multiple mages working to cast a single spell together, the spell didn't simply become easier to cast. Their power increased dramatically.

From the sky, these massive spell formations were larger than the castles below.

"Players, prepare to sortie!" Esa's voice rang through the command channels.

Players who had been on the walls moved off, forming into parties and groups.

Deia continued to watch the destruction being waged through the air.

The Dragons' spell formation unleashed a hellish rain that descended upon the Xelur-occupied castles as if meteors returning to the planet. Massive glowing barriers covered the castles. The Xelur burned their souls in order to gain cover from this oncoming barrage.

Those castles that weren't under attack unleashed their own attacks at the four newly arrived Dragons. Among these attacks, Demon Lords raced into the sky, treating the sky as if it were land as they went to meet these Dragons.

The Dragons wheeled apart, dodging the beams of light with aerobatics that made Deia watch in awe. Hits peppered their personal Mana barriers as spell formations unleashed spells at their attackers.

The Xelur burned soul energy, enhancing their natural abilities as they fought against spells as if they were spears and swords, not magical formed creations.

It was a terrifying sight as these forces clashed in the sky above the portal.

"They're nearly at the walls!" Lox yelled over the sound of fighting. His sword and axe formed in his hands.

Deia looked to everyone. They were all looking to the sky in wonder of the fight there. But with Lox's words, their looks of awe hardened as they checked weapons or started to circulate their Mana so as to instacast their attacks.

The Mana barrier of the northern castle was quickly failing as the roars of the oncoming Xelur were clearer than ever. The very ground shook with their progress.

"Ready yourselves!" a commander called out. His deep voice made those on the walls brace themselves. Hundreds of small white beams illuminated the Mana barrier. The charging forces now added in their own attacks; for them to display their full power, they needed to get rid of this Mana barrier.

The Xelur might be a techno race that fell backward but they were as smart as any of the people on Emerilia.

The Mana barrier shone with brilliant light, weathering the impacts for a time. Finally it was unable to take the attacks. Holes appeared within the barrier before suddenly the runes that were supporting the Mana barrier stopped lighting up with power and the Mana barrier collapsed!

"Use individual Mana barriers!" Esa called out.

In different areas, smaller barriers were activated to cover the people within their area of effect. They weren't as good as the Mana barrier of the castle but they could blunt the worst attacks and give those underneath a better chance.

The main gate closest to the eastern side shook with an impact. More and more impacts sounded against the gate as the sound of metal hitting stone could be heard along the walls.

"They're trying to break down the gate and climb the walls!" someone called out.

"Area attacks outside the gate and the walls. Archers, hit anything that moves out there," Esa ordered.

With the Mana barrier down, they had lost their protection; however, they had regained their visibility. Mages and ranged attackers unleashed concentrated attacks that they had been holding back. Arrows left the castle in droves, whistling overhead to land among the Xelur and cutting them down as they continued to race toward the castle's outer walls.

The Xelur didn't let this pass as their Demon Lords started to reach the walls. With their soul-enhanced strength, they smashed into the walls, leaving large impacts as they continued to swing their weapons. Others got to the wall, leaping onto them, using their claws or weapons to climb the walls.

The castle's outer walls were covered in a thick cover of Xelur fighters working their way up the wall. There were simply too many of them to be all killed by the spells and ranged attacks.

"We've got Xelur in the seventh and ninth area!" someone called out.

Deia looked to those areas, where Xelur were fighting with the Terra Alliance people. They'd created an opening on the wall; more and more of the attackers rushed to get into that gap and reinforce them. With each death, the Xelur would grow stronger, pulling the souls from their own fallen and the fallen from the Alliance. Much as Dave's armor did.

With each death the Xelur were absorbing their soul power, their average power keeping up with their consumption or even slightly increasing.

This made them a terrifying enemy as they wielded their blood rune weapons.

Lu Lu unleashed a lightning attack from Suzy's shoulder, stunning the Xelur Demons that had made it over the wall in the seventh section of the wall. Most would have been killed by the attack but the Xelur were tough opponents and were merely stunned for a while.

Thankfully, this gave the people on the wall the opportunity to drive them back.

The first Xelur Demon made it to the wall. They roared in victory; from their body, it seemed that their soul aura erupted, killing off the POEs within the area. It twirled its spear and smashed through three others that had been nearby. His strength was so great as to throw them from the wall and into the Xelur waiting below.

All across the walls, there was fighting. There wasn't a single place where people weren't fighting for their lives.

Deia pulled out her bow. Drawing the string back, she sighted the Xelur and unleashed her arrows. Her accuracy was uncanny, as if she were some war goddess who had trained with the bow all of her life.

Xelur fell to her attacks while Induca and Malsour created lances from their respective Mana and started to add their own pressure to the Xelur forces. Steve now wore his own modified Devastator armor, increasing his defense and his abilities. He, unlike Lox and Gurren, instead of being sealed away, in a space of holding, was actually connected to the armor.

He, Gurren, and Lox put their weapons away. The runes around their wrists lit up as they fired Mana spears into the oncoming attackers.

Streams flew from Jung Lee, each of them a condensed spell. Jekoni linked to these spirits and was able to draw on their power with the bond that he had with Jung Lee.

From Dave's bag of holding, he threw out Mana grenades that Suzy's Air creations gathered up and headed out toward the walls with. Moments later, the rumbling explosions of the grenades could be heard as the creations returned for more of the grenades.

Deia concentrated on the Xelur Demon Lords. She hit one in the arm, making their attack go wide as a POE who would have died continued with their own attack, driving their spear into the Demon Lord's chest.

The Demon Lord let out a howl of rage. Its other hand was covered in a soul glow as it smashed into the POE, crushing their helmet and dropping them to the ground.

The Xelur Demon Lord looked directly at Deia. It leapt into the air and pulled out the arrows from its sword arm. Its wounds on its chest and arm healed at a visible speed.

Deia drew and released arrows faster than one could blink. The Xelur Demon, now with nowhere to go as it was in the sky trying to attack Deia, was able to defend against a number of the arrows but because it had not made it to a high enough rank, it didn't have the power or the ability to walk through the air as other Xelur Demon Lords could.

Deia's arrows tore through the Xelur where they hit. Even as the Demon Lord tried to heal itself, its body grew smaller. With the consumption of so much soul force, it was thrown backward with the impacts of the arrows.

Deia, seeing that it would escape her and fall back over the wall, clicked the runed wheel on her bow over. A magical formation appeared in front of her bow as she released the arrow; the magical formation empowered it. It shot through the air like a red streak.

The Xelur Demon wasn't able to bring its sword up in time and looked at its chest in confusion. A wide hole, from where the arrow had hit, appeared in his chest as he dropped lifelessly over the wall.

Deia didn't spend any more time on the Demon Lord as she looked back to where other Demon Lords were fighting along the wall. With her enhanced arrows, she was able to help those on the walls and quickly bring down these Demon Lords.

"The gates won't be able to hold much longer!" a Dark mage yelled.

The gates had been sealed up with metal and stone to make it harder for the Xelur but they didn't care.

A massive, full-grown Grand Demon Lord at fifteen meters tall landed outside the wall. It had run and jumped from the castle that it had been in. When it landed, a massive crater was imprinted into the ground.

He pulled out his sword, piercing the wall in front of him. With an eager laugh, the Grand Demon Lord was covered in his soul aura. The aura passed down his hand and covered his blade, appearing like flames as the demon swung his sword once again.

It hit the wall, this time making it shake as the half-foot cut from before turned into a foot-and-a-half deep gouge. The reinforced and rune-covered stone showed signs of burning and melting around the edges of the cut.

"Concentrate on the Grand Demon Lord!" Deia called out to the rest of Party Zero.

Deia flicked the wheel on her bow. Angular sheets appeared around her as they did when she cast the plasma cannon spell. The sheets surrounded her bow as a series of magical formations appeared in front of it.

Deia drew an arrow of blue flame. It tore through the sky. But even as the air around it seemed distorted, there didn't seem to be any heat leaking from the arrow made from condensed flame.

The Xelur Grand Demon used their massive sword, which was nearly as big as Steve's axe, and hit the flame arrow. It diverted some of the strength of the flame arrow as it exploded on hitting its sword.

The space beside the Xelur Demon Lord turned into a blue sun for a moment. The Grand Demon Lord's aura flickered and fought the massive power that was contained within the arrow.

The Demon Lord stumbled sideways for a few meters. His sword melted and distorted, even with the protective and enhancing soul aura around it.

The Grand Demon Lord looked up as the rest of Party Zero unleashed their attacks.

From Jung Lee's hand, a gray spear was released. The Grand Demon Lord was able to hit the gray spear but it was only slightly weaker than the blue arrow.

As it passed, a shock wave of air hit the Demon Lord. Although it didn't explode like the arrow, the force of the wind was enough to shock and disturb the Demon Lord.

Induca unleashed a plasma cannon spell, which hit the off-balance Grand Demon Lord.

Its soul aura weakened, flickering for a moment before returning. The Xelur Demon Lord seemed to grow slightly shorter, pulling on its deep power reserves.

Anna's attack didn't leave the Grand Demon Lord much time to react as a tornado of wind was sent flying from her sword. This twisting and cutting attack found his shoulder, cutting deep into the creature's arm and revealing muscle underneath.

His body started to regenerate as Gurren, Lox, and Steve's attacks seemed to only increase in ferocity.

The area around the Grand Demon Lord seemed to fluctuate as Dave's orbs appeared around him. A spell formation from these different orbs was created, pinning them down as it was hit with another round of attacks. Its body went from fifteen meters tall to just ten meters.

The Xelur soldiers all noticed this as well. Their attacks became wilder as they hit the walls and tried to climb the walls to engage those on top. Those that were closest to the Grand Demon Lord were attacking the different orbs that were around them.

They were trying to break him out!

One of the orbs failed, and the Xelur focused on the others.

"I can't hold him for much longer," Dave said.

"I'm nearly done," Malsour said as a spell formation appeared around him.

Deia looked at the spell formation, understanding it was one of Malsour's stronger attacks.

Party Zero had been doing their best to suppress the Grand Demon Lord without going all out. The night was young and the battle had only just started. If they were to use up all of their power now, then there would be no time for them to regain their strength later.

There was no knowing what life-and-death situations they would find this night.

Even with Party Zero's power, they weren't able to kill the Xelur Demon Lord one on one—unless they were willing to sacrifice deep reserves of power.

Another orb failed and then another. The Grand Demon Lord's aura erupted, going from ten meters tall to eight in an instant. Burning all of that supporting soul power made him look like some kind of war god of destruction, with his Xelur minions aiding him in his escape.

With a shout, the Grand Demon Lord pulled out a new sword from the dead around him and cut at the wall with it, letting out a wild howl filled with rage.

A blade of soul energy refined into a single slash crashed against the wall, making it shake violently as a hole appeared within the outer walls.

"Kill them all and refine their souls!" The Grand Demon Lord's voice carried through the air, reaching Party Zero as he stared at them, his eyes filled with pure anger.

They had made him burn so much of his soul power that he had been building up for nearly a century.

"Got it!" Malsour said as Xelur started to swarm toward the breach within the wall. The Xelur now gained access to the corridors that ran through the outer walls where the archers, mages, and ranged attackers lay.

Esa could be heard calling for people to move to the breach and push back the Xelur. The defenders who were within the area stopped firing on the Xelur outside and started to fight for their own lives within those corridors.

The Xelur, now with less ranged attackers firing on them, were able to push forward with larger numbers, swarming the breached wall and making it over the top.

The Grand Demon Lord rushed forward, making it ten meters.

A realm of darkness descended over him, blocking out all light. Shrieks of pain filled the air as Xelur around the Grand Demon Lord were affected by the attack.

Flashes of white soul energy rippled through that dark dome.

Party Zero added their own aid to the people on the top of the wall, unable to see into the corridors where Xelur and the people of the Terra Alliance were fighting a fierce battle to control the breach.

A beam of light hit the walls, leaving a half-foot-deep groove as it swept across the wall, catching casting balconies and arrow slits.

The balcony shields were powerful but the Xelur had been hitting them this entire time, trying to get the mages who were using these platforms to rain powerful spells down on them. These balconies' Mana barriers weren't as strong as the castle's original Mana barrier and quickly fell under this powerful beam's attack.

Some unlucky mages and archers were hit by this soul-powered attack, letting out screams of pain. Some died immediately, while the wounded were left in a terrible state.

Others tried to pull them away, adding to the groups of wounded that were being funneled through the ono within the castle, back to Terra.

More forces that had been held in reserve were pushed through the ono and to the walls around the castle to try to keep up with the casualties.

"Grand Demon Lord!" someone called out. A marker appeared in front of everyone. A second Demon Lord had made it onto the battlefield.

They had been the one to cast the focused attack. They launched themselves from where they'd been reaching the base of the outer wall.

Party Zero couldn't see down to the base of the castle and were unable to attack the newly arrived Grand Demon Lord.

"Another one!" someone else called out. A new marker appeared as a Grand Demon Lord that was almost parallel with the ground charged forward. Within his hands, he carried a massive war hammer.

Attacks rained down around the Grand Demon Lord but he was able to dodge as he moved closer, his aura erupted, defending him from these attacks and his speed increased even higher.

"He's going for the gate," Dave said.

"If he comes through, we have to put him down," Deia said.

If the Grand Demon Lord made it inside, then he would slaughter nearly all of the POE within.

The majority of players who were within the castle were actually logged off, dealing with real-world life stuff or getting sleep so that they were ready for the battle tomorrow morning. Some were coming online in a hurry after learning about the battle that was happening now but it was only a thousand or so of them.

The POEs within the castle were mostly mages, dwarven artillery, and people who were good at ranged attacks.

The reinforcements they were getting were good and they were also more melee-based. But they didn't know this castle or what threats they were facing that well. They were just reacting, which, although it helped, didn't make them as effective as they could be.

The Xelur were driven; they had the numbers and the powerful forces to put to use. They were able to fight weaker Dragons in the air and could group together to try to take down the more powerful creatures.

"Looks like we'll get to go all out pretty soon," Anna said.

"Remember, always make sure we're close together. If we get separated, we can't help one another," Deia reminded them. She had changed back to regular arrows, killing Xelur that had unknowingly entered her range as they stepped upon the outer walls.

"Dammit!" Malsour's realm of darkness was banished as the Xelur Grand Demon Lord standing within an aura a meter wide seemed to be burning off his skin. The Xelur bodies around him shook as their soul energy was all pulled into the Grand Demon Lord, growing from his reduced five-meter-tall stature back to ten meters.

It activated one of its Legendary abilities and hurled its sword. A massive magical formation appeared around the now mangled sword from blocking Party Zero's attacks.

The sword smashed into the outer wall, cutting inside it and passing through the inner corridor to the wall on the other side. It smashed into the ground between the outer wall and the castle in the middle of a group of players.

Dave's hands moved as he worked to break apart the spell formation but being a Legendary ability, it was a complicated and powerful spell.

"Get away from that sword!" Dave yelled out.

The players started to move, not all that fast, thinking that Dave was overreacting.

A massive area around the sword seemed to come alive with runes made from blood. Anyone who was within this one hundred-meter-wide circle let out cries of agony as the circle pulled at the nanites within their bodies that supported their consciousness and their bodies.

Those with a higher Willpower were able to resist, becoming slower in many cases as they had to force their way out of the area of effect spell, pulling others with them where they could.

All of this power shot through the wall where the sword had been launched, tearing through it and opening up another breach as it rushed into the Grand Demon Lord's body.

Bloody runes were illuminated across his body as he drank in that overwhelming power.

At the same time, the Xelur Grand Demon Lord that had been rushing over to the eastern gate finally reached his destination. Soul energy covered his body and his massive war hammer. Its war hammer seemed unstoppable as it slammed into the gate. Waves of power tore apart the wooden gate and the intervening barrier that had been formed in the tunnel behind the gate.

Rocks and debris flew out of the gate's tunnel, killing and injuring those on the other side. The Dark mages who had been working to reinforce the gate were the worst affected.

There was no time to look to the wounded as the Xelur took this opportunity to rush through the rubble- and dust-filled tunnel, around the war hammer-wielding Grand Demon Lord and into the castle.

"Dave, Jung Lee, and Anna—on me. We'll deal with that Grand Demon Lord absorbing the soul energy. The rest of you—get to that gate, stop the Xelur and kill that Grand Demon Lord," Deia yelled.

"Let's go!" Lox led his group toward the breached gate where the Xelur were pouring out.

In Dave's hands, a sword and shield formed, he stood there looking to Deia, Jung lee and Anna who were also waiting for Deia's directions.

"Jung Lee, Anna—up front. Dave—mid-range support. I'll be long-range support and overwatch," Deia said. The others nodded.

"Let's go." Flames sprang into life around Deia as she flew into the sky. A gray light covered Jung Lee as he followed. Anna swept up into the air while Dave floated with them with apparently no support.

Chapter 6: To Glory or Defeat

Lox twirled the sword that had formed in his fingers, getting a feel for its balance and keeping his hand limber.

"Hah! Seems like someone's excited!" Gurren said as they rushed toward the tunnel. Steve was at the front, followed by Gurren and Lox on either side of him and back a bit. Behind them was Anna; Suzy, Induca, Malsour, and Lu Lu followed as well, using their various methods to fly through the air.

"Been some time since we got into a fight like this," Lox said, a smile on his face. He had been a warrior since a young age, taking his training and his position seriously as he looked to improve his skills constantly. He had followed the dwarven War Clans and then struck out to join the Stone Raiders, finally attaining his position within Party Zero. He hadn't felt deserving of the position at first, thinking of himself as too weak compared to the others.

He wasn't able to throw back powerful creatures with a wave of his hands; he fought with his fists, sword, feet, and shield. His actions were more savage than the mages' and seemed to be born through desperation instead of thought-out and choreographed movements.

While fighting was a mad melee, Lox had learned to fight and to fight well. His power had increased in leaps and bounds so that he would no longer think of himself as a hindrance to Party Zero. It had driven him to become the warrior he was now. He didn't wish to fight, but he would do it—for himself, for those beside him and for his beliefs.

"Malsour, as soon as we get there, make up a defensive wall. We've got a lot of ranged people—let's see if we can't get them some cover so that they can put their skills to use! Anna, you've got the best eyesight out of all of us. Call out when you see anything happening. Induca, Suzy—support us as best as possible and let us know when you're going for a large attack. Induca, I want a wall of fire down the center of that tunnel and a plasma cannon round down there to give us some space! Steve, don't Steve up too much!"

"How is that a saying?" Steve asked.

"'Cause you do dumb shit, you crystal blockhead," Gurren said.

"Hey, it's fun for the entire family!"

"I rest my case," Gurren said.

"Ready yourselves!" Lox said as they reached the first of the Xelur soldiers.

From behind, a blade of Air curved over the three at the front. Anna's Air blade cut through a number of the weaker Xelur, opening up the Xelur's haphazard formation as they swarmed out.

Lox lowered his shield and slammed into a large Xelur, tossing them backward with his enhanced strength. His sword shot out, opening a nearby Xelur's neck before it sliced down, taking out a knee as a war hammer clanged on his shield. He shifted his stance thrusting his sword out and upwards through the side of the war hammer attacker.

Lox turned. His sword grew longer as he dodged a spear. His sword edge struck the side of the attacker.

Steve's fist smashed into their face, propelling them backward as Steve stepped forward with a grunt. His axe slammed through three Xelur as it started to build up momentum.

Lox and Gurren looked to each other, turning back and defending Steve's sides as his axe gained more and more momentum. Steve twisted and turned his body; the axe rotated and moved at greater speeds as he cleaved through those in front of him.

"Advance!" Lox called out. They had the initiative. As they moved forward, the Xelur were being pushed from behind, making it harder for them to fight effectively in the tight quarters while Party Zero, who had fought and trained together for years now, moved like a single organism. They rotated and moved seemingly out of place but always giving the rest of the party room as they continued forward.

"I'm laying down a soul drain formation! It might take some time but it will pull the power to the citadels and tear it away from the Xelur so the survivors don't gain power every time they kill or someone near them is killed," Malsour said over the half party chat.

Lu Lu unleashed her lightning attack overhead. Thick lightning ran through the Xelur ranks, killing a few and stunning others.

Steve, Gurren, and Lox didn't hesitate and pushed forward.

Anna lay behind them, plugging any gaps and helping them out where needed. She was stronger individually than them but unless they came up against an opponent that they couldn't take on, she had the reaction speed and powerful attacks to help out the three up front.

Suzy's creations added flank security, helping to push back the other Xelur around them and making sure that they didn't hit them in the sides and rear.

They had been the first to react but other groups were now coming to the gate's aid.

Induca unleashed fireballs from one hand as she placed down a thick fire wall at the tunnel entrance into the courtyard of the castle to halt the Xelur advance.

"They're attacking the spell with their own magic. The wall will only hold for about five minutes." Induca lay down Fire tornadoes among the largest pockets of Xelur and blocked them from advancing on the walls that lay to either side of the gate.

Induca and Suzy were on crowd control and limiting the Xelur movement as they pushed forward into the Xelur.

The farther they went, the stronger the Xelur became, soul energies covered the ground. As one died on either side, dozens of Xelur would collect their soul energy, making it their own as their bodies grew with their abilities.

Gurren ignited the runes on his armor, increasing how much the Devastator armor increased his own abilities. It consumed more power faster and wouldn't last as long, but right now he needed that edge in order to keep up their forward momentum and make it to that tunnel.

A massive magical formation appeared in the air before passing through people without affecting them and slamming into the ground.

"Done!" Malsour said. The runes carved themselves into the ground as the soul energy that was being released started to be pulled into this magical formation instead of being reclaimed by surviving Xelur.

"I hate necros and I hate Xelur!" Steve grunted. His axe moved so fast it was hard to follow. His movements were erratic; he looked as if he were trying to dance, awkwardly crossing his arms over to always keep his axe moving. The power it unleashed was enough to kill anything that was in its way.

Steve was barely adding strength to the axe's rotation. With its momentum, he only had to alter its direction to tear through those near him, or cut down attacks aimed his way.

"Aren't you and Jake good friends?" Gurren asked.

"Yeah, but he's *our* necro—it's different. I came in like a wreeecking axe!" Steve slammed his axe into a shield-holding Xelur and tossed them to the side. Steve laughed. "Gets me every time!"

Anna let out a pained sigh as Lox focused on fighting.

Soon, there was no time for talking as they advanced.

"I have the ground in the tunnel ready to close it up, but we need to take out that Grand Demon Lord or else he's just going to smash through it all over again," Malsour said, blessing the front line fighters with necrotic damage to their weapons.

Even if their attacks were stopped, then they'd melt through the weapons and armor in their way, or upon touching the skin, it would then start to decay and inflict damage onto the one hit for a period of time.

"Seems like he's coming to us!" Induca cast down repeated fire walls over the tunnel entrance. "I can feel them breaking up my spells by attacking them within the tunnel."

The ground shook as the fire wall Induca had been making, exploded. Induca stumbled her face pale from the failed casting and rebounding power that raged through her body.

Standing at the entrance of the destroyed tunnel was the war hammer-wielding Grand Demon Lord. It surveyed the battlefield, looking over the defenders as one might look over prey, his eyes filled with bloodlust.

Lu Lu unleashed a powerful lightning attack from her beak, sensing that this creature had hurt Induca.

The Grand Demon Lord raised his war hammer to hit back the attack but it instead traveled down the war hammer and into the Demon Lord's body, making him twitch slightly.

The amused look on the Grand Demon Lord's face turned to one of anger at having such a weak creature inflicting pain on him. With a roar, the Grand Demon Lord shot forward, pushing the Xelur out of his way as he raced toward Party Zero.

"Plasma cannon!" Suzy called out. Her Air creations moved into a special formation in front of Induca.

Induca had mostly recovered after downing a Health potion.

Red sheets formed, as did magical formations, lining up perfectly with Suzy's creations.

Additional white magical formations by Anna appeared in front of the barrel that formed in front of Induca, integrating perfectly with the other spell formations.

The Xelur, with fear in their eyes, looked up at Induca, who was wreathed in these multiple spell formations as well as supported by Suzy's creations.

The Xelur Grand Demon Lord swiped his war hammer up at Induca. A white beam of light cut through the sky at her.

Induca's eyes changed to red as her skin became scaled. Her power increased as she allowed herself to change slightly into her Dragon form.

Power surged through the massive conglomeration of items. The plasma cannon unleashed a cyan stream of light that was twisted, fueled, and compressed to a terrifying degree by Anna and then directed with incredible precision by Suzy's creations.

A plasma cannon spell usually just fired one spell. This was a continuous spell, much like the flamethrower spell that one might use, burning through Mana continuously for a longer time of effect.

This cyan light smashed into the soul-powered beam that seemed to pierce up through the heavens.

The impact from the two magical powers sent out a shock wave over the castle, clearing away any dust and debris and shaking the people below.

A crater appeared underneath the Grand Demon Lord's feet. He was nearly thrown off-balance but he shifted his weight and stomped his foot down,, grounding himself as he faced off against Induca, who had been pushed back ten meters in the sky.

The flames that surrounded Induca grew stronger, turning from red to blue as she held her position in the sky.

The Grand Demon Lord's aura increased in power as his body grew smaller, increasing the power in his magical attack. He could only direct his power against Induca, unable to move unless he'd be thrown off-balance and destroyed.

"I can hold him for a while. I'm stronger than him but if he ignites all of his soul energy at once, then I don't think I can keep him suppressed," Induca said through gritted teeth.

"Forward while she has the Grand Demon Lord suppressed!" Lox yelled. They advanced—Suzy and Lu Lu with Induca in the air, defending her from attacks and letting her concentrate.

Malsour unleashed a fog from himself that decreased the reaction time of the Xelur within fifteen meters of him. This allowed those at the front to easily kill of anyone who lay in their path.

They cut a path through the Xelur. The other parties lent their help, watching the flanks of Party Zero, holding their ground so that they could advance without care of the Xelur that they left alive.

"Shoot the mage!" the Grand Demon Lord yelled out.

The Xelur on the ground that were in life-or-death fights directed their power into beams, aiming at Induca.

Suzy held her staff outward. Waves of power distorted the air around her as the gem in her staff was released, starting to rotate and move higher into the sky.

From Suzy's belt and her bag, creations started to appear.

"Creations of Gray!" Suzy yelled. These creations came together. Instead of being limited to their own singular Affinities, these creations were made from all of the Affinities. They carried within them seven cores: one for each of the different Affinities and another to send out orders and regulate the other six.

Ten of them formed, all taking on a similar appearance to Suzy. These creations didn't have any emotion on their faces as they looked at the incoming attacks. Gray light formed from their hands as they erected a Mana barrier around Suzy and Induca, only allowing the beam of Induca's attack to continue.

"I can't keep this up for long!" Suzy said. The attacks were blunted but the power necessary for these creations were on another level compared to the regular creations she had.

She sent out three of the creations. They dove toward the ground, brimming with energy. They fired simple Mana beams, like the Xelur utilizing Mana barriers.

They moved, dancing around like the wind, hitting as fast as light and as hard as earth and metal, flowing through the Xelur's defense like water. They weren't as powerful or fast as Lox and Gurren, but because they were inanimate, they didn't have to care about wounds that would have killed others. As long as their cores were unaffected, they could continue to fight.

Lox let out a roar, his movements picked up in speed as he pushed forward, not worrying about the consumption from his soul gem reserves any more.

More and more of the Xelur now unleashed their ranged attacks on Induca and Suzy.

Steve, Lox, and Gurren broke through the Xelur lines and appeared at the edge of the thirty-meter-wide crater around the Grand Demon Lord.

Lox shot forward. His armor glowed white as he flew toward the Grand Demon Lord.

It instantly combusted its soul reserves as Gurren, Steve, Malsour, and Anna followed behind Lox's wild charge. Its ranged attack grew in power, forcing back Induca, who didn't have time to change her Dragon form as the new power output from the Xelur Grand Demon overpowered her own attack.

She was hit straight on, crying out as her Health dropped to just ten percent.

"No!" Suzy yelled. The Air creation on her back allowed her to shoot across the sky and grab Induca, who was falling from the sky. The different components of her attack came apart without her there to ground it all.

The Grand Demon let out a terrifying roar, a ghost-like apparition formed in front of it. The ghost paused in the air for a moment before taking off like a dart and entering the opening within Suzy's defenses.

Her great creations moved to try to intercept but they weren't quick enough. The attack smashed into Suzy, making her cough blood. Three of her gray creations fell apart as she could no longer control them.

Lox's sword smashed down at the Grand Demon Lord.

The Grand Demon Lord moved its war hammer across to block the attack. It made to counterattack as Steve reacted. Lox, attacking the Grand Demon Lord's side, forced him to defend instead of continue his attack.

"Anna, go get them!" Lox barked as Gurren added himself to the fray. His sword lashed out like a viper, the Grand Demon Lord again forced to defend.

Steve, Gurren, and Lox fought on the ground or in the air, attacking anywhere they saw a weakness, working together unconsciously so that they would open up the Grand Demon Lord for another one to hit them.

"Got it!" Anna yelled. An explosion ripped through the area around her, blowing away any who were close enough and not stable on their feet. The Grand Demon Lord and the rest of Party Zero around him didn't even regard the shock wave as they fought with everything they had.

Malsour protected their backs, using his spells to kill as many Xelur as possible.

Lox knew that Suzy and Induca's fall from the sky was pulling at his very heart but the rest of the party needed him where he was or else this could all come apart.

Anna reached into the air, grabbing the falling Suzy and Induca. Lu Lu had turned into a raging demon as she tore through the sky, unleashing the most powerful attacks on those below.

The Xelur tried to hit her with their ranged attacks but her flying skills were no less than that of a Dragon's. Now she wasn't resting on Suzy or Induca's shoulders; her size expanded from a housecat to that of a four-door car.

Each of her attacks was more powerful than the last. As she killed or assisted others, her experience constantly rose, giving her more levels. Unlike the players or people of Emerilia, she couldn't assign her increase in stat points; they were automatically updated—meaning Suzy didn't need to go into her stats and increase them.

"Lu Lu!" Anna's yell cut through the sky.

Lu Lu let out an angered call but seeing Anna carrying her mom, the fight went out of her. She turned, displaying her greatest speed as she followed Anna, Induca, and Suzy back toward the castle.

Lox didn't have time to look anymore as he, Gurren, and Steve all stepped up to take the damage, fulfilling their role as tanks. They could barely keep the Grand Demon Lord pinned. They needed someone to get in heavy hits to start pulling the Grand Demon Lord's Health down.

"We need mage support and DPS! We can hold the Demon Lord but we can't kill him as he burns so much soul energy!" Lox cried out on the command channel.

"Lord Indas! We need your scouts!" Esa yelled out.

"They're on their way!" Lord Indas yelled.

Gurren, Lox, and Steve continued their attacks, tirelessly attacking the Grand Demon Lord.

Gurren, in his frustration, went for a risky attack, finding the handle of the Grand Demon Lord's war hammer coming for his head. It smashed into his helmet, but being within the separate space of the bag of holding, he swung his shield up and pressed forward with an attack.

The Grand Demon Lord, surprised that Gurren wasn't at least stunned, had to sidestep Gurren's second attack, his own follow-up going wide.

Steve and Lox both attacked at the same time. Steve's blow was deflected but Lox's hit cutting into the Xelur's side.

The wound started healing as soon as Lox's attack had passed. Steam rose off it as the soul aura around it burned fiercely to defeat the attacking gray Mana that worked its way into the Grand Demon Lord's body.

They moved around the crater. The sound of their weapons rang out with each crushing hit that broke the ground or made the ears of those nearby ring.

With a flickering movement, Indas and six of his people appeared. All of them wore loose and baggy clothing, as well as veils that covered their faces. Weapons were held in their hands and there was not an inch of armor on their bodies.

By looking at these people, one might think them as weak, but their movement speed was incredibly high!

Blades on chains moved like live snakes, moving between the three tanks and striking the Grand Demon Lord.

Unable to fight off all of the attacks, the Grand Demon Lord was hit by the blades, cutting down on his Health. Still, he defended against Lox, Gurren, and Steve. If one of their attacks hit, then it would severely impact his Health, more so than the attacks by Indas's people.

The Grand Demon Lord cried out in anger and frustration as the attacks kept on whittling down its Health.

"It's nearing seventy-five percent!" Gurren yelled out.

"Be ready for a Legendary ability!" Lox said.

The Grand Demon Lord fell to seventy percent and still there was no sign of the Legendary ability.

Steve hit the Grand Demon Lord's war hammer wide. Gurren's sword jabbed out low, cutting deep into the Grand Demon Lord's thigh and making him stumble.

Even at that, his wounds were healing but thankfully it wasn't instantaneous.

Indas's people used the time to their advantage, dropping his Health more than fifteen percent.

"Coming up on fifty percent. Maybe he's not got a Legendary ability?" Gurren said, sounding unsure.

Fifty percent hit and the Grand Demon Lord's soul aura climbed to new heights as his Health bar started to quickly refill.

A magical formation appeared around the Grand Demon Lord. Gurren, Lox, and Steve were unaffected but Malsour and Indas's people were.

"It's a soul attack," Malsour ground out, fighting the attack with all of his Willpower. Indas's people were brought to the ground, crying out in pain within the area of effect.

"Pull back and use your ranged!" Lox yelled.

Steve and Gurren jumped back five meters. Steve dropped his axe; the head embedded itself into the ground as his wrists glowed. Gurren and Lox's weapons fell away, dissipating into fog as they activated their wristbands, pushing them to full power.

The Grand Demon Lord was still in the air. Soul energy from all around rushed toward him, filling his Health and also returning some of his lost power.

The trio didn't hesitate. From their hands, gray Mana bolts appeared. The smoky balls came out so fast that they looked like solid streams.

These attacks impacted the Grand Demon Lord as he tried to regenerate his abilities and reserves. The rate of his Health returning decreased as their damaging attacks were faster than his regeneration.

The Grand Demon Lord whirled out his war hammer. It glowed white with soul energy. His movement ended his Legendary ability of regeneration as the other Legendary ability of soul domain continued to affect all of those within the area of effect.

Gurren and Lox, within their Devastator armor, couldn't be touched, and Steve didn't have a soul nor did he use nanites that powered the Xelur, so it had no effect on him either.

The white light rushed outward, becoming weaker as it was hit by the Mana bolts.

Lox brought his fist back, wreathed in gray Mana. He punched forward and smashed against the attack.

The attack failed. Lox continued to fire his attacks. The Grand Demon Lord now smashed his hammer toward Gurren's attacks, advancing on him. The pressure from the attacks made it impossible for him to close the mere ten meters quickly.

Steve broke through the war hammer attack at the same time as Gurren. The both of them added in their attacks onto Lox's. The Grand Demon Lord howled in pain as the three streams of Mana bolts kept it contained. Waves of Mana flew from the three as they looked like demigods trying to restrain the full might of a god between their efforts.

The Grand Demon Lord was completely suppressed as it tried to move; to get past the Mana bolts holding it back.

The power consumption was incredible with runes across all three sets of armor lighting up to collect rampant Mana. The wind was whipped up with this intake sucked in like an ancient beast was trying to breath in the planet's air.

If the Grand Demon tried to move in one direction, then the three would also move to block him.

The Grand Demon's soul aura was still strong enough to stop the attacks but it was burning off its soul energy at a massive rate to stay alive. It dropped its hammer, staring directly at Steve, it raised its hands slowly, fighting the streams from Lox and Gurren. Its soul aura spun and twisted down its arms, concentrating in the palm of its hands before light tore outward. The twin streams pushed back Lox and Gurren's bolts, defeating them before they reached the Grand Demon Lord, just as it had done with Induca.

However, Induca was much stronger than Lox and Gurren and their armors' attacks; even though they were powerful, they didn't have the complexity or power of Induca's attacks.

Steve, seeing the two dwarves being suppressed, altered his coding, pouring more and more of his Mana into his arms as he stepped forward.

The Grand Demon Lord laughed crazily, its soul aura taking on the attacks from Steve. It looked as if its entire body was aflame with brilliant and powerful soul energy. Motes of light of all colors danced around in the soothing miasma of energy.

"Not again!" Steve's voice boomed. He continued forward. Each step left a crater from the force of his attacks.

The Grand Demon Lord's attacks pushed Lox and Gurren's attacks back farther.

Fear started to form in Lox but he clamped down on it. He could burn out this Grand Demon Lord's power—then someone might be able to kill it! If he lost the armor or even his life, it would have been worth it. He planted his feet firmer, thinking of Suzy and Induca, who'd been seriously injured to the point that they'd fallen from the sky, unconscious.

The light beam from the Grand Demon Lord reached Lox and Gurren's hands. They didn't flinch as their hands were melted away and their wrists were destroyed, breaking the magical coding.

The attack raced back and their wrists slammed into their chests.

To get the most power to their attack, they had both stopped powering their Mana barriers. They were thrown backward, craters in their chests.

Lox saw all kinds of warning lights on his interface as his armor was severely damaged. He looked over to see Steve cancel his ranged attack. His hand shot backward; his axe responded to him and flew into his grip.

The Grand Demon Lord grasped his war hammer and swung it around at Steve, who brought his axe up and around, smashing into the oncoming war hammer.

They had both imbued their power into their weapons. Steve's was covered in a dark miasma while the Grand Demon Lord's was covered in that soul aura once again.

With the impact of their weapons, the dust at the wall that had been churned up by the trio's attacks was dispersed, showing the outside world.

Runic lines across Steve's armor lit up with darkness as the two separated. Hammer and axe met again and again. The two of them fought with everything they had: Steve burned his soul gem reserves while the Grand Demon Lord burned up his soul energy.

Lox made to get up but found that his armor was too badly damaged to be of much use. Restorative runes had been activated across his armor, repairing his destroyed hands and forearm as well as his chest section. Lox knew that getting out of his armor around these two would only make him a hindrance to Steve. He focused on pouring as much power in getting his armor functional as he watched the two giants battle in the middle of that crater.

Xelur were now moving into the area as the Grand Demon Lord's Legendary attack soul domain had worn off. The Legendary ability didn't care whether those within it were allies or not; they would consume all.

Malsour regained his feet as people tried to charge into the crater. Malsour let out a roar that shook the very heavens as his body grew at an alarming speed revealing his Dragon form!

In the eyes of Malsour—once he was in Dragon form—these low-level Xelur weren't much of a problem.

"We have a breach in the southeastern wall! The Grand Demon Lord there has made it through!" someone called out.

Around the crater, black flames rose to ten feet in height, burning all of those who were less than ten meters away. Some were simply turned to ash in the face of the attack.

From these flames, darklings stepped out. Four hundred darklings looked upon the Xelur, amassing their numbers. Malsour looked down upon them like a titan making his judgement.

The flames surged outward for forty meters in every direction, killing tens of Xelur.

As they were recovering from the sudden attack, the darklings that had advanced in those flames brought forth from the abyss itself descended upon the Xelur ranks. In the early morning darkness, the darklings were in their element, moving through shadows as easily as one might walk.

The Xelur used soul energy, which was highly effective against the darklings. But they were within the Terra Alliance's walls—they were being cut down by ranged defenders as well as melee types.

The eastern side of the castle was in chaos. The eastern gate was still open and Xelur were coming in but at a much lower rate than before. Outside the northeastern wall, Deia, Jung Lee, and Dave were fighting against the Xelur there and the southeastern wall had been breached.

Lox looked to Steve and the Grand Demon Lord as they continued to clash with each other. Lox moved his legs, to prop himself up and try to get upright. All around him, people were yelling out their roaring cries as they clashed with Xelur and those of the Terra Alliance.

Indas and his people rose to their feet as well, anger in their eyes.

Lox watched as they rushed forward; their chained blades darted outward as they seemed to dance with their weapons. They flowed through attacks, looking exotic and beautiful even as their blades struck the Demon Lord's vital areas.

The Grand Demon Lord's wounds healed at a slower rate but they were still sealing up.

Steve, however, did not have the fighting experience or power reserves of the Grand Demon Lord. His armor was scratched, dented, and opened in several areas. His body underneath was exposed, with some attacks cutting open his soul gem construct.

Still, these titans clashed with each other—only now with Indas's men was Steve approaching parity with the Xelur Grand Demon Lord.

Lox couldn't help but feel his heart moved as he conjured new hands, and a sword and shield for his armor. It wouldn't be as strong as if they were real but they would function.

"On your right!" Lox yelled, rushing forward to support Steve, who was quickly weakening under the Xelur Grand Demon's attacks.

"What took you so long!" Steve said, trying to hide his happiness.

"Thought you could handle it!" Gurren stepped up to Steve's left side. The three of them stood side by side to hold back the Xelur Grand Demon Lord.

"Die for me!" The Grand Demon Lord hacked at all three of them.

Steve blocked the attack; Lox and Gurren darted forward, their blades piercing the sides of the Grand Demon Lord.

He coughed blood and retreated a meter or so. Several chained daggers came from behind and sliced open his back, making him stagger forward. He let out a bellow of pain, just blocking Gurren's attack in time and brought his Warhammer across to hit Steve in the side.

Lox interposed himself against the war hammer; his conjured shield shattered and he was tossed sideways. But Steve didn't let the opportunity pass by. His hand, covered in Mana, punched the Xelur Grand Demon in the side, which pushed him back two steps as he tried to defend against Gurren's attack. He was thrown back while Steve turned, gaining momentum with his axe, and smashed up against the Grand Demon Lord, who was just able to stop the attack.

Lox rolled over, conjuring a new hand to grab the ground as he threw himself forward. The runes on his body made him fly as he came across and behind the Grand Demon Lord, cutting his calves.

Steve and the Grand Demon Lord's attacks were broken off. The Grand Demon Lord let himself drop, barely missing Steve's axe that swung over his head. He came upward from the ground and under Steve's swing. His hammer slammed into Steve's chest and sent him back five meters. He made to attack Steve again as chained daggers went for his face.

He smashed them away with his war hammer as Gurren stepped up in front of him, cutting down with his sword. The Grand Demon Lord's defense was strong enough to break the conjured sword.

Gurren jumped backward and out of the range of the war hammer. The Grand Demon Lord cut out with his war hammer and a soul gem light filled the air.

The light spread outward and smashed against Gurren's hips. His Mana barrier was active so there wasn't any damage to his armor but it sent him tumbling away.

Steve— who'd recovered from being hit back, the armor around his chest dented inward from the war hammer's impact—now ran forward as Lox, who'd overshot the Grand Demon Lord, came on a right angle from him.

With the two of them, they were able to pin the Grand Demon Lord in place.

They were evenly matched. Steve and Lox had both burned so much power that they were no longer able to show off their strongest abilities.

Likewise, the Grand Demon Lord had burned through his soul power. With Malsour's new magical formation, less and less were making it to the Grand Demon Lord and he had already needed to burn most of it in order to stay alive.

In the shadows from behind the Grand Demon Lord, a claw as big as the Grand Demon Lord emerged, striking out so fast that the Grand Demon Lord didn't even know that it was there. The claw pierced through the Grand Demon Lord's back and exited his front.

He looked at the claw in shock and horror.

The claw turned around as the Grand Demon Lord found itself looking up at a Dragon with scales that seemed to be made from obsidian and black flames darker than the night across its body and resting in its mouth.

The Grand Demon looked up in horror, powerless to resist and unable to restore itself with a claw through its body.

Malsour looked at the Grand Demon Lord with disdain. "This is for my sister." Malsour opened his mouth. Flames shot out from his maw, covering the Xelur Grand Demon Lord completely.

After a moment, the flames disappeared. There was no sign of the Xelur Grand Demon Lord's existence.

From within the castle, a familiar noise shook the castle and the grounds its foundations were buried in.

"The War Clans have arrived!" Lox yelled out. He would know those drums anywhere.

The dwarven War Clans had finally reached the castles. The drum beat was fast and fierce as dwarves' feet jogged through the castles. They swarmed out of the main corridors, pressing out and into the open area between the outer walls and the inner castles. As they stepped out of the castles, dwarves would turn and plant themselves. Their shields faced toward the eastern side; from the north and south, dwarven walls formed quickly as dwarves moved into place, the first rank filling in and the second rank lining up behind them.

Lox climbed to his feet and conjured his hands, sword and shield once again.

"Well, let's see if we can't give them some time to form up!" Lox yelled, looking to the players and POEs nearby.

They checked their weapons, nervously looking to the Party Zero members.

"Malsour, clear us a path to the tunnel. If you can seal it up, we can cover your rear," Lox said.

"Understood." Malsour's voice was deep and powerful, like the ancient, powerful, and wise beast that he was.

"Let's show these Xelur Demons what we're made of! With me!" Lox yelled, jogging toward the gate tunnel to the east.

Malsour unleashed his terrifying breath over them all, scouring the ground clear of Xelur and anything that was in their way.

A few of the Demon Lords that were within their ranks were able to resist, only to find themselves alive but without support of their weaker soldiers and facing the forces that Lox was able to rally.

"Leave none standing!" Lox yelled as he clashed with a Xelur Demon Lord, their power easily matched as they fought each other.

Battle was once again joined. The others cleared the path for Malsour, who was breathing down the gate tunnel, killing those in his way.

Chapter 7: Live or Die

Anna caught Induca and Suzy as they fell, she could tell they were both badly injured as she used healing spells on them both. She didn't have time to look backward.

"Lu Lu!" Anna yelled out.

The lightning phoenix, hearing the familiar name, turned and rushed toward Anna, who was already entering the castle, holding both Suzy and Induca and covering the trio in air.

Anna continued to use healing spells, not having enough time to pull a potion from her bag of holding as she rushed through the halls into the main area of the castle. She followed the stream of wounded passing through the ono.

As soldiers and forces moved in through one side of the teleport pad in Terra, on the other side people were rushed through the intake area, which doubled as a triage area.

Anna raced in, putting Suzy and Induca on two different beds. Anna pulled out Health potions, pouring them on Induca's wounds and pouring it down Suzy's throat.

Suzy only had blood on her mouth but Anna could tell that her Vitality was weak. Knowing that Suzy could re-spawn Anna focused her efforts on Induca. Her armor was in tatters; her body was cut up from the ravaging energies of the attacking soul energy.

A healer came past and put his hands on Induca.

Healing light came from his hands even as he talked. "She needs to get to intake right away! Priority one!" the healer said to the bearers behind them. Without hesitating, they picked up Induca and moved for the underground tunnels that would take them and Induca right to the Stone Raiders' tower and the hospital that lay within.

"Odd—looks like a soul attack to me. Take her to the shamans," the healer said after touching Suzy's head.

Another set of bearers whisked her away as well.

Anna followed Induca. Suzy would win her fight or come back again. She would lose some levels but that would be it. If something happened to Induca, she could truly die. Anna followed the bearers to the underground stations; her identity was confirmed before she was allowed to pass.

When they found out that Emerilia was real, Dwayne and Jules had enforced rules on the activities within Terra. This was to make sure that no one from the Jukal or from groups that wanted to attack the Terra Alliance or the Stone Raiders would ever be given the chance. Such as allowing wounded into the hospital but keeping them in secured zones compared to the Stone Raiders and vetted personnel.

They stepped onto a platform, all around there was nonstop movement, with capsules constantly on the move, some arriving while others were leaving.

Seeing it, Anna was surprised with just how modern-looking it was. She followed the bearers onto a capsule.

A Mana barrier formed over the entrance as they shot off. Gravity and inertia magic kept them in place and not feeling anything while also accelerating them at incredible speeds to the towers.

They reached the towers. Underneath the towers there was another platform; this one was not laid out simply like the first but had defenses in place, as well as automatons.

They were checked once more as they reached an elevator on the capsule.

Other elevators shot capsules upward or brought them back down before sending them on their way through Terra.

The capsule they were on finally reached an elevator that shot upward.

They came to a stop. The capsule's barrier disappeared as the bearers walked out. A door opened beside the capsule, as they walked out of the capsule and into the hospital.

"Stage one! Soul energy attack!" one of the bearers yelled out at the waiting people facing the doors.

"Room E-73!" One called out.

The bearers rushed down the halls with Induca. The stretcher underneath her had magical coding that was constantly healing her and trying to keep her stable in transport.

They passed wards filled with all manner of wounded. People from castles all over Emerilia were transported to this hospital.

The bearers entered the ward for E-73. A a healer nearby rushed over; a team followed them.

"Stage one, Xelur soul energy attack," the bearer repeated.

"What kind of Xelur was it?" the healer asked.

"Grand Demon Lord. His spell was too powerful, broke through hers and hit her," Anna said.

"Looks like she was able to blunt the power of the spell. Instead of hitting her right in the chest, she broke the beam and it hit most of her body. Thankfully, she directed it downward," the healer said grimly.

Anna felt lost as she looked at her friend barely holding on to life.

"Immediately start healing. Focus on the head. Be ready with ventilation. We're going to need a grand healing potion bath!" the healer called out. One of the group ran away to carry out their orders while the healer placed his hands on Induca's head, another healer in the group moved to the other side. Golden light fell down on Induca as her face started to return to its original shape.

"Let's make sure she stays unconscious. We don't want her waking up to all of this," the healer said.

Induca was put down on a cart, next to what looked like a large bathtub made from straight lines. Along the sides of the bathtub and inside it there were runic lines. The base of the bathtub was made of soul gem connected directly into the floor.

The bearers looked at Induca, unsure how to get her from the cart they'd put her on to the bathtub.

The healers moved out of the way, moving to the bathtub to receive her.

Most of Induca's legs were gone and from below the neck, she was in a terrible state.

With a wave of her hand, Anna lifted Induca off the stretcher and cart, over the healer and into the bathtub.

Immediately, the lines around the bathtub came on. Induca let out a rasping and terrible breath.

The healers placed their hands on Induca's head.

"Set her bones and have her prepped for healing!" the lead healer said, still concentrating on Induca's head.

The bearers left to help move more people as the group of healers examined Induca's body, putting her bones back in place and healing them enough to hold their position. Their focus then moved on to her vital organs.

The person who had been sent off to the side of the room was now carrying massive potion jugs.

"Stamina potion, good idea," the lead healer said. "How are we with the lower body wounds?"

"There are a lot of them but we need to get those organs healed fast," one of the healers working on the lower body said.

"Do it," the lead healer said.

The one with the jugs poured the Stamina potion into the bathtub.

A vitality started to spread through Induca's body as she took in this Stamina potion throughout her body.

The person with the healing potion handed out cups of the potion to the healers, who guided it into different areas for the maximum effect.

Anna could only stand there and watch, helpless, as the healers worked tirelessly to bring Induca back from the edge.

***

Deia, Dave, and Jung Lee saw Induca in the sky as she had been fighting the Grand Demon Lord but they shot over the outer walls, unable to see her anymore as they locked onto their own target: the Grand Demon Lord who had first attacked their castle.

Jung Lee called upon his Free Affinity spirits. As he descended toward the ground, a gray ethereal smoke formed around him. Jekoni appeared next to his shoulder. Instead of his normal sitting, now Jekoni stood; his hat, instead of dropping, was upright and ready, as if becoming serious. Across Jekoni's body, power fluctuated as Jung Lee felt the spirits imbued within the sword where Jekoni resided stirred.

The Grand Demon Lord, upon seeing them, charged forward, his body covered in the white flames of soul energy.

Jung Lee Walked ahead of them, his pace quickly closing the gap as he pulled his sword from the sheath, a grey light shining in front of him.

The Grand Demon Lord's forward momentum was halted as he was smacked with the sword light formed of gray Mana. It left a deep cut in his body, his soul aura tremble.

"Looks like I've found a great harvest in your souls!" The Grand Demon Lord laughed and rushed forward at Jung Lee. His hands grew talons made out of soul energy that whistled through the air.

Fast and in control of his soul energy. Jung Lee's sword snaked out, directing the blow to the side. A fifteen-meter-long line was

cut into the ground where the blow passed over. The Grand Demon Lord didn't slow his pace, advancing as he clawed at him. Jung
Lee deflected the attacks, his movements nimble and agile as that
terrifying force rushed past him.

With each blow, the ground was torn apart. The remaining dirt
and grass turned to a shredded mess, creating dust and debris in the
air.

"I can hold back the Xelur. Deia—help Lee," Dave said.

Lee caught Dave out the side of his eye. Dave was now on the
ground, armed with twin axes. Down his arms, runic lines formed,
directing and enhancing his power. The twin axes gave off a gray
smoke similar to Jung Lee's own attacks and spells.

Dave pushed off the ground, shooting forward to meet the
Xelur. As his axes shot out, Mana grenades flew from his bags
of holding, shooting outward to meet the surrounding Xelur and
keeping them back.

Disks and other orbs were also unleashed, creating magical formations and traps that activated nearly immediately and killed any
Xelur within their area of effect.

Jung Lee continued to dodge blows from the Grand Demon
Lord, moving side to side and using his blade sparingly as he got a
better idea of the Grand Demon Lord's abilities.

As he moved to the side, he felt a rush of air from behind him
as a blue arrow passed in front of his face. *So fast and precise. Deia
must have read my very movements so as to not hit me.*

The arrow passed Jung Lee, the Grand Demon Lord, seeing it,
was able to increase their soul aura to try to defend themselves better. He rushed forward so instead of the arrow hitting him in the
head, it struck his shoulder.

The aura blunted the attack but a big chunk of the Grand Demon Lord's shoulder was turned into a bloody mess. In front of
Jung Lee's eyes, it started to recover.

Jung Lee pressed forward. He changed his grip on his sword, moving from defending to attacking. With the recent attack, the Grand Demon Lord was in close with Jung Lee, whose power was ignited.

Around him, gray smoke seemed to form and trailed his movements as his sword struck out. The Grand Demon Lord parried the attack, a look of utmost confusion on its face. The Grand Demon Lord was one of the most powerful beings within the Xelur realm, yet these insects could actually hurt him!

There were few people who would anger a Grand Demon Lord and few who would openly challenge them.

Even Grand Demon Lords challenging each other was a rare occurrence. Not because they didn't want to fight, but that fighting between Grand Demon Lords could exhaust the soul energy that they had built up over decades, if not centuries. Losing that power would reduce their rank and also open them up to attacks by those they stepped on in the past.

The Grand Demon Lord's face turned from confusion into open joy as he met Jung Lee's blade with his claws.

"Try to get his back facing me so I can hit him," Deia said over the party chat.

"Okay." Jung Lee changed up his movements and put pressure on the Grand Demon Lord to try to give Deia a shot.

The Grand Demon Lord, wary of Deia and her attacks, continued to place Jung Lee between them, going so far as to take light wounds.

"Why are you not doing anything?" Jung Lee asked Jekoni.

"Lee, you're a lot more powerful than you were before but you've yet to display it. Here and now, you can put your strength to use and temper your abilities that you've just touched on. Dave needs my help in order to keep back the Xelur around you. Do not let this opportunity go to waste." Jekoni floated away from Jung Lee.

"It's been some time since I played with Mana." Jekoni laughed. His body became more physical and detailed as Jung Lee felt Jekoni pull from the sword as well as from the link he shared with Jung Lee. "Dave, you deal with the northern side—I can deal with the south!"

"Thanks, Jekoni!" Dave said.

Jung Lee was stunned by Dave's fighting style. Myriad different weapons and movements seemed to form into one terrifying whole. Dave's weapons changed nearly instantly, going from axe to sword, to shield, to spear to war hammer, and back to axe or any combination in between.

The Xelur were constantly kept off-balance as he continued to change up his fighting style. As the Xelur died, instead of their power being dispersed, it was pulled into Dave's armor, growing stronger each time.

Even if the Xelur hit Dave, they would instead find a Mana barrier in their way, deflecting their attack as a weapon whistled through the air to finish them off.

Jung Lee felt a smile rise to his lips. He had felt distant for quite some time. He was attached to the people of Party Zero but Emerilia—although he had been born here— it didn't feel like his home anymore. Jekoni was one of the only people he had known while he had been free within Emerilia who was still alive.

His friends, family—all of that was taken from him by time, leaving him trapped within the Six Affinities Temple. He had suffered loneliness, loneliness so terrifying that he had thought about letting go, of releasing his bond to Emerilia.

But he hadn't. When he was released, he was filled with excitement and joy. He could do everything that he had dreamed of!

Now, these creatures and this event wanted to once again seal him up, to take away that freedom.

A fire that Jung Lee had not felt for a long time built in his stomach. It turned and shook the very fiber of his being. It was anger; it was fear; it was all the emotions that came with fighting. He could die at any moment and all of his dreams would be left unrealized, unattained. His freedom would count for nothing.

Jekoni had been right: Jung Lee had come to know of the six Affinity spirits within his body, but he hadn't come to understand or use them in any manner.

Jung Lee saw the Grand Demon Lord in front of him and the aura that surrounded him—the aura of soul energy from all the Affinities, just out of equilibrium by the smallest amount. Jung Lee had an idea.

He called upon the Affinity spirits under his command. They swirled and moved from their slumber, eager to let their energies loose upon the world. They stepped out of Jung Lee and formed human-looking shapes.

The Grand Demon Lord looked at them as they continued to trade blows, wary of these smoky apparitions of Earth, Fire, Water, Air, Light, and Dark.

The apparitions turned formless, once again returning to Jung Lee. But instead of returning to their rest, they entered Jung Lee's body.

Behind him an ethereal looking Jekoni floated in the air, he raised his head, hat moving out of his way as his eyes glowed with arcane light. This was the imprint Jekoni had left on the weapon of power, this was his might. The affinity spirits moved to enhance Jung Lee under Jekoni's guidance.

Lee let out a satisfied noise as he felt their power enhance his own. His senses grew sharper and his mind clearer as his body felt as light as a feather but as strong as a pillar of metal.

Jung Lee's speed increased as he hit harder. His mind moved at a speed that allowed him to look upon his techniques, critiquing and improving upon them. With the six Affinity spirits improving the power of his own body, he came to understand them more, to know the effects of their enhancement, as well as their weaknesses and strengths, forcing him to adapt and understand how to use them to his advantage.

The Grand Demon Lord, sensing Jung Lee's power rising, combusted more of his soul energy. From a bag of holding, he crushed a soul gem. Power filled the air and centered on the Grand Demon Lord, increasing his power to its peak as his aura increased in power.

"Yes! Yes!" The Grand Demon Lord seemed like a battle fanatic as they exchanged blows. Jung Lee's sword was covered in gray Mana while the Xelur Grand Demon Lord's was covered in the chaotic and powerful soul energy.

The area around Jekoni seemed to turn into a desert as all of the moisture was pulled from it. A number of the weaker Xelur were drained as their bodies weren't strong enough to resist that pull.

"Oh no you don't!" Jekoni pulled the power from the souls toward himself instead of allowing the other Xelur to power up from it.

Deia, seeing that the Xelur Grand Demon wasn't going to let her hit him, turned her attention toward the breach in the wall. She fired her bow as fast as a repeater could fire. The runes that she had picked made the arrows faster and made them multiply in a horizontal line instead of creating an area of falling arrows. A half-dozen arrows took the Xelur down. Deia seemed to rotate back and forth. In front of her bow, the weaker Xelur were just wheat to be harvested.

She dodged from side to side with an almost ethereal grace, not even needing to pause as she fired a seemingly continuous stream of arrows at the Xelur. She advanced without pause or fear. The Xelur rushed her and her team to concentrate their attacks and tear Party Zero apart.

Jung Lee pushed that from his mind as he fought against the Grand Demon Lord.

"Come out!" Jung Lee yelled. Six humanoid shapes made of colored mist shot out from his body, and stood around the Grand Demon Lord.

Jung Lee could only use a fraction of their power in order to reinforce his body. If he was to use it all, then his body would start to come apart, unable to contain that power in his mere flesh. All of their power that he was not using he allowed free, forming their individual bodies.

Jung Lee and the Grand Demon Lord continued to fight, smashing against each other over and over again, trading blows at a speed most couldn't match. Their abilities were many times stronger than their base attributes.

Jung Lee cut in close, attacking the Grand Demon Lord's stomach.

He jumped backward. As soon as Jung Lee saw the Grand Demon Lord retreat a meter, he flashed back three.

The six Affinities flashed outward to surround the Grand Demon Lord.

The Grand Demon Lord looked toward them but didn't have time to react as six different elemental energies illuminated the world, pinning him in place.

Jung Lee moved his hands, his eyes closed as he made a seal in midair. Mages could use their hands or their voices in order to help assist in forming magical spells.

Between the six rays of energies, a magical formation appeared. A spell formation appeared in the midst of these different colored streams. As they touched one another, these spell formations combined the power of them all. They transformed from their six colors into gray threads that burned through the Grand Demon Lord's protection faster and faster.

Jung Lee ran his hand down his blade, pulling on the spirits' power that was tapped into Emerilia's different Affinities.

The soul gem appearance of the sword transformed becoming a solid gray that shone in the early dawn sunlight. The gray smoke from before was all sucked into this polished gray sword.

Jung Lee opened his eyes. Red, blue, green, white, gold, and black seemed to swirl in his eyes before they turned solid gray, glowing with power as Dave's did.

The ground broke under his feet as he charged forward.

"No!" The Grand Demon Lord burned all of the soul energy that it could, inflicting damage on itself as it tried to fight the six Free Affinity spirits.

They increased their power. How could a being that relied on tearing energy from others compare to them that had been born from the energies of Emerilia?

Jung Lee passed the Free Affinity spirits, his face expressionless as his fully gray eyes looked at the Grand Demon Lord as if he were nothing but a pebble in a sea of rocks.

His sword rushed forward, piercing through the struggling Grand Demon's head and coming back out in a flash.

The six Affinity spirits lowered their hands. The power disappeared as the spell formations faded away.

The Grand Demon Lord dropped to the ground, an expression of disbelief etched on his face for eternity.

Jung Lee waved his sword, sending out a mental command to his Affinity spirits.

They floated forward, doubling themselves, producing lower-class Affinity spirits. As they stepped forward, they doubled again, going from six to twelve to twenty-four and forty-eight and then ninety-six. The main Free Affinity spirits returned to Jung Lee as the ninety copies held out their hands.

"Destroy them." Jung Lee looked to the Xelur.

Jung Lee might not be a mage but the six Affinity spirits had the innate ability to use the energies within their bodies. They didn't even need to create spell formations as the natural energies of Emerilia obeyed their commands.

Fire storms ripped out at the Xelur surrounding Deia's party. Tornadoes carved paths through with their cutting winds. Darklings emerged from the shadows, appearing among the Xelur and cutting them down. Golden light fell upon the Xelur, burning their bodies and tearing the soul energy free from them. The ground revolted against the Xelur, unbalancing them and making them unable to react as grasses and vines attacked them, cracking against their soul auras. Storm clouds formed above with lightning and rain hammering those below.

Jekoni let out a maniacal laugh, he had been using the water from the ground and air in order to augment his abilities. Now, with the surplus of water, he formed a sphere of it that extended outward, creating blades along the surface. He rushed forward, these blades cutting against the off-balance Xelur.

Deia had cleared out the area around the breach and was targeting Demon Lords. Her arrows found an opening as they fell to the ground, no longer a threat.

Dave was among the ranks still. Using his gravitational manipulation, he was able to make any of the Xelur that he was fighting, off-balance, allowing him to plant a weapon in whatever weaknesses he could find.

Now that he didn't have to try to protect Jung Lee from ranged attacks, his speed only increased. His weapons transformed in a blur: one moment it would be a sword; then next a bow; the next a claymore. As he moved, he left bodies in his wake.

Jung Lee rushed toward the Xelur. Deia, Dave, Jekoni, and now Jung Lee pushed outward in different directions.

The Xelur were stunned by the turn of events.

The Grand Demon Lord had been an all-powerful existence, akin to their gods.

Now that they were gone, they understood the disparity between them and these members of Party Zero.

It was only due to Jung Lee's high levels and abilities that they had been able to deal with the Grand Demon Lord. His power was a third of Malsour's; however, when combined with the power of his six Affinity spirits, Jung Lee's power rose to new heights, making it hard to accurately guess his overall power.

Jung Lee's hearing was enhanced so that he could easily hear the drums of the War Clans as they entered the castles and advanced toward the area between the castle and the outer walls.

"Esa wants us back in the castle to deal with the last remaining Xelur Grand Demon Lord!" Deia yelled over the party chat.

"Ready when you are," Dave said, cutting through Xelur.

"I can leave these spirits here. If they consume all of their power, it will take only a few hours for the originals to regain their lost energy," Jung Lee said after having gained a better understanding of the Free Affinity spirits within his body.

"Okay, let's go!" Deia shot off into the sky, a ray of fire, conjuring a raging fire storm in the midst of the Xelur.

Dave jumped into the air, dumping a bag of grenades that created a trail behind him. The runes lit up on them as they were hurled out by different fields created by the orbs that circled Dave.

Explosions rippled out of the Xelur ranks, killing and severely wounding many.

Jekoni was the nucleus of the massive water sphere, blades shot out, spinning so fast as to whip up the air around it. Jekoni charged forwards the blades tearing through the Xelur, as the blades were broken here adn there the sphere became smaller as new blades emerged. Jung Lee followed in its wake, their efforts serving to free the Dwarves trying to contain the Xelur that had broken through the eastern side.

Their lines started to get reorganized, not letting the time go to waste, knowing that Jung Lee and Jekoni wouldn't be able to keep it up forever. The two left destruction in their wake, the Dwarven Veterans felt their hearts pound faster with their faces turning pale. They gripped their swords and shields tighter the war drums sounding out the advance as they moved in behind the duo.

***

Dave looked at the crater that the remaining members of Party Zero, frowning as he saw no signs of Induca, Suzy, Lu Lu, and Anna.

They altered their course to meet up with Party Zero.

The southeastern wall exploded outwards, the rocks stopped before reaching the crater. Malsour threw them at the Xelur around those in the crater as a Grand Demon Lord let out a roar of victory as they exited the wall, entering the open area between the castles.

Dave, Deia, and Jekoni dropped to the ground.

Steve, Gurren, and Lox were all showing signs of heavy fighting. Their armor was broken in places, with Gurren and Lox conjuring up hands as well as weapons in order to fight. Their chests were slowly reforming where it looked as if a hot poker had been stabbed into them.

"Where are Suzy, Anna, and Induca?" Dave landed in a run, a claymore in his hands as he smashed into a Xelur Demon Lord, cutting them down and whirling away under another's attack. His claymore turned into a war hammer as he smashed it into their side and threw them backward.

"They were hit badly by the Grand Demon Lord—they're in Terra." Lox savagely punched a Xelur in the face with his shield to vent the anger that he turned in on himself.

"Advance!" The dwarven War Clan leader's order carried over the castle as the dwarven lines moved forward. Behind them, lines of ranged fighters, from mages to archers, javelin throwers and destruction staff users, unleashed their attacks, tearing into the Xelur Demons' lines. With the victory of Lox's group and Deia's group emerging victorious over their Grand Demon Lords, the dwarven lines were sweeping up the Xelur soldiers and lower-ranked Demon Lords within the castle's defenses. This allowed their engineers to repair the walls and counterattack the Xelur.

"For now, we need to focus on killing that final Xelur Grand Demon Lord. If we can get rid of him, then the Xelur's morale will break and we can push them out of the castle and chase them back to the ones that they came from," Deia said.

Deia was as close to Suzy and Induca as sisters might be but right now she couldn't let that distract her from her position as leader of Party Zero.

"If Steve, Lox, Gurren, and I are to attack, we can fully suppress the Grand Demon Lord," Jung Lee said.

"Malsour and I can weaken him," Dave added.

"Jekoni and I should be enough to support you all and hit him with strong spells. Together we can destroy him," Deia said.

"Then we will need a path." Malsour's voice carried over the open area as he stomped his leg. The black flames that surrounded the crater parted in front of the party, spiked walls appeared from the ground, impaling the Xelur in the way.

The Grand Demon Lord looked down the corridor that connected him and Party Zero.

A circle of stone appeared around them, cutting them and the Xelur within from those outside.

Malsour leaned forward. Black flames rushed forward, the corridor serving to direct the flames. The weaker Xelur couldn't even defend against the attacks.

Party Zero rushed down the corridor as the Grand Demon Lord took to the sky, his aura becoming more powerful.

"It's whack-a-mole!" Steve's whole body glowed with power as he shot upward into the sky. Lox, Gurren, and Jung Lee were beside him as they appeared above the Xelur Grand Demon Lord.

"Come on then, you big bastard!" Gurren yelled. He and Lox attacked together, distracting the Xelur Grand Demon Lord and putting him on the defensive.

"Down. You. GO!" Steve yelled, his armor glowed with runes as his soul gem-constructed body lit up the holes in his armor as he brought his axe downward, glowing with its own runic lines.

The Grand Demon Lord looked like a meteor tearing through the heavens as he rose. His twin swords stabbed out at Steve.

"Didn't you hear the man?" Jung Lee yelled, his own power ignited. It was less than when he had fought the other Grand Demon Lord but he moved in a flash, his sword expanded until it was ten meters long and smashed against the Xelur Grand Demon Lord's seven-meter-long swords. He grunted with exertion as he pushed them backward slightly, opening the Xelur Grand Demon's defenses just enough for Steve's hit to connect.

The Grand Demon Lord turned ping pong ball was slapped down ten meters, still in the air.

Malsour created metal spears that killed off those who hadn't died with his flames while Deia and Dave raced forward, their bows letting loose arrows that tore through the Xelur.

Jekoni gestured; water droplets sped through the air, leaving holes in the Xelur's foreheads as they dropped to the ground. He floated beside Malsour as they moved forward at a relaxed pace.

Steve had been tossed back by the impact of his attack had the Grand Demon Lord more angry than anything that the hit had impacted his soul energy but not his Health.

Again, Lox, Gurren, and Jung Lee kept the Grand Demon Lord wrapped up as Steve pounded on the Grand Demon Lord as if he were nothing more than a nail to be hammered into wood.

At their backs, the Dwarven War Clans were advancing, opening to allow POE and players to pass through their lines as they cut down the Xelur without mercy.

Archers on the castles and mages supporting the dwarves took out the Demon Lords, allowing the dwarves to only deal with the normal Xelur forces.

These War Clans had been trained at the Mithsia Mountains for months and tempered in the Ashal wilderness around Aldamire Mountain. Their strength and fighting abilities were greater than most other War Clan's that had been fielded in the past.

They took injuries here and there but it was hard to notice as they pushed onward like an unstoppable juggernaut of shields and swords. Even in the eyes of these venerated shield bearers, there was a look of respect as they looked upon the members of Party Zero. They were powerful and decisive. Even if they were weak and wounded, they continued forward against any that stood in their way.

Dave and Deia rose up into the air, Malsour between them as the Grand Demon Lord was smashed into the ground by Steve's axe.

"And stay there!" Steve slammed against a wall from the recoil of his attack, using the wall to push off and return to the fight.

Dave was linked to Steve, as well as Deia, Lox, and Gurren's armor. The fighting had not been easy on Lox, Steve, and Gurren's power reserves.

He directed the power that was being captured by his armor through specialized circuits and shared it with the other three instead of storing it within the vault soul gem that he carried in his bag of holding as his own armor was fully charged.

The others' power levels climbed upward. Their strength increased as Lox and Gurren's missing hands and melted chest started to repair at a faster rate.

The three's attacks increased in speed and power while Jung Lee continued to add his own attacks. The four of them were able to fully suppress the Grand Demon Lord, even getting hits on the Grand Demon Lord who was now fully enraged, unable to escape or move, being treated as nothing more than a demon punching bag.

In no more than it would take a person to blink, Deia clicked the wheel on her bow over to a new setting. Power surged through the bow, lighting up new runes as blue flames flickered over the bow. She pulled on the bow's string; an arrow of solid blue appeared between her fingers. She drew the string fully back before she released it.

The air shuddered and exploded outward in a pressure wave. The blue arrow turned into a ray of blue light as it passed under Steve's raised arm and over Jung Lee's shoulder before it hit the Grand Demon Lord straight on.

The Grand Demon Lord was thrown backward at Gurren, who turned his shield and sword into a war hammer that he swung with all of his strength, his runes blinding as they were overclocked by the power surging through them.

The war hammer halted the Grand Demon Lord's momentum.

Gurren's conjured war hammer and hands were destroyed by the forces placed upon them.

From around Dave, orbs shot forward, creating a hexagonal prism with orbs digging through the ground to create all of the various major points. Gray light spread between them all; magical formations appeared along the faces of the prism that surrounded the Xelur Grand Demon Lord.

The Grand Demon Lord didn't have time to get from its knees when the ground around it shattered, gravitational forces acting upon the Grand Demon Lord.

If we weren't restricted by the AI's damn parameters, I could just make it so that he couldn't move at all, Dave hissed in his mind.

The Grand Demon Lord's injuries from Deia's attack were repairing; his soul aura took a few moments to stabilize itself. Deia's attack had actually blown off his arm. The soul energy still regrew the limb at a speed visible to the eye.

The Xelur Grand Demon Lord, because of his size, was having more trouble in the gravitational prison than a smaller person might, but he still regained his footing. He was in the center of the gravitational forces.

Lox and Gurren hurled out conjured javelins; their wrists and hands were still broken, so they couldn't fire out Mana bolts. The javelins, upon reaching the edge of the gravity prison, sped up even more, smashing against the Grand Demon Lord.

He howled out in anger as Jung Lee and Steve unleashed their powered attacks with their weapons, axe, and sword light racing toward the Grand Demon Lord. He blocked Jung Lee's attack with his right sword, waving his left hand as his other sword leapt from the ground and raced to meet his newly formed hand.

Steve's hit made him stagger backward; the gravity prison pulled him back into place even as his aura fought against the pull of the prison.

At this time, there was no one left. Malsour had killed the last of the Xelur soldiers that had been trying to escape the walled area, not caring for their Grand Demon Lord that was being completely suppressed.

Deia fired another arrow at the Grand Demon Lord as Malsour looked upon them, unleashing his most powerful attack, flames of the abyss. Wherever the flames passed, the ground was torn asunder, reduced to its molecular components.

The Grand Demon Lord pushed his aura to the maximum, creating a solid shield of pure soul energy in front of him as he wildly attacked one of the gravity prison's orbs that created it.

Even the soul energy was slowed as it passed through that gravity prison, hitting a Mana barrier around the orb.

Dave laughed coldly. "You think that you will be able to break my gravity prison? Think again. I might not have your soul energy, but I'm a dwarven master smith. I work with soul energy every day and I made magical coding. With just your strength, you won't be able to defeat my creations," Dave said with the utmost confidence.

The Grand Demon Lord let out a roar of anger, not willing to accept his fate as he pushed away from the center of the prison, wildly slashing out at Party Zero.

"Finish him off," Deia said. With his power reduced by twenty to thirty percent in the prison and his speed cut to a third, he was a much easier opponent to deal with.

The Grand Demon Lord wasn't given time to gather himself as all of Party Zero unleashed their finishing moves. Deia used her modified plasma cannon with her bow. Dave continued to enclose the Demon Lord, altering his orbs' coding here and there to keep continuous pressure on them. Gurren and Lox hurled javelins while Steve unleashed powerful slash attacks that penetrated through the octagonal gravity prison. Jung Lee held up his hand; a swirl of all the Affinities came together to focus into a gray stream of Mana that pierced through the Demon Lord's soul energy. With the Free Affinity spirits now being allowed more freedom, these creatures that had tried to take over Jung Lee for hundreds of years now tore through the Demon Lord's own soul, weakening his control over the soul energy he had collected. Rain fell from the sky, each drop as fast as a bullet and concentrated on the Grand Demon Lord as Jekoni looked on with cold eyes. Malsour's breath was concentrated and condensed, eating away at the Grand Demon Lord's soul energy.

The Grand Demon Lord's Health rushed downward. Even though it had Legendary abilities that it could use, it needed to have control over itself, its body and its soul energy in order to use them. Right now it didn't have control over anything; racked by pain, thrown off by the attacks and the suppression, its mind was frantic and filled with panic.

Its size greatly reduced as its soul energy was spent, shrinking from a dominating fifteen meters tall until he was only two meters tall. He combusted his own soul but it was under attack by Jung Lee's Free Affinity spirits, reducing his control over it and making it more chaotic.

The attacks tore through the Grand Demon Lord's body. Malsour's breath reduced the Grand Demon Lord to nothing more than ashes.

The attacks stopped as all of Party Zero looked at where the Grand Demon Lord had been. All of them looked at the spot, as if not believing that it was truly over.

"Stamina, and Mana potions!" Deia said, bringing everyone out of their stunned state.

"Lox, Gurren—get over here. Let's see if Malsour and I can't help fix up your armor," Dave said.

They wandered over as the orbs around the Grand Demon Lord's ashes powered down and faded away from view as they moved toward Dave. They were still there but their stealth abilities made them practically invisible.

"What happened with Induca and Suzy?" Dave inspected the armor, pulling metals from his pack.

Around them, the sounds of fighting could be heard as the dwarves moved past the walled-off area Malsour had created, pushing the Xelur backward.

Many of them, no longer sensing their Grand Demon Lord, were completely disheartened. Even the Demon Lords were having trouble in trying to keep them fighting. They understood that if the Grand Demon Lord had been killed, then it would be easy for them to die.

Even though they lived in a world of fighting in an attempt to gain more soul energy, they didn't want to throw their lives away. They wanted to survive to use that energy and not lose it to anyone else. As such, they were giving ground, allowing themselves to be pushed back to the breaches, fighting those that they could.

Before Lox, Gurren, and Malsour could respond to Dave, Esa sent a message to Party Zero.

"Good work on the Grand Demon Lord. The Xelur are in disarray, as soon as you're ready, I want you to get out there and hit them with everything you have. As you do, I'll unleash everything we have in reserve. If we can break them here, then they'll pull back to their castles."

"We'll be ready in five minutes," Deia said.

Chapter 8: Rout

Anna watched as Induca's body started to repair itself.

The healers talked to one another, directing their healing spells as well as using the healing potions in order to speed up recovery. The healer in charge and his assistant continued to focus on her head. Induca's face was still covered in blood but it had recovered to her original structure.

"Seems that she's coming around," the healer in charge said.

"Damn, looks like she's got a strong Willpower. It's a pain to keep her suppressed so that she doesn't come to with her body in its current state."

The lead healer and his assistant grunted and sweat as they fought Induca, who was trying to wake up, her face wrinkling with effort.

"Induca, let them work!" Anna yelled out in a panic, seeing how Induca's stubborn personality could let her wake up, see her injuries and then make everything worse for the healers to deal with.

Induca's face relaxed.

"Looks like she was conscious enough to hear you," the lead healer said with clear relief as the other healers continued to work. Together they repaired what was left of Induca before allowing the healing potions to get to work. The healing potions could have done it all themselves, but with healing, they took energy from the person they were putting back together. With Induca, that kind of strain might be too much on her weak body.

Also, with them repairing what was left, it meant that they didn't have to use as much healing potion and that the patient would heal faster.

As sections of Induca were set in place, the healers would then spread the healing potion over Induca.

Bit by bit, her body was coming back. Already her organs were working; her bones were fused together and regrown in places. Muscle and skin reformed as Induca started to look more like a person.

Anna didn't know how much time went by as she looked on anxiously before Induca's body was fully recovered.

The healers, all tired from their exertions, drank Stamina potions, while one of them laid a cloth over Induca's body.

"Okay, looking good. She's well on her way to recovery. Get, a Mana potion for her— seems that she's got deep Mana fatigue. It's a good thing she didn't wake up or the fatigue would have been too much for her body and it could have affected her Mana pool."

Someone pulled out a Mana potion from their bag of holding and poured it into the bathtub. It was absorbed into Induca.

After a few moments, her eyes fluttered and she looked around. "What's going on?" Induca pulled on the sheet over top of her.

"You were badly wounded. You're in Terra." Anna pulled out a set of clothes from her bag.

"You're going to need some more healing, and Mana and Stamina potions. But you should make a full recovery. Don't go out and fight for the next five hours. If you'll excuse us, we have other patients that we need to see to." The healer moved away.

Doctors from Earth might be surprised by how fast Induca recovered. To be told that they didn't want her fighting for a few hours after the injuries she had sustained? That was complete lunacy. They would have kept her in a hospital for months, and then have maybe a year or more recovery time.

With magic and potions, people could be healed back to their peak in a matter of hours, however they would need to eat and sleep in order to fully recover their Mana and Stamina without the cooldown of the different healing spells that were placed upon them.

The healers left. The last one pulled a curtain around the bathtub that Induca was in.

Induca got out of the tub, there was a shower off to the side, which she moved toward. She was still covered in blood and bits from her injuries.

"Where is Suzy?" Induca asked.

"She's being treated for a soul attack that the Grand Xelur Demon Lord used. She should recover in a bit. If not, she'll re-spawn in a few hours or so," Anna said.

Induca's face froze for a moment as she let out a shuddering sigh. "I keep forgetting that she's a player. I know she'll be fine—even if she dies, she'll come back. But there's a disconnect between that, which I know is right, and knowing that if we as people of Emerilia die, we're just gone." Induca shook her head and moved to the shower, turning it on.

"I know." Anna still felt slightly guilty about leaving Suzy to follow Induca. Suzy had Lu Lu watching over her, after all, and even if she did die, she could come back. If Induca hadn't made it to the hospital in time, she would have died.

Now, in just a few hours, she had been able to recover from her terrible injuries that would have killed anyone on Earth, or anyone who hadn't been right next to a healer. It truly showed how useful and vital the hospital with its healer wards was to the people of the Terra Alliance.

Anna opened up the Party Zero chat, finding the others talking about their options. "Hey everyone, just wanted to give an update. Suzy is still under a soul attack, and Induca has made a full recovery. She should be okay to go in a few hours," Anna said.

***

Deia looked over Party Zero. Dave and Malsour worked to repair Lox and Gurren, parts of their broken hands as well as melted chests reforming. Steve pulled out replacement parts from a ring of holding, exchanging them for his broken armor while his soul gem body affixed to the new armor plates and repaired itself. Around him, various soul gems were being drained to fill up his power reserves.

Everyone else was downing potions to recover their spent Mana and Stamina faster.

"Party Zero, are you ready?" Esa's voice was tight; she saw the opportunity to turn this battle around and she was having to wait.

Deia looked to the others.

"A minute or two." Dave kept his focus on Lox's hands as he used his soul smithing art to finish off Lox's hand and repair all of the Magical Circuits that had been destroyed. It was not a simple process, but under Dave's guidance, it was hundreds of times faster than letting the armor repair itself.

"We'll stick to the air for this one, provide support. If we get in the midst of the Xelur, then we're just going to make it harder for the dwarves, as well as their support," Deia said, talking to Party Zero and Esa.

"Understood. It would be nice to have you clear a path through the Xelur. Basically, we just need you to show that you're fine and ready to kick more ass, put the fear of Emerilians into the little bastards and maybe make the Grand Demon Lords think twice about fighting us," Esa said.

"That we can do." Malsour looked to the sky.

The five Dragons who had been engaged in fights with various Grand Demon Lords had won their fights; most of the Grand Demon Lords had made good on their escapes, fleeing back to the castles that the Dragons couldn't attack by themselves unless they were willing to take heavy injuries.

Two of the Dragons were badly wounded; the other three had wounds but they were still ready for a fight. They cartwheeled in the sky, dropping down toward the ground, their attacks and flames raining down upon those who were caught out in the open between castles.

Otherwise they would combine their attacks to hit the Xelur castles that looked weaker, trying to open up their defenses so that the Terra Alliance could rain down attacks on the Xelur before they had a chance to recover their soul-powered shielding or barriers.

"Ready as we're going to get," Dave said.

Anna connected to the party chat. Everyone tensed up to listen.

"Hey everyone, just wanted to give an update. Suzy is still under a soul attack, and Induca has made a full recovery. She should be okay to go in a few hours," Anna said.

Some of the hard edge that showed through everyone's faces dimmed somewhat. Knowing that Induca was all right took a weight off their minds; no matter what, Suzy would be able to come back from the brink.

"Thank you, Anna." Deia's voice was soft.

"No problem. Now , go kick some Xelur ass!" Anna cut out of the party chat.

"All right, I want it as such. Malsour, you'll be center. Jung Lee, Steve, Lox, and Gurren to either side. Jekoni, on the right side with Dave, and I'll be on the left side. Everyone good?" Deia asked.

"Sounds like a plan to me," Lox said as they moved into a line facing the walls that Malsour had made to contain the Grand Demon Lord and any of the forces that had been around to support him.

"Time to push them back," Malsour said. A pillar pushed him up into the sky as the others of Party Zero rose into the sky with him. They emerged out of the dust-covered coliseum they had made like Legendary warriors of the gods.

As soon as they were able to see the Xelur, they started to attack. The dwarves were moving past the corridor and coliseum that Malsour had made, putting Party Zero right in the midst of the Xelur.

"I'll work the Mana barrier!" Dave called out as orbs appeared around them. Xelur ranged attacks hit the barrier that snapped into existence.

The party spread out above the coliseum and unleashed their attacks. Malsour opened his mouth; a spell formation came into existence in front of his mouth. Spears made from smoking shadows appeared like a cloud. They shot out in a straight stream. As soon as one was sent flying, another would appear.

The effect was like watching a machine gun cut down unarmored people. Malsour might feel reassured with hearing Induca was okay; however, the Xelur had put her in that healing ward and they had also hurt his nieces and nephews who had come to aid the people of Emerilia.

There was no room for mercy in his eyes or in his attacks as they tore up the ground and washed away the Xelur that stood in the path of his attack.

Gurren, Lox, and Steve unleashed their Mana bolts. Now fully charged, their bolts could take out most regular Xelur's soul aura in a few hits before taking down the Xelur. For Demon Lords, they had to focus their attacks, leading to them calling out to one another when they found a heavy.

Jekoni used his water magic to cut through Xelur, pulling more and more water out of the area; the water came together to form a massive water snake that seemed almost sentient in the way it attacked.

Around Jung Lee, his six Affinity spirits stood in midair, unleashing their own attacks: Fiery phoenixes that screeched into the air before racing through the Xelur. An Earth-formed rhino. A shadowy reaper and a Light paladin. Water krakens and Air eagles. He himself unleashed blade attacks as if he were practicing his swordplay. With every cut or stab, he would imbue his sword with Mana, unleashing gray Mana attacks that cut through the Xelur.

Deia was covered in flames as she loosed arrow after arrow into the Xelur ranks.

Dave focused on the Mana barrier, taking on multiple hits from the now panicked Xelur from below. He stood in midair, his eyes closed. The runic lines over his body glowed with power. Finally, he opened his eyes. Three-meter-wide magical formations appeared in the sky. Metallic beams slowly emerged from these magical formations, growing from one meter wide to three. Suddenly they dropped from the spell formations and slammed into the ground. Runic lines across these beams lit up as energy started to flow from them.

Under his hood, Dave's face was pale, but Deia could see the satisfied grin on his face as she looked at those beams. All of the dying Xelur and ambient soul energy that was drifting through the battlefield was pulled toward these beams as if they were a black hole. All of that soul energy that would have gone to the Xelur was now being captured by these beams.

They made a wide formation around that castle, overlapping one another so that there was not one place where their touch wasn't felt.

The Xelur's spells were affected as the power that they poured into enhancing their abilities or their ranged beam- like attacks was pulled in by these pillars.

Even the attacks that would come in from the other castles were being pulled into these pillars.

With every second, their runes started to glow brighter.

Now, every bit of energy that the Xelur might be able to capture and use was being drained away, making it so that they could only use what was within their bodies, and with only slight chances that they would gain power from the fallen.

***

Esa grabbed onto the side of the balcony as Dave's pillars dropped from the sky. Esa looked in shock at these pillars as they slammed into the ground. Energy rushed into them; even ranged attacks were affected under these pillars' influence.

Malsour rose into the air with powerful beats of his wings. The others rose up behind him before they spread out, all of them unleashing attacks upon the Xelur below.

The Xelur were thrown further off-balance by the attacks from the dwarven cannons and other players that were also claiming a huge number of their people.

As the attacks landed, the ground that had been filled with Xelur was being cleared of people.

The Xelur already had low morale after seeing their Grand Demon Lords fall to Party Zero. Now the dwarves were advancing into their lines as Party Zero hit them from the air. A Mana barrier appeared around them, stopping any attacks from hitting them.

"All ranged attacks, focus on the courtyard!" Esa yelled out, seeing an opportunity.

Artillery cannons, spells, and anything that could reach the Xelur was redirected. Grand workings exploded into firestorms and massive domes of darkness, with oily black tentacles that pulled Xelur into its depths.

That eastern corner of their castle had turned into a hellish and chaotic scene of combat in nearly every direction.

The Xelur held for a moment and then, all at once, like the tide going out, the Xelur ran back toward the breaches.

The dwarves continued to press forward, not letting anyone past them as they slaughtered all that lay in their path.

The Xelur were broken. However, they could regroup, find their courage again and continue to fight. Here they could inflict the most injuries.

Players, sensing the Xelur's weakness, moved out from where they had been playing it safe and unleashed their most powerful attacks to try to get the most experience possible.

The Xelur retreat was illuminated with vicious and powerful attacks that wiped out dozens in one go. Hundreds died as one as they passed through the walls, running for the east and west castles.

"Call the DCA and Dragons to rake the Xelur as they retreat!" Esa yelled to her aides.

The Dragons in the sky who had been supporting in the distance now turned, forming up on the eldest to create an arrow-like formation as they turned toward the northern castle.

Underneath the tower in the castle, the ono switched from Terra to Devil's Crater. Wounded continued to be funneled through to the medical areas that Devil's Crater had adopted after seeing the Terra Hospital and working with Jules.

On the other side, Efri and his forces rushed forward.

"Move it!" Efri ran through the ono and out into the inner castle. As soon as he was in the castle, he spread out his wings, taking to the sky in a few flaps. His speed increased, as he rushed through the corridors, out of the castle and into the open area between the castle and the outer walls. He tilted toward the heavens, seeing the sun coming over the horizon as he gained altitude. Behind him, DCA aerial forces followed in a stream.

They grouped together into their wings as Efri looked over the battlefield, comparing it to the real-time updates that he had been watching through his Mirror of Communication.

"Wing commanders, take over. Hunt the Xelur bastards down!" Efri's voice had no room for mercy in it.

He and the DCA aerial forces had been all over Emerilia, supporting different castles' groups around the portals. Many were thankfully under the control of the Terra Alliance but a number of them were being contested. But none of them had had the degree of fighting that these castles had gone through.

He banked to the side, watching as four Dragons whistled out of the sky, unleashing flames of different colors from their mouths, illuminating their polished scales as the ground and Xelur below were annihilated. Their wings snapped outward, catching the wind as they rushed over the Xelur. Four lines of destruction cut through the fleeing Xelur.

Efri's eyes thinned as he looked at these Xelur Demons. It was after these creatures that his race had been created. The Dark Lord and his minion Boran-al were not able to make the demons of Devil's Crater able to use soul energy to enhance their abilities but instead increased their physical abilities and made it so that they would grow stronger and faster than other races, at the cost of having a low ability with magic.

The Xelur lived to tear power from one another and their victims.

Esa watched that line of DCA aerial forces that took to the sky, spreading out like vengeful spirits. They rushed over the Xelur that were retreating or still within the outer walls killing them all with brutal efficiency then soaring away to look for the next prey.

From their chests, Mana bombs dropped. Their impacts made the ground rumble as Xelur were destroyed by the bombing runs. The DCA held out their hands; shooting out Mana bolts raking the panicked Xelur, who were now in full retreat, trying to get away from the northern castle that had turned into a death trap.

With the change of events, the defenders surged, retaking the walls and sections that the Xelur had held.

The Xelur that were still waiting to get into the castle were now running back toward their castles while the breaches were now the exits for the Xelur streaming away from the northern castle. However these breaches were getting smaller and smaller as the conquest points were poured in to repair them.

The western wall, which had only been breached in a few places, didn't know what was happening at the eastern side. One moment, they were still trying to gain access to the castle and had a few places where they had gained a foothold on the top of the walls; the next, the Dragons banked low around the walls, unleashing a combined breath that was four times their original power and size of their individual attacks.

They tore through the Xelur as if they were nothing, inflicting thousands of casualties in one pass.

The Xelur, stunned by this sudden attack, were thrown into disarray turning from an army into an uncoordinated mob.

Then the DCA wings appeared, their bombs and Mana bolts raking those below.

The Xelur attacked with their ranged soul-powered beams. But their ranged attacks were totally ineffective because of the Soul Draining beams that Dave had created.

The DCA's Mana barriers took hits but with their speed and evasive actions, it was hard to get a solid hit on them long enough to take down their Mana barrier.

Mana bombs made the ground rumble as every hit killed tens of Xelur.

The eastern wall advanced faster and faster. The dwarves advanced at walking pace now, pushing over the cratered and broken ground and stepping over the fallen Xelur.

Players and POEs of all kinds hovered in the air, attacking with all their might, or along the walls above the breaches, raining down attacks on the Xelur.

The western group of Xelur broke and ran for their castle.

Esa watched as they retreated in a panic. "Repair the walls and hit those bastards in the back. Get the outer castles to assist where they can," Esa said, not looking backward as her aide carried out her orders.

She wiped her forehead with a dirty hand, not caring as she looked over the ruins that was her northern castle. "Prepare the assault. We're going ahead with it as soon as everyone is ready." Esa turned and walked into the command room.

"Esa, we just won—shouldn't we take a rest?" a player asked.

"The Xelur are in a panic. They have their people coming back scared and uncoordinated. If we hit them now, while they're off-balance, our actions will have the greatest effect," Esa said.

"But some of us need to deal with real-world things," the player complained.

If it had been before Dave had told her and the rest of the Stone Raider leadership about the truth of Emerilia, Esa might have entertained the idea of waiting to let the players do their stuff on Earth to go ahead with their full strength.

Now—well, now she knew that real lives were on the line. She wasn't willing to wait for anyone.

"Well, too damn bad! Those who are online or can get online will get the best loot for taking the eastern castle." Esa looked to the other aides who had been listening and watching the byplay. "See that everything is ready as soon as possible."

Chapter 9: Counterattack

Malsour landed on the wall of the northern castle and watched the Xelur flee toward their nearest castles. His fellow Dragons and the DCA wheeled away from them as they now came under attack from the castles' Xelur defenders.

Malsour snorted, his eyes cold as he looked at the eastern castle.

"Well, looks like the Dragon's out of the bag," Steve said on the party chat.

Malsour looked to Steve and then the others who were on the walls, looking to the Xelur and Malsour.

"It was bound to happen sometime," Dave said.

"At least this way I can use my full power." Malsour looked at a breach, commanding the wall to repair itself. The rocks moved as if they were alive, coming back together as they filled the breach.

"Esa just passed down the order. We're to prepare ourselves to counterattack the eastern castle as soon as possible," Deia said.

"Looks like we're far from done." Gurren sighed.

"One thing at a time," Lox agreed.

"I'll help with repairing the wall," Malsour said.

"And I'll see what I can do about fixing Lox and Gurren's armor." Dave gave the two dwarves an unimpressed look.

***

Esa was once again in the command center of the northern tower. She had reviewed the plan with all the different commanders and Dwayne had even come over to personally lead the Stone Raiders who were a part of the plan to attack the eastern castle.

Still, she was stuck up in the command post, watching over all of it as people rushed into battles. She understood that she needed to stay behind in order to deal with anything that didn't go according to plan. At the same time, she wished that she could be down there with everyone.

"Well, looks like you've got everything in hand."

Esa jumped at the voice and her hand went to her sword.

"Seems I can still creep up on people." Josh grinned. His face turned solemn as he continued to look over the forces that were arrayed within the outer walls and castle.

"Goddamn rogue types," Esa muttered, also looking to the forces. "And yes, they're ready."

In the distance, Dragons and DCA aerial forces were well above the eastern castle, hammering the Xelur below with every attack they had. Artillery spells and cannons activated against Xelur soul barriers. Here and there, barriers would give way as sections of the walls would explode inward or Xelur would bear the brunt of the incoming attacks.

It was a hellish scene but neither Josh nor Esa had an ounce of pity for those within those defenses.

"Each time that we kill some of them, the others get stronger. It's nearly as bad as fighting necros," Esa said in frustration.

Josh clapped her on the shoulder. "Don't worry. We'll get through this."

"I hope so."

Commanders yelled out their orders. The time had come.

The sound of marching feet could be heard from the command post as players led the way, moving through the south and northern gates; Malsour, had completely sealed the eastern gate already.

The forces marched out of the gates, moving to the east and coming together.

Guild leaders organized their people into rectangular fighting formations, their long sides faced the eastern castles. Their lines were only three deep, with the tanks in front, ranged and DPS fighters in the second row; the third rank held ranged fighters.

The players moved forward at a brisk pace as more and more flowed out of the gates to join on the ends of the player groups. Each of the guilds were in separate fighting formations.

In the middle, the Stone Raiders were with other guilds, from largest to smallest, spread to the right and left side. Here and there, players moved faster forward than the other sections; the guild leaders snapped on them to stay together.

Players worked well together but they were also greedy when confident. They were in a massive fighting force of players, the biggest player versus monster fight that had happened in Emerilia thus far. They were excited, leading them to advance in front of the others and also wanting to reach the enemy faster in order to gain more experience instead of losing it to the other players.

While these thoughts were going on, they also wanted to win and they would do anything to keep one another alive so that they could continue fighting.

It seemed like the two thought processes were in opposition to each other, but with players, it somehow made sense.

Everything but experience they would help one another with.

The Xelur must have noticed their advance as they started to fire their ranged beam attacks from the eastern castle. They smashed into Mana barriers along the length of the moving formation.

"Looks like those Mana barriers are working well," Esa commented.

"Well, after seeing how useful they were to Esamael's army at Verlun, we made some purchases and then Dave modified them a bit so that they aren't as easy to break as he did with the ones at Verlun," Josh said.

The fighting heated up as the Xelur started to attack the airborne forces of the Terra Alliance as well as the approaching players.

The Dragons and DCA's forces continued to stay high in the air, making it hard to be hit as their attacks continued to pressure the Xelur, not allowing them to devote much of their strength to attacking. Instead they had to hole up and defend themselves as artillery spells continued to blossom on their soul barriers, with Mana bombs and Dragon flames tearing at the energy constructs.

Josh and Esa stopped talking, looking down upon the forces that moved like an unstoppable juggernaut across that desolate rock and dirt.

The no-man's-land between castles had been hospitable when the Dragons had laid claim to the Densaou Ring of Fire that spewed heat and magma into the sky.

Now, with the vicious fighting that had been going on for weeks, the ground had been split apart, forming craters and gouges in the ground. Weapons and items that the dead left behind rested there; tombstones that marked Xelur that had died in their retreat flashed here and there. People collected the loot from these tombstones as they advanced forward. Hits lit up their Mana barrier but it did not slow or deter them.

The players started to use ranged attacks as they got closer. The Xelur could only use their soul energy. Although they could regenerate their own energy, they couldn't regenerate the energy that they used from others who had died.

Attacking them like this served to burn off more of their energy to make their assault easier and the Xelur a less ferocious target.

Their attacks reached up the large outer walls where Xelur fired down their own attacks onto the players.

Support mages and players cast out their spells and chanted their enhancing spells.

The fighting got more intense as the players reached past the range of the beam-like soul energy attacks. The Xelur within the wall were now able to attack with their arrows and physical weapons.

The players continued to advance. The commanders had a hard time keeping them in check instead of letting them rush the walls.

The distance quickly closed, and the fighting became so fierce between the two groups that the groups were torn apart, light from the intense magical attacks cris crossing from the walls were nearly blinding.

Just one hundred meters from the wall, the strongest players among the guilds and groups who were in front of the wall unleashed their own attacks.

In that dawn light, as the sun moved over the horizon, the brilliant light of ranged attack lit up the eastern castle's wall.

Each of these people were not as strong as the Grand Demon Lords but they were all hitting the same areas and had much greater control over their Mana and their spells than the Xelur Grand Demon Lord. Their attack scarred and broke the wall in sections. Arrows whistled through walls as spells smashed apart rock; light based spell attacks left gouges in the walls as the real attack was thrown out.

Grand workings that had been held in reserve were activated and shot out by Air mages. They hit the walls of the eastern castle. Some were destroyed in flashes of light that made Mana and soul barriers shiver under the power of their explosion. Shock waves of air threw out debris and dust.

The first grand working hit a wall.

It was like a missile striking a battleship. An explosion of light and heat appeared where the impact had been. A section of wall was blown apart. The top section of the wall turned into flying boulders and shards of stone that peppered the inside of the eastern castle.

The artillery of the other castles had stopped as the players' formation had got closer.

Now everyone watched the destruction of the eastern castle's walls.

Recoiling from the first attack, the second hit. The wall exploded outward again.

To Esa, it felt as if time had slowed down, that eastern castle's wall igniting with explosions that blew the wall in, like that attack by the Grand Demon Lord that had killed her.

Even in the dust and rock that was thrown into the air, the clear lights of magical spells was seen, lighting up the dust from inside and cutting through that destruction, hitting stunned Xelur that were trying to fight back.

Arrows and javelins came through the air, finding breaks in the Xelur's armor and dropping them to the ground with ease.

The explosions moved away from the major breaches.

Dark mages solidified the rubble around the breaches, creating ramps.

With a yell, the players rushed forward into that mayhem as walls continued to be torn apart. The Xelur within the eastern castle lit up the sky with their soul energy, letting out their own war cries as they raced to meet them. Knowing that there was no room for them to retreat anymore after having faced them taking back the northern castle, the Xelur fought with everything they had to meet the players.

They came together in a flash of weapons and magic. As the forces connected, chaos reigned as people fought against one another with all they had.

The Mana barriers that had covered the players fell apart, the lines and area too chaotic for them to keep up.

Malsour unleashed his Dragon breath, creating a path in front of him as Deia called down a rain of her fire arrows.

The Stone Raiders formed behind them, forcing their way toward the main castle. Dwayne led the way. Steve, Gurren, Lox, and Jung Lee were beside him. Their blades tore through any that opposed them. Dave hovered in the air. With a wave of his hand, spikes would drop from the sky. A grenade would appear among the Xelur or a barrier would form around an ally.

With a wave of his hand, five grand workings appeared.

"What workings are those?" Esa asked.

"I don't know. He had a factory that builds them but he makes a lot of things he doesn't or can't tell us about." Josh also leaned forward.

The grand workings spread out at an incredible speed, activating as their power surged outward. They smashed into the ground, breaking their containment.

All around them, it seemed as if space had been ripped open as black shadows that seemed to connect to the abyss appeared. Affinity spirits started to step out of these portals. They looked from the players to the Xelur. With screeching noises, they raced toward the Xelur.

"He formed Affinity spirits?" Esa said in shock.

"Looks like he took a lot more from the Six Affinities Temple than others. Looks like that is some kind of conjuring formation he's created and then pumped it full of Dark Affinity Mana; pulling from that, the Affinity spirits are formed and can go on a rampage. Unlike the shades Loughbreck used at Verlun, these Affinity spirits can use Mana," Josh said.

Both creature types could only last for as long as they had energy and the Affinity Spirits used it faster than the Shades, but their attacks were much stronger. The Affinity spirits blitz attacks killed or weakened a ton of the Xelur and took a lot of pressure off of the Players.

"Dwayne is halfway through the castle," one of the aides called out.

"Come on, get us that eastern castle." Josh looked at the fight. Players were fighting Xelur all over the place. Dark Affinity spirits rampaged through the ranks of Xelur, not caring about injuries— only caring to attack the Xelur.

Dragons and DCA came in from overhead, their attacks accurate enough to pressure the Xelur and not put the players into danger.

"We're at the capture point and we're taking it!" Dwayne yelled out over a private chat. It was clear that he was fighting.

A bar appeared in Josh and Esa's view, showing that they were capturing the castle from the inside.

The Xelur now pushed inward to the castle, leaving the walls that were on the southern side to try to push the players out.

It was too late. Esa checked the feed from Aleph automatons and those that were live streaming from inside the castle.

There were already barriers and defenses in place. It was a violent and chaotic fight but the Stone Raiders had made a castle within the castle over top the capture point. Area heals were going on constantly as tanks fought back the Xelur. Soul energy attacks broke the walls that had been formed around the capture point. Arrows and Mana bolts destroyed the inside of the castle and the tower above to try to kill the Xelur that attacked them from all sides.

It seemed like a valiant last stand as Stone Raiders yelled out to one another, attacking with all they had. Heal spells flew around; magic crossed the air in streams of destruction, colliding with shields, tearing up the ground, and sending people to the ground with injuries.

Tanks placed themselves in front of the ones with weaker defense, taking on all the damage possible in order to let them live and continue their attacks.

Xelur weapons smashed against Stone Raiders, who were hunkered down, not giving in to their impulses to race out and end the Xelur, playing the objective.

The Xelur pressure was so strong that the Stone Raiders within the castle had been cut off from those outside.

Now the other players, hearing their fellow players trapped within on their final stand, pushed themselves to the limit, melding reactions with tactics that they had worked on and perfected. They had built their characters, come to understand themselves on a level that they could now react and draw them out. They took enhancing potions and applied gear that would improve their lethality as they pushed their builds, used their stats and played. For now they were not players; they were not people of Earth: they were their avatar; they were Emerilians. This was their world and they would win.

This was the thought of every player. Instead of fear and anger, their faces showed joy as they came together. Even experience was pushed aside as parties reorganized, bringing their most powerful offense into play.

The Xelur that had been holding the players back were shocked as the players pushed back, more vicious and deadly than before.

These players had come together to work with their parties, with their guilds. This was what they lived for!

Esa and Josh watched as the players surged forward, burning through resources that entire kingdoms would weep if they would see it.

They didn't care. To them, saving up these resources and gaining them was a challenge. To put them on display like this—they were excited beyond all reason.

Here they weren't bankers, mothers, and fathers; they weren't students, or wealthy business owners, teachers or computer programmers; they came from all walks of life, all different backgrounds.

Here they were gamers, they were living the world of Emerilia even as they died. They would yell and swear and curse, but before they did, those moments that would be forever remembered and would bring them back to the game time and again

They were mages, warriors, fighters: they were people of Emerilia.

"They broke through to Dwayne's group!" someone yelled out in the command center.

The Xelur that had been fighting from the balconies and corridors that led into the capture point underneath the tower were now getting hit from behind as players swarmed through the castle.

The Stone Raiders attacked back at the Xelur, suppressing them. As more of the Xelur were killed off, the capture speed increased, moving from a turtle's pace until it seemed to be sprinting upward as the first players reached the group of Stone Raiders within the inner castle.

A prompt appeared in everyone's view, across the entire battlefield.

Castle Conquest

The Terra Alliance has captured a contested castle!

Rewards:

2,000 Conquest points

Castle Conquest

You currently control (5/8) Castles

Earning: (5) conquest points per minute

Bonus: For controlling five of the Castles, you earn an additional (1) conquest point(s) per minute.

Total points: 15,781

Rights: Administrative (Can spend conquest points to upgrade Castle infrastructure and repair castles. Can also delete Castle infrastructure.)

Eastern Castle 1

Status: Under Control by Terra Alliance

Earn: 1 conquest point per minute

Evolution: 1 (Second evolution 0%) Can increase evolution to Level 2 by paying (100,000) Conquest points.

Upgrades: None

Durability: 12,548/60,000

Esa dismissed it and continued to look at the eastern castle as players, their minions, and the Affinity spirits surged forth, sweeping away the Xelur. A mix of emotions rose in her chest. She let out a shaky breath, her body weak as she tried to take in what she had seen.

It took another hour or so for the players to finish off any remaining Xelur in the castle. Once they had cleaned them all out of the castle and surrounding area, the Xelur southern castle started to fire at them.

The Mana barriers that the players had used as cover were placed all over the castle, giving them cover from the fire as they looted and repaired the castle to the best of their ability.

"They've got a request in for an ono," Josh said.

"Well, let's get it in there. We can start to build it up and we can hit more of the Xelur coming from the portal to the southern castles."

As this had been going on, more and more Xelur had come out of the portal, streaming toward the occupied castles. Artillery that couldn't reach the contested castles fired down upon these streams of Xelur, trying to kill as many of them off as possible so that they couldn't reach the various castles and reinforce them.

"Bravo—looks like we've reclaimed the eastern castle." Josh looked to Esa.

"We lost a number of players who aren't going to be too happy about losing all those levels."

"But they aren't POE. They can come back," Josh said.

"Yeah." Esa smiled slightly before she looked over her own castle. There were still signs of the fighting that had been going on just a few hours ago. Her smile dimmed as she thought of the POEs who had stood alongside players, knowing that if they were to die that they wouldn't re-spawn.

That took a lot more guts than what she'd done.

People were already checking the loot they'd gathered and checking out the class upgrades they'd received and some had even gained levels and stat points to increase their attributes.

It had been a bloody fight but their hard earned gains would be needed in the near future.

Chapter 10: Force Multiplier

Suzy let out a gasp as she opened her eyes.

Lu Lu, seeing her master wake up, made pitiful squeaking noises and rubbed her face against Suzy's.

Suzy made to pat Lu Lu's head but found that she was too weak to do so. Her Stamina and Mana were at their lowest point and she felt completely drained. She shivered as she thought of the nightmares she had seen.

"Suzy?" someone asked.

"Hi. Where am I? What happened?" Suzy asked.

"You were struck by a Xelur soul attack. When you were using the skill on your Weapon of Power, your Willpower was boosted a lot higher than normal. It weakened the attack that targets the power of your soul, attempting to rip it from you and be absorbed by the Xelur attacker. But, the backlash from the skill is to greatly impact your soul energy and leave you in a weakened state. In this state, the soul attacks were much more powerful. It took a number of people skilled in the ways of the soul to increase your strength and to weaken the attack that you were hit with. They reduced it as much as possible and there was nothing to do but let you fight it off yourself," the lady said.

Suzy nodded before her expression froze. Her eyes went wide as she looked to the lady. "Where's Induca? She was hit by that Grand Demon Lord's attack!"

"Calm down, please. You might be awake but your body is incredibly weak!" The lady stepped forward to press a hand down on Suzy's chest, holding her in place.

Lu Lu, feeling ignored started to licked Suzy's face.

"You damn animal, stop that!" Suzy giggled as Lu Lu's tongue tickled her.

Induca pushed open the door, smiling at the scene before her.

Suzy looked to Induca. Time seemed to stop as relief filled her; tears fell down her cheeks as she started to sob.

"Oh, come here dear," Induca said, her voice soft as she wrapped her arms around the fragile Suzy, who grabbed her as if she were some kind of lifeboat.

Suzy couldn't stop crying as she grabbed onto Induca, not wanting to let go.

Induca made comforting noises, stroking Suzy's hair as she held her close.

Suzy looked up to Induca, finding that she wasn't the only one crying. She pulled Induca close, kissing her and once again finding refuge in her arms. "I thought I lost you!" Suzy sobbed.

"Take a lot more to get rid of me," Induca said comfortingly.

"Don't do that again!" Suzy said, remembering the scenes of Induca being hit by that soul energy ranged attack.

"I'll do my best, love," Induca promised.

The two of them held each other. Relief filled them both at seeing that the other was all right.

Anna simply stood by the doorway, looking at them both, with a smile on her face.

There was the sound of feet and rushing air in the corridor.

Anna looked to where the noise was coming from before hastily stepping fully into the room. "Incoming!" Anna warned.

Party Zero crammed through the doorway. All of them looked to Suzy and Induca.

Malsour was like a black shadow, looking over Suzy and Induca at the same time.

"Are you okay? How do you feel?" Dave asked, right at his shoulder.

"Healer, what do they need?" Deia asked the healer who was stuck in the room.

"Well, Suzy needs bed rest and a good meal," the healer said.

"Induca needs the same but there was no stopping her coming here," Anna said.

"Should take better care of yourself." Lox gave Induca stink eye.

Suzy couldn't stop crying. She wasn't normally a person to show her emotions but she had been stretched so far that right now, seeing the care and the way that the rest of Party Zero were doting on them, the way that some of them were still wearing their armor that showed signs of recent fighting, she didn't doubt that they had raced from the battle to be with her.

"What happened with the castle?" Anna asked.

"We secured the northern castle and retook the eastern one." Steve admired his nails. "No big deal."

Suzy and Induca laughed at Steve's antics, finally coming down off the emotional high they had both been at.

"If you want, I can discharge Suzy right now. She's stable, just needs to rest," the healer said.

"We'll look after her," Deia said. The rest of Party Zero nodded unconsciously. There wasn't even a question in their minds that they would do everything in their power to see that Suzy and Induca got better.

Suzy had thought of the rest of Party Zero as her family many times, but it was only now when seeing them all together like this her words became more than just words; she saw them turn to action. She saw their acceptance, their love and fears. She bawled again, hiding her head in Induca's chest.

"What's wrong?" Dave asked.

"Nothing!" Suzy said, her voice muffled. "Everything is perfect." She muttered that part into Induca's shirt softly, as if saying it any louder might break the moment.

***

Party Zero all accessed the Mirror of Communication conference room.

Waiting for them was Josh, with a complicated expression on his face.

"Hey, Josh. What did you want to see us for?" Deia asked. The rest of the party took seats around the actual conference table.

"I came to ask a question, I guess," Josh said, not sounding too sure himself. "My question is, do you think fighting is the best use of your time? I know that you're working on something or things—I don't know what but I know that you place importance on them. You're one of the most powerful parties within the Stone Raiders but I need to know if your time would be better spent on working on these inventions."

Party Zero looked to one another before their eyes turned to Dave.

"As much as I want to say that being on the front lines would be the best use of our time, I can't. Malsour and I are working on multiple projects. However, these projects won't be useful for now and in these fights, well, actually some of them will." Dave looked to Malsour, who nodded before he looked back to Josh. "The others we can't use simply because they'll send the Jukal AI off. They're too powerful and they're seen as weapons of war that could be used to attack the Jukal Empire. We can only bring out these things as a very last resort."

"What is the thing we can use now?" Josh asked.

"The citadels. However, we only have one that is mostly operational and we haven't tested it out yet. We've got another three in various stages of production. In a week, the first will be complete; in three weeks, the second will be ready," Malsour said.

"What can I give you in order to speed this up?" Josh asked.

"People," Dave said. "Right now we've got maybe a half-dozen people and the Blood Kin besides Steve, Malsour, and me working on these projects."

"How many people do you need and in what capacity?" Josh asked.

"We need coders, people who can manipulate Dark and Earth Mana. We also need Water mages and Light mages. We need laborers—everything." Dave waved his hands.

"We also need people who would be willing to work for us for the next three years but they would be kept where they work," Malsour said.

"What for?" Josh asked.

"We can't go into that," Dave said. It wasn't that Dave didn't trust Josh; it was that he didn't want to put more things on his plate. He was already the binding force of the Terra Alliance. Throwing more on him would only add stress to his day.

"Okay, I'll do what I can. Now, what about the rest of you?" Josh's eyes passed over the rest of Party Zero.

"I'm good to fight," Deia said.

"I am too," Induca said.

"Same," Gurren said.

"I'll join in." Anna raised a hand.

"Might as well help this lot out." Lox smiled.

Lu Lu let out a screech.

"Looks like we're in," Suzy said.

"I'm just computing things anyway. With the upgrades Jeeves has got, he's much faster and more useful than I am," Steve said.

"Okay, well, let's go off that then," Josh said.

***

Dave sat down at a desk within Pandora's Box. His eyes slid over to his angrily blinking notifications.

He opened up the menu. Different prompts cascaded down.

Quest: Weapons Master Level 3

One handed and shield 1000/1000

Two handed 325/1000

Dual wielding 458/1000

Archery 1000/1000

Rewards: Unlock Level 4 Quest

Increase to stats

Passive skills from other weapons increase from 25% to 50% when designated weapon is not equipped. (Example: While using Dual-wield blades, one is able to gain 50% of the archery skill's abilities.)

"Close." Dave sighed and continued through the prompts.

Level 240

You have reached level 255; you have **75** stat points to use.

It was only through killing hundreds of the Xelur as well as their beasts that he was able to get such a large increase in stats. There really was nothing quite like killing other sentients in order to raise one's level.

Dave felt guilt but at the same time he knew that he would do the same thing again in an instant.

He moved to his character sheet and placed down his stat points. Twenty-five went into Intelligence, twenty into Endurance, another twenty into Willpower and ten into Agility.

With all of his projects, he needed to prioritize attributes that would allow him to work longer on these projects and make them as powerful as possible.

He checked over his new character sheet. His mind seemed clearer and his fatigue and hunger seemed to drift away as an inner strength filled him. His body felt rejuvenated and light, as if he could run forever.

Character Sheet

Name:	David Grahslagg	Gender:	Male
Level:	255	Class:	Dwarven Master Smith, Friend of the Grey God, Bleeder, Librarian, Aleph Engineer, Weapons Master, Champion Slayer, Skill Creator, Mine Manager, Master of Space and Time, Master of Gravitational Anomalies
Race:	Human/ Dwarf	Alignment:	Chaotic Good

Unspent points: 0

Health:	50,100	Regen:	24.82 /s
Mana:	16,280	Regen:	59.95 /s
Stamina:	5,520	Regen:	51.90 /s
Vitality:	501	Endurance:	1,241
Intelligence:	1,628	Willpower:	1,199
Strength:	552	Agility:	1,038

With a nod of approval, he dismissed the character sheets and focused on the Mirror of Communication in front of him. He used the menu to find the right conference room; he entered a password and placed his hand on the Mirror of Communication.

He was sucked into the conference room.

"How are they doing?" Dave asked Malsour, who was watching the people in the simulation.

"They're getting better every time. They've only been at it for a few hours but they're already better than I thought," Malsour said. "Watch."

"Power levels are looking good. Okay, let's power up the flight drive. How are we looking there, weapons?" the captain sitting at the back of the room asked.

"Weapons seem to be good," a person in front of the captain, sitting at one of the consoles, said.

"Very good. Flight, situation?" the captain asked.

"Captain, all checks are good on the magical coding. The flight systems are good and ready to go," the flight officer said.

"Barrier?" The captain looked to the barrier officer.

"Barriers are online above ground; as soon as we're in the air, ready to transition to full coverage. I've tweaked them a little from last time so we should have greater defense," the barrier officer said.

"That's what I like to hear. Keep it up." The captain bestowed the barrier officer with a smile. "Okay, well, seeing as we're all ready to go, Flight, shall we get going?"

"Yes sir. Powering up flight drive."

A deep humming filled the room as it shook slightly. Power seemed to thrum around the citadel and deep within Emerilia.

For a few seconds, nothing happened; then, slowly, they started to move.

Dave looked to a feed, watching the simulated citadel. This simulated citadel was complete, unlike the ones that were around Goblin Mountain. The ground around the citadel shook as it started to rise into the air.

As it rose, the mana barrier that had been covering just the Citadel now extended downwards, light shining out from under the rising construct.

"Power, how are we looking?" the captain asked.

"We're good for power. Once we're in the air, then I'm going to work on the heat and cold exchangers to see if we can't get more power while we're in the sky." The power officer glanced to the captain.

"Good." The captain nodded. They were still learning about how to use the citadel.

The citadel continued to rise, exposing what looked to be a massive soul gem underneath it. The roots that had spread throughout the rock underneath the citadel had worked with the soul gem construct to change the rock underneath into a massive soul gem. Right now, magical formations circled this massive soul gem construct; these formations were the flight drive that moved the citadel.

Rocks and debris that weren't part of the citadel fell off the soul gem construct.

The soul gem underneath the citadel was massive, taking a few minutes just for the citadel to get high enough so that it was fully out of the ground.

"Moving to cruising altitude," the flight officer said as the citadel moved away from the crater where it had been and pushed upward three kilometers into the sky.

Dave's eyes shone as he looked over the flying citadel.

The massive soul gem supported the Level 3 citadel on top. The sight made one's heart clench in awe.

The floating citadel dominated the sky, resting there.

"Okay, make any adjustments you want and test out your theories. You have ten minutes, then we'll continue with the live fire exercise and see how we do up against an enemy," the captain said to his officers.

Dave and Malsour shared a look, excited expressions on their faces.

"Not bad," Dave said on a private channel. As they were in observer mode, no one in the command center could see them.

"With these, we can bring an entire citadel with us wherever we need to go. We could just stop above an occupied castle and jump down into it, take it and move onward," Malsour said.

"Definitely increases our striking power." Dave nodded. "What about weapons?"

"We've been testing them out. I've had Jeeves watching over all of these simulations and improving the coding to make the floating citadels easier to manage. Right now we've only got weapons that are based on the soul gem construct. However, I want to get in some dwarven master smiths and engineers to retrofit some artillery cannons to the walls of this beast. Having the ability to launch grand workings with this thing—this is how we're going to win this event and portal opening," Malsour said.

Dave nodded.

"Can we use the new cannons?" Malsour asked.

"I've been debating that. I think it would be best if we had some of them ready and fitted to the citadels but keep it hidden—I don't want anyone to know that we have them. Only if we have to will we use them. Also, we're going to have to secretly retrofit the secondary systems we've been working on."

Malsour took a deep breath before he let it out. He looked at the command center, where the command crew were talking to one another, getting a good feel for their stations and working through issues they'd had and working to improve their abilities.

"I really wish that we could use those measures now," Malsour said.

"I do, too. However, we can't—we don't have the strength yet," Dave said. "Oh, and Bob wants to see us both. I can go by myself but do you want to come?"

"What, don't want to go across star systems by yourself?" Malsour grinned.

"Fine, if you don't want to come, don't." Dave rolled his eyes.

"Screw that—I'm coming. If Bob says that he's figured something out, then I want to see what that crazy gnome's done. Also I want to see just what has happened to the different bases in the Nal system," Malsour said.

"Someone wants to get mining," Dave teased.

"Hey, so what if I like rocks and asteroids?" Malsour shrugged.

"Uh huh." Dave exited the Mirror of Communication and once again appeared in Pandora's Box. Next to him, Malsour also opened his eyes.

"To the ice planet!" Dave stood and headed out of the room for the portal that connected Pandora's Box to the ice planet within the Nal system.

There were even more carts moving through the various portals that connected the ever-growing network of bases that they had created.

Dave and Malsour expanded their shields, capturing the air around them in a large area, and stepped through the portal. They exited, coming out to find the industrial complex and apartments made from the ice planet.

The industrial complex was taking in carts filled with ice blocks that were stuffed into the refinery, which then spat out purified resources that were stored in specialized storage chests. Off to the side, there was a heavily armored building where the fusion reactor powering all of this hummed away.

Past it, there were massive greenhouses that took up most of the room within the ice city.

Then there was a small-looking laboratory; off to the side of it, there were storage areas. The rest of the ice city was filled with apartments that didn't look too different from those within Terra.

The ice was being quickly replaced by a soul gem construct. The progress was visible as they walked down from the portal and through the defensive structure covered in trap runes.

"We're going to need to make our own automatons to man these places," Dave said as they walked through the city. With the power output from the fusion reactors as well as the new heat exchangers that had been prototyped with the flying citadels, the soul gem constructs were growing at a speed visible to the human eye. Plants were being harvested every few days, quickly converting the different gases that had been released into the greenhouses into a combination that could be inhaled by people from Emerilia.

Factories pumped out miners that continued to widen the city or move through another portal at the other side of the city. This portal led to the asteroid belt.

The area was lit by strip lighting that came from the soul construct buildings.

"Well, you're the factory man—that would probably be best for you to look into," Malsour said.

"I'll tinker with it, but I've been thinking on that whole hiring thing. We need more people to manage all of this—there are just a few of us to manage everything here. Do you think Ela-Dorn would be interested?" Dave asked.

"I think so, as long as she can bring her pup and husband." Malsour nodded. "I think it might be good to get quite a few of the Aleph. They're more open to new ideas and they know how to keep a secret. Plus, here with the new technology, they love that stuff, so adapting over won't be too hard. However, I still suggest creating contracts with them."

"Trust but verify." Dave nodded. "Some people aren't going to like that, but feelings don't matter as much as trying to keep this secret does."

"Exactly." Malsour nodded.

They stepped onto a runed circle that pushed them upward.

"These repulsor lifts are pretty awesome, though the version that goes down isn't as much fun," Dave said.

"That's just because you're afraid of heights," Malsour said.

"I was. Now that I can fly, it isn't too bad." Dave stepped off the runed circle that was pushing upward, into a hallway.

"While they're interesting, I still think that having elevators on the different ships and in the bases make sense," Malsour said.

"I agree. Steve must have put that one in." Dave opened a door into the one laboratory on the floor.

Malsour walked in and came to a stop.

Dave nudged past him, and then also halted. His eyes went wide as he looked at the contents of the room.

It was three stories tall. The floor they were on merely overlooked the first floor, with panes of see-through soul gem cutting them off from the area inside.

On the first floor, several stations faced one another along either side of the wall. They looked like medical wards from some futuristic video.

There were pods in each of these bays. Most were lit up by internal light while others seemed to have gas converging inside them.

Bob stood at a console on the second floor, overlooking the first. When he noticed that the two had entered, he turned to face them.

"Welcome to the first growth laboratory, gentlemen!" Bob waved his hands.

Dave's eyes fell on a pod that was raised up from the first floor by metallic arms. Inside there was a woman. She looked as if she were asleep.

"You did it?" Dave looked to Bob.

"I did it." Bob smiled. Malsour and Dave moved up toward the glass; Bob turned around to look on his creation as well.

"It was harder than I thought it was going to be. Not being able to pull apart an Altar of Rebirth makes things a little harder. However, I helped to make all of the original races that made up the population of Emerilia. I had to get some information from my old notes back then and make a lot of the machinery from the beginning. It took me trial and error like crazy and while I've made bodies, I'm not yet sure if they'll be ready for a consciousness transfer. And if it does work, then we've got to think of just what the hell we're going to do," Bob said.

Dave and Malsour looked at the fourteen pods—some lit up, others not. In each of them, a person was being born. Their true body.

"So you've been able to make your own version of the Altar of Rebirth?" Malsour asked.

"Kind of. This can create people in a dormant state. It takes uploading their consciousness afterward to make them actually people. However, I do not have the capture and processing systems that the Altar of Rebirths have and can use in order to make people respawn. Also, with most people re-spawning after dying, their minds are broken and they can't do it. With the players of Emerilia, it is different as they don't linger on the fact that they've actually died as they don't know that they have. Basically, their psychological stress is so reduced it doesn't have a detrimental effect. But, someone knowing that they're going to actually die and can only rely on the Altar of Rebirth to save them—they can be forever changed by the psychological stress, turning catatonic and even dying."

"Lovely. So what are the chances of this working?" Dave asked.

"I'd put it at seventy to eighty percent. I still need to do a whole bunch of tests and I can get that rate up to ninety percent. At the same time, I am working on creating an AI program to take over the person's life within the Earth simulation, much like how the AI took over as you became a bleeder," Bob said.

"Sounds rather complicated," Malsour said.

"Well, the AI just run off information data, which is easy enough to fake. The problem is going to be the other players within the simulation starting to notice people acting weird. We can only pull out a small population of people from the Earth simulation. Hacking through the simulation isn't too hard as I have admin rights. Though I'm having to hide my tracks as I find the more isolated people who are only surrounded by non-player characters," Bob said.

"How stable are they going to be, finding out that they've only been surrounded by characters made up to try to get them to game?" Malsour turned to Dave.

"Well, that is the question, isn't it?" Bob shrugged.

Dave was wrapped up in his own thoughts as he looked over those players.

They all looked into the lab for a few minutes before Dave broke the silence.

"It's weird. In a way, we're all brothers and sisters—us players, that is."

"Most of your genes are really similar to one another. The argument could easily be made that you're brothers and sisters. Every player pool is very similar in genealogy. It is only really the people of Emerilia who have a more diverse genetic background. I went a bit mad with making sure that they had multiple parent couplings, to make sure that there wasn't regressive genes to come out. Some of the elves are closer in genes to the dwarves and orcs than they would ever think to guess," Bob said.

Dave made a thoughtful noise as he looked over those pods. Before, they had just been brains in vats, people that he felt sorry for as their entire being and existence had been made and fabricated together by the Jukal Empire.

Now, however, seeing their bodies, he wasn't all that different from them. They had all the same genes; they had gone through the simulation of Earth at the exact same time period but just in different simulations and the majority of them were gamers.

They could have just as easily been Josh, Suzy, Cassie, Esa, Dwayne, or any one of the millions of gamers on Emerilia right now.

Dave let out a shaky breath and cleared his head. "When will you start trying to see when you can shift their consciousness to their real bodies?"

"About a month. Then, if it goes well, I can pull out all the outlying people, have Jeeves cover it over—then I have to pull people in groups from across the Earth simulation. These groups are going to be thousands to tens of thousands big, ripping out entire networks of players before reviving them here, inserting in Jeeves immediately. For that, we're going to need facilities much bigger than this, but then hopefully some people will be willing to help us and can learn through the Mirror of Communication school to improve their stats and skills," Bob said.

"Damn, that's a lot faster than I thought." Malsour shook his head.

"Our plans are slowly but surely coming together," Dave said. Suddenly he clapped his hands together. "Okay, so we're going to be trying to hire people on to help us out with all of this and are from Emerilia. Let me know any names you have for people to help us or be hired on. Suzy will do her best to get them to join us. In the meantime, Malsour and I need to go check on the asteroid facility."

"I haven't been able to look into the asteroid facility much. I re-positioned the portal within the asteroid, as you know, so that no one might see the light coming off the portal. There are also drones moving through the thing and eating through everything. As you've requested, half of the soul gem base constructs created by the industrial sector here have been sent to the asteroid facility, with the rest going to Emerilia and through Pandora's Box."

"Awesome. What about those portal materials?" Dave asked.

"I've also placed them out there. Be careful, though—need to test it all first," Bob warned.

"We'll do our best," Malsour said.

"All right, well, stop keeping this old gnome waiting—go and get that asteroid base sorted out!" Bob shooed them out of his laboratory with his hands.

"Very well." Dave sighed. He snapped his fingers; a spell formation appeared around Malsour and Dave in an instant, orbs floating around them.

One moment, they were in Bob's laboratory; the next, they were in front of a portal that seemed to look into the abyss, with occasional beams of light.

"Was that teleporting?" Malsour said in shock. It had to be understood that only the gods and goddesses could teleport on Emerilia; they used the AI and their massive divine well power in order to do it.

However, Dave didn't have an AI and nowhere near the power that they did.

"Well, I told you that I've been working on my teleportation." Dave laughed.

"Yes, but I thought that was in relation to the portals, the teleport pads, and the onos. I never thought that you were going to do it to yourself! And to me! Have you even tested it out before?" Malsour's voice went higher and higher with every moment.

"Well, I've done some tests with small objects, mostly when I've been off Emerilia. I'm not sure how sensitive those sensors really are and if they might pick up a foreign signal and link it to tele-portation," Dave said.

"So not really is your answer. Do you know what could have gone wrong?"

"Oh, don't worry so much. I pulled it from what I have seen of Fire, Water, and Bob's teleportation spells. Then I mixed it togeth-er with the knowledge that I have from working with the teleporta-tion array, onos, portals, teleportation pads and all the rest that you just mentioned. If I am not qualified to do it, then I don't think that there is anyone else on Emerilia who is," Dave said with a con-fident smile. "Now let's go and see this asteroid, shall we? I want to practice it some more."

With that said, Dave appeared in front of the portal in a flash and stepped through it.

Dave looked upon the pure darkness that was all around him. The portal gave off a faint light as he looked around. The faint light was enough for his high-leveled night vision to pierce through that inky darkness, revealing that he was in a portal control area, just like the ones on the ice planet. These centers were made to control who came in and left through the portal.

Malsour appeared through the portal, right behind Dave.

With a wave of his hand, once again Dave and Malsour disap-peared from their spot, finding themselves on what looked like a balcony.

To their right and to their left, there were golden lights that were eating into the walls of the asteroid. These were the miners that had been created in the ice planet's factories. They moved as one solid entity, creating a tunnel through the massive ten-kilome-ter-long asteroid. Other miners that had come from the ice planet later were cutting in straight ahead before angling to follow their fellow miners.

Dave's senses spread out through his Touch of the Land spell, finding the different areas of the asteroid. There was a fueling station for the miners, as well as three fusion reactors that had been laid down along the side of the asteroid Dave and Malsour stood on. There was no gravity within the asteroid yet but Dave was unconsciously using gravity magic so that they didn't go flying away.

"Okay, looks like the reactors are just running at around five percent of their total output. Do you want to get with the soul gem constructs? We've got that shipyard plan from Sato and his people—we can use that in order to create this place faster and modify it as we need to. Then we also need to make soul gem factories. I'm thinking not the normal soul gem factories, but rather we take something from the citadels—see if we can't create hybrid soul gems, linking together multiple vault gem-sized soul gems and then interlinking them with magical coding. If it works out, then it can create the kind of soul gems we need for our current power requirements."

"I can do that. What are you going to be working on?" Malsour asked.

"I'll get some of the soul gem constructs and I'll start them working on making asteroid miners and spaceships to move material within the asteroid fields. Also I'm going to hook up some more powerful sensor units so we can figure out what kind of materials are hanging out around us. Then I can start working on the warships, proper warships, not just the arks that are within Emerilia and the moon," Dave said.

"Aren't you building battleships on the moon? Don't they count?"

"They do, kind of. I modified them a bit. They're not really true battleships but more of missile boats. If this goes down, we have a lot of targets to hit at once if we want to survive. Those missiles can take out a fair amount of the Jukal's infrastructure in one shot," Dave said.

"Okay. I'll put down the soul gem constructs and have them run power lines out to the berths first," Malsour said.

"Thanks. Well, we better get started then." Dave was standing there one moment; the next, he disappeared, taking with him the artificial gravity.

Malsour had to hurriedly reach out to the wall, willing the stone there to create handholds. "And we're making gravity and inertia runing after that so everyone else isn't spinning off into space!" Malsour yelled to Dave, who was at a berth a few hundred meters away.

"What did you say?" Dave yelled back.

Malsour was about to yell back but instead waved his hand, giving up on it, and pushed himself along the wall toward the fusion powerplants, as he passed, ladders appeared along the walls and the rough outline of the walls firmed up, looking like polished stone.

Dave turned to the cart next to him. He opened up the storage crates, finding soul gem base constructs inside. He pulled them out one by one. As he touched them, a three-dimensional picture of what they were set to appeared in front of him. As he cut and pasted in different plans he had into the base construct, these images changed.

There were two types of automated asteroid miner. One had a simple drill bit that was covered in Dark Mana that would disrupt the bonds between inanimate objects like rock and metal; the drill section would grind these apart. Gravity scoops on either side would pull the materials into storage containers to the rear of the asteroid miner, which could be switched out.

It was covered in a variety of repulsors that would allow it to move through space and through asteroids. There were sensor units that would be built into the body of the miner so that it knew where it was at all times and, as it was mining, it could pick up the different materials that were in its path.

This miner was meant for two things: to open up asteroids for the second miner to get into it and to also be used outside of asteroids to cut into different ore veins. This miner used Dark Mana instead of Light so that it would be harder to detect. Unless someone was specifically looking for the miner, then they would have a hard time finding it, between the Dark Mana drillbit and the amazingly effective stealth runes that covered the exterior of its hull.

The soul gem constructs consumed the power that they had stored within them, making the base structure of the different things that had been programmed into them.

The second miner didn't have these stealth runes. It was nearly ten times the size and it was hooked up directly to storage chests that would stay behind it, ready to be changed out by carts and cargo shuttles.

This had multiple Light drills that would create a beam of golden light that would cut through the interior of an asteroid at an alarming rate. These would be as fast as twenty of the original miners that were running through the asteroid. With it, hollowing out an asteroid would be much more efficient, taking much less time.

While it cut out the main thoroughfare of the shipyard that would be inside the asteroid, the smaller miners would be able to cut out the hallways and slips that would run down the asteroid shipyard.

Dave finished making ten soul gem constructs of the first miner and two of the large-scale miner. As he finished with them, they would disappear from his hands as he teleported them across the asteroid to the few catwalks that jutted out from the wall that the portal corridors and fusion plants were located behind.

These small little sections of rock that jutted outwards were about ten meters wide and one hundred long and were spread out every five hundred meters. These were what the slips of the shipyard would be built out from, the slips would then hold one or more ships as they were being held at readiness or were being worked on

It would take some time before all of the slips were filled with working ships. But now with the soul gem constructs, all it took was enough power. Their fusion plants were operational and the ice planet was refining enough fuel to meet the demands that Pandora's Box's creators needed.

They were stockpiling more for the fusion reactors that would be built within the different warships. The Mana expenditure was simply astronomical.

Once he had finished with the different base soul gem constructs that were now growing where the slips would be constructed, he started forming the cargo shuttles. These were automated creations that would handle most of the cargo within the system. So, Dave went ahead and put in the right coding so that Jeeves could command them.

They would be covered in the ovaloid-looking repulsor units and drive units that would allow them to cross space. Its rear section was one entire box of holding. They could be chained together, much like how train carts were attached to one another.

The shuttle could drop them off and then attach all of the filled containers and fly back toward the main asteroid mining base, dropping off the storage boxes to be separated down by ore and then stuffed into automated carts that would take these back to the refinery on the ice planet to be processed.

The shuttles were, like the miners that would operate outside the asteroids, covered in stealth magical coding. Even heat exchangers were being put in to simply make sure that the ambient temperature around the shuttles wasn't more or less than the surrounding area.

If someone was able to plot where the shuttles were, then they could figure out where the bases were within the asteroid belt.

Dave made three of these, teleporting them out to different areas to allow them to grow. Dave looked toward where he and Malsour had entered the center of the shipyard. The soul gem constructs powered by the fusion reactors of the asteroid base were now racing across the floor with runic lines in them, guiding the power outward. They spread out at an incredible speed, covering the floors and then reaching out across the interior of the shipyard. They reached the slips, diverting with runic lines of power leading the way.

As they touched the different soul gem constructs that were resting against the slips, they started to grow at an incredible rate.

The soul gem construct from the fusion plant brought with it gravity and strip lighting as it raced toward either end of the shipyard, where the miners were currently hard at work.

Dave held a soul gem construct in his hands. Above it, there was a sharp-looking ship, with missile tubes and gun tubes that looked like bristles. The drive units on it were larger and the Mana barrier projectors were massive.

This was what the battleships in the moon should have been. It was a melding of the magical coding and technology that Dave knew of and matched with information he had got from Bob about the Jukal ships, as well as human ships and the information that Sato and his people had shared.

From all of this amassed information, Jeeves, Steve, Dave, Malsour, and Bob had created something that demanded respect. This melded technologies that the Emerilia AI would have freaked out over and Dave wasn't willing to use even in his secret bases within Emerilia or its moon.

The soul gem construct in Dave's hands disappeared. Reappearing in a slip, it grew rapidly. From it, support beams that ran the length of the ship creating its "spine," extended; other supports spread outward, creating the superstructure of the ship.

Dave created a half-dozen more of the soul gem constructs and sent them outward into the various slips.

In these slips, nearly twenty different items were being created at the same time.

Dave's focus was not on the miners, nor the cargo shuttles or the impressive battleships. Instead, it was on the simple ring-looking three-dimensional image that floated above the soul gem he had just modified.

The Jukal made hundreds of portals. Let's see if I can make one or two.

Dave lowered the soul gem construct into a groove at his feet. Runic lines flared around the soul gem construct as the asteroid base's soul gem interior poured power into Dave's soul gem construct.

From the catwalk, much slower than the beams or the other soul gem constructs, a base started to appear—a base, that looked similar to a portal's.

His notifications, which had been blinking for a while but he'd forgotten about, now once again blinked rapidly.

"Seems that I've churned up a notification storm."

Dave opened his notifications, blinking at the number of prompts.

"Lovely—stat points." Dave rubbed his hands together and went through the screens.

Quest Completed: Librarian Level 7

Use research to prove a theory (8/3)

Rewards: Unlock Level 8 Quest

+10 to all stats

700,000 Experience

Quest Completed: Librarian Level 8
Use research to prove a theory (8/4)
Rewards: Unlock Level 9 Quest
+10 to all stats
800,000 Experience

Quest Completed: Librarian Level 9
Use research to prove a theory (8/5)
Rewards: Unlock Level 10 Quest
+10 to all stats
900,000 Experience

Quest Completed: Librarian Level 10
Use research to prove a theory (8/6)
Rewards: Unlock Level 11 Quest
+10 to all stats
1,00,000 Experience

Quest Completed: Librarian Level 11
Use research to prove a theory (8/7)
Rewards: Unlock Level 12 Quest
+10 to all stats
1,100,000 Experience

Quest Completed: Librarian Level 12
Use research to prove a theory (8/8)
Rewards: Unlock Level 13 Quest
+10 to all stats
1,200,000 Experience (5,700,000 Experience accumulated)

Class: Librarian
Status: Level 12
             +120 to all stats
Effects: Read 10% faster
             Understand 15% more of the information that you read

Quest: Librarian Level 13

Use research to prove a theory (8/9)

Rewards: Unlock Level 14 Quest

Increase to stats

Dave turned pensive.

"These must be not only from starting work on the portal but actually the anchors and moving portals around as well as my own teleporting around.'" As Dave stopped talking, his eyes went wide. "Wait. If, if I had six theories I researched and proved, what were theories about?"

Dave's voice shook a bit as he continued through his notifications.

Quest Completed: Master of Space and Time Level 15

Come up with new possible theory (6/3)

Rewards: Unlock Level 16 quest

+15 to Willpower

+15 to Intelligence

+15 to Endurance

+15 to Agility

1,500,000 Experience

Quest Completed: Master of Space and Time Level 16

Come up with new possible theory (6/4)

Rewards: Unlock Level 17 quest

+15 to Willpower

+15 to Intelligence

+15 to Endurance

+15 to Agility

1,600,000 Experience (3,100,000 Experience accumulated)

Quest Completed: Master of Space and Time Level 17
Come up with new possible theory (6/5)
Rewards: Unlock Level 18 quest
+15 to Willpower
+15 to Intelligence
+15 to Endurance
+15 to Agility
1,700,000 Experience (4,800,000 Experience accumulated)

Quest Completed: Master of Space and Time Level 18
Come up with new possible theory (6/6)
Rewards: Unlock Level 19 quest
+15 to Willpower
+15 to Intelligence
+15 to Endurance
+15 to Agility
1,800,000 Experience (6,600,000 Experience accumulated)

Class: Master of Space and Time
Status: Level 18
          Greater understanding of Space and Time
          +270 to Willpower
Effects: +270 to Intelligence
          +270 to Endurance
          +270 to Agility

Quest: Master of Space and Time Level 19
Come up with new possible theory (6/7)
Rewards: Unlock Level 20 quest
Increase to stats

Dave could feel as his body was already starting to change. Cold sweat fell down his back. He'd had four theories related to space and time that he'd proved; there were still two more theories that he'd proved right.

He quickly sent Malsour a message saying where he was as he felt a torrent of power only barely being held back. Knowing how dumping in stats could overload a person, Dave didn't dare to think about trying to keep working with all the changes that were happening in his body.

He quickly continued onward, a mix of excitement and nervousness.

Quest Completed: Master of Gravitational Anomalies Level 11
Come up with new possible theory (4/3)
Rewards: Unlock Level 12 quest
+10 to all stats
1,100,000 Experience

Quest Completed: Master of Gravitational Anomalies Level 12
Come up with new possible theory (4/4)
Rewards: Unlock Level 13 quest
+10 to all stats
1,200,000 Experience (2,300,000 Experience accumulated)

Class: Master of Gravitational Anomalies

Status: Level 12

Effects: Greater understanding of Gravitational Anomalies
+120 to all stats

Quest: Master of Gravitational Anomalies Level 13
Come up with new possible theory (4/5)
Rewards: Unlock Level 14 quest
Increase to stats

Level 255
You have reached Level 261; you have **30** stat points to use.

Dave's character sheet showed up as power started to surge through every part of his body.

Character Sheet

| Name: | David Grahslagg | Gender: | Male |

| Level: | 261 | Class: | Dwarven Master Smith, Friend of the Grey God, Bleeder, Librarian, Aleph Engineer, Weapons Master, Champion Slayer, Skill Creator, Mine Manager, Master of Space and Time, Master of Gravitational Anomalies |

| Race: | Human/ Dwarf | Alignment: | Chaotic Good |

Unspent points: 30

Health:	50,100	Regen:	27.62 /s
Mana:	16,280	Regen:	66.95 /s
Stamina:	5,520	Regen:	58.90 /s
Vitality:	581	Endurance:	1,381
Intelligence:	1,768	Willpower:	1,339
Strength:	632	Agility:	1,178

Active Skill: *Teleportation*

Level: *Master Level 3*

Effect: *Able to create a device to teleport across distances.*

Dave closed the screen as an almost tyrannical energy seemed to be tearing him apart from the inside and re-creating him. The surge of over seven hundred stat points rushed through his body. His mind became clearer as his body's strength increased in leaps and bounds. The runic lines across his body surged with energy; he glowed with power as his aura underwent a massive change with the increase of power.

With the interlinking of classes that were suited toward what he was doing, these kinds of surges were possible. In the space of a few minutes, it was as if he had gained over a hundred levels—a nearly impossible feat even if he was to kill thousands, but with the progressing classes it was possible to break past these barriers.

Dave was unable to do anything as his body surged with strength.

The world went dark as he collapsed, his body and mind no longer able to support him as his attributes skyrocketed.

Chapter 11: Shifts to Emerilia

Sato watched the stealth remote that was set up in the Emerilia system. Everyone within the command center was silent as they looked at the various scenes on the different screens.

There were a dozen or so stealthed remote buoys that watched the Emerilia system at all times, recording and sending back everything that they saw.

"What the hell happened?" Sato said under his breath, his face pale.

Each of the screens showed a different battle or fight happening on Emerilia.

There were entire armies that were clashing all across Emerilia. People were sieging and defending castles.

A number of the creatures had been pulled up on the Deq'ual's database.

"Looks like the portals have been activated and all of the aggressive species that were on different planets are now connected to Emerilia and fighting it out with the Emerilians." Adams, at his side, looked at the video feed that was nearly an hour old.

The power that was being unleashed in some of these battles could be seen from orbit.

"Adams, I want remotes within all of the aggressive species systems. I want to know what Emerilia is up against and what threats we might have to deal with in the future. Or who might be allies," Sato said.

Even if they were attacking Emerilia right now, there might be a way to use them to fight the Jukal in the future.

Sato hated himself for saying those words but he needed to. His duty was to the people of the Deq'ual system first and he needed to deal with that. Even as much as he wanted to help out the people of Emerilia and Dave, he couldn't, so he needed to use this to learn about his possible enemies and allies.

If he could find out something to help Dave and the people of Emerilia, then he could pass it on.

"Yes, sir." Adams worked on her screen to organize certain stealth ships that were out providing recon and scouting the other systems around the Deq'ual and certain points that interested the leadership.

Sato watched the battles that continued to rage on, burning those images into his mind. He stood there, straight-backed, emotions roiling as he kept up a professional facade. Hundreds—maybe thousands—of people died and he couldn't do a thing but watch.

And so he would watch as they were overrun or pushed back the enemy, the moments of brilliance that turned a battle and all too many last moments that people went through.

He stood there like a statue, taking on those images and wishing nothing more than to reach out in help and aid.

***

Josh looked over the various maps that showed dozens of portals and the castles around them.

So far, only five of the portal locations had been secured. The rest were still being contested, with the Terra Alliance fighting to capture more of the castles or to hold what they had against the enemy.

There was a constant murmur in the room of people talking. All of these people and Shard were working to put the forces at their command to the most use.

People, like the DCA aerial forces, were being pulled from one battlefield to another to support or reinforce.

The Terra Alliance had nearly half a million people under its command, from healers in various hospital areas, to the quartermasters who moved munitions, food, water, potions, and all the materials a fighting military needed on Emerilia. Then there were the actual soldiers who could fight on the front lines against the enemy.

Using all of their strengths together and finding a place for them was difficult.

Cassie walked through the room and handed Josh a piece of paper.

He held it in his hands, frowning as he read it. "What? Is this real?" Josh asked in a private chat with Cassie.

"I just had the ambassador from Markolm give it to me," Cassie said.

Josh didn't know what to say for a few moments. "When will they start pulling back their forces?"

"They've already begun," Cassie said, her face and voice solemn.

"Shit. All right, well, if Markolm is pulling out of the Terra Alliance, then wasting people on helping them is useless. Inform the commanders in Markolm what is going on and order them to pull back to Terra to receive new orders."

"Got it." Cassie reached out to squeeze Josh's hand.

He smiled to her.

"Nothing stops the Stone Raiders," Cassie said.

"I thought you were a golden sabre?" Josh joked.

Cassie's eyebrow lowered, as if she saw Josh in a whole new light.

"I'm joking," Josh laughed, squeezing her hand.

The corners of her mouth lifted into a smile.

"I'll see you later," She said, giving him a deep look.

With that, Cassie turned around to carry out his orders and Josh contacted Lucy.

"Josh?" Lucy answered a moment later.

"Did you know about Markolm?" Josh asked.

"Is it official—did they pull out of the Alliance?"

"Yeah." Josh sighed.

"That bitch. Damn, she's good," Lucy hissed.

"What happened?" Josh asked, at a loss for what had happened while he hadn't been watching.

"The Lady of Light had Khanundra and her generals of Light step in and save the people of Markolm. They almost singlehandedly moved through the entire continent; Light teleported them from battlefield to battlefield just as it looked as if all hope was lost.

"They valiantly defended the people of Markolm in a way that the forces of the Terra Alliance couldn't. It looks like she made the generals and Khanundra her champions. The power that it must have taken to do that would be immense, but they're all now some of the strongest people on Emerilia.

"They sealed the portals as well. Now the people are turning to them, the angels denying that they killed anyone who might argue against joining the Lady of Light. Without those powerful figures, few are willing to deny the Lady of Light now that the people are starting to get behind her.

"The angels are calling the deaths of those people a fabrication of the truth. She was smart about it. She took out the resistance ahead of time—then, just as everyone was in a panic, ready to sell their souls to the devil, her angels rush in to save them. She has already inserted some of her people as priests and priestesses within Markolm."

"In desperate times, people are willing to look to anyone who offers them hope." Josh shook his head.

"She's growing in power with every day the elves of Markolm are devoting more and more of their energy to her. However, she's not the only one from the Pantheon who's increasing their power," Lucy said. "The Dark Lord has been oddly quiet but here and there, Dark forces have been pulled from different locations. We think this is him bringing his strength together. The Earth Lord has also been gathering creatures from Emerilia. Even if they are not the same Affinity, they are still of Emerilia and they trust the Earth Lord and his more simplistic ways, as well as bow their heads to his power."

"So, the beasts went to the Earth Lord, the Dark Lord is pulling those who practice his arts to him, and the Lady of Light is growing her power base through the people of Emerilia, shoring up her position as she waits for her Legions of Light to return." Josh held his head, rubbing it with his hand.

"In the meantime, we can do nothing but fight among ourselves and try to counteract all of the creatures and species that have been unleashed upon us," Lucy said. "This is but the first wave of the war. The mortal war has started but the war of the Pantheon is about to start."

"Well, isn't that just lovely." Josh looked at the chaos across Emerilia. The people had holed up within their cities, fighting off the things that came out of the wilderness or the portals. The castles surrounding portals were heavily contested in most areas.

They were in a state of chaos; the Terra Alliance was , reacting and making adjustments where they could. Through this they might forge themselves into a stronger entity or they could be torn apart, too weak to resist the forces on Emerilia that were on the move or being put into play, and nothing but ants in front of the gods' growing power.

We dance the blade, to gain levels and increase our strength fighting through this hell, only to step deeper and continue against the gods of Emerilia, always courting failure and instead being stripped of that power and once again having to climb higher to hopefully fend off destruction.

"Esa reports that her people are ready to assault the eastern castle." Shard appeared next to Josh.

"Thank you." Josh looked to the screen that was relaying information back from that battlefield.

Josh switched back to Lucy's and his chat. "I've got to go. Keep a watch out for the gods and see if there is anything we can do to try to decrease their power gain."

"Okay. Talk later." Lucy ended the chat.

***

Induca and Suzy watched from above, as the rest of Party Zero led an attack on a captured castle.

They were fighting against Ooinfa, which made it hard for casters with low Willpower. With the Ooinfa's ability with illusions, the mages were much more likely to hit their own people. Thus, the fighting had resulted in melee fighters coming to the fore.

Suzy commanded half of her creations to protect her mind from the illusions while Induca laid down supporting fire walls to block off the Ooinfa's attacks and also limit the amount of Ooinfa that could clash with the player formations advancing toward the Ooinfa-controlled castle.

Although the Ooinfa were formidable with their illusions, their actual attacks came in the manner of sneak attacks. In this kind of straight-up fight, they might get one or two lucky hits but the players worked together to neutralize their attacks and push forward.

The Ooinfa's hidden and weak bodies fell before the players in droves. Anna, Deia, Jung Lee, Lox, Gurren, and Steve moved through the Ooinfa like an unstoppable wave. They might not be able to see the Ooinfa's actual bodies but their speed and strength made it nearly impossible for the illusion-loving creatures to escape.

"It seems that the world has changed these few weeks," Suzy said as they watched over the battle. It was furious at times but without their main advantages and fighting players with a high

Willpower, the Ooinfa found themselves being driven backward, the players using them to increase their skills and class levels.

"Everyone has hunkered down in cities and towns, with only player alts or massive party groups moving between cities. Markolm has pulled out of the Terra Alliance and their continent and people seem to be devoting themselves to the Lady of Light, who's amassing her power and getting her angel generals to train up a fighting force of the more radicalized followers, or the devoted. People are flocking to Markolm in search of safety and pledging themselves to the Lady of Light in turn. It has given us more people who were originally aiding Markolm, allowing us to hold all of our castles with full strength," Induca said.

"Don't forget that with every minute we hold the castles, the coders are getting to work in using the soul gem constructs to reinforce them," Suzy said.

"Even with all of this, we've just attained a draw. We're stretched over far too much area. We're growing Terra faster than ever before, with the third section being connected tonight and the fourth already about twenty five percent completed. We've got people pouring in from all over Emerilia who can't fit in these cities and towns. Food is running low and while we're building more greenhouse towers with the Aleph, dwarves, Devil's Crater, and Terra, it won't be enough to feed everyone," Induca said.

"We've come this far. We'll find a way." Suzy looked to Induca as a spell formation appeared in front of her. A new fire wall cut through the Ooinfa.

"I fear that this is just the beginning," Induca said.

***

Ela-Dorn looked to Dave, who sat across from her, bouncing Koi on his knee, who looked shocked but amused by the action.

"You want me to leave the Aleph College for at least two years, and I won't be able to talk to anyone without first having it vetted by an AI?" Ela-Dorn repeated what he had just said to her.

"That's about the gist of it."

"Why would I want to?" Ela-Dorn leaned back in her chair. Her hand fell to her summoned wolf and scratched behind his ears.

"To see more than you've ever seen before." Dave's eyes shone as he smiled at Ela-Dorn.

"Sounds mysterious, but I'm used to that with you." Ela-Dorn laughed.

"You will see things that you would have never thought were even possible. You will have resources at your disposal that make the materials that the Aleph get in a year look like mere crumbs. You will work with and create technology that rivals the portals that you've worked with. What we do will change the face of Emerilia. It could change the balance of power in the known universe," Dave said.

"What have you done?"

"Come with me." Dave smiled, standing and putting Koi on his shoulder.

"Okay." Ela-Dorn followed Dave. He led her out of the Aleph College, and through the teleport pad to the power station.

"Are you taking me to your lab?" Ela-Dorn asked through a private chat. She knew all about the Jukal and had become extremely paranoid about what she said out of private chats and Mirrors of Communication.

"Yes. It's gone through some changes," Dave said.

The power station had been fully automated so that there was no one to see them as they passed through the secret passage that linked the power station to Pandora's Box.

Ela-Dorn entered right behind, looking at the various workstations covered in different items. With her arcane sight, she was able to see what these different items were. Her eyes widened as she looked at the walls and floor. "There's so much power going through this place. How can you have so much power and keep up power production to Terra?"

"We've created something called a fusion reactor. Basically, it harnesses the same energies that we find in Emerilia's sun and uses that to create electrical power, which is, in turn, free Mana. We also have Mana wells, which give off continuous Mana and will do so for millions of years," Dave said.

"Okay, so you've got all this power, but what do you need it for?" Ela-Dorn looked over missiles that she knew Frenik from the Aleph Council was in charge of building, as well as the Band-Aids that were now being issued to all members of the Terra Alliance. They provided a good boost in defensive stats and they had been turned into a mandatory piece of kit for all people. Being relatively cheap, people from all over Emerilia were buying them in job lots, from the lowest peasant to members of leadership, everyone wanted one.

There were Dave's orbs, pulled part, and sheets of magical coding next to drawings of Magical Circuits and spell formations.

Ela-Dorn was already blown away with the array of items that covered the workshop. Dave led her through it all, looking back at her as he stood in front of a wall.

"Well, we need them for this." He stepped through the wall.

"I couldn't even sense it there with my arcane sight." Ela-Dorn pushed her hand forward, finding it go through the illusion that had been put in place. She took a breath and stepped forward, entering a space easily as large as the rest of Pandora's Box.

Automated carts moved between portals, carrying all manner of resources and materials.

Ela-Dorn simply stood there, looking at the room. Her eyes moved from portal to portal. "Y-you have working portals?"

"Yes, I do." Dave smiled. "All that power is used to keep these portals activated. They're connected to other locations, I can't tell you where these locations are or what's at them, but I can tell you that the stuff there makes everything in Pandora's Box look like child's play."

Koi, supported by her father, looked at the portals before flopping onto his shoulder, her little arms encompassing Dave's neck.

Ela-Dorn's pup Kelo rubbed his side against Ela-Dorn. By reflex, she patted his side, still looking at these portals. "I knew that your understanding of teleportation was advanced but I didn't think that it had yet reached this level," Ela-Dorn said, stunned by what she was seeing.

If the Jukal could see what she was, they would have spat blood at the resources and power being used in order to create this network of bases.

"Do you want to learn more and go further than you have before?" Dave asked.

Ela-Dorn's face became solemn as she saw what she had never even dreamed of in her life, just waiting for her beyond those portal event horizons.

She cracked a smile. "Well, with modern treatments, I can live for another hundred or two hundred years. What's just two of them trying to broaden my horizons?"

"Then I welcome you to the Pandora's Box team." Dave held out his hand to Ela-Dorn. She shook it as Koi moved once again, using her dad's face in order to right herself.

"Hey, this was supposed to be a serious moment, missy," Dave said to Koi as he moved her hand away and moved her into a different position.

"So, what now?" Ela-Dorn asked.

"First, we're going to need more people to help, and then, we see if we can't write our own future." Dave smiled.

***

"We need dwarven master smiths now more than ever, but you and Dave want to hire away as many as possible in order to help with some mysterious project that you can't tell us?" Sola asked as the Council of Anvil and Fire was all in attendance.

"Correct," Kol said.

"We need something more than that. I trust you and Dave, but he's not even here and this is a large request," Jesal said.

"I will be honest. Most of the things that Dave wants to work on are not something that will assist us here and now. Most of these projects are aimed to be of use in a year or two. I have never lied to this council nor will I ever. However, there are things of importance that are hard to explain. To know more, each and every one of you must make an oath on smithing," Kol said.

"You don't trust us?" Rola asked.

"I trust you, but this—" Kol shook his head before he looked directly at Rola. "This is larger than anything we have ever worked on or done before."

"I'll swear," Quino said.

"I will too," Endur said. "However, no matter what, we must keep a number of dwarven master smiths working within the dwarven mountains or at least helping out in the smithies and keeping everything running. If we all disappear, then it will create instability."

The other dwarves all agreed and swore on their smithing that they wouldn't say anything about what they would see to anyone else.

"Very well. Meet me in Terra," Kol said.

He exited the Mirror of Communication, finding himself in the conference room of the Terra smithy. The other dwarves also left the Council of Anvil and Fire conference, all of them looking to Kol.

"Follow me," Kol said. They went to a teleport pad. It didn't take much time before the other members of the Council of Anvil and Fire teleported to Terra and joined them.

People talked to one another but the atmosphere was tense. As everyone was gathered, Kol indicated for the controller of the teleport pad to connect to the power station.

He guided them through the teleport pad, and then through the power station. The dwarves were a bit shocked when they walked into Pandora's Box through its secret entrance. When they were inside the workshop, their eyes went wide as they looked upon various machines and items that surpassed what they had been working on.

Kol saw that a number of them just wanted to grab onto these items and never let them go. They contained themselves, their voices excited as they followed Kol through a wall and into the portal room. Just as Dave had shown Ela-Dorn not more than a few hours before.

As they all reached the portal room, the dwarves let out various noises.

"You got portals working?" Endur asked.

Dave stepped out of one of the Portals carrying Koi and walked over to the group.

"Yes, indeed we do have working portals," Kol said. "I was going to take them to the ark shipyard."

"Good idea. It's been some time since I was there myself. I need to check it out and the moonbase before I get this one off to bed," Dave said. "Also, while we can make portals work, we can shut them down."

There were angered and frustrated noises from the dwarves. Endur held up his hand and the dwarves quieted.

"Dave doesn't usually do these things on a whim, so before we start jumping to conclusions, it might be best if we asked him why he hasn't shut down the portals that different races are currently exiting through in order to attack us." Endur couldn't keep a bit of heat out of his voice. A number of people from Emerilia had died because of these open portals.

"As you all know, there is a power that usually keeps the balance within Emerilia, a person by the name of the Grey God, or Bob as he is going by now. You all know that he gets his orders from someone else. These people are called the Jukal, who nearly wiped out our ancestors and only created Emerilia and us so that we could fight off the species that they didn't want to—the creatures that are currently coming through the portals. Now the Jukal made this place and they monitor us. If I was to shut down the portals, then it might take some time for the Jukal to figure out just what the hell is going on and then when they did, they'd start raining down hell from the sky and kill us all off," Dave said.

The Dwarven Council of Anvil and Fire had learned about the Jukal a long time ago from Bob; however, they were powerless to do anything. They kept their meetings in the Mirrors of Communication to make sure that they didn't hear of their plans and did their best to stay under the radar.

The dwarven master smiths paled at all of this.

"What we've been working on—well, it would be better to show you." Dave looked upward. "Jeeves, carts please."

Carts came out of one portal, creating a line in front of the dwarves.

The dwarves climbed onto the carts; as soon as they were all on, the carts started to move. They passed through a portal and entered a hallway where there were carts moving up and down in two lines, splitting off through doorways on the right and left side of the corridor.

"This base is mostly a shipyard called the ark," Dave said. As they moved, the doorways on either side were so close together and their speed so great that they could see into the massive areas on either side.

"Here we assemble missiles that are shipped off to different bases. These missiles fit into two categories: one a surface-to-space and the other a space-based missile. The first is made so that we can take out the different systems that are around Emerilia so they can't destroy us right away. The second are for our own ships."

They passed the factory and Kol smiled as he saw the expressions on the dwarven master smiths' faces as they reached the real beasts that lay hidden within the ark shipyard.

When Kol had come here previously, there were just four ships being built and they were being formed from metals and other precious resources. Now there were eighteen different berths, nine on each side of the corridor.

"Originally we wanted to make battleships, to fight the Jukal in space and secure our skies so they couldn't wipe us out. Building these ships, we ran into a number of difficulties. At first, we were spending a lot of resources on creating the armored hulls. With the advances with soul gem constructs, we can cut down on these materials usage. But then we were still left with these heavier hulls. So now they're all going to be turned into arks, ships that can hold the people of Emerilia and protect them from nearly anything," Kol said. "As well as supply our frontline forces and act as a support base for operations."

They passed what looked like massive cylinders. There was little grace to them as they had engines on both ends of the cylinders. Massive corridors extended from the main corridor with entrances all along the ark.

"When the time comes, we'll we'll evacuate people on these arks to other bases that we have secured," Dave said as the carts changed directions and moved toward one of the completed arks that floated in midair.

"These gravity runes—I've seen nothing like them before," Helick said.

"When making the ships in gravity, we had to use a lot more materials. We didn't have all that much, so we created these runes in the soul gem construct that makes up all of the shipyard in order to make these slips have zero gravity. The ark's engines and inertia runes work so that it won't move an inch unless it's commanded to do so," Dave said as the carts turned and they advanced through the slip.

"How are the carts flying?" another asked.

"Well, we needed to test out the flight drives someway and it makes it much faster to move materials around with." Dave shrugged as if it were the most natural thing in the world.

A massive door was open, as large as a dwarven mountain's main gate.

Inside, the ark looked more like a warehouse than a ship.

"These arks were made for one purpose: to move people from Emerilia to the safety of other areas. However, they're they're going to be turned into haulers." Kol looked to Dave.

"What we need is to test them somehow," Dave said as they flew to the ark's command center, a boxy-looking structure that extended through the open and bare decks of the ark.

The carts stopped outside the command center. Dave and Kol guided everyone through it. They displayed the various flight drives and the magical coding that ran them, as well as the structure of the ark and different technologies they'd incorporated and even the missile systems that had been added on just in case of emergencies as well as the Mana barrier and shield.

The dwarves were filled with questions that Dave and Kol worked to answer.

Dave let out a sigh of relief as he kissed the side of Koi's head; she was getting sleepy now. Dave had been nervous about bringing more people in on his projects; that possibility of something leaking was high. Though, right now, he couldn't with a clear consciousness hold all of this to himself; he needed other people to help him. *The Council of Anvil and Fire and the Aleph College—two down and one to go. I hope Bob can convince the two of them.*

***

As Dave and Kol showed the dwarves around, Bob was looking at the Lady of Fire and Lord of Water, as well as Oson'Mal.

"So this is what my son-in-law has been up to," Mal said with a note of approval. They were within the ice planet base.

"And what we need people's help with." Bob led them through the ice planet city. "Air, you can come out now."

"Ugh, how did you know?" The Lady of Air appeared off to the side; her minder Venfik also appeared beside her.

"You breathe too loud," Bob said before his tone turned serious. "Also, do you think I would let you enter a place like this without me knowing about it?"

"No, but I wanted to see. Fire and Icebergs over there didn't notice anything," Air said with a note of satisfaction.

"Why did Steve have to be so similar to you?" Bob questioned the heavens, holding his face with his hand before getting back on track. "All right, children, listen up! As I was saying, we've we've got this and other bases all across Emerilia and this system. What we need is people to help us run all of this and more. Right now there's Malsour, Dave, sometimes Steve, Jeeves, and me working on everything. We've been able to do a lot, but now we have the resources and power so that we can expand!"

"So you want people who are good at coding, with weapons and thinking outside the box? I think I know a few people like that," Fire said.

"I know that my people have been harassed near constantly—there will be a number of them from the mer people's college who'd be interested in joining," Water added.

"Eh, gimme a list—we'll find them." Air waved her hand as if this were no big deal.

"No kidnapping," Bob said with a look toward Air.

"Hey, they don't know what they want to do until they're in our care," Air said innocently.

Venfik moved a bit away from Air as they walked.

"Where you more or less forced the choice on them or dropped them from the sky repeatedly so that their brains were so addled that they would imitate a chicken for the rest of their lives!" Bob's voice rose as he talked.

"That was one time and it wasn't a big deal." Air shrugged.

"It was the emperor of an Ashal empire!" Bob said.

"Well, he wasn't playing nice with others. He did afterward, when his son took over everything." Air put her hands on her hips.

"You're five hundred years old and you still have a child's argument," Bob complained.

"Maybe a child's argument is better!" Air harrumphed, stomping her foot and pushing out her bottom lip.

"Oh, how I love family reunions," Fire said.

"Shut it, zippy," Bob snapped.

Fire and Water looked to each other, grinning.

"I'll show you this and then you can get out of my hair," Bob complained.

"But you don't have hair," Water said.

"Why in the hell did they tell me to make gods and goddesses? Would would have been perfectly fine with just AI, but *nooo*—had to have real *human* gods and goddesses," Bob muttered to himself, doing a good impression of a mad scientist as he opened a door. The facility from the outside looked like nothing more than a warehouse; inside, it was a warehouse but just not what others were thinking.

Even Air went silent as they looked at the rows upon rows of people who rested within the warehouse. There were empty pods that were being transported to the growing labs that were continuously creating bodies for the players locked within the Earth simulation, there was so much to take in.

As they walked through the warehouse, they passed storage containers of organic materials being fed into the bodies or used to create them. There were also refined materials from the expanding refinery district that ran continuously.

"These are the bodies of players within the next two rotas of players." Bob waved to them.

"This ice planet's two main objectives are to refine materials that come from the asteroid base and what it mined out of the planet, as well as grow the players who are still trapped within the Earth simulation. In time, we will be waking them up and seeing how they react to being in reality. It will not be easy but it is a step that I believe we must take. We need people who can grow the organic material needed to build their bodies. We need people to enhance our own plans and technology. We need miners and refiners to make sure that this doesn't all fall apart. We need people to help us make automatons that can do these jobs—we're still reliant on the Aleph repair bots! We need people who are good with factories to speed up our production and people who can learn our power systems and soul gem constructs to manage and improve them. We've got the basic groundwork here but we need people to take what we've got and push the boundaries. We can do a lot, but we're just three people and *sometimes* two AI constructs."

"What you're building here is the resistance—a resistance to the Jukal," Fire said, her tone solemn.

Desmond, who she was cradling, chose this moment to start crying.

"Exactly," Bob agreed.

The group looked to one another. They might play around and joke a lot but this was something that affected them all.

"I will field it to the mage's college and guild as well as the Dragons. I know a number of them might be interested in coming here if they know that not only they, but their family, will be safe from the threats on Emerilia," Fire said.

"The seas have become a lot rougher, we have a number of portals that we are dealing with, as well as creatures not seen in centuries. A good portion of my people would be willing to move here just to be safe," Water said.

"I can find the hidden experts and people who might be good for this. I can also work on making sure that the Jukal and the rest of the Pantheon or people of Emerilia don't figure out any of this," Air said.

"Thank you." A weight fell from Bob's shoulders. "Ela-Dorn is already working to invite many of her peers to help while Dave is talking to the Council of Anvil and Fire. I hope that we can get some more support from there."

"Well, it looks like we've got a lot to do," Oson'Mal said with a look of excitement in his eyes.

"You're not thinking of coming here as well?" Fire bounced up and down slightly so as to try to calm Desmond down.

"Well, I've been looking after Desmond all this time and been going through the Per'ush libraries.I wanted to test out what I had learned and look to gain a deeper understanding away from prying eyes. But this," Mal raised his hands to encompass everything around him. "The ideas and things people are coming up with around here. Well, this ice planet and the other bases give me an opportunity to push my boundaries," Mal said, visibly excited.

.

***

Dave had left Kol and the dwarven master smiths to talk. After seeing everything, they had become interested—eager, even— in learning more about what they were doing. A number of them pointed to different magical coding that they had created and the Pandora's Box people had hacked together to create the different magical systems.

Kol knew what was going on with Pandora's Box and all of the bases; however, with managing the smithies of the Grahslagg Corporation, he didn't have the time to help out with many of the major items.

Dave looked around what was the moonbase. Originally it was to be the base of operations for the Pandora's Box group. However, with going to the Nal system and establishing a base in the ice planet as well as the asteroid belt, they had picked the ice planet to hold all of the laboratories that would grow the bodies of the players as well as storage facilities. The growing areas had been left here, as well as the fusion reactor, factories, and the miners that were still working to hollow out the moon. Now, the moonbase had gone under some radical changes. The portal exited onto a catwalk on either side, which crossed over between five-hundred- meter long and three-hundred-meter wide sections that lay below all of them were occupied by missile boat frames in various stages of completion.

They were boxy-looking ships with missile tubes covering most of their surface area, with only minimal small weapons otherwise.

They lay underneath the catwalk with the moonbase's soul gem constructs creating tube-like extensions from the floor and the catwalks to the missile boats. Runic lines guided power from the now five fusion reactors of the base into the ever growing missile boats.

Carts loaded with missiles in storage crates moved to the missile boats, loading them with missiles.

The overhead catwalks made a box that was five bays across and nine deep, each holding a missile boat that was held in a cradle of soul gem constructs. Most of them were still under production; a few of them had powered up their own fusion reactors and secondary Mana wells that increased the speed at which their soul gem constructs interior complete its build-out.

Automated carts and repair bots could be seen floating around the missile boats, as well as moving in and out to add in the various other materials needed to create the armor and superstructure of the missile boats. The soul gem constructs were great for internal components but relied on beefy structural members, beams and braces for strength and protection. Heavy armor panels as well as Mana barrier projectors were their defenses against enemy attacks.

If those shields and barriers went down, then he didn't want his ships to get smashed apart in just a few volleys.

Dave quickly stepped into the air. His body moved over the catwalks at a high speed. He moved past all of the growing warships and moved to where the fusion reactors that were powering the entire base as well as the different offices that looked over the moonbase were located.

Plans and screens rotated around him he moved from one to another, adjusting Koi on his shoulder as he opened up these various screens. He looked at the different launchers that had been buried throughout the moon's surface.

They were covered in stealth runes so that Dave couldn't even find them with his touch of the land spell, even if he was within fifteen feet of them.

He checked the stocks of weaponry and looked over the growing towers that were supplying the warships with the breathable atmosphere that was stored in their tanks.

Dave had wanted to go to the stars to be a discover, but now he was creating weapons of war that he would use to conquer it. Many people might be thrown off by this change but Dave understood it. He only had to look down to Koi to see why he was doing this.

"Looks like you need your bed," Dave said in a whisper, looking at Koi, who was oblivious of the world around her.

He disappeared from the offices and appeared in front of the portal building he passed through the security automatons returning to Emerilia.

***

Josh looked at the people around the table. They were all within a Mirror of Communication conference room. As the event and the portals opening had gone on, they had all taken more measures so that if there was ever an attack on the Terra Alliance heads couldn't be eliminated in a single attack.

As time had gone on, the Alliance had actually grown. The benefits of being in the Alliance outweighed not being in it by far.

The fact that the elves of Markolm weren't there wasn't missed by anyone. They had returned to their island and shut up their borders to all but the believers of the Lady of Light.

It was a problem but there was nothing that the Alliance could do. And they weren't in the business of telling people what they could and couldn't believe in.

"We have alt player accounts that are running around outside of cities and towns, allowing us to get a better idea of what is going on. Right now, it looks like the creatures and people from the Event are attacking not only the cities and the towns, they are also attacking one another.

This means that their numbers have been greatly reduced. But it also means that the ones that survive are going to be much more powerful than they were originally," Lucy said.

"This is why we need to send forces to destroy these people and creatures and then we can go back to pushing back the people at the portals," an Amazonian-looking woman from Strabon Kingdom said.

"If we start splitting our forces now, then we're just going to invite defeat," a noble-looking man from Egas Nation said.

"Well, it's better than holing up and doing nothing!" the woman shot back.

"This is not the time for us to be fighting among one another," Josh said, his voice bringing the room back under control. "We're in a stalemate right now. We're holding off the forces of the portals, but they're still coming through and reinforcing the castles that they do hold. Even the locations where we hold all of the castles, we can't relax our guard lest they break through and then get in behind us and start wreaking havoc. Or they can lead massive assaults that take all of our castles to react to. With the loss of Markolm's support, we have lost a large number of fighting-able people. We have made new friends and we have also regained the forces that we had based in Markolm. Right now is not the time to throw away our people. We need to grow in strength and ready ourselves for the next part of our offense."

The room quietened down in the face of Josh's words.

"We have Band-Aids, we have summoning halls, and we have the schools within the Mirrors of Communication. Our people were off-balance with this first attack. We need to focus our efforts to get them ready for what is to come. This war has only just started. For us to win, we need to get stronger. This is an anvil that we can forge ourselves through or be broken by," the dwarven master smith Quino, who was on the Terra Alliance council, said.

Everyone listened; the Dwarven Master Smiths were known for being wise as they were decisive.

"What is our plan going forward?" Alkao looked to Josh.

The heads of the Terra Alliance all looked to Josh. Alkao was a respected leader. At first, they hadn't thought that he was all that much, but after the reports of what his forces were capable of and what he had created in Devil's Crater, all of their doubt had been wiped away.

Josh and Lucy smiled at each other before they turned back to everyone.

"This," Josh said. A hologram of a floating citadel appeared in front of everyone.

***

The Dark Lord looked over the different seer pools that allowed him to look upon Emerilia. He opened and closed his hand, feeling the power at his command.

In his hall, multiple Alturarans stood around, like immobile statues. The Dark Lord paid them no attention as he watched the various forces he had brought under his control. With the Event, he had been able to increase his number of followers greatly the power in his divine wells swelling with each day.

His Dark Champions controlled them, sending them out to raid different cities or kill forces that were under the command of the other members of the Pantheon.

This was all in order to increase his forces' strength.

He turned his head and looked at a seer pool that rested over top of Markolm. His aura started to roll around his body as he looked upon Light's nation. *I will tear her out from that nation and kill her in front of all those angels and believers.*

Someone who might look upon the Dark Lord would feel a deep chill run through their spine.

The Dark Lord didn't care about what was happening to the rest of Emerilia. He loved this kind of chaos that allowed his forces to move freely. The people of Emerilia didn't even rate as interesting in his eyes, other than possible experience that his people could use to increase their strength.

He was focused on the battle between him and the Lady of Light.

Those angels will be a problem, especially if she makes them all her champions. It seems that I should ask the Earth Lord to make an alliance. Then when the battle enters its final moments, I can call upon my true forces and power to destroy them both.

His bone-like fingers formed into a fist, a satisfied smile on his face. "As I bring my true forces to bear, then the Lady of Fire will know of true despair as I kill off her college and guild. Then I can defeat the Earth Lord and the Lady of Light. Then there will just be Fire herself and Water to deal with." The Dark Lord didn't even put Air into consideration as he let out a laugh that would make one shiver in fear.

The Dark Lord didn't even hold the Lady of Air in his eyes; she was an unimportant figure to him—a woman who dealt with secrets and worked behind the scenes. The only power that he respected was fighting ability.

The Dark Lord looked over to the side of his hall; resting there were four different pools of what looked like tar. People who had seen the outside of the Six Affinities Temple would recognize the Dark Mana concentrated liquid. These were divine wells brimming with Dark Mana. Ten more holes lay around these four, waiting for more divine wells to fill them.

His carefully laid plan was ready. Now he just had to wait for the pieces to come together. He would wait, letting the Lady of Light gain her confidence before attacking her. He, would let her get wrapped up in the fighting before he unleashed his trump cards.

***

The Lady of Light looked over her own hall.

Her divine well was overflowing. A flash of golden light appeared in the air as a new well slid into the ground; the pool doubled in size.

The Lady of Light couldn't help but smile. When a member of the Pantheon gained energy from their people's devotions, once it reached the limit, another divine well would be called down to Emerilia.

The Dark Lord hadn't waited for his followers to devote their Mana to him but had instead forcefully supplemented energy and Mana wells, with Boran-al creating more Mana wells from the original.

Light smiled as her first divine well dimmed slightly, reducing to half of its capacity and sharing it with the second divine well.

"My lady, your ascension comes closer with every day." Khanundra bowed to the Lady of Light.

"Thank you, Khanundra. With every day that we grow in power, we are able to better fight off the scourge that threatens our followers and Emerilia," Light said with a caring smile. Her eyes flickered to Daeundra.

And those who don't follow will be cleared from Emerilia.

The people in the hall looked to the Lady of Light with reverence in their eyes, thinking that all of her actions were done for their benefit.

Cattle, to think that I wish to support them. As soon as their use runs out and I gain my higher position, I can truly control them and shed this veil.

"I only hope that your brothers and sisters are freed from their prison as soon as possible. I miss my sons and daughters deeply." Light let out a shaky breath as she pressed a hand to her chest, her eyes misty. "Soon we will be reunited. I cannot express the joy I feel," Light said, tears of pain and joy in her face as she looked to Khanundra and the people within her hall, moved by the emotions showed by the Lady of Light.

***

The Earth Lord sat on his throne as a green light appeared in front of him. A Dwarf Champion appeared, on his knee.

"Lord of Earth, I come bearing a message from the Dark Lord." The dwarf pulled out a scroll from his bag of holding and raised it above his head.

The Earth Lord moved his eyes, glowing in interest. A root reached up from the ground, grasping the scroll that was covered in moving shadows that looked like people screaming in agony.

The Earth Lord checked the scroll for any traps before the roots unfurled the scroll and brought it to him.

The Earth Lord read the words within, actually lifting his large head off his hand, showing interest in the scroll held in midair.

"Good." The Earth Lord's mouth of rock and dirt spread open into a cold smile. "Look to increase our strength by either recruiting more of these creatures and people of power, or by destroying them." The Earth Lord looked to the Earth Champion.

"I will pass on your orders, my lord," the Earth Champion said.

The Earth Lord nodded. The green lines of the spell formation lit up before the Earth Champion disappeared from his sight.

Chapter 12: Stalemate

The action at the portals had calmed down, there was the occasional skirmish but it wasn't too big anymore. The real action was happening in the Emerilia wilderness, with the various creatures and people that had been released with the event of Myths and Legends.

There was fighting going on every day. The alt scouts run by players were reporting that it wasn't just the different things from the events but it looked as though there were champions of Earth, Dark, and Light moving about and killing creatures and people or accepting them into their ranks.

It was making the people in the higher up positions nervous but most of the people of Emerilia were working to increase their own combat power and thus their ability to survive.

The third section of Terra had already been spun up and was connected. The Blood Kin were even better than Malsour had hoped. Fueled by blood essence crystals as well as some potions that Jung Lee had concocted to enhance their natural abilities, they were quickly finishing off the fourth section of Terra while also working on the seventh and eighth citadels around Goblin Mountain.

Since learning about the plan with the citadels, all of the different nations had been pouring their resources into the Terra Alliance in order to get them operational.

More and more Dark mages as well as Earth mages were helping out to get them operational. Command crews had been drafted up. Dwarves worked on adding cannons to the citadels for the best effect. Mages and ranged attackers as well as melee units that would use them to go into battle amassed on the citadels.

Dave and Deia were within the Densaou Ring of Fire. Deia sat on Dave's lap, holding Koi. Mal was cooking in the kitchen and Fire watched over the crawling Desmond and talked to them both.

"Okay, so we've got these melee units on the citadels but how are they going to get into battle? Land the damn thing?" Fire asked.

"Well, while we could do that, I've been working on flight drives for the citadel and my other projects. Steve was playing around one day—he was actually sitting on one of the flight drives and said, 'I'm a peacock, Dave—you've got to let me fly!' While it was ridiculous and doesn't make sense because peacocks don't fly, it gave me an idea—why don't I just create flight drives that people could wear? They jump off the citadel and then they can use the flight drives to reach their target," Dave said.

"So we're going to have dwarves jumping from the sky now?" Deia asked.

"Pretty much." Dave grinned.

"Well, that's a terrifying thought," Mal said from the kitchen.

"Well, other than your dive bombing dwarves, I think that the recruiting for your different bases is going pretty well. With the surety of security, a lot of people are excited to help out with getting all of the projects Pandora's Box are working on. I don't think that they have the faintest idea of what they're going to be getting themselves involved in." Fire smiled.

"It's certainly going to be eye-opening for a number of them," Dave agreed. His arm tightened around Deia.

"So when are the two of you getting married?" Mal asked.

"When are you two getting married?" Deia fired back.

"Someday," Fire said.

Mal caught Dave's eyes, shaking his head and sighing before he returned to his kitchen duties.

Dave drank his Scotch and kept quiet.

***

Suzy and Induca strolled through Per'ush without any apparent care in the world. Lu Lu flew through the air above them, letting out happy noises as she flew freely. She had now grown to the size of a small car when she wanted to. When she decided to go back down to rest on Suzy's shoulders, she would shrink to the size of a housecoat once again.

Induca and Suzy talked idly as they walked through the gardens of Per'ush, their fingers intertwined. They had been fighting for three weeks nearly constantly, finally they had taken a break in the fighting to be with one another and play with Lu Lu. However after only a few days, they were going back to the battlefields of Emerilia.

Steve had left for a period of time and was working on his armor while Lox, Gurren, Anna, and Jung Lee moved from fight to fight, all of them working to improve their abilities. In the last couple of weeks, their strength had increased greatly. It wasn't always a factor of their levels or their skills and classes improving but their knowledge of how to fight.

The more they fought and lived on the razor's edge of life and death, the more understanding into their own abilities and how to use them to their maximum effect came up.

Lox and Gurren had been powerful when the event had started, but now they were on par with Steve's abilities, maybe even stronger.

Anna was constantly improving on her understanding of wind; with her speed and her devastating attacks, she blew through enemy formations, killing all of those that faced her.

Jung Lee had become more composed; his and Jekoni's cooperation grew more and more as he could use his Free Affinity spirits more easily and to greater devastating effect.

The normally relaxed atmosphere of the park had been dulled slightly. It was hard to stay relaxed when all around Emerilia war had erupted.

Suzy and Induca sat at a bench overlooking a small lake that streamed through the gardens and ran underneath small bridges.

Lu Lu dove and spun in the air, diving into the water and shooting back up, happily playing around.

There were a number of other summoned creatures around the park. With the summoning halls, more and more people were getting soul bound creatures to increase their combat and defensive power.

Induca and Suzy watched Lu Lu's antics.

"Looks like there's no going back now." Suzy looked at the lake.

"What do you mean?" Induca asked.

"Everything is in motion. The portals, the event, the Pantheon—all of it is moving now. Emerilia has already changed. There are few safe havens left and those that are left are filled to the brim. Even Per'ush has filled all of their residences and they're starting to put people up in their parks. It won't be long until this is filled with tents and refugees." Suzy gestured at the park.

"I know, but we can get past this." Induca rubbed Suzy's fingers with her thumb.

"I know, but it's going to get to a stage where we can't do anything but go all out. When it comes to that, everything is going to change," Suzy said, unable to keep the fear out of her voice.

"What's got you all worked up?" Induca pushed Suzy's hair behind her ear.

"I'm scared about losing you. I'm scared about losing everyone." Suzy's eyes misted.

"Come here." Induca's heart hurt, seeing Suzy under so much stress as tears fell down her face. Induca hugged Suzy, who wrapped her hands around Induca tightly.

It was not lost on Suzy how close Induca had come to dying. It weighed heavily on her, to the extent that she found it hard to leave Induca on her own. She had proposed the idea of taking some time off because she just wanted to have some time with Induca outside of fighting.

She didn't know what the future would bring or that they would survive what was coming.

**

Dave, Malsour, Steve, and Bob all stood in the main area of Pandora's Box. The workstations had been moved to the ice planet and Steve's workshop had also been moved to the asteroid base.

His workshop had been right next to the teleportation array room. Now the wall had been knocked out and there were cranes attached to the ceiling that ran from Steve's workshop, into the teleportation array room and back to Steve's old workshop.

Through the door to the power station, people were filing through the secret doorway, all of them looking to their guides who greeted the four at the front of the room.

They looked around the room with curiosity. They had been given a brief description of what was going on but then the rest had been kept from them. For most of them, this was a leap of faith and a hope for their families to be protected from what was going on Emerilia.

Over the space of an hour, more and more people funneled through the secret doorway and into Pandora's Box.

Dave wasn't scared that anyone would figure out where they had gone. Thousands of people moved through Terra all the time; it was hard to sense what was going on in the rune-covered city and the Jukal's signal there wasn't too strong.

Once they reached the power station, the fluctuations of Mana running through the place was good enough to cover up most signals, and in Pandora's Box, there was virtually no way that the Jukal—or anyone else, for that matter—would find out where these people had gone.

There were nearly four hundred people within the workshop when the door to the power station was finally shut and secured.

"Has everyone signed the contracts?" Malsour looked to the guides.

All of them nodded. These people had been checked out by Air, Lucy, and Bob, as well as Fire and Water. They were all verified and had been trusted with guiding everyone here and would guide later groups through Pandora's Box as well.

"Good. Then I think it's time to tell you what this is all about." Dave clapped his hands, a smile on his face.

Everyone became silent as they looked to the four people at the front of the room. They looked to Bob out of curiosity. Most of them knew about Malsour, Steve, and Dave, but Bob was an unknown.

Bob smiled to himself as Dave started to talk.

"Okay, all of you were invited here as we need help on multiple different projects that we're working on. Though most of you were told that already, what these projects are for and what they will do—all of that will come. But I can promise you that the work that we do here will change the future of Emerilia forever." Dave's smile faded away as he looked at the people facing him. "First, let's get you into your new homes and we can start going over what the different projects are and see what works for you all."

Behind him, the wall fell away to reveal different portals to the various locations that Pandora's Box was connected to.

There was excited mumbling among the Aleph and those from the mage's college and guild who knew more about portals. All of them looked at the portals and the four people in front of them with stunned eyes.

"This is only the beginning," Bob said with a teasing smile.

"We'll be going to a place covered in ice. Don't worry—we've heated it up a bit and it's filled with breathable air," Dave said.

Bob had been working for weeks to make sure that people could live within the ice planet city without needing clothes that had heating circuits in them or needing to capture air in a Mana shield every time they moved through the city.

This would serve as the base for all of their projects and the new nucleus of Pandora's Box.

***

Dwayne watched over his different castles. He controlled the outer castles around the portal but the interior castles were controlled by the expansionistic race called the Jakan.

The Jakan were an overpopulated race that practiced war as a measure of population control. They weren't like many of the other races and had a true military structure, from generals down to privates. They were also well versed in offensive and defensive tactics. However, their healing abilities were nearly nonexistent. Dying in battle was a great honor; healing one another up would be going against that warrior code.

Although the Jakan wished to die on the battlefield and attain honor for themselves and be risen up into the planes of the Oidf, their version of Valhalla, they weren't going to sell their lives short. Just going in waves and waves of attacks was seen as cheap and useless and their gods wouldn't look down on them with favor if they did that. So, instead, they were building up their strength; their various leaders communicated with one another and made plans to attack the Terra Alliance that held the outer castles. They were constantly sending out probing attacks that would check to see whether there were any weaknesses within the Terra outer castles.

Dwayne had been posted to the outer castles with three other highly decorated veterans who had taken command of the other four castles. Dwayne had been named as the commander of this location but after meeting with the other veterans, Dwayne— who had been a sergeant when he was with the military on Earth— turned to them for their opinions and they worked together in order to deal with the Jakan.

They used a combination of swords that could cut through nearly anything—but dulled really quickly and were fragile—and their destruction staffs.

The Jakan used to use rifles but after coming to Emerilia, over time they had come to learn about destruction staffs and their offensive abilities. They'd incorporated it into the battle plans and through fighting with one another, they'd come up with tactics in order to deal with being attacked by destruction staffs.

The Jakan were also not just warriors but builders.

From their castles, they had made networks of trenches that spread outward, making it so that they could hit anyone who tried to attack them face-to-face. This network of trenches also made it impossible for the Terra Alliance to simply attack their walls.

They had to get into the trenches and clear them out, which was a process in and of itself. The Jakan made them fight for every inch in the trenches and used traps and tricks to kill as many of the Terra Alliance as possible.

Until the flying citadels came online, the leaders of the four outer castles had agreed that they would defend their positions. Attacking the Jakan would take a lot of resources and lives with little gain. Only when they had overwhelming superiority would they hammer the Jakan and attempt to remove them from Emerilia.

Dwayne didn't understand the Jakan's reasoning but he respected them. They were one of the few aggressive species that had come up with plans of how to fight. They were one hell of an enemy not simply because of their numbers but because of their actions and tactics.

They had sent messages to the Jakan, asking whether there was a peaceful way to resolve their issues. The Jakan had respectfully declined and then gone on to say that they would make a good sacrifice to their gods.

Apparently that was pretty high praise from the Jakan. That or Shard was pulling my leg with translating their message.

Even though he respected them, Dwayne knew that there would be one victor and one loser. If he lost, then Emerilia would be opened up for the Jakan's advance, which would turn into a war similar to World War Two, but with creatures coming out of the forests and wilderness that could easily wipe out entire battalions of people on both sides.

"We need those flying citadels," Dwayne said to himself. Eight of them at Goblin Mountain had been altered already and would be ready to move soon enough. The castles that had been defending against the Erach invasion to the northeast of the Gudalo continent were also being converted.

Dwayne shivered as he thought about that portal location.

The Erach hadn't stopped trying to come through the portal to reach Emerilia. The lake around the portal was filled with their bodies. If they had been allowed to spread across Emerilia, he couldn't even start to guess what the damage would have been.

As the different engineers, mages, and the Blood Kin worked on the floating Citadels more forces were being pulled into training, ready to man the citadels.

Each would have heavy long-distance mages, as well as archers and dwarven artillery crews. There would also be dwarven War Clans and quick-reaction mounted forces and DCA or aerial forces.

As they prepared, then it was up to the forces that were left in the castles to keep the creatures that were coming through the portals back. If they could just hold them off for a couple of months, then the citadels could come in with their heavy support and push them back, holding over the portal to make sure that they weren't capable of coming through again.

The portals were nearly indestructible but they could still fire cannons down onto those that came out of them, wiping them out.

"Just need to hold the line." Dwayne looked out over the castle walls. In the distance, he saw light illuminating the sky as two beings from the event clashed in the air.

Blue water Mana clashed with green Mana, creating thunder-like explosions as the trees shook with the impacts of their attacks or misses.

This was the new world that Dwayne lived in.

***

Lox, Gurren, and Steve looked over the various War Clans that were all lined up within Terra. Since the summoning hall had been made available to the public and those who were part of the Terra Alliance, the dwarves had been the first group to work up a strategy to use the summoned creatures. Each of the dwarf shield bearers were to get one summoned creature. It was supposed to be able to hit at range and fly if at all possible—but not too high.

Many of the dwarves were getting some kind of magical flying beast that could change shape and rest on their shoulders and could give overhead cover when possible.

The dwarven artillery crews were, in turn, getting creatures that didn't fly but were strong and could move heavy loads and fight. If they got into a battle, the creatures could fight for them while they continued to man their guns. The summoned aerial creatures would allow the dwarven shield bearers to gain a ranged attack ability that they had not had before.

The dwarven formation with them already had showed that they were to be feared in the practice that they had carried out. The summoned creatures needed to be trained but within the Terra Alliance, the number of summoners and the beast tamers was the largest in recorded history. They had been lent out to the other races and groups that were a part of the Alliance to foster better relationships and to increase their military might.

Now was not the time to care whether their neighbors had a better fighting force or not. Here they were all people of Emerilia and they were fighting for their home.

Gurren, Lox, and Steve continued onward, moving through all of the people in Terra. Even with the third section complete, there were still more people who wanted to move to Terra and there were military barracks throughout the city. Many of them weren't filled but ready in case forces were pulled off from the castles and reinforcements were slotted into the castles that they had been manning.

"So, what are we going to be doing exactly?" Gurren asked.

"Training," Steve said in a glum voice.

"We're going to be working on the doctrine for using the flying citadels," Lox expanded.

"Okay, so that's not too bad. Still wish that we were fighting more, though," Gurren said.

"Well, it looks like most of the groups are building their strength up or that the ones that go for wave-like attacks to try to overpower us are already dead or there just aren't enough of them to be a threat," Lox said.

"But I miss axe golf!" Steve complained.

"You just kept saying fore and smacking people with the side of your axe!" Lox yelled.

"I know! It was great!" Steve waved his hands in the air.

"Give me strength." Lox looked to the other side of Terra.

"Now that you say it—you could use a few gym sessions," Steve said.

Gurren cleared his throat, trying to hide his laughter.

"Let's just get to Goblin Mountain before I can see how far I can boot your shiny ass down the street," Lox said.

"Does this armor make my crystal ass look big?" Steve looked back at his ass.

"Where the hell did that come from?" Lox asked.

"Well, I saw these hot pink pants that Clara was wearing and I have to say she can work it. I'm just not sure if I have the kind of figure for it. You know, I was wondering about updating my wardrobe," Steve said.

"It's a set of armor, not a bloody handbag!" Lox yelled.

"You seen my handbag?" Steve said in a squeal of excitement.

Gurren looked as if he were going to burst a blood vessel listening to the two of them.

Lox let out a noise of frustration as Steve pulled out a handbag made of pink hide. To most, it would have looked like a duffel bag but in the crook of Steve's arm, it did indeed look like a handbag.

Gurren couldn't stop himself from laughing as Lox simply stopped in the middle of the road and stared at Steve as he moved the handbag around from the crook of his arm to his shoulder to the other arm.

"Pretty styling, right? All the crystal constructs are doing it." Steve smiled.

"I wish all of the soul gem constructs were buildings." Lox walked onwards.

"Aww, come on—I'm much more fun than a building!" Steve said.

"Yeah but the fecking buildings don't talk nor do they have vibrant flipping pink handbags that look like they're big enough to hide a ruddy elephant in!" Lox yelled.

Gurren laughed as he followed behind them, tears in his eyes.

***

"Where are the others?" Deia looked to Jung Lee and Anna as they were waiting within Goblin Mountains' southern Citadel number one.

"They're on their way. They went to check out the dwarves at the summoning halls and get a look at what kind of creatures they have so that we have a better idea of what kind of abilities the new War Clans will have," Anna said.

"Why do you have a sequin top! How are there that many sequins in all of Emerilia!?" Gurren asked.

"Fashion has no limits!" Steve replied. Lox, Gurren, and Steve had walked out of the ono that was underneath the tower in the inner castle.

Deia didn't know what to say.

Steve wore a pink hat with a rim that extended outward nearly three feet and had a bright green feather in it. He wore a sequin-covered crop top in blue and that was so shiny that Deia thought of investing in sunglasses.

Coupled with his Devastator armor he was still wearing underneath and the pink handbag, all of the members of Party Zero waiting within the castle just looked at the scene without knowing what to say.

The others walking through the area stopped, their minds misfiring at Steve's ensemble.

"What's up, homies!" Steve said.

"Anna," Deia said, her voice monotone as she continued to look at Steve. "The hell did you create?"

"I don't know, but something went wrong—horribly and utterly wrong," Anna said, also unable to take her eyes off the train wreck that was Steve.

"Heeeey!" Steve waved his hand daintily.

"I think I just threw up in my mouth a little bit at his style sense," Suzy said.

"I think it's snazzy," Induca said.

Suzy looked at Induca as if she had just declared she was the devil. "Dear, we'll talk about this later." Suzy patted Induca's hand.

"We're here. Now please give me something to do before I lose my mind," Lox said in a pained voice.

"Uh, well, we need you, Gurren, Suzy, and Steve to teach all of the War Clans as well as units with ground units how to use the flight drives that will allow them to jump from the citadel and reach the ground," Deia said, still sounding pretty shell-shocked from Steve's appearance.

"I can do that," Lox said.

"Anna, you and I will work with the different casters and get the DCA situated. We've dealt with them before and so we should be able to get them used to what's going on pretty easily. Induca, you can deal with the Dragons as well as help out with the casters. Jekoni and Jung Lee can get with the mages and make sure that they're all sorted out as well.

"Dave and Malsour will be around later to check on all the major systems of the citadel and to make sure everything is running well. We have one week to get everyone used to what they're doing. Another week to go through any problems and then we're going to be doing training drops and scenarios.

"Steve, why are you wearing what you're wearing? Is there a reason for it?" Deia asked, unable to hold back any longer.

"Made Lox uncomfortable?" Steve shrugged.

"I'm going to go jump off really tall things now." Lox walked away quickly.

The rest of Party Zero couldn't stop from laughing at it all.

***

Ela-Dorn found Dave in the asteroid base, working with the different slips where one of the first massive miners was launching from and heading toward the end of what would be the main thoroughfare of the asteroid shipyard.

"Hey," Dave said over a private chat with a smile on his face.

"Hey, Dave," Ela-Dorn said, her voice subdued.

"Something the matter?" Dave looked to her.

"No. Just—do you know what you've made here?"

"Just what we needed to." Dave shrugged.

"Only what you need? All of this together—it's beyond *anything* I've ever thought of. I and most of the people here have been so focused on the fact of surviving or thriving on Emerilia that we haven't really ever thought of moving past it. Now we find out that there is an empire that is using Emerilia just to entertain themselves. We're part of a race that was killed off hundreds of years ago because they caused the empire more problems and could have destabilized it. You're here and making ships and vehicles of war so that we can try to make Emerilia free and fight against these Jukal. Just...I can't even try to get through it all. I understand it and I've come to recognize it all, but I just, well, I see it as truth. My scientific brain makes me see all of the proofs and the evidence that you've put forth and it's irrefutable, but Dave, this is not to simply win the war on Emerilia—this is to end the war on Emerilia and to fight the Jukal in their territory," Ela-Dorn said.

"Welcome to Pandora's Box—once it's open then there's no going back," Dave said with a smile as he conjured two seats and sat down.

Ela-Dorn fell into the seat opposite him.

"Okay, so you understand about the Jukal and you understand about what we're trying to build here. What are you having difficulty with?" Dave asked.

"I just can't believe that three people and an AI did all of this," Ela-Dorn said.

"Well, we've had some help with the Mirror of Communication." Dave hadn't yet told them about Sato and all of his people; that was just too much right now and if that was to get out, then they might be wiped out. As long as Sato and his people were safe, then even if Emerilia fell the human race would live on, and be able to fight at a later date.

"Dave, you're building dreadnoughts, battleships, and missile boats. You have arks that can act as cargo haulers of millions of tons of resources. The technology and the magical coding that you're working with—most of us are playing catch-up with."

"We'll, see if Jeeves can help you out with that. We got him to code mostly everything; he makes much better code than us. We basically gave him parameters and took that code for what we needed. However, we need you to go over what we gave him and what he made to see if there are room for improvements. We made the shell— we need you to check it and add in the extras," Dave said.

Ela-Dorn just couldn't put together all she had seen over the last week with the unassuming man in front of her. With his easy smile and his excitement at making something new and then these weapons of war—he had come up with nuclear warheads that worked on fusion, created grand working spells that could destroy a three-hundred-meter area and be felt from kilometers away.

On one hand, he was offering redemption; on the other, he was holding hands with death—a war god incarnate, ready to destroy and carve a path through the enemy.

Ela-Dorn felt a chill run down her spine. "Dave, why are you doing this?" Ela-Dorn asked in a small voice.

"Why?" Dave made to answer but then pursed his lips instead before he laughed and rested his head on his fist. "To most people, I would answer because of all of those lost and because it's the right thing to do, blah blah human race and so on," Dave said. "Honestly, I started all of this and I was just swept up in it. I was doing it because I was scared. I don't want to die—no one wants to. I had Deia; imagining me leaving her behind—leaving the people I've met here behind and being nothing but a footnote in life—it pushed me to do things that I never thought possible. To attain heights that amazed even me. Nothing is a greater motivation than knowing that." Dave clicked his fingers. "Like that, it can all be gone and you have no control over it. Now I've known that for a long time, but having someone else deciding when I'm done and pressing a button—that's something that I couldn't just sit back and accept. I didn't know what I was going to do but everything that I would do was going to be aimed toward once again putting my life back into my own hands."

Dave paused. An unreadable look passed over his eyes. "You want a drink?" Dave pulled out a can of beer from his bag of holding.

"I, uuhh..."

"I've got a nice wine, some different whiskys, ciders and the like. Try this one out." Dave pulled out a small vial of amber-looking liquid, pouring it into a small glass and handing it to Ela-Dorn.

"Thank you." Ela-Dorn took a sip of the drink. It was chilled and sweet but with that relaxing sensation as she swallowed, it warmed her.

Dave cracked the can in his hands and poured it into a glass. The beer was so dark that it almost looked black. He took a deep drink from it and let out a sigh. "At first, I was doing this all to prolong my life. Then with the people I came to know, it was about getting us all out of this. Then Koi came along." Dave took a sip of his beer, a smile on his face.

"I'll never forget the look in Deia's eyes as we looked on Koi—kicking, screaming and *alive*. I didn't realize how much of an impact that had on me until later. Well, until now, really. All of those people lived on Earth, taking shit or being treated a certain way to make them play video games, they grew up, came to Emerilia and were watched by the Jukal as if they were some kind of interesting toy. Their lives didn't matter and for the people of Emerilia it was even worse. Deia can come back but there was no guarantee that Koi would've, there still isn't now. I felt so protective over her, as I feel with the rest of my party who aren't players and even with Deia when she was pregnant with Koi. Those smug fucking Jukal— they sit in their ships, they watch everything that's happening and they don't give a flying fuck. We're nothing to them. Creatures that can be ignored, the laughingstock of the universe. Do you know that they watch our camera feeds at times when we're with our loved ones? They pollute every moment that we're not in a Mirror of Communication or within a stealth rune-covered zone.

"I want my daughter to be free to make her decisions. That was when the true weight of all that the Jukal have done hit me. How many sons and daughters have the Jukal killed? How how many brothers and sisters like mine have died? And what? All of this just so that they could stay on top of the economic pile. Fuck them and fuck their empire. I might die— I might never see the end of this—but I sure as hell am going to let the Jukal know that those people mattered, that the people of Emerilia matter, that my daughter matters and that no matter what, even if they look down on us, they should never treat us any differently. My daughter deserves freedom—the sons and daughters of Emerilia deserve freedom to not live in fear of some random event, to know that they're going to be safe at night. So why am I doing this? It's not for some noble reason. It's because I care for my daughter and the people around me. For them, I am willing to do horrible things so that they might live a good life," Dave said with fire in his eyes as he drank from his beer.

He would take on all comers and not bat an eye. The Jukal had killed off trillions of humans. Dave might not know them and he might not have a connection to them, but any one of those people could have been someone in his family; any of them could have been his daughter.

Ela-Dorn drank from her glass as she looked away from his eyes and looked over the different slips where various machines were being built, with repair bots creating superstructures while soul gem constructs grew over top.

Ela-Dorn didn't think of the people of Emerilia; she thought of her mother and father who were hunted down for the simple fact that they loved each other and had had a child together. She remembered how her father had fought them off for as long as possible before her mother was set upon by them. She killed herself to create a protection spell around Ela-Dorn that sped her away from the violence.

She shouldn't have lived but through their love and sacrifice she had.

It didn't make logic or sense why it had to happen that way. She had devoted her life to science and the Aleph College, looking into mysteries, making what seemed to be miraculous make sense, pulling it apart and coming to understand the world.

This cause was right. She knew that there might be times that she would look upon this moment with regret, but she also knew that if she didn't do it, then someone else would have to take up that weight.

Ela-Dorn finished off her drink and let out a sigh. "Dave, what can I help you with?"

The area around them shifted as she found herself still on the chair but now at a different slip, where what looked to be a portal was growing.

"Did you just use teleportation?" Ela-Dorn asked.

"Yep. I'm getting better at it. I think that I'll get to a stage where I'm not using so much Mana pretty soon." Dave smiled, drinking his beer as he stood.

"Is that a portal?"

"Yes, yes it is—well, if it works, that is. I'm not really sure how good it's going to be. I made it so that it should be able to work with the Jukal portals but it has the ability to connect to different ones, faster and with not using as much power as the original portals. And it also has a shield function so that we can stop people from just walking through," Dave said.

Ela-Dorn walked around the portal with a shocked look on her face. "Our best minds are still attempting to unravel how these even work and are having partial successes in Portal theory and here you are Building improved Portals on your own!" Ela-Dorn could only shake her head in shock.

"Well, I did break a teleport pad and then a portal to try to understand them while I was under the effect of a ton of increased stat points." Dave shrugged.

"Though this is way more advanced—you've got magical coding down to runic lines and you've got multiple plates set up so that you don't need to have the rotating Magical Circuits so that they all line up. Changing from one portal to another will be a lot faster." Ela-Dorn examined the portal. "To get to this level of understanding..." She shot a look at Dave.

"I didn't tell everyone how much I knew about it. I wanted people to figure it out for themselves and it wouldn't point to me.

I might have sent you on a longer route to find the solution simply because I didn't want the Jukal to see that you're messing around with portals," Dave said.

"The more I see, the more I understand why you did it." Ela-Dorn sighed.

"Well, now I need your help with something else." Dave shared a project with her.

She opened up the file and looked at it, frowning at first before her eyebrows rose. "This..." Ela-Dorn didn't know what to say as she read on. "This is...how? It's? It's massive."

"Well, we're going to need this soon enough to move around," Dave said. "Whether it works or not, that remains to be seen. This portal here is a prototype, to see if it will work. If it does, then that later version might be possible." Dave said with a tired grin.

Dave saw the image that Ela-Dorn was looking at. It was a portal just like the one that was growing a few meters away from them. Only, *this* one was big enough to fit ships through, not just people and their carts.

"This is meant to move ships, but where to?" Ela-Dorn asked.

"Well, we're going to need more than just missile boats at Emerilia. I don't think that we will need to use the arks to move people now that the ono network is up and running. We can use the arks to move resources in massive quantities between different bases."

"Wait, the onos—what do they have to do with anything?" Ela-Dorn asked.

"Well, when you were done with them, we put Mana wells on them, as well as soul gem constructs. This was so that we could store up their power and then make them usable anywhere without having to supply them with soul gems constantly. This was part of the reason; the second is they're a defensive net. We're using them as focal points so that they can project Mana barriers outward to cover all of Emerilia," Dave said.

"What better to cover Emerilia with than a teleportation network that covers all of Emerilia? That's cunning and smart."

"Well, I didn't get here on my good looks alone." Dave laughed.

"Though the network's not complete yet," Ela-Dorn said.

"I know, but it will be soon. And when it is, then we will have complete coverage. With the Mana wells storing up all of that energy within the soul gem constructs and then making an interlinking Mana barrier that works off one another. Jeeves will handle all of the power output and make sure that we're presenting the strongest barriers. Even if the Jukal fleet that is hiding out at the military base in the second moon starts to try to bomb Emerilia, it will take a lot of work for them to do that and deal with our own fleet," Dave said.

"Okay, but the people needed to man these ships is quite high."

"Well, hopefully some of the people who wake up want to do it. Otherwise, our second plan is to jack into the Earth simulation and then allow them to play a space game, which would actually be them fighting the Jukal," Dave said.

"Would we be any better than the Jukal if we did that?" Ela-Dorn said.

"We would be doing it for survival while they were doing it for entertainment. But, when you get down to it, I don't think so but needs must at that point." Dave shrugged. "I just hope that the players we start to wake up will want to work with us."

"That's a lot of ifs and maybes," Ela-Dorn said.

"It is, but it's all we've got at the moment," Dave replied.

Chapter 13: Build Up

Deia held little Koi as she looked out over the practicing DCA aerial forces, all of them huddled around Mirrors of Communication within the main tower of the citadel.

She looked to her Mirror of Communication that looked in at what they were seeing.

All of them were launching from the citadel's tower. Shooting outward in aerial formations, they dropped down below the citadel that was unleashing hell upon the target below. Dwarven cannons as well as Mana attacks from the citadel itself slammed against the walls of the castle below.

The DCA came over top of the castle and unleashed their bombs. As they had the castle fully suppressed, Dwarven Legions started to leap from the citadel. All of them had their shields in hand and their hands on their swords as they dropped. On their backs there was a teardrop-looking backpack covered in runes.

Steve had made them, melding a flight drive, a stabilizing mechanism, and a sensor together with programming that would stop the wearer's descent before they smashed into the ground.

The dwarves let out their war cries but it was more to deal with the fact that they were dropping through the air when the rune-covered teardrops fired up and their fall slowed just a few meters from the ground.

This was so that the people within the castle wouldn't get the time to kill them on the way down. It put the dwarves under more stress but they still all got to the ground.

The teardrops were also programmed in groups so War Clans all landed together or at least near one another.

The War Clan leaders yelled out their orders as the dwarven war drums were beat. The Dwarves that had now made it back to the ground moved into their formations and started to advance as soon as they were all situated.

"We need to increase that speed," Lox said, looking at the different screens.

"It is their first drop—they'll get better," Deia said.

"Yeah but they don't rely on them yet. We have to get them to a stage where they are willing to trust their drop packs with their lives, literally," Gurren added.

Deia smiled and looked at the two dwarves who were both staring at the screens, muttering to each other as they looked over mistakes that the dwarves had made as well as things that they had done well.

The walls of the flying citadel were covered in mages and ranged attackers unleashing their attacks upon the castle. With all of the attacks, it was hard to think that anyone would be able to weather all of the fury that was coming down on them.

After the dwarves came the quick-reaction groups. The beast riders tried to get their beasts to leap off, using the teardrops to reach the ground. But the creatures, even though they were highly trained, stopped as soon as they saw the edge of the citadel disappearing. Some fell off the castle simply because of those behind them.

Deia frowned. "Okay, so don't like jumping out in wide open spaces. Maybe we can rig up some kind of platform for them to go down on?" Deia muttered to herself. Her eyes moved from screen to screen as she looked at the different people, from the rangers and casters to the dwarves on the ground who were constantly communicating with the citadel in order to not get hit by their own fire.

"Communication is all messed up, but that's something that will get better with time," Deia said.

After another hour and a half, the training exercise stopped.

"Okay, well, it looks like we've got a good base to work from. I think we're going to need to change a few things," Deia said to Lox and Gurren. They had been testing the forces of just one of the Citadel's they now had sixteen full citadels of people to work with.

Nearly all of the training was carried out in Mirrors of Communication.

The current simulation disappeared and the battlefield was removed. Everyone reappeared within the flying citadel. In the training area, there was all sixteen citadels were manned, with their people floating about in one large circle.

Sometimes they would be brought together to train them on items such as the teardrop backpack. At other times they would be left on their own or work as a long citadel. Just like with this training exercise.

This sped up their training quite a bit. They didn't need to burn through resources and the citadels were now in fierce competition with one another to get themselves better.

Anna and Deia had been a big force in making them start to compete with one another. Gurren and Lox had done it almost unconsciously. Pitting them against one another and making them prove themselves to one another, this made it so that they were constantly improving.

"Got a lot of kinks to work out," Lox said.

"Well, it has only a week and a half," Deia said.

"Yes, but they're dwarves, dammit. I don't expect anything but the best from them," Lox said. Gurren, beside him, nodded as well, both of them with fierce expressions on their faces.

"Well, I'll let you get at it." Deia smiled.

"See you later, Koi." Gurren's," Gurren said his fierce look fell away as he touched Koi's back gently. Even Lox's face seemed to soften for maybe a moment as he looked upon Koi.

In a very real way, the members of Party Zero had become Koi's aunts and uncles.

The two of them touched their hands to the Mirrors of Communication, closing their eyes as they disappeared into the training grounds to unleash their training pointers upon the dwarves and the others under their command.

Deia sighed and moved Koi around.

She didn't seem to like this and started to cry.

"Someone's a bit moody today." Deia tried to calm her daughter down. She felt guilty. She wanted to spend as much time as possible with Koi but it seemed that as soon as she saw her, something came up and blocked her from being with her daughter.

She felt as if she were a bad mother.

It was something that weighed heavily on her mind. At this point, she believed that her mother and father had seen Koi more than she had.

She wanted nothing more than to go to Cliff-Hill with Dave to just look over Koi and watch her grow up. Instead, they were in the middle of this stupid war and there was nothing that they could do. If they were to bow out now, then neither of them would be able to live with it.

I just wish the sacrifice wasn't the time I spent with my daughter.

Deia smiled sadly at Koi, feeling her heart being pulled by the crying girl in her arms.

"It's going to be okay, baby girl," Deia said sweetly, emotions filling her.

She had been a strong and defiant woman her entire life. A Fire mage, an elven ranger, and attached to the Dwarven War Clans, she had joined the Stone Raiders and been part of some of the biggest battles that Emerilia had seen. She had helped three different races come back from the brink and to reclaim their home. She'd seen her friends die and be heavily wounded. She lived her life on the edge of her swords and arrows.

Now, inside she felt that hardness crumbling.

She had a family. She had not only her father but her mother, countless nephews and nieces within the Dracul clan. She had Party Zero, Dave and Koi. All of those things together—she now had so much that she could lose.

It pulled at her heart and it made it difficult, but she knew that they were all doing their part so that they might live in a place that they were free to do as they wished, to be free from this fighting.

Deia saw that Anna was talking with the DCA leader over the training exercise.

She sat down in the citadel, looking out at Goblin Mountain. She saw the battle that had happened there as if it were yesterday. But as her eyes moved to Koi, who was finally calming down, she thought of Koi growing up, of seeing her walk, talking, going on her own adventures.

A smile covered her face as she thought of that future, excited for it, but tinged with the doubt of what was to come. That they would get to that future.

Deia took a deep breath and wiped Koi's tears away.

"No matter what happens, we're on this path now. We've got on this tiger—we've got to ride it until the end." Deia played with Koi's lips. Today she would let herself be a mother and let the world deal with itself, for just a few hours. That's all she wanted. Then she would go back to figuring out how to defeat the enemies that beset them on all sides.

***

Anna cleared her throat as she tried to calm herself.

She looked at her hands accusingly, as if willing them to unclench and stop laying around as she rested them behind her back.

She let out a frustrated noise as she moved them to her pockets, unsure of what to do with them.

She opened up her interface, looking for something to distract her but finding nothing that needed her attention.

She played around with it a bit more before the door in front of her started to open. The sounds of a meeting just ending came from the other side of the door.

She was almost startled by it, causing her to close her interface; a number of people that she knew came out from the meeting, there were mostly military commanders.

They gave her a cordial smile and went on their way. With everything happening, every military across Emerilia had been called upon to defend the land that they held. The areas outside of the cities and defensible walled areas had turned into a battlefield.

This made Devil's Crater a safe haven as the natural crater and the newly built walls were perfect for keeping out anything that might threaten the people inside. Already, nations and various groups were looking to Devil's Crater, making the move to taking up residency within Unity City.

Growing towers were being prioritized as was the DCA and the growth of Devil's Crater, Unity, as well as the different settlements within the crater, was all expanding, with more people coming. The walls and the keeps around the crater walls were also being improved.

She looked past these important figures. Her heart seemed to shift in her chest as her hands became clammy. She unconsciously ran a hand through her hair as she looked at Alkao. He was talking to a few of the people who had stayed behind in the briefing room to go over some last details.

She gathered herself together and moved into the room past the flood of people. Aides moved through the room and cleared up what was left after the meeting.

Alkao was focused on what he was talking about with the group that had remained behind. After a few minutes, their small group collapsed and they also started to leave the room.

Alkao had a hard look on his face. He was a leader with his people, not the entirety of Emerilia now plunged into war. He had to do everything in his power to combat not only these forces but to push Devil's Crater ahead, to make sure that they didn't fall in the coming violence.

His eyes found Anna, softening as his hard smile became more playful and mischievous. "Anna," Alkao said in greeting.

Anna was unable to keep a smile from forming on her face.

Alkao hadn't hidden his affection when meeting with Anna.

Even as she lay down conditions that would have made most men turn away in defeat, he had accepted her challenge. Even through the challenges, he had carved out a place in her heart. He was a great leader, but when it was just the two of them, he was a romantic, a funny man who made every day brighter and better.

"Could we go somewhere to talk?" Anna asked.

Alkao's eyes became thoughtful. She saw a flash of nervousness and fear in his eyes. It touched her heart, seeing him scared for what she might say.

"Sure. Let's go to my office." Alkao's smile seemed a little more forced.

"Okay," Anna said.

Alkao started to lead out of the room as Anna slid her hand into Alkao's. He acted as if he had been shocked by lightning and paused mid-step to look at Anna in shock.

She smiled shyly up at him. His face bloomed into a smile as he moved forward, his footsteps light and quick instead of the somber footfalls from earlier.

It didn't take long for them to reach Alkao's office.

Alkao's guard and secretary all saw the two of them holding hands, smiling to themselves. Anna tried to hide her head and the growing blush on her cheeks.

Finally they made it into his office. He closed the door and looked to her, unable to contain himself anymore. "What did you want to ask me?" His eyes shined and he had a wide smile on his face.

Anna couldn't help but feel her heart beating heavily in her chest, as if she were just watching this moment. Her mind warred once again before she pushed forward. "Would you want to date me?" Anna asked, unable to stop playing with her damn hands.

She couldn't help but be frustrated with how nervous she was.

"Yes!" Alkao said, as if he said it any slower that she might escape his grasp.

Anna bit her lip, unable to look at Alkao.

His one hand moved to the small of Anna's back, pulling her closer; she moved without resistance as Alkao lifted her chin with his large finger. "Will you finally be my girlfriend?" The corner of Alkao's mouth lifted in mirth.

As she looked up into those eyes, she thought of all that had happened in the last couple of weeks—the uncertainty of it all, not knowing what was going to happen.

When she had been near to despair, a single face had surfaced in her mind: that easy smile of Alkao's when they were in private and the hard eyes and focused look when he was working. She had realized that he had made a place in her heart a long time ago. Though it had taken this crisis in order to push her past her reservations.

"Yes." Anna smiled up at him.

Alkao looked as if he was the happiest man alive as they looked into each other's eyes. He lowered his head. His lips found hers as he pulled her tight; her arms wrapped around him as she felt relief, as if she had come home in his embrace.

"I have something that I wanted to give to you." Alkao's hand finding hers as he walked to his desk, he opened a drawer pulling out a box and opened it, showing her the necklace displayed inside.

It was made from spun silver, creating a flat spiral.

"Something for you to remember Devil's Crater wherever you go, and know that there's someone here waiting for you," Alkao said.

Anna smiled, not at the necklace but the meaning and the heaviness of his words as he talked. She moved her hair out of the way as Alkao put it around her neck. She let her hair drop, holding the necklace in her fingers, her eyes wet with emotions that surged through her like a comforting sea.

"Thank you." Anna looked to Alkao.

"Who would think that after beating my ass in a dungeon you'd agree to being my girlfriend." Alkao laughed.

Anna pouted and playfully hit his shoulder. He laughed harder, putting his arms around her and kissing her again as if he could never kiss her enough times in this life.

***

Malsour was on a cart, inspecting the progress of the asteroid base.

He watched as the beams of golden light broke through the asteroid rock. The materials were sucked up by scoops behind the beams. Carts waited behind them, gathering up these materials into storage chests before shooting off toward the portals that would allow them to take this back to the ice planet to be refined.

"How's it going?" Dave asked in a private chat before teleporting right next to Malsour, making him jump.

"Would be better if I didn't have the human jack-in-the-box making me jump out of my skin!" Malsour got his breathing under control. He let out a frustrated noise. "I like it better when you weren't testing out your teleportation magic. You'd be pretty deadly with that."

"Oh, I know and it was also why I was so willing to let Deia participate in fighting or at least be near it when she was pregnant with Koi. If anything went wrong, then I could teleport her away in the blink of an eye," Dave said seriously.

"Well, that's good to know." Malsour glanced at the miners. "I never thought that our projects would turn into anything on this scale. I still don't quite understand it all."

"It is pretty damn impressive. It it still hasn't sunk in for me." Dave sighed.

"I know," Malsour said. "Me either. Though it's here now so we have to do something with it."

"I was wondering if I could use your mind for something that I've been thinking on," Dave said.

"What is it?"

"Teleportation related and I also want to go over the new designs for the battleships and destroyers," Dave said.

"Okay," Malsour said. They disappeared from in front of the miners and appeared next to the portal.

Dave stepped through, Malsour following right behind him.

As soon as he was through, Dave teleported them both to the workshop and laboratory buildings that were filled with people working on different projects or coming to understand them.

Ela-Dorn was in the room, sitting in a chair, her hand on a Mirror of Communication.

Dave swiped his hand over the surface of the workstation in front of them. A complicated series of spell formations appeared in midair, overlapping one another.

"What does it do?" Malsour looked at it.

"Well, we've been looking at what the flying citadels are doing with dropping everyone off and I had to think that there is a better way to drop off troops than have them use those teardrop backpacks," Dave said.

"Okay." Malsour waved for Dave to go on.

"This is what I call teleportation drop. I know it needs work but anyway—these spell formations would be turned into runic lines that people could stand on. Then we cast a spell on the ground below the runic lines, use that as an anchor and we send people to the surface," Dave said.

"Okay, so basically we have a teleport but it only teleports people to whatever's below it," Malsour said.

"Exactly! So we could have a whole bunch of say War Clans—they're standing inside these teleportation circles, then we just drop them right onto the battlefield. Instant reinforcements!" Dave smiled.

"Okay, that does sound like a good idea, but that anchor—there has been a reason that we've been using drop pads and the portal anchors," Malsour said.

"Yes, but this anchor isn't crossing three-dimensional space, a lot less things to deal with. Here the anchor is basically making sure that we don't stick people in the ground." Dave's excitement built.

"I don't think that we should tell the people that we're going to be using this on that we might stick them into the ground."

"Well, of course not. We're going to fix that up before it happens," Dave said.

"Okay, well, it makes sense to me." The more Malsour looked at the spell formations, the more he could understand what it was trying to do.

"Now the other thing that I want your help on." Dave flicked his hand, using the interface menu to change what they were looking at.

Two large ships appeared. One was a kilometer long, the other about three hundred meters long.

"Okay, so these are our designs for the battleships and the destroyers. The destroyers were made to be a multi-platform ship. Though the more I talk with the people who have been going through history and are working to become buffs on this stuff, the more I'm starting to think that we should make them farther apart. Able to cover the other's weaknesses. What the eggheads have been thinking is to adapt the battleship so that it is faster and can move between atmosphere and space. However, the destroyers will be a complete space warship. They can then have much heavier armor, better long-range weapons, and fusion reactors dedicated to the shields and Mana barriers.

"The battleships are good for close-in defense and patrols but they're not good to slug it out. That will be the destroyer's job. We can fit the destroyers with the new jump drive while the battleships can just use portal jumping. The destroyers clear the area, then call in the missile boats and battleships through portals," Dave said.

"It's a good thing that the flight drives run off gravity and Mana so it doesn't matter if they're in atmosphere or space—they'll still work. This scale up on the destroyer—it's going tot cost a lot more resources than we originally thought." Malsour looked at the ship.

"Yes, but it will still take about the same time as the battleship to make. The destroyer is much bigger and its armor plates are really simple. The battleship, however, is streamlined to make sure that it doesn't face too much resistance when moving from atmosphere to vacuum," Dave said.

"Which brings us to the automatons. How has development gone with those?"

"Well, the Aleph we've got are looking into it and we've got Jeeves running through multiple simulations to see which of them would be the best for our needs. It looks more and more like we're going to have to make multiple types for all kinds of jobs." Dave scratched his head.

"Which means multiple factories, which means more time up front to build up the infrastructure to create them," Malsour added.

"Yep, but thankfully we have all of these people here so it's coming along a lot faster than I thought. We should have finalized ideas within a few days, it looks like. But anyway, back to the ship types," Dave said.

"I think it's smart. We've got missile boats heavy on armor and defenses, with storage crates filled with hundreds of missiles. Those are good for just saturating the enemy's defenses with weapons fire— make their defense work for it. Then we've got the battleships that can wade through the fires of hell to reach the Jukal ships and smash them apart at long range and up close. I would think about even increasing the power on the engines. With the inertia information that we've got from Sato's people, we can handle a lot more gravities on these ships and still be fine.

"Let's use that to our advantage. The destroyers have missiles and weapons. And they've got high speed, and can enter and exit planets. They have less armor and have way less striking power than the battleships but they can escort them and enhance their striking abilities." Malsour looked at the ships.

"Someone has been doing their homework." Dave smiled.

"Well, we're making a fleet of warships— I thought it might be a good idea to know how to use them and what they're going to be doing. I was thinking of bringing it up before but we just didn't have the resources in order to have multiple kinds of ships. With all of the bases and what we have now, it's possible for us to increase our striking power and our abilities."

"Good. That was what I was thinking, too." Dave pressed another command on the console. The ships started to change, with their weapons and emplacements being pulled out and changed, as well as their forms. Their armor changed shape and also densities.

It was as if someone had gone over them and started to remove all of the useless extras and beefed up what needed to be touched.

Malsour looked at the final products.

The battleship was shaped like an octagonal prism. Mana shield nodules covered the ship. Runic lines ran across it, lighting it up with an ethereal glow. Flight drives lay on either end of the ship and then along its body to allow it to maneuver in every direction. Heavy armor covered the surface of the ship as rows of massive heavy cannons lined the different faces of the battleship. Missile ports were sealed up, ready to launch.

Looking upon the ship, Malsour felt reassured. This was a ship of war seemed to combine clean lethal lines while seeming dominating at the same time.

The Destroyer was much smaller. It was streamlined with two wings midway up it's body for atmospheric flight and they also held missile racks and even a few smaller cannon attachment points.

armor was more polished and less rough, with lighter weapons and less missile ports than the larger battleship.

"The destroyer will have the drop teleporting ability that I was talking about earlier, allowing it to move into hostile territory and drop off reinforcements quickly. It will have surface-to-space as well as space-to-space missiles. It will have automated cannon turrets that can fire all types of rounds, from the plasma cannon rounds to the nuclear warhead grand workings. When entering and exiting atmosphere, it's going to be pretty nimble, but people better be strapped the hell down. Wait—we'll just boost the power of the gravity runes and we should get Jeeves to code out something that will make it so that everyone's good at all times. It's damn useful having an AI around."

"Good to know my services are appreciated," Jeeves said from the ceiling.

"Hello, Jeeves." Malsour smiled. Jeeves was the hardest working of them all. In the beginning, they had needed to code everything by themselves. Now they coded some of the more complex stuff that Jeeves didn't understand. Like Dave's portals. Though, for the most part, they could tell Jeeves what they wanted and he could whip up a code to be inserted into a soul gem construct and with enough power it could be built. It was why and how they were able to change between designs like they were now.

If they were an Earth military, then they could adapt their designs but to change them completely, they would have to remake the entire hull, rip out everything and try again.

"Hello, Malsour. Did the miners within the asteroid belt meet your approval?" Jeeves asked.

"Yes, they did. Good work," Malsour said.

"Thank you," Jeeves said. The AI didn't get any happier than when someone praised him on doing a good job. When something went wrong, he would sit over the shoulder of whoever was working on the project and try to help them figure out what went wrong. He was a perfectionist and within Pandora's Box that was necessary.

"Jeeves, do you want to tell Malsour the specs on the battleship?" Dave asked.

"The battleship has multi-layered armor, similar to the armor used by the Devastator suits. Once impacted, the layers of soul gem within the metal will repair itself and then where it has been hit; as long as the ship is powered, it will recover. It has five large fusion reactors, ten small reactors like the one within Pandora's Box on Emerilia. It has twenty-four Mana wells that are spread throughout. The soul gem construct within all of these ships is the most complicated construct ever made. It is grown on a reinforced and runed metallic superstructure made up of a Mithril composite."

"Wait—what? A Mithril composite?" Malsour interrupted.

"With the information from Earth, the Jukal Empire, as well as the various texts from the dwarves, we were able to work out how to make the Mithril composite. It is rather expensive to make but with our large amounts of resources, it is not impossible. With this surplus, we have been looking at using it with a combination of other materials in different processes to retain the integral strength of the Mithril material without having to use just purely Mithril. With this composite material, we are able to have that strength throughout the battleship. It is actually needed in order to support all of the armor as well as the acceleration you two have been talking about. A lesser material could warp and then the entire ship could break apart or have weaknesses.

"The Mithril composite material is part of the superstructure that the soul gem construct is grown upon. The soul gem construct will look after things like power distribution, breathable atmosphere, command and control circuits for the various items within the ship. It will also be able to seal off sections of the ship that are heavily damaged and repair them. It can also act as a reservoir of power for the different magical coding within it. All of the coding will be compressed to runic lines but can be altered at any time To do that at the ship level, Administration rights would need to be assigned and delegated. Also, with having the soul gem construct as the base material, it is possible to replace out items like burnt-out Mana barrier coding automatically. As Mana shields go down from overheating, then you could code in heat exchangers that remove the excess heat or replace the soul gem construct completely. With Earth warships and Jukal Earth ships, it is necessary to take out banks of hardware stacks and replace them out due to overheating or damage. Also, they are more likely to have faults. Any issues that are detected by me will automatically be repaired so that there is no loss in functionality," Jeeves said with some pride.

"Every time I think of these soul gem constructs, I just can't think how it would be possible to do it without them," Malsour said.

"I know. Terra wouldn't be at half of its progress, we wouldn't have flying citadels lying in wait, or be able to create the places we have," Dave said.

"Do you wish for me to continue?" Jeeves asked.

"Please do," Malsour said.

"Then we move to weaponry. There is no need for massive missile holding areas like the Jukal or the old Earth ships had. With the bags of holding and storage crates, each ship can store hundreds of missiles easily, each one armed with a fusion grand working warhead.

"Same goes for the various cannons. They will be controlled by the ship's AI, which I am currently undergoing training on and working with in simulations to improve the accuracy and abilities of the cannons. The cannons are based off Deia and Induca's plasma cannon as well as the dwarven cannons, and information from the Earth archives and the Jukal fleets.

"The cannons will use grand workings and their base unit will be similar to the dwarven artillery cannon, but more heavily reinforced and able to channel much more power through in order to reach near relativistic speeds.

"It will be enhanced by magical formation and magical coding, similar to the cannons that Deia and Induca make out of their fire. While this will increase the power of the artillery cannons, it will also make it impossible for the ships to remain within stealth. Each time that they fire, they will also create these glowing sheet-like apparitions that the enemy will be able to see," Jeeves said.

"Are we still going with the stealth runes? I thought that would be impossible?" Malsour asked.

"Not impossible but really difficult. But Jeeves—"," Dave, a grin on his face, pointed to the ceiling.

"The problem with the stealth runes is that they make an entire area look as if it doesn't exist and cuts it off from the outside universe. A Mirror of Communication will still work but everything else is dulled.

"What we worked on was with the heat exchange system as well as the adaptive abilities of the soul gem construct, we can mimic the surrounding area's heat, reduce our own and also fake the stars and other light sources around us. This will not allow us long, but with the increased speed that I am simulating out right now after yours and Dave's discussion, I believe that it will give all of the battleships a much better chance at surprising the enemy. However, the destroyers will be unable to use this to such great effect.

"Their ships, with their smaller power units and their more reduced design, would not have the power or the technological abilities in order to carry this out. However, they could hide in the shadow of a battleship to get in close with the enemy. The missile boats would be in much the same situation," Jeeves said.

"Okay, so the battleships will have massive cannons, a hell of a lot of armor and they can stealth pretty well until they fire and they will have the ability to jump between different locations.

"The missile boats will be heavily armored, have good missile defenses and shields. It will also be able to pump out missiles like crazy. It won't be too fast and it will need to rely on an anchor or a portal in order to move across solar system distances.

"The destroyers will be able to move between atmosphere and space. They will have decent weaponry to deal with most threats. They will also be able to use Mana barriers. They are also faster than the battleships but they also cannot move between star systems without anchors or portals," Malsour said.

"Correct. However, the battleships, due to their mass, will have issues with slowing their momentum as well as changing their heading. Once they are going in one direction, it's going to be hard to move in another. Unless you want to burn through the battleship's energy like no tomorrow," Jeeves added.

Dave and Malsour both looked on the warships that floated above the workstation, turning around as they showed off all their sides.

"Well, it looks like we're going to have our fleet soon enough," Malsour said.

"As long as we can get the materials for them," Dave said.

"With current production and the predicted rates of expansion, we are well on our way to meet our needs," Jeeves said.

"Shouldn't we be helping out the people with the flying citadels?" Malsour asked.

"They know what they're doing and they've done so many of them while we've been working on the designs and getting that sorted that we're not really needed. They have a plan they've refined—we're extra hands but here we're needed to deal with the issues that crop up, not just build things," Dave said.

"You make a fair point," Malsour said.

"Which is why I could use your help in building something," Dave said.

"Didn't you just say that we're better at solving problems instead of building things?" Malsour said.

"Why, yes, I did but this is a portal. The one I've been making in the asteroid base? Well, I finished it and we're having issues with it." Dave walked past the workstation and into one of the many workshops.

There were people all around working on different projects, from cannons to flight drives and armor. Although they had the basis of what they wanted to make and Jeeves was working off of that, it was basic and simple: integrating all of these systems together—although theoretically possible—hadn't been done before. They were trying to figure out any problems that might happen beforehand and solve them.

Dave and Malsour entered a room where a portal rested, it was made from soul gem, with runic lines spiraling throughout the ring and the base of the portal.

Malsour's sense spread out to the portal. His eyes opened with a blue light as he activated his arcane sight. "Impressive. Your power regulation is way off, though, and your runic lines are so close in places that they might have overlap."

The two of them moved forward to the portal. As Malsour talked, Dave used his soul smithing art to change and transform the portal so that it would work out the kinks.

***

"Listen up and listen good, because if you mess this up, then it's not going to be you turning into meat paste but the man or woman beside you! And they're a hell of a lot more useful than you!" Deia barked as she looked at the forces in front of her.

None of them dared to say anything.

Party Zero had become the trainers of the different citadel crews. They had brought with them the trainers Deia, Quindar, and Anna had worked with in Devil's Crater to get the DCA army up to their current standard.

The DCA were regarded with great respect by their peers; their fighting skills and their tactics weren't any less than other groups. Coupled with how they fought and their supporting abilities, they had earned a place within the hearts of all the soldiers within the Terra Alliance. Nearly no other force had been so active: many times, the DCA aerial forces provided support and the DCA ground forces lay down traps and went out into the no-man's-land between castles and searched out creatures around towns and cities to finish them off and give the people peace.

"We have been training within the Mirror of Communication for a number of weeks. All of you have come to understand your gear and your roles. Obviously we have not trained in real life with the flying citadels. Today, we will be lifting Citadel One. We will move it near to Citadel Two. We will be going through practice drops throughout the day. Make sure that you follow your training and follow the orders of your leaders. We're here to get you used to dropping and carrying out your various duties. Safety is paramount. I don't want any screw-ups. If you see something going wrong, I want you to point it out immediately. If you don't, I'll have your damn asses and by the time I'm done with you, I'll have you jumping out of those citadels in your nightmares." Deia looked to them all.

A few made snide comments to one another about being around Deia. She was a good-looking elf and many held her in their eyes with interest. Some of their peers shot them dirty looks while others gave them looks of pity.

Deia and Dave were completely devoted to each other. If Deia was to hear their comments, then many of the people would wish that they had died from the training that she would put them through.

"Once you are down on the ground, you will move to Citadel Two, where you will move through the ono back to your citadels. From there, you will go over after-action reports on what you did well and what went wrong. We will be doing one drop per day this entire week. If we can, I want to get to two or three for next week.

Get used to the drop backpacks and the platforms! After this training, we will be using them to directly attack the enemy," Deia said.

The officers and the training staff looked over the twenty-five different citadel groups that were arranged in rows.

There were five dwarven War Clans, a unit of ten thousand mounted, two thousand mages and two thousand archers, followed by forty-five dwarven artillery gun crews, four hundred Aleph controllers and their four thousand automatons, and then a flying force of a thousand. There were sixteen flying citadels under construction right now. The nine extra units were there so that if the citadels needed reinforcements, they could assist without needing to be familiarized in the middle of battle. They could also completely switch out with citadel fighting forces, rotating units that had been fighting from the citadel outward without any problems.

It had been a pain to deal with everything but Lucy and Florence had kept everything organized and equipment flowing. They were still waiting for some gear but the industrial complexes of the Terra Alliance were rushing to meet their needs. The flying citadels could alter the balance of the war, after all.

"Okay, let's get going. Citadel One crew, you will be up first, moving down through the crews. While waiting, I want everyone doing drops within the Mirror of Communication," Deia said. "That's all I have to say. Citadel commanders, I turn them over to you."

The different forces started to disappear as the citadel commanders talked to their people and disseminated information to their leaders and their troops.

Party Zero, as well as Quindar, exited the Mirror of Communication, finding themselves in the command center of the first citadel.

"Captain Farul, take us up please," Deia said.

"You heard the lady. Flight?" Farul looked to the woman in the flight chair.

"Yes, Captain. Power is looking good; flight drive is looking good. Power retention at eighty percent and charging. Ready to push off. Powering up the drive to five percent." The flight officer's hands moved across the different buttons and the screen in front of her.

The citadel started to shake slightly.

"Shaking free the dirt and rubble." The flight officer increased the power to the flight engines.

Around the citadel, the grass, trees, and dirt was pushed away as power pulsed out from the citadel. For a few moments, it seemed to pause before it lurched upward slightly. Then it gradually rose up above the massive crater below.

The citadel's polished walls shone in the early morning light. The runes and the soul gem that had grown through the wall lit up even in the early morning sun. Dirt and debris fell from around the outside of the citadel as the soul gem base was revealed. Glowing with motes of light, the citadel rose upward.

"We are free. Moving to altitude of one kilometer and moving toward Citadel Two." The flight officer said, her voice sounded both nervous and excited at the same time.

"Well, seems that it works at least," Anna said.

"If there is one thing that those guys can do, it's build things," Induca said.

"Yeah, it's a pain in the ass to get them to do anything else." Deia sighed.

"You've been training people the entire time," Anna rebuked.

"So, have you and Alkao, but you've still been sneaking off together," Deia said with a sly smile.

Anna turned red in embarrassment. "Well, that's none of your business," Anna muttered, hip checking him and looking around shyly, at complete odds with the commanding force she was on the training grounds.

The forces of Citadel One were roused from their different barracks and quarters. Mages and ranged forces moved to the various casting balconies, as well as weapons. The Aleph automatons manned repeaters along the wall. Dwarven artillery crews checked their guns and made them ready for battle.

Mages stepped onto the specialized casting balconies that were inscribed with runes that would allow them to recover their Mana faster and make it harder for them to go into Mana fatigue.

Aerial forces moved to the new flight deck that had been added to the main tower. Here people could launch and land from all manner of beasts. Runes were used to create a jet stream that people could drop into and use to reach impressive speeds right from launch. The other sides were landing areas that didn't have any wind to make it easier to land.

DCA forces lined up within the tower, ready to throw themselves into the launcher runes.

Dwarves and their mounted compatriots moved out from their barracks and to the different areas where they could drop from.

The mounted actually took large lifts through the soul gem underneath the castle to large bay-looking areas. Off to the side, there were racks of metal plates with runes and a fence around them. The creatures stepped onto these plates, now trained to get past their original fears.

A gravity field encompassed them as they moved over the bay doors so that it didn't even feel as if they were flying.

The dwarves were split up between groups that marched onto this landing platform to others that were ready at chutes buried deep inside the soul gem island that the Citadel rested on. These were basically slides that the dwarves or other single-person forces would jump in, the slide guiding them through the soul gem construct and out below the citadel.

Then they would use their teardrop-shaped backpack to guide themselves to their drop zone.

All over the place, there was training staff. All weapons and armor had been removed so that they couldn't get in the way. Here, they were just doing the basics; later they would get into holding weapons and more complicated maneuvers like the kind that they might need to use if they were getting attacked at range.

The massive flying citadel crossed the sky. The other training forces in the different citadels looked upward, staring at the monstrosity in the sky.

The only floating creations they knew of were the Per'ush Islands. To see an entire citadel flying across the sky— even though they had seen it in the Mirrors of Communication training—was much different in real life.

The citadel came to float near the second citadel's location so that forces, once they were done, could pass through the ono to allow the next citadel fighting force to move through.

Trainers who could fly took to the air around the citadel, looking about to make sure there were no threats and ready to intervene if any issues arose.

"We are hovering outside of Citadel Two," Flight said.

"Good. Keep us on a hover. Make sure that we get the information on crosswinds to the groups dropping today," the captain said.

His command crew did their tasks with economic movements. Nervous at first, they relaxed more and more, getting used to their roles. They had practiced for weeks in the Mirror of Communication. They knew how to work their stations; it was only the pressure of practicing it and then actually doing it in real life made their nerves hit an all-time high.

Deia, Anna, Quindar, Steve, Lox, Gurren, and Induca were within the command center.

"So, anyone else want to jump off a perfectly good flying citadel?" Steve rubbed his hands together.

"We'll go check on the different ground forces." Lox indicated Gurren and Steve at the same time.

"I'll check in with the aerial forces quick," Anna said.

"I'll join," Quindar said.

"Want to go and help those on safety?" Induca asked Deia, looking to the people who were floating around the citadel, making sure that no one got into too much trouble and that everyone got to the ground in one piece.

"Sounds good to me—be able to see just what they get up to." Deia smiled. She was nervous as the people who were doing this for real for the first time. If something went wrong, it would reflect back on her. She'd got a lot of help from Anna and the others but this was her show; she was the training commander of everyone here.

They took elevators from the command center heading to the different parts of Citadel One.

Deia and Induca took to the sky, twin fireballs as they moved.

"I'm surprised that Dave and Malsour aren't here," Induca said in a private chat with Deia. Talking with the air rushing past would have been impossible.

"I know. They probably wish that they were here too, but they've been wrapped up in their own projects. It seems that everything has just gone mad in the last couple of weeks," Deia said, her voice quiet. She missed spending time with Dave. It felt like a lifetime ago that they had let loose and relaxed in Per'ush.

Deia shook free those thoughts and smiled at Induca. "So after Malsour showed that he was actually a Dragon, how have people been?"

"Well, they've mostly figured out that I'm a Dragon too. The players are all losing their shit and the people of Emerilia are a bit stunned. However, I think it's still hard for them to try to understand that I'm human and I can also turn into a massive red Dragon. I think that it might be good that way as most people aren't treating me too different," Induca said.

"Now that it's out of the bag, are you going to fight in your human form or Dragon?"

"I'm thinking my Dragon form for most things. We're coming up against creatures and groups that are much stronger than us. We need every advantage that we can get," Induca said.

"Yeah. I thought at one time that anything higher than Level 100 was powerful. Though Emerilia and the portals are showing me just how foolish that idea was."

"Well, there's no limit to how powerful someone can be on Emerilia. There's bound to be people who push those boundaries—look at Denur," Induca said.

"You have a point." Deia laughed.

"First drop, ready to go," one of the overseeing trainers said over the trainers' channel.

Deia changed over.

The various people who had been flying around now moved closer to the flying citadel, ready to help where needed.

"Five, four, three, two, one. Drop, drop, drop!" Bay doors slammed open underneath the citadel as platforms dropped downward like rocks. Beasts yelled out as they dropped even though they couldn't feel the dropping sensation but saw the ground all around them, and the sudden change of scenery made them feel disoriented.

The platforms shot down toward the ground and into various formations. They flew in separate groups, following programmed flight plans so that they weren't ontop of one another or that they were in the flight path of the others who were leaving the citadel.

Dwarves dropped out of the chutes; their teardrop backpacks took over as soon as they left the citadel in a stream. They raced toward the ground as well. All of the forces were spread out so that it would be headed to kill a large number of them in one hit.

It looked as if the citadel were a bee's nest and that all of the bees inside were rushing to attack something that had disturbed them.

From the flight deck, the DCA-based aerial crew jumped into the different jet streams, launching into the air. They curved around and turned toward Citadel Two.

Mages and ranged attackers went through the motions of what they would do without actually completing the action of firing their weapons or releasing their spells. Right now, they were just seeing how they could deploy their forces and the kind of effect it would have. Adding in live fire as well as testing out all facets of the citadel could come later, once everyone was used to dropping from the citadel and launching.

The sight made Deia's heart clench as she continued to watch on the interface that was tracking everyone who was dropping. Shard managed all of the different flight's so that they wouldn't hit one another. The trainers hovered around, ready to aid if needed.

The dwarves with their backpacks hit the ground first. Their creatures followed them as they moved into their armored formations. The creatures screeched and flew above their heads.

In battle, they would continue to attack whatever was in the dwarves' way as they advanced forward, allowing them to hit the enemy at range instead of only being a close-quarters fighting group.

The platforms flared before settling on the ground. The fences around the platforms dropped as the mounted forces rushed outward, headed for Citadel Two while the Dwarven formations on the platforms marched off, their creatures jumping into the sky.

With every group that made it to the ground safely, Deia felt slight relief. Still, there were hundreds of platforms and thousands of people and moving parts all going at once.

There were some complications but they weren't too bad and they were easily solved. Still, the first drop took about forty-five minutes before everyone was deployed.

"We're going to need to work on that time," Deia said, even as she had a smile on her face.

"No one injured and only a few mess-ups—room for improvement but not bad," Induca said.

"I want those platforms and the landing backpacks reset and ready for the next group. I want this reset and ready for the next citadel crew coming through in an hour and a half." Deia moved toward the forces that were now walking toward Citadel Two, talking to one another about what had happened.

"How long until we can get more platforms and backpacks?" Induca asked.

"We're getting more every day. Florence says that in three weeks, we'll have all of them," Deia said.

"That's cutting it close to when the Alliance wants us to hit our first target." Induca frowned.

"Yes, it is, and we're going to need to test every single piece of gear. We're dropping from the sky— I don't want to have any complications," Deia said.

"Do you think that the trainees will be able to keep up with everything?" Induca asked as they moved to where a group of platforms were rising back up into the air. As they could land, they could also return to the citadel. All of it was under the guidance of Shard.

Each platform could hold a hundred warbands, or five hundred dwarves, or two hundred mounted.

"I know that it's one hell of a punishing schedule. We've got them training for real right now, then we're going to be doing multiple drops and introducing them to live fire and full gear by the end of next week. The week afterward, I want to have them working with those barrier trainers that I used with the DCA. If we slack their training, then we're doing them a disservice. The more sweat we spend here, the less blood we'll have when it's real," Deia said, her voice firm.

Induca looked at Deia. Deia was a driven woman, much more driven than Induca had been before she had left Emerilia. She had even gone into hibernation when she and the Dracul clan were moved to their other planet. Now that she was back on Emerilia, she worked to improve her abilities to the utmost.

Deia had a stronger base to go from, being the daughter of a goddess. However, combined with her work ethic, she had struck a powerful figure that Induca looked up to.

"I was wondering if you wanted to train together?" Induca asked.

"Sure." Deia smiled.

Induca smiled as well. Her fight with the Xelur Grand Demon Lord had shaken her up more than she let others know. She'd come close to dying and even Suzy had been badly hurt. She wanted to protect her girlfriend but now even her Dragon form that she had relied on before to fight others wasn't strong enough to fight the opponents they were finding.

They reached the ground and collected the different backpacks that had been laid out. Once collected, they headed back up to Citadel One so that they were ready for the next group to come through.

***

Within the asteroid base, a miner moved away from a slip as automatons started to lay down a superstructure. The pre-made parts came together as the repair bots with their flight drives and carts moved from the nose of the craft toward the rear. As it moved downward, a soul gem construct was placed in the fore of the craft. Reaching out from the asteroid base, bundles of runic lines running through a soul gem construct reached out from the base, connecting the fusion plants of the asteroid base to the superstructure of the craft.

The soul gem construct spread across the superstructure, corridors started to form with runic lines across it. Different supports and panels were attached to the superstructure; the soul gem construct grew over it at a rapid pace as the craft started to take shape.

Wings were brought together by repair bots and joined together into a single form as the main body of the craft extended backward. The three sections met up and came together as the soul gem construct continued to grow through the ship. Mounts appeared, and holes where missiles would be held. Fusion reactors started to take form as power continued to flow into the craft.

People came to watch the craft as it grew. A few moved inside, checking on the progress as other superstructures were laid down. As the asteroid shipyard grew, more and more hulls were laid down. Two more destroyers were started in front and behind the original. On the other side of the shipyard's main thoroughfare, a massive mile long hull was under construction. Multiple soul gem constructs were already laid down, flowing over the Mithril frame and creating the rooms where the fusion reactors would be held and Mana wells were inserted strategically throughout the Battleship. Repair bots and carts moved continuously as missile tubes, gun mounts, and other structures that couldn't be made from the soul gem construct were placed within the different ships.

Miners and cargo shuttles left while it grew, moving to other asteroids that contained materials needed to fuel the ships' progress.

Malsour and Dave were once again within the asteroid base, watching as the first of the battleships was finished. Its reactors were working but it still needed armor and its coding was an issue. That meant over a hundred people were swarming over every inch of the craft, checking it—along with Jeeves—to make sure that everything functioned properly.

Dwarves were some of the best Magical Circuit making people known. But when they had been working with Magical Circuits in order to enhance weapons, they were dealing with maybe a hundred characters and they were within a formation. They could copy them over and it would be completely fine. With magical coding, they were used to hundreds of different runes that could be put into simple combinations and greatly enhance the original effect.

The difference between using magical coding to decrease the weight of an item or allow it to have an ice attack was like comparing a math test to someone solving out how to fly from Earth to Mars with pure math. The learning curve was sharp but they knew it on a small level. They were just adjusting what they already knew and placing it onto the coding that was running through the battleships.

"Bob says that he's ready to wake up the first of the players," Malsour said.

"I know." Dave looked out over the ship.

"Nervous?"

"A bit. These people are going to just be torn from their lives and shown this truth—it's going to be a bit incredible," Dave said.

Malsour made a noise of agreement but didn't say anything else. There was no knowing how the players would react.

Dave touched the wall of the asteroid base, sending his consciousness through the wall and into the first destroyer that was the closest to completion. It might look complete on the outside, but inside there were still runic lines growing through the soul gem construct and unfinished hallways were coming together.

The fusion reactors were pouring constant power into the soul gem construct; , the walls around them were the strongest and the most complete. From there, power lines ran outward toward the different areas across the ship. All of these would need power and were ready for the components that were to be inserted.

Although most of the interior was made with soul gem construct growing, here and there the more complicated magical coding was compressed down into runic lines were made in factories, assembled, and then placed into the craft. They were fully integrated into the soul gem matrix of the ship melding with these complex constructs to make them one and the same.

There were greenhouses that were busy converting the atmosphere in the ship into breathable air. With the speed at which the different plants grew, they were able to easily scrub the air, making it possible for the people of Emerilia to walk through the ship without needing to bring their own air in a Mana shield.

Support beams spread through the ship. The armor bolted onto these different hard points as the soul gem construct created the command center, missile tubes, hallways, light strips, sleeping quarters, and drop circles—as they were being called by the development team.

Dave felt a sense of excitement and apprehension. He had never built something as complicated as the warships and he was scared that they might not work.

Everything was coming together but he was filled with nerves and a feeling of uselessness. He could do nothing but sit back and support his party from the rear. He wanted to be up front and on the front, where he could use his devices and tricks.

"Damn Jukal." Dave sighed and pulled his hand from the soul gem construct.

"What's the matter?" Malsour asked.

"Just—I have all of these weapons and I know that I could finish off a lot of groups that we are fighting with just a few moves. But I can't because everything that I use would tip off a damn AI or some kind of sensor. We have warships. We're working to develop our own massive portals. We've got nuclear fusion bombs in grand workings. We've got grand workings and cannons that make what the dwarves have look like they're playing with water guns. All of this and we still have to sit and wait, hoping that we're ready for what the Jukal bring to bear on us once we go to war with them," Dave said.

Malsour nodded. He, too, felt these pressures; at least he was able to use his gifts to fight. Dave's abilities didn't always come from his magic—it came from what he had made, greatly enhancing his abilities and making him a force to be reckoned with on the battlefield.

"The time is coming closer and closer. With these bases in Nal, it won't be long until we can reveal some of our strength." Malsour paused. "I think it might be time to talk to Sato about our plan to undermine the Jukal."

Dave looked to Malsour, thinking on his words. His face became harder as he came to a decision and nodded his head. "You may be right."

Chapter 14: Welcome to the Neighborhood

"Ready for jump," the navigation officer of the Deq'ual navy's latest stealth ship, the *Sprite*, said. After seeing all of the different aggressive species that were attacking Emerilia, they had been deployed in order to gather information on the various aggressive species systems with stealthed remote drones.

"Take us to the Nal system," Captain Xue said.

"Engaging jump drive," the navigation officer called out.

The space around the craft distorted as they entered jump space, exiting outside the system and deep in the asteroid belt of the Nal system.

"Looking for recon and communication platforms," the sensor officer called out. His eyes darted across his screen as information came into his terminal.

The more systems they went through, the better they had become at sensing out platforms that the Jukal had put throughout their controlled systems.

"No portal in-system. We've got basic communication arrays. Looks like some sensor satellites around the planet Nal, which the Nalheim live on." The sensor officer looked at light readings that were coming in from a few minutes ago.

"One day of silent running, then I want to start seeding the system with remotes." Captain Xue relaxed slightly. He wouldn't fully relax until they'd completely scanned the system for a few hours and knew about everything within the system.

"I'm picking up some odd readings," the sensor officer said after a few moments.

"What?" Xue sat up in his chair, trying to not appear too alarmed by what sensors was calling out, even as his heart raced and his palms started to sweat.

"It looked like a flicker but I thought that I was reading an asteroid reducing in mass—its orbit changed slightly. I'll need a few more minutes to check it out in more detail," the sensor officer said.

They had the best sensors possible; they combined multiple different sensor types and were centuries ahead of anything that the Jukal had made. The Jukal were happy, making the same thing over and over again while the innovated sensors used by the Deq'ual system's navy were highly accurate and effective.

**

Dave and Malsour had finished looking through the asteroid base and all of the various projects that were underway.

Dave's skill had gone up when they'd been not only looking over the projects but lending their help.

New Active Skill: *Teacher*

Level: *Apprentice Level 8*

Effect: *You can teach people skills that you have prior knowledge of, up to your level of ability. Your students are 5% more likely to understand what you're teaching them. Teaching on subjects you have a higher knowledge on will yield higher results. Teaching skills you have mastered or created give a higher chance for students understanding your lessons.*

It was odd to have so many people around. They had become used to having just a few of them working in cramped quarters.

It was slow going at first but they were quickly coming to understand what Dave, Malsour, Steve, and Bob had been working on and it was opening up a number of avenues of projects.

"Okay, your power distribution is all off. With the soul gem construct, it's an easy fix— you just increase this line of code." Dave pointed to a screen that showed lines upon lines of magical runes. "Then the soul gem construct will alter its size so that it can fit it. You've got to take off these restricting lines of code here for the size. If you can't make it bigger due to there not being enough space, run a second power line conduit," Dave said over the dwarf's shoulder.

"This?" The dwarf looked at the new code that Dave had entered. The hologram to the side showed a different image than before, with an increase on stats on the side.

"You'll get the hang of it." Dave smiled and clapped the man on the shoulder.

The dwarf laughed, looking to Dave. "Well, we're not all magical coding crazies like you lot."

Dave joined in. The atmosphere within the different bases was greatly relaxed. Without the threat of monsters and creatures in Emerilia, these people were able to unleash their minds on the problems that they found.

Dave and Malsour found that most of their time was not spent on dealing with issues that they had run into but instead trying to get everyone else up to date on all of their practices and understanding the various items that they were using to push the development in the Nal system and through Pandora's Box.

Instead of hindering them, as they taught others, they were both coming to understand what they were working with more and more. As they discussed issues with more people, it was possible for them to have more breakthroughs.

At the same time, Dave was increasing the level of his teaching class.

"We have sensed someone searching one of the asteroids currently being mined," Jeeves said through a private chat to Dave.

Dave looked up from the dwarf he'd been talking to, to Malsour in alarm.

"Ready our defenses and get me a look at what they are. Ready Battleship One." Dave disappeared from the lab, before he appeared inside Battleship One. Malsour appeared next to him; a circle appeared next to Malsour as Ela-Dorn, who had her finger raised into the air, looked around in confusion, finding herself within Battleship One.

Power surged through the massive ship. All of its reactors surged up to their maximum. Dave's hands moved through the air as he checked through the queue of things that were being worked on.

"Malsour, Ela-Dorn—we need weapons online as soon as possible— at least one bank of cannons and some missile tubes. Malsour, you work on that. Ela-Dorn, I want you to raise everything that will get the jump mechanics working, as well as the flight drive. We've got twenty minutes to work on as much as possible. Get Jeeves to help you to prioritize. Also, see if we can get some of the shields and barriers online if at all possible," Dave said, not stopping his own work as he turned off everything that wasn't required to bring the ship up to combat readiness,. freeing up power and resources to devote to what would bring the ship up to fighting condition.

"I have been analyzing the information on the unknown ship. It uses magical coding for its stealth covering and it's rather impressive. Also, by the drives, it seems that they are using ideas from our own flight drives," Jeeves said.

He had met with Sato and Edwards within the Mirror of Communication but there was still no way for the two groups to meet up and try to talk to one another and create some kind of mutually supporting agreement.

Dave didn't know where they were and they were a paranoid group. They had survived on the outside of the Jukal Empire's reach for hundreds of years, doing everything that they could in order to not be found out. Dave and his groups had aided them out a lot but still they were hesitant to help him with more than just a few ideas here and there, fearing that he might use this information to turn on the Deq'ual system or undermine any advantages they might have.

"Bob." Dave said, using a Mirror of Communication to get his voice chat through the portal linking the asteroid base and the ice planet.

"What?" Bob sounded irritated.

"I have what looks to be a ship paying attention to one of our asteroid mines. We've shut down everything but we're getting readings that the ship looks like it might be from the Deq'ual system," Dave said.

"Really? They've made it this far already?" Bob's annoyance turned into a voice filled with praise.

"Well, it looks like it. However, I want to check with Sato. Could you ask him?" Dave asked.

"Give me two minutes and I can message him," Bob said in a panic.

"Got it," Dave said. "Thanks Bob"."

"I'll let you know what he says."

Dave cut the channel, going back to his party chat with Ela-Dorn and Malsour.

"Okay, let's do everything we can to get this beast combat ready and see just how good our stealth runes are," Dave said.

"We're not going to engage them?" Ela-Dorn asked. She didn't know about Sato and his people.

"They might be a group that we've been working with," Dave said in a hesitant voice. *She's come this far—telling her, there isn't much risk.* Dave continued. "We made contact with a group of humans who are hiding out in space. We gave them a whole bunch of information and we told them about our own practices and most of the technology we're working with here. The technology we're seeing on their ships is based on magical coding, which makes me think that they could actually be these same people."

Dave wore an apprehensive look on his face but there was also hope and happiness. If they hadn't made it to this stage already, Dave didn't think that they would be able to truly support what he was doing. However, it looked as if he had underestimated them.

Though, why are they in the Nal system?

Ela-Dorn had a look of shock on her face.

"We can think on that later. Right now, we need to get this battleship ready to fight," Malsour said, his gruff voice bringing them all back to their work.

They worked to get some weapons, shields, and drives online. The armor was mostly complete. They had some firepower but basically if it came to it, they would need to bluff the people on the other ship, or unleash an unholy shit storm of missiles and hope the targeting circuits weren't too bad on the cannons.

Dave worked, hoping that Bob could get Sato as soon as possible.

"Oh shit—it looks like they're readying weapons and shields! Strap in!" Dave yelled, jumping to the captain's chair. Malsour and Ela-Dorn sat down at the navigation and engineering consoles in front of the captain's chair.

"Damn, these seats are pretty comfortable." Dave tried to keep the nerves out of his voice as he connected to the soul gem matrix of the ship. Runic lines across his body lit up as his eyes glowed gray. Runic lines spread out from the soul gem chair underneath him.

Runic lines spread out from the chair as he took complete control of the ship. He couldn't teleport the entire ship based on his strength alone, but by altering the coding of the ship, he could use it to boost his own power and do the heavy lifting while he simply acted like a guide for it all.

Still, it was a risky business and the amount of power he was talking about was enough for him to pucker right up.

***

"I'm not picking up any more readings from the asteroid. I'm going to switch to optical scopes," the sensor officer of the *Sprite* said. His screen changed to an image of the asteroid instead of a three-dimensional representation of all the light coming off the asteroid.

The main screen showed the asteroid. Everyone stood ready at their stations, able to carry out their captain's orders immediately.

Xue watched over it all, his palms sweaty as he looked out over various readings.

The sensor officer made a noise of interest and zoomed in on the asteroid.

A boxy-looking device with what looked like a drill bit on the end of it stuck out of the asteroid. Behind it, there was a shuttle with a massive cargo box attached to the rear of it. As the asteroid spun, more of the drills were revealed and there were only a few cargo hauling shuttles.

"Why aren't they doing anything?" the sensor officer said.

Xue wasn't picked for this mission for his good looks. "Bring to battle stations and seal the ship. Prepare to leave the system and warm up the missile and cannon tubes!" Xue yelled.

One moment, they were looking at the asteroid belt; the next, a mass of armor appeared in front of them.

"They're trying to contact us!" the communications officer said as everyone started to panic.

"What are they saying and look to get us the hell out of here!" Xue said. His biggest priority was to get everyone home undetected; other than that, he was to make sure that the Jukal never knew there were humans still in the universe.

Xue looked to the secret panel in his chair, knowing that it would destroy the ship completely, leaving no trace of those within.

"Hey! This thing working?" someone yelled.

"Yes, it's on. They're only receiving." Another voice sounded as if they were talking through their teeth.

"Oi, you lot with Sato?" the voice asked.

"They're still not talking back." The second voice sounded frustrated.

"Well, shit! How do I get them to talk? I know Edwards! And Sato! I'm Dave!" The last part was yelled out.

"No need to shout—the pickup is from your seat," the second voice said.

He knows Sato and Edwards—is this a ploy? Xue cut off the audio.

"Contact Deq'ual immediately! How are we for jump?" Xue asked.

"We need to get clear of the asteroid belt some before we can jump again. If we do a micro jump, we can do it in two goes. However, the chance of not hitting a rock or something isn't high," the navigation officer called out, no hesitation in her words as she laid out their options.

"Captain Xue, what's going on?" Admiral Adams appeared on the main screen.

"Admiral, we have someone who has appeared in front of our ship in a massive warship." Even as Xue looked at it, he couldn't believe its size or the weapons that covered it. "We don't know how it got to our position but there is someone saying they know Edwards and Sato."

"Prepare to escape and hold readiness but do not fire! Do you have an image of them or know who they are?" Adams asked.

The communications officer turned and looked to Xue; he indicated for her to say whatever was on her mind as an image appeared on the main screen.

"The man in the commander's chair calls himself Dave," Captain Xue said.

"How the hell?" Adams said to herself before she turned away from the Mirror of Communication.

"Get me Sato right now! Wake him the hell up! Tell him Dave showed up in the Nal system!" Adams barked, an irritated look on her face as she looked back to Xue.

"Ask Dave what's his last name in both realities," Adams said to Xue.

"My voice only," Xue said to the communications officer.

"You're live," the communications officer said.

"Hello. I wish to know what Dave's last name is in both realities." Xue felt odd saying it.

"Whoa—there's life! See, Edwards is a smart cookie! Didn't think that he'd actually be able to build stealth craft out of everything. Must've really applied himself, you know," the one called Dave said.

"Dave, I know you're Mana fatigued—but last name," Malsour said in calm tones.

"Okay, so this is reality, so Grahslagg. Earth simulation, Zane," Dave said.

Xue looked to Admiral Adams, who had a shocked look on her face that quickly turned to one more serious.

"Hold position and do not fire. Tell him Sato is on his way."

"Yes, Admiral," Xue said.

***

Sato woke up to alarms in his room. He smacked the intercom next to his bed as he jumped up and pulled on his clothes.

"Report!"

"In the Nal system, one of the stealth ships has been intercepted by a larger ship. Bob is also trying to contact you through the Mirror of Communication and Admiral Adams is asking for you to report to the command center as soon as possible," the person on the other side said.

Shit, just what the hell happened? Sato clamped down on his emotions as his face hardened and he finished putting on his clothes. "I'll be there in three minutes." Sato hit the com and rushed out of his door toward the command center.

He passed through the different checkpoints; the various guards opened the doors for him ahead of time so that there was no need to slow down. He reached the command center and his eyes found the main screen, filled with a diagram of a truly massive warship. He looked over the highlighted cannons and missile banks.

"Sato, Captain Xue and the crew of the *Sprite* were supposed to be placing down remotes within the Nal system in order to watch over the Nalheim race and see if Dave and his group were up to anything within the Nal system. As they were doing so, they found anomalous readings. They looked into it more and found out a number of mining drills that had been stopped.

"They started to power up their weapons and looked to escape when the ship on the main screen appeared. The person in charge of the large ship has tried contacting them. His name is Dave Grahslagg," Adams said.

"How the hell?" Sato asked under his breath, unable to keep the confusion off his face. His solemn expression quickly returned as he frowned. "I'll contact Dave and see if this is really him." Sato moved to a free console with a Mirror of Communication. He used his contacts and dialed Dave.

Dave answered after only a few moments. "Hey, Sato. Have a nice nap? Seems you lot have been busy with the ship making department. If I didn't know stealth coding, then I wouldn't have been able to pick up your little scouting ship. Sorry if I sound a little out of it. Mana fatigue, ya know—just need a big ole nap." Dave sighed.

"Dave, that's really your ship?" Sato asked.

"Well, one of them—can't have just one." Dave yawned.

Sato couldn't stop himself from looking at the main screen and the warship on it. It was bigger than Sato's main line warships that were being built within the asteroid shipyards. It had more weapons, more armor and the thing looked terrifying. *The amount of resources and the people needed to work on it must be astronomical.*

"Dave, why are you in the Nal system?" Sato asked.

"Well, when we came into contact with the Nalheim and they surrendered, we traveled to the planet Nal—you know, get the treaty signed...well, there wasn't a treaty and Malsour was basically made their king."

"Dave," someone said, outside of the Mirror of Communication's field of view.

"Oh yeah, sorry. Brain's all over the place. That's Malsour." Dave picked up the Mirror of Communication in his seat and pointed it at Malsour before he put it back in its holder.

"Okay, so Nal. We were there, portal, ice planet—well, you know we were looking for fuel. Found it, by the way—thanks, guys. Then from there, we expanded, we needed more resources and so we got to work on a few surprises for the Jukal." Dave grinned.

Sato had thought that they might have found a way to get to the ice planet, but he would have never thought that they would have taken that and then continued outward and go on to make these massive ships in such a short time. It was simply outside the realm of possibilities in Sato's mind.

"So now you know where we're at. Pop in and say hi at any time. Jeeves will send you a signal to use so that we can confirm it's you. We don't want the Jukal or anyone finding out about us. Which, by the way, how did you find us?" Dave asked.

"Umm, well." Sato scratched his head. "We took the data from the ice planet that you gave us, compared it with our records, then made a few deductions of what we were seeing on Emerilia. We added it to our list of places to visit. We didn't really know how you were going to get to the ice planet. And after the portal disappeared, we didn't think that it would actually happen. So we sent along Captain Xue and the *Sprite* to seed the system with stealth remotes so that we might be able to see what's going on in the system. However, with the aggressive species rampaging across Emerilia, we diverted the *Sprite* a few times in order to seed other systems that hold aggressive species so that we might come to better understand them," Sato said, not keeping anything back.

Dave looked thoughtful for a few minutes before he shrugged. "Well, you're here—well, your people are. You're welcome to visit, though we can't show everything. We can certainly give them a tour them around our facilities, fill up their fuel. If you want, you can set up a supply depot here. Would give you additional range. We could have you an asteroid ready within a few weeks with the extras." Dave looked off camera.

"Sounds doable," Malsour said.

"Don't look at me— I deal with portal tech," said the woman in the bridge who Sato had seen a glimpse of when Dave was turning the Mirror of Communication around.

"If I allow my people to enter, they will be transmitting constantly and they will be allowed to take their weapons," Sato said.

"Sure," Dave agreed, sounding uninterested. "Everyone I know carries around enough weapons to make Earth's old United Nations piss their pants."

Sato didn't know how to respond to that.

"All right—we'll send them directions to where they can park their ship as well as an access point into our asteroid base. Jeeves, could you sort that out?" Dave asked.

"I can," Jeeves said.

"All right. Well, one more jump, and I'm going to take a nap. If they want to come over in, say, nine hours after I've slept off the worst of this Mana fatigue, that would be *awesome.*" Dave made a circle with his fingers.

"I'll pass it on." Sato smiled, clearly seeing that Dave was exhausted.

"Awesome. See your people in a bit!" The Mirror of Communication to Sato as well as to the *Sprite* was cut.

On the *Sprite*'s sensors, the massive warship simply disappeared from their sight.

Everyone who hadn't seen the ship appearing at first was now looking at the screen in shock, as if something had gone wrong.

"Are they jumping within the system or are they cloaked?" Adams muttered next to Sato, sounding jealous.

"I don't know but it seems that we've underestimated just how much they can get done in a short period of time." Sato held his chin as he thought on what would happen when the people of the Deq'ual system found out about this new base Dave had set up in the Nal system. His thoughts turned to the politicians.

"I'm going to meet with Council Leader Wong." Sato rose from his seat. He needed to work with the councilwoman to control how this was seen by the public and to see whether they couldn't use this in order to become closer with the people of Emerilia.

"Understood." Adams nodded to Sato.

Dave had shown that he was innovative and driven. Time and time again, Edwards and his team, as they were going through the information Dave had given them, found out ways to speed up their production and also increase the abilities of the military forces as well as improve the lives of the Deq'ualians.

Sato called up Council Leader Wong as he marched out of the command center and through the Deq'ual station.

A guard detail fell in around him as he sent a message to her secretary.

In mere moments, he was told that Council Leader Wong would be ready and available to meet him as soon as possible in her private quarters.

Sato changed directions and headed for her apartment. It didn't take him long to traverse the station. The security detail outside Wong's residence informed her of his arrival and allowed him to pass in.

Council Leader Wong sat at her open-plan kitchen, sipping on coffee as her husband made up a few more cups. He was an elderly gentleman who worked in hydroponics and always had a kind smile on his face.

"Commander Sato, would you like a coffee?" Mister Wong asked.

"Please." Sato smiled. Coffee sounded like a great idea. He'd only had a few hours of sleep and he hadn't integrated with the Jukal nanites or interface so he didn't have stats or the abilities to raise his Endurance so he didn't have to sleep for days on end.

Edward's people had largely assimilated the tech, allowing them to work constantly and make more and more breakthroughs.

Still, the higher-ups refrained from using it, due to fears within the government.

Mister Wong poured an extra cup of coffee and put out sugar and cream, moving so that he hugged Council Leader Wong from the side. "Let me know if you need anything. I'm going to work on the garden," Mister Wong said.

"I will, thank you," she said. The two of them had a quick kiss and Mister Wong headed for their private hydroponics area to tend to the plants held there.

"One of our stealth ships came into contact with Dave Grahslagg," Council Leader Wong said, getting right to the point as Sato mixed cream and sugar into his coffee.

"Yes. It seems that he was doing more than playing around with the ice planet. He mentioned something about using a portal." Sato glanced to Wong.

She paused and raised her coffee to her lips; her eyes went wide as she lowered the cup in shock. "He knows how to use portals?"

"I don't know. He was under a lot of Mana fatigue when I was talking to him, made him seem pretty wishy-washy. He has agreed to allow a group of the people from the stealth craft the *Sprite* entrance into his asteroid base. They will be armed and transmitting at all times," Sato said.

"This will allow us to better understand what Dave Grahslagg is capable of and if working with him will be of a gain to us," Wong said.

"He has already helped us out more than we could ever imagine." Sato frowned as he looked at Wong.

"I know, but this is how the council will look at things." Wong sighed. "They will want to see what we can get from him and how it could benefit Deq'ual."

"Do you think it will help change their thoughts on helping Emerilia?" Sato asked, trying not to raise his hopes too high.

Wong let out a sigh, looking older as she gave Sato a sad smile.

He knew what she was going to say before she opened her mouth.

"We've become conservative to the point that any change is hard to pass through the council. It is changing with time as we see the benefits of these changes but as you know, it is slow to develop.

We've got a council that overlooks what tech we put into the different warships. They move slower than a turtle going uphill and they can hardly agree on items. It should be under your purview but the more that the politicians see the power going to the military, the more that they try to 'assist,' which usually means putting shackles on the military so that they can feel a larger sense of control."

Wong hadn't always been a politician; she had been a doctor before but seeing that there were issues within the system, she had stepped up. She didn't like politics and before Sato had made her his point of contact within the council, she had been gradually pushed to the sidelines by the "real" politicians who wished to continue to play their games.

Sato sighed. The higher he had become within Deq'ual, the more he had needed to deal with these characters. He fought to hold control over the military but the politicians wanted as much strength and bartering power in their pockets as possible.

As he drank from his coffee, Wong continued.

"However, we might be able to use this," Wong said, a light in her eyes as a devious smile spread across her face.

"How?"

"Well, it's clear that Dave is a capable man and he's not bound by a government or anyone watching over him. We already have a lot of trust in him and you have built up a steady relationship with him. While your hands are being bound tighter and tighter, we can possibly offload some of these projects onto Dave or at least see what he thinks of them, improve upon them and make them. We can pay him with resources and assistance. A few people might be interested in paying an asteroid base in another system a visit. We gain a better understanding of what Dave is building, we gain more knowledge, and we help Emerilia and Dave indirectly, allowing them to build up their own strength. Once we are assured of our trust placed in Dave, then we can start to discuss things like possible ways to attack the Jukal and see about decreasing their influence and bringing about a time when we won't have to hide. Then we can figure out a plan that if we bring to the people that they will agree to it," Wong said.

"Not the council?" Sato asked, feeling excited. It was only a small gesture of help but it was more than the Deq'ual system had been capable of giving Dave and the people of Emerilia in the past.

"The council will wrap it up in red tape—this is a decision of all of Deq'ual. Not just the council," Wong said.

Sato looked at the small and fragile-looking woman in front of him. Her face was set in hard lines, determination in her eyes. A smile bloomed on his face as he drank from his coffee.

I picked the right council member to talk to when I found out about Dave. Sato was eager to see what the future would bear.

Times had certainly changed from when the military forces of Deq'ual had tested out their defensive networks and systems as well as their few fighters with most of their forces actually being communication experts and guards who policed the system.

Now they had a sprawling military complex. They had been able to pull their population within cryo back out. Their population was booming and their technology advanced in leaps and bounds. They had true warships, scout ships, and had a growing network of stealth remotes that covered multiple systems. They watched the sensor readings of Jukal fleets, their merchant vessels and watched the populated outer worlds of the Jukal Empire.

They had never been stronger and Sato had never felt as alive. He'd never felt Deq'ual so alive and driven. It filled him with energy that no coffee could give him—a mix of hope, determination, and the pressure to excel.

Chapter 15: Second Stage

Dave finished teleporting the entire battleship back into the asteroid base.

"We need to finish those doors," Dave said, as the runic lines on his body and the gray glow of his eyes dimmed. He leaned back in the captain's chair, his head lolling forward as he fell asleep.

"Well, that was a lot of excitement for one day." Ela-Dorn slowly taking her shaking hands off the console and put them in her lap. Her green face had taken on a lighter hue.

"Seems that we're going to have to increase the speed at which we finish up these ships," Malsour said in a grave voice.

"Who are those people?" Ela-Dorn asked.

"They're humans who have been hiding outside of the Jukal Empire. They're survivors of the Jukal and human war," Malsour said.

Ela-Dorn sat back in her chair, her mind working overtime. Everyone who was now part of the Pandora's Box team had been told the full history of the Jukal and human war, how it had ended with humanity being practically wiped out until Bob had come along and created Emerilia in order to deal with the aggressive species.

After all of that, now learning that there had been survivors, she didn't know what kind of hardships they had to have gone through in order to survive.

Still, they were venturing out of their homes and looking to search out the Jukal and to find out what was happening outside of their system. This kind of bravery was not easily put into words.

"Don't worry— when they visit, you'll have plenty of time to talk to them. However, they probably won't be interested in talking about their homes, family, or anything of the like," Malsour said.

"I understand. The Aleph were the same way before we were betrayed." Ela-Dorn nodded, a new fire in her eyes. "If you want to look after Dave, I'll talk to the development teams and finding ways to speed up production. From what I know, the biggest bottleneck we still have is resources, so we're going to need to focus on more miners and cargo shuttles instead of ships for a bit."

Malsour nodded. "Understandable. See if you can talk to those working with the refineries as well as the mining operations."

Ela-Dorn seemed to have a flash of inspiration. "If we were to hollow out an asteroid, create a separator as well as line its interior with mining drills, we could teleport other asteroids inside it, thus reducing how easy it would be for someone to see the drills and pick up on us. Also, the cargo shuttles would be inside unless they were moving from one of the mining/separating asteroids to the main asteroid base to take the materials back to the ice planet and the refinery there. The mining drills could eat through the entire asteroid, taking out the precious materials. They, too, wouldn't need to be transported from the asteroid base to each of the asteroids around. It could increase the speed at which we mine and it could also reduce the amount of items we have floating around that could get someone's attention." Ela-Dorn's eyes narrowed slightly as she thought over the idea.

"If it gets to a large enough stage, we could bring the arks in. They could go through portals within the asteroids, picking up the separated out materials from the crusher asteroids and transport them to another asteroid refinery that could send them out to the various bases. Already the refinery within the ice planet is being taxed heavily and it's only going to have more demand upon it to refine out the various gases and materials that are mined from the planet," Malsour said thoughtfully, working through the problem. His age allowed him to step back from the problem instead of be wrapped up in it like Dave and Ela-Dorn. He still got excited but the ability to pull back and look at things from a practical perspective was hard to do.

"Come up with a plan and run it past Jeeves to see if it's viable. If if it is, then we'll look into carrying it out." Malsour nodded and looked to Ela-Dorn.

"I'll do that!" Ela-Dorn said.

"Docking clamps engaging," Jeeves said from overhead. He was piloting the ship back into its slip. Once again, the umbilical soul gem lines from the asteroid base connected to the battleship. Automatons swarmed the battleship, continuing the work on the massive ship.

Ela-Dorn rushed off to start on her new project.

Malsour checked the work queue. As much as he knew the trust that Dave and Bob placed within Sato and his people, Malsour was still cautious. They were building something here that was supposed to rival the Jukal Empire.

All of the systems at the top of the battleship's to-do list were to get it in fighting condition as fast as possible. Everything else was put on a back burner until these essential systems were completed.

Malsour turned around and saw Dave sleeping on the main chair. They weren't sharing the same Mana shield, so Malsour couldn't hear the snores in the nonexistent atmosphere. Dave's orbs silently floated around him, maintaining his shield.

Malsour sighed and threw out some metal plates from his bag of holding as he stood. He stepped into Dave's shield, being recognized as a friend by the orbs.

Malsour shook his head. The coding that Dave had put into these orbs—even able to recognized friend and foe—was simply extraordinary. The metal sheets picked up Dave; Malsour walked out of the ship and through the asteroid base. When he reached, the ice planet, he quickly came to the Dracul quarters.

People all knew the secret of the Dracul now but still they had come together over their love of technology and their drive toward pushing the boundaries of what was known. They were more interested than scared by the Dracul and the fact that they were Dragons.

Fire was still within the Densaou Ring of Fire but Oson'Mal lived within the ice planet apartments, looking after Desmond and Koi most of the time. Quindar and Fornau's children, as well as the younger generation of the Dracul family, were there, as were a number of Dragons who looked after them when Mal was working on projects or even helped him out when he was with the kids.

This allowed the older generations to concentrate on what was happening in Emerilia without worrying about their young getting into harm's way.

Malsour smiled. Fire's boyfriend Mal, had truly turned into the grandfatherly figure of the Dracul family.

He dropped Dave off in one of the free rooms, letting him sleep off his Mana fatigue.

The ice planet's city had mostly breathable atmosphere. The different buildings and sections of the city all had Mana shields and barriers that were put in place to secure various areas if there was ever a pressure loss within the city.

The ice buildings were being changed to soul gem constructs over time, but the resources were mostly going to the different projects being worked on, as well as development within the asteroid base.

If we were still working with only the materials that Bob gave Dave, we would have run out long ago. Malsour shook his head, thinking about the resource drains they were under. Even Dave's slow bleed of resources were already claimed by the flying citadels as well as Terra and the various other constructs under the Stone Raiders' purview.

Pandora's Box, the ark shipyard and the moonbase were all producing some materials. However, most of the items they needed were now coming from the Nal system.

"If only we had more time." Malsour sighed. They were balancing which projects to fund with resources over how useful they would be. A large portion was going to the mining and refining, as the more it built up, the faster they would be able to grow the other projects. However, building it was easier said than done, as the resources were being used to improve the mining and refining abilities!

Malsour let out a frustrated sigh as he started to walk out of the apartment buildings. As he passed a room, he heard giggling inside and the sounds of children playing. Malsour was about to continue past when a small hand grabbed his pant leg.

"Hello there, Desmond. Looks like you've escaped again." Malsour smiled and looked at—technically—his uncle, who waved his small hand around, still clenched on Malsour's pant leg. Malsour laughed at the little one's antics, picking him up and disconnecting him from his pants.

Desmond made annoyed noises, grabbing at Malsour's face before pausing and staring at him with wide eyes.

Malsour walked back into the room where the children were playing with one another, or off with various toys. The smaller babies were being looked after by nearby minders who also kept a watchful eye on the young in the room.

All of them had their bloodlines sealed so that they would remain in human form. Only when they reached the age of fifteen would this restriction be removed unless they were within the Densaou Ring of Fire. There they could freely use their Dragon form.

"That's where you got off to!" One of the minders who had been looking around saw Malsour coming back in with Desmond.

"Who's a naughty boy." The minder shook her head at Desmond but with no real anger in her voice. She looked to Malsour. "I heard that something happened over at the asteroid belt?"

"Over in the asteroid belt? Yora, you make it sound as if it's a house down the street." Malsour shook his head.

"Well, the portal isn't too far away," Yora rebutted.

"There was an issue but it was solved," Malsour said, starting to realize that since he'd been back, he hadn't told anyone what had happened. Seeing the battleship disappear and reappear might have made them all a bit nervous. He could see the relief in the minder's eyes as he smiled awkwardly, quickly handing off Desmond.

"Sorry—just need to write up a message." Malsour tapped on his interface a message to let everyone know who had showed up near the asteroid and that they would have visitors tomorrow.

"So what was it?" Yora asked, not willing to let it go. Malsour knew that she was the type to love gossip.

"Well, we're having some visitors come over. They were coming here to put down stealth remotes so that they could watch what was happening in the system. We picked them up, found out that Dave knows them and they're coming over to the asteroid base tomorrow," Malsour said, focusing on the message he was still writing up.

"What!?" Yora yelled, her face pale as everyone in the nursery looked to her and Malsour.

"Look—it's okay. We know them. They're people who hid away from the Jukal. I'm putting it all out in this message. There's nothing to worry about—they'll probably be coming for a stroll tomorrow." Malsour finished off the message and gave Yora a reassuring smile.

"Uncle Malsour, you might be a brilliant man, but you can't scare me like that!" Yora complained.

"Everything will be okay, Yora." Malsour hugged her from the side. He could see Yora was having a lot of trouble with the stress that she'd been under.

She wasn't all that old, just thirty or so, and the threat of the fighting on Emerilia and the sudden surprise here made her feel listless. Malsour hugged her tightly and some of Yora's emotions settled down.

"I have to get back to work. I leave these rascals in your care," Malsour said. A few of the older kids in the group frowned at Malsour's words; one blew raspberries at him.

"Rickard! Put that tongue away!" one of the minders admonished. Rickard frowned and gave Malsour the stink eye.

Malsour laughed inside, smiling as he left the room. Feeling a little more at ease, he went to his workshop.

***

The training staff were all together in the air. The first week of drops had gone better than they hoped. There had been a number of injuries and people hurt; however, even the most serious injuries had been healed up and everyone was okay.

By the end of the first week, they had gotten better and better at the drops and coordinating between the ground forces and those in the sky and the support from within the citadels, taking what they had built up within the Mirror of Communication training and polishing it.

They still didn't drop in their full gear but the different mounted creatures were getting used to the air launch system as well as the drop platforms.

Their coordination with the drop packs and platforms had also increased. Shard had created a mini-game where those with the packs would have to reach circles in the air; once they crossed through them, another circle would appear, leading a path down to the ground. If they were dodging around, trying to get away from enemy fire, then the circles would also move to give them a flight path down to the same position as before.

In addition to the training staff, Florence was there, currently addressing them all.

"We've delivered enough drop packs and platforms to equip two more citadels. Production has picked up and we hope to have another two sets of platforms and drop pads ready within a week. The week after, we should be able to supply three, which is our current limit of production," Florence said to them.

"So two more—that brings us to three. Then we have thirteen remaining citadels. However, the eight in Gudalo are still under development. They will take anywhere from three more weeks to a month to get ready, while the citadels around Goblin Mountain will take two more weeks to be ready to fly." Suzy was managing the citadels' progress; with her organization abilities, she had been able to streamline the citadel upgrade process.

"We mustn't forget that the citadels around Goblin Mountain will also undergo a change, except for Citadel Three in about a week's time," Anna said.

Deia nodded, listening to all they had to say and incorporating it into her own plans.

"Good. I want Citadels Five and Seven to receive the drop packs and the platforms. I want them to move into holding patterns around Citadel Six and Eight respectively. With them up in the air, we will be able to have faster rotations of people doing drops and can extend the training time so that we can add in training fights.

"I want us to ramp things up. We might be only having eight of these crews going into battle in two weeks so I want the best ones to be going. So everything, from now until then, I want you to evaluate them on, while keeping that in mind. We need to have the best crews ready. If they need more time, they can get it while the other citadels are being completed." Deia looked to the training staff.

Seeing their understanding in their eyes, she continued on.

"I have also received word from the Dragons. They will be supporting the citadel offensive. Each of the citadels will have a flying complement of five Dragons. They will be coming this week to work with the flying forces we have already. Each citadel group is to figure out how they wish to incorporate the Dragons into their battle plans."

The people who made up the fighting forces within the citadels were all veterans. Although jumping from a flying citadel was new for them, being able to fire down on their enemy with their spells and cannons was different. They had taken the basics the training staff had given them and were quickly adapting it with their own tactics and thoughts, teaching the training staff a number of things that they hadn't thought of.

"When the citadels undergo their upgrade to stage three defenses, we will have Citadel One hold position in the air while Citadel Five will land in a new position. The rest will land in the craters that they came from. We need to find out if the changes will happen while we're in the air or in different locations or if just in their original positions," Deia said.

Some people made notes on their interfaces while the rest continued to listen.

"Are there any other issues or problems?" Deia asked the training staff and the overseers of the flying citadels.

No one made to raise their hand or indicate that they had anything to say.

"Okay, then let's move on to today's training rota. Florence, can you get those platforms and drop packs out to where they need to be? We'll rotate people through as needed. For today, we'll be doing drops in full gear. We'll gauge each group on how good they are.

From there, we will either have them drop in gear a few more times or have them move on to training battles. First, we'll allow live fire from the ranged forces on the citadel as well as the aerial forces. Once everyone and all the creatures are used to that, we can move to assaulting and defending the citadels. One force will protect the citadel on the ground, while the other will attack them. From there, we let them figure out tactics and see what works and what doesn't."

Deia was just going over what they all knew, hitting the major points to make sure that they hadn't forgotten.

"Questions, issues?" Deia looked at them all. Again, there was no one with anything to say.

"Good—let's go drop some people out of a citadel." Deia rose. The rest of the room moved about as they exited the Mirror of Communication, appearing wherever they had connected to the briefing room.

***

Dave woke with a start. He had a faint headache that came with Mana fatigue. He pulled out a Mana potion, quickly consuming it. His headache fell away.

"Seems that my teleportation skills have increased." Dave let out a short laugh. His eye twitched as he remembered the last time he'd made a breakthrough in theories and collapsed from the excessive stat points. He took a deep breath and looked at the notifications on the side of his screen. His finger stabbed forward, and the notification panel dropped down.

Quest Completed: Master of Space and Time Level 19

Come up with new possible theory (7/7)

Rewards: Unlock Level 20 quest

+15 to Willpower

+15 to Intelligence

+15 to Endurance

+15 to Agility

1,900,000 Experience (6,600,000 Experience accumulated)

Class: Master of Space and Time

Status: Level 19

          Greater understanding of Space and Time.

          +285 to Willpower

Effects: +285 to Intelligence

          +285 to Endurance

          +285 to Agility

Quest: Master of Space and Time Level 20

Come up with new possible theory (7/8)

Rewards: Unlock Level 21 quest

Increase to stats

Active Skill: Teleportation

    Level: Master Level 3

    Effect: Able to create a device to teleport across distances.

He went to check his new character sheet as he felt once again that awe-inspiring power of increasing one's stats. It was a constant feeling that he chased, not only for the physical feeling but the mental goals he had set himself as a gamer.

Character Sheet

Name:	David Grahslagg	Gender:	Male
Level:	255	Class:	Dwarven Master Smith, Friend of the Grey God, Bleeder, Librarian, Aleph Engineer, Weapons Master, Champion Slayer, Skill Creator, Mine Manager, Master of Space and Time, Master of Gravitational Anomalies
Race:	Human/ Dwarf	Alignment:	Chaotic Good

Unspent points: 30

Health:	51,600	Regen:	25.12 /s
Mana:	16,430	Regen:	60.70 /s
Stamina:	5,670	Regen:	52.65 /s
Vitality:	516	Endurance:	1,256
Intelligence:	1,643	Willpower:	1,214
Strength:	567	Agility:	1,053

He had worked with using portals and other devices to teleport with before. He had also used his own abilities to teleport before. Though he hadn't used a combination of his magic with magical coding before.

"It bears looking into. Even with the orbs, I was having them make the spell formation, only putting in information of where I wanted to go. Melding that and my own teleportation abilities might allow me to reach farther and at a greatly reduced cost of Mana," Dave pondered.

He let the thought slide to the back of his mind as he stood and went for a shower. He checked his messages, finding one from Malsour detailing when Captain Xue and his protection detail would be meeting them in the asteroid base. Dave was about to step out the door, before he turned around and headed for the shower.

"If Deia was to hear that I had greeted the only known group of human survivors from the Jukal war in two-day-old clothes, she wouldn't be very happy with me!" Dave said. "Though I wouldn't mind if she was here to shower with me."

Dave had a wide smile on his face.

"Been some time since we got free from it all—I should surprise her." Dave thought on the problem as he showered, got dressed and stepped out of his apartment. He found that he was near the Dracul-run daycare and wandered over.

It was always open and a number of children even slept there as their parents got wrapped up in work, or in some cases they were in Emerilia or on the asteroid base and didn't want to bring them there for fear of being hurt.

Dave walked into the room. The minders around saw Dave and pointed in Koi's direction. He wandered into a room where the children and babies were sleeping; minders were also in here, watching over the children.

They all came from different time zones around Emerilia, so some of them were sleeping while others were awake.

Dave found little Koi sleeping without a care in the world. He stood there for some time, looking at his daughter, a smile on his face.

Malsour contacted him with a party chat. "Dave, you up yet?" Malsour asked.

"No, I'm still asleep. What's up?" Dave shook his head.

"Bob wants to see us and then we're to greet the people from Deq'ual. I've already sorted out the protection detail on our side and Jeeves has locked up the different areas that hold some of our more powerful tech. Our people will be free to walk around but it's to make sure they don't get their hands on too many secrets," Malsour said.

"Nice work. I'll be at Bob's in five minutes," Dave said.

"See you there," Malsour said.

Dave focused on his Touch of the Land spell. He saw Bob working in his laboratory, overseeing the creation chamber where players' bodies were being created every minute. Bob had nearly a dozen helpers who were talking to one another or working on various machines. The science and technology was advanced but they were smart people and quickly coming to understand it.

Dave looked out over all of the ice planet's city. There had originally been nearly one hundred people who had been accepted into the program. Now there was nearly five hundred and more people were being recruited every day.

The wives, husbands, and relatives of those who were working in the asteroid base, moonbase, or the ice planet had all started to look for jobs. Most of them were working with the growing facilities or looking over the running of the city while their other family members worked in various workshops, laboratories, shipyards, and slips.

Pandora's Box within Terra's power station acted as a hub for all of the various locations but all of the materials and projects had been moved from there to the other facilities. Now the facility was a portal hub, with the first teleportation array waiting.

There was also a command center there, as well as armories of different items that they were building.

Dave smiled as he looked out over it all. Ice City, as it was coming to be called, wasn't massive but it was growing at an incredible rate.

Miners were being created from soul gem constructs outside the city to go farther across the ice planet in order to search out deposits of materials that the Pandora's Box Initiative needed.

Everything was starting to come together.

Dave looked down at Koi, just watching her as she slept.

Dave's five minutes ran out in what felt like seconds.

He smiled and disappeared from the room. Using his Touch of the Land, he found a clear spot and appeared in Bob's laboratory.

Malsour was already waiting.

"Looks like we're all here. Okay, so when the *Sprite* showed up, I was going to tell you two that we're ready to start waking people up. I was actually going through some preliminary tests beforehand," Bob said. Dave and Malsour's eyebrows rose in shock. "Now we have to think about how we're going to do this. I suggest that we bring Air in on this. She might be a bit of a prankster at times but she knows how to deal with people and she might be of help to transition these people from Earth's simulation into reality."

"I don't see any issue with it." Dave looked to Malsour.

"I was worried that the transition might create issues. We are, after all, pulling them out from everything they know," Malsour said.

"That's another thing. We're going to have people of all ages coming through—some will think they're eighty; some will think they're twelve. Air is adaptive enough to deal with that. At least I hope," Bob said.

"Well, we're going to be pulling them into a universe they don't know. I think it would be best for Air to not only ease them through the transition but inform us on how these people are. Some of them might lash out at us in anger," Dave said.

"Exactly. Not a discussion I thought I would have in my life, but there it is." Bob shrugged.

"All we can do is our best by them," Dave said.

They were silent for a bit. Facing an uncertain future, they wondered what would happen.

"It's about time that we went and greeted Captain Xue," Malsour said, breaking the thoughtful silence.

"See you later, Bob. And let us know how it goes with Air," Dave said.

"Will do," Bob said.

Dave teleported Malsour and himself across Ice City and to where the portal to the asteroid base was located. The runes in the building around the portal wouldn't allow anyone to teleport within them and cut off all power emissions from the portal.

Dave and Malsour stepped through, passing Aleph fighting automatons that manned the building around the portal, resting in charging racks, ready to be called upon at a moment's notice.

"I've got to remember to go check in on the automaton development team," Dave said.

"We can do that with Captain Xue. I don't think that it would be a secret that we need to hide from him and Sato's people," Malsour said.

"We've got to find out a better name for all of them than just calling them Sato's people," Dave said.

"Well, maybe we can ask them?"

"Always a possibility but how much will they tell us?" Dave captured some atmosphere within his Mana shield and passed through the portal.

"They have been hiding for centuries—giving out where they live and that kind of information will be hard," Malsour said as they appeared in the asteroid base. A number of people were waiting for them, most of them from the Dracul family. Who wouldn't feel safer with a bunch of Dragons backing them up?

"Hopefully this meeting can act as a bridge between our groups, opening up the communication from just sharing information to working together." Dave looked to the waiting guards. "Hello, boys and girls. Ready to go meet some humans?"

"We are humans most of the time," Gelimah said in a grouchy tone. He'd been working to develop magical coding that would reduce the power needed to create a gravitational field.

"I know, but these are like direct descendants from Earth. We're all like vat babies. Go vat!" Dave smiled.

Gelimah shared a look with Malsour.

"Don't ask me—he's always like this. I think Steve's been having an effect on him," Malsour said.

"I-I'm not going to even grace that comment with a response. Steve's..." Dave looked around, as if trying to find the right words to describe Steve. "Well, he's Steve, all right!"

"Very descriptive." The corners of Malsour's mouth rose in an amused smirk.

"Come on, let's go meet the humans. Also, we figured out any way to retain more atmosphere yet? Having to use our shields nearly constantly is a pain." Dave moved away from the portal and toward the shipyard.

"I don't think that we do—the shields work for now," Malsour said.

"I could rig up some orbs for everyone. That way, they'd have defensive capabilities and they would adapt to the gravity, atmosphere, and temperature of the various planets and places that we go," Dave said. "Using just Mana shields to capture the heat and then relying on coded clothes to retain heat seems like an easy way for someone to forget one spell and get injured."

"Your orbs could do that?" Malsour asked. Dave was always pretty secretive with what the hidden orbs around him could do.

"Yes, though the ones that I'm using are rather complicated and need me to manage them. However, for someone else, I would need to take out most of that command function and make them automatic." Dave pondered on this for a while.

"It would be a good project to work on. We've got people who have to come in from the outer reaches of the ice planet and the asteroid base every few hours or so because their Mana pool can't keep up with the draw," Sola, who had been put in charge of the mining projects for the asteroid base and the ice planet, said.

"We can't have that. It's a safety concern. I'll get working on it once we're done with this meeting," Dave said. "We might also be able to pass it on to the Terra Alliance. If we altered the wavelengths of the shield or Mana barrier, working with the Band-Aid it might be able to block out the Jukal's kill signal. Would raise our chances of stopping people from being hit by it. The onos and their transmission Magical Circuits are good at covering a large area but the possibility of the signal making it past without expending a truly massive amount of power is too high."

"Let me know if you need any help with the coding. I don't have any projects currently on my hands," Malsour said.

"Sounds like a good idea to me." Dave smiled at Malsour. The two of them worked well together.

"Sensors have picked up a shuttle departing from the *Sprite*," Gelimah said.

"Well, let's go say hi." Dave smiled. They disappeared from where they had been walking, Dave once again using his teleportation abilities.

***

Captain Xue sat in the shuttle's main bay. Ten people were within the bay, eight of them crew members who had advanced weapons training. All of them were armored up. Their armor covered their entire bodies, leaving only a black face shield. They were all carrying standard rifles and side arms.

Underneath the armored exteriors, there were multiple coded panels that augmented the people underneath.

If Dave was to look at them, he would think that there were a lot of similarities with his original Abscondita armor.

All of their weapons had faint runes on them that had been machined into them.

Captain Xue wore armor as well but his face plate was clear, unlike the others.

The two pilots were talking to each other and to the *Sprite* as they flew from the ship toward a massive asteroid. Even with scanners going at full blast, they hadn't been able to detect anything within this monstrous rock.

They proceeded to the marker that was set down for them.

"All right, remember we're here to learn and meet with these people, no overt combative actions. Only on my command or unless we come under fire are you to react. We are here as representatives of the Deq'ual systems. Make sure that your Mirrors of Communication are active at all times and report anything suspicious." Captain Xue repeated the same instructions he had given them before boarding the shuttle.

The repetition calmed them down.

"Five minutes till we reach the way point," one of the pilots reported.

"Check your weapons and your safeties," the chief in charge of the security detail said.

Everyone pulled back the charging handles, chambering a round, and placed their weapons on safe, pointing them at the shuttle's floor.

Captain Xue connected his visor; the shuttle's sensors allowed him to see in front of the shuttle. Just as they were about to reach the way point, a section of the asteroid depressed inward a few meters, rolling apart in sections to reveal a tunnel with running lights leading into the asteroid.

"Captain?" the pilots asked.

"Proceed inward." Xue sounded calm even as inside he felt his nerves rolling about.

The shuttle stopped decreasing its speed and instead increased, passing into the tunnel.

The asteroid's walls closed behind them. They were covered in runic lines that started glowing as soon as all the sections of the hatch were once again in place.

Xue was looking at the walls that were made out of what looked like a smooth glass-like material.

"What are the walls made of?" Xue asked.

"The composition looks to be soul gem," the secondary pilot said.

We've been experimenting with making the inside of large areas with soul gem constructs, but even those areas are not even a hundredth of the size of this. If this asteroid is all made out from soul gem on the inside? How much power must that take? Xue knew that soul gem constructs needed a ton of power in order to keep growing and running. The coding that was placed on them was highly complex. To cover this entire asteroid was a massive achievement.

Armored doors opened ahead of them and closed behind them as they passed through. Finally, an armored door opened and they found themselves coming out of the side of a massive open area.

Xue's eyes went wide as he looked around. They were inside a massive shipyard.

There were slips for new ships along one of the walls, floor, and roof. It was clear that the shipyard was still under construction by the fact that mining drills were still cutting away sections of the wall to create more room for slips on the floor and roof, as well as carve out more slips on the wall. To either side of the shuttle, the asteroid stretched outward, excavators and mining drills at work to expand the interior of the shipyard.

"We have been given a way point to a landing position," the secondary pilot said.

"Take us in slowly," Xue said, still looking around the massive shipyard. It was already three times the size of the third shipyard in the Deq'ual system. He looked at the slips where superstructures were being formed even as soul gem constructs were growing over them. He looked at three destroyers that looked almost completed from the outside as well as the massive battleship that calmly looked over all, its hull complete. But shuttles and various automatons crawled all over it, entering and exiting through hangars and access points to work on the interior. Another battleship was being created behind it.

The rest of the slips were filled with the same miners that sensors had picked up on the asteroid, as well as the massive excavators that could hollow out asteroids.

How are they thinking of getting these massive ships out? How did they do it before with the battleship? Xue looked at the battleship and then the rest of the base. There was only one access point in and out of the asteroid base right now and Xue had entered through it. Shuttles now moved past them, leaving the asteroid to go and pick up cargoes from the various miners and excavators around the asteroid belt.

So the question remained, how did the battleship leave?

Xue's eyes fell on a slip that was growing something completely made from soul gem constructs. He was linked back to the Deq'ual system and was able to talk to them. He opened up a channel to them through his Mirror of Communication. "Does anyone know what this is?"

"It—it looks like a portal."

Xue was shocked as Edwards's voice passed into his ear. He never thought that Edwards would be there.

"Isn't it a bit large?" Sato asked.

"It isn't if you mean to put ships through it!" Edwards said excitedly.

"Still, it isn't operational and I don't see any way that the battleship would have been able to get out of this shipyard," Xue said.

"Well, they must have a way to jump in-system then," Edwards said simply.

Even with the things that Xue had seen, he wasn't able to stop his eyes from going wide at the revelation. To have the ability to teleport in-system was something that had only been theorized. One would need extremely powerful sensors as well as a jump drive that was calibrated to the highest degree so that there was no chance of it being off course.

"Seems that Dave has been busy," Sato said. Xue could hear the amusement in Sato's voice.

"It looks like he's come to understand the Jukal portals to the point of knowing how to build them himself. He's probably the only person outside of the Jukal Empire," Edwards said.

"Those ships are heavier than ours and look at the rate at which they're being completed. With those soul gem constructs, the power usage must be astronomical—however, they're completing one as fast as it would take us to build a stealth craft," Adams added.

Xue was silent, taking this all in as the shuttle made its way across the shipyard.

Here and there, the sensors on the craft picked up people who were working on different items. Most of them wore magically coded clothes and shoes but they didn't wear atmospheric suits at all.

"Are these readings right on the atmosphere outside?" Xue asked.

"Yes sir—little atmosphere, low gravity," the secondary pilot reported.

"And they're out there working in pants and shirts," Adams said, sounding shocked.

"Seems that Dave is well ahead of us," Edwards said.

Xue looked at the different people around: dwarves, elves, Beast Kin, demons, orcs, gnomes, and all manner of races that he had only read about in fantasy books. It was all a bit too surreal.

The shuttle slowly came in to land. There was no one to greet them as the shuttle passed through the hangar bay doors, into an area filled with containers and shuttles. There were automated carts collecting storage crates from the massive containers and whisking them off across the asteroid base.

One second, there was no one near the shuttle; the next, there was a party of six standing at the rear of the shuttle.

"Individual jumping? How is that even possible?" Edwards said incredulously.

"Ready to lower ramp," the primary pilot said.

"Everyone ready!" the chief reported.

"Lower ramp," Captain Xue said.

The ramp at the rear of the shuttle came down, revealing the soul gem-covered hangar and the six people waiting for them. Four were humans; one was a dwarf and the other looked to be a taller dwarf.

Xue recognized Malsour and Dave. Dave wore casual pants and a t-shirt; Malsour wore a black cloak and leather vest with comfortable black pants.

The other humans also wore cloaks with various colored interiors.

The dwarf studied everyone as they filed out of the shuttle, crossing her arms as she watched. She wore a tool belt and her beefy body filled out her smithing clothes that were burnt and stained in places.

They were talking among one another but Xue couldn't hear anything.

The protection detail looked around, alert but not overtly hostile.

Xue left the ship, passing the security detail, and moved toward the group of six.

Dave moved forward, saying something, before he frowned. He continued forward more.

Xue's armor's sensors registered that he had passed through a barrier of some kind that had breathable atmosphere and was comfortably warm inside.

"Sorry about that. Forgot you didn't have the party chat feature and weren't in the same atmosphere as me. My name's Dave. You must be Captain Xue. You got Sato and Edwards listening in?" Dave held out his hand.

Xue took the hand and shook it. "Thank you for having us. That's correct and they are listening in," Xue said with a nervous smile, his actions wooden. He was still in a bit of shock. This was the first time anyone in the Deq'ual system had ever shook someone's hand who didn't come from the same system.

"All right, well, have we got the tour for you!" Dave smiled, letting go of Xue's hand. "What do you think of our asteroid base?"

"It's rather impressive," Xue said.

"Pretty cool. Though we're in the midst of expanding so should be a lot more going on in the near future." Dave smiled and then looked back to the group that had come closer. "Malsour, what's the plan for the tour?"

"Well, they've seen the asteroid base, so on to Ice City, have a look around at various ongoing projects—some food and talking. I was thinking the moonbase but their Mirrors of Communication won't reach that far in signal," Malsour said.

"Shame—that'd be pretty cool. Oh well, on to Ice City?" Dave looked to Xue.

"Please, lead on," Xue said. Whatever he had been expecting, it had not been that Dave would treat this like just showing people around his house. He was so relaxed and laid-back that Xue was a bit in shock at it.

Dave did so. His group held off to the side as Xue's security detail did the same on the other side, looking around for threats and also keeping a close eye on the people who had come to greet them.

"Okay, so here we're building some large projects—warships, portals and the like. We hope to use these in order to attain Emerilia's freedom. To supply this, we've got many miners and excavators working in the surrounding asteroid, as you saw. All of those raw materials pass through here, and currently go to a refinery in Ice City, located on the ice planet that you lot found out about from the spectral analysis I asked for," Dave said.

"Once materials are refined, they're sent to factories in one of the bases to be turned into useful components that are shipped out to various bases in order to fulfill their needs. We're using a network of portals to move materials and people from the different bases. Makes it a lot easier to move items and faster. However, it's a massive power draw," Dave explained as they walked.

Captain Xue naturally knew about the portals; they were one of the biggest reasons that humanity had been pushed back and then destroyed. They were seen as the backbone of the Jukal Empire. They allowed fleets to pass over vast areas in an instant, allowing the Jukal Empire to continuously bring fresh forces up and send back their wounded ships and people to bring them up to fighting condition.

This was how humanity had been destroyed: the Jukal, with their unending waves of reinforced and re-armed fleets and forces.

Dave was talking about them as if they were as simple as a wooden doorway.

Xue pushed down his immediate reactions, thinking on the portals that he had seen being built in the shipyard. If they were to be completed, then they, too, would allow the forces under Dave's command, to move between systems.

"I see that other than the weapons on the ships that you don't have any personal items," Xue asked, perplexed. His people were all wearing armor while Dave and the others were just in simple clothes.

"Not everything is as it appears," Dave said. In a moment, he was wearing armor and twin batons; the next, they had changed back into his normal appearance.

"Also, those guns don't mean much of a threat to us. With their highest power setting, it would take hundreds of rounds to penetrate any one of our barriers here. Also, the runing on the powered armor—while it is good and allows you to move freely—your power sources and the power retention in them isn't good enough," Dave said. "I have the ability to look through nearly anything that isn't stealth runed—which, by the way, good work with the stealth ships there. They're not bad. We've been constantly working on upgrading our ability to sense stealth ships as well as increase our own stealth. Tell Edwards to start working on improving—I'm not going to give him the answers every time," Dave said in an admonishing tone.

"Well, I would if it wasn't for that damn board jumping all over my ass saying that I'm going to blow up the shipyard," Edwards, who was still connected to Xue's headset via the Mirror of Communication, mumbled.

Xue felt awkward, being in the middle of the conversation between these groups.

"Malsour, am I forgetting anything?" Dave asked.

Malsour had been watching all of them, studying their actions and their gear. He seemed like a reserved man, but in his eyes; he looked like a wise old man, even with the appearance of being in his late twenties.

"Most of the people you will see here are not military experts. They haven't been in battles. Most of the people here are actually researchers and those we have taken on in order to lighten the load of the work we have been placed under. So please don't react with hostility. There are a number of children about as well in Ice City. Everyone has been informed that you are coming, so there might be a number of people staring and talking to one another," Malsour said as they stepped out of the hangar and into a main corridor.

They were now deep in the asteroid's side. Runic lines ran through the walls. A strip of them created light; the others connected to the various ships.

They passed a corridor where people were walking up and down, some of them on carts. There were various workshops and different rooms, all with runic lines going into them.

"Ask what those lines are," Edwards said.

"What are the lines on the walls and floor?" Xue asked.

"They're called runic lines. The magical coding for this place, if it was to be all laid out, would need something like fifteen times the size in order to just fit them all. The AIs compressed down the magical code, thought it didn't work when carving it out. We found that with the soul gem constructs, it is possible to create runic lines. They can carry information, power and even be turned into light sources," the dwarf said.

"That's Sola," Dave said.

She grunted to them all.

"I never thought of magical coding being compressed down to such a state. If that's possible, then I could tear out those old cannons and replace them with the modified cannons we've been working on!" Edwards said in a rush.

"Edwards, we're here to watch what's going on. Make a note of it and stop dancing around." Sato sighed.

Xue kept silent as he listened to the byplay.

"That's impressive," Xue said.

"Well, it certainly makes things easier," Malsour said.

People looked up from their work and stared at the party. All of them wore magically coded clothes but didn't seem affected by the fact that there was no atmosphere within the asteroid base.

"What's this?" Xue asked as they walked toward a hardened-looking building that stuck out of the asteroid. There were rune-covered machines patrolling the area.

"This is a portal location. We have automatons on staff so that they can deal with any threat that comes through these portals. If one of the portal locations is found out, we can shut down the network and make sure no one else comes through," Malsour said, his voice somber.

"We didn't have the manpower to hire not only people to help with the projects but also those who could help with defense. We don't have much room here and the more people who are helping out here, the more who disappear from Emerilia. Too many people and then the Jukal and the AI might start paying attention and then bring everything right down on top of our heads," Dave said.

Malsour sighed and shook his head.

"What? They know we're here and they're seeing us, so what? We have a low defense force right now—but we have enough grand workings to blow up a sun," Dave said.

Malsour stared at Dave.

"Shouldn't have said that?" Dave asked.

"Probably not the best idea," Malsour admitted.

"Sorry, dude," Dave said to Xue. "Just got a lot of firepower here. We're working on upgrading our automatons and we have a bunch of people working out our offensive abilities."

They stepped past the automatons standing guard around the hardened portal location. People who were walking out of the portal location stopped their conversations upon seeing Xue and his people.

Xue stared at them. It was hard not to, seeing them up close and finding out that they were real. It made his heart beat faster to know that Deq'ual was truly not the last human group in the entire universe. They were so different from him but they had been all grown from human DNA. He had seen people in weirder styles back on Deq'ual at times so he didn't pay too much attention to the different forms that they came in.

Carts raced past the groups in a near constant stream, passing through special doorways built into the building holding the portal. Carts were constantly moving, piled with storage crates or towing storage containers like the ones that the shuttles carried back and forth from the miners. They passed through a number of open hatches before coming in front of a portal. The room they were in was filled with automatons that watched the other side. The room that they could see through the portal looked identical to the one that they were in, complete with runic lines and guards.

Dave and his party led the way, the carts pausing to allow them through.

Xue stepped through the portal, expecting to feel something. Instead, he just found himself on the other side.

They quickly stepped off to the side. Carts came out behind them in one direction as other carts entered the portal in the other direction.

"Welcome to Ice City, currently the home for the development team of the Pandora's Box Initiative," Dave said as they weaved through armored doors once again and battle automatons before they reached the exit.

Dave and the group continued on but Captain Xue stopped. Even the security detail paused in shock as they looked out over the true city.

Carts raced through the air, moving people and materials to and fro.

A massive sprawling industrial complex was growing off to the side of the city. The city was still undergoing growth as miners and excavators mined out sections around the city.

Flying automatons were pulling out metal structural pieces, adding it together as if they were parts of a jigsaw, creating the inner superstructure of multiple buildings.

Soul gem constructs across the city were growing up these support members. As they traveled upward, they expanded outward to meet up with one another, creating floors, then walls and then ceilings, complete with room for elevators, stairs, and the rest.

The refineries and factories were a buzz of activity as raw materials were taken in and finished products shuttled outward. The soul gem constructs all took on a bluish appearance, with flares of silver and transparent areas. The soul gem constructs were easily able to mimic any possible color.

The light was delicate on the eyes instead of overpowering. All around the city, there was ice. The city looked as if it belonged to some realm of old.

Even though they were surrounded by ice, the temperature was comfortable and there was an actual breathable atmosphere. In various buildings, plants could be seen growing and people walked around and talked to one another.

There were gardens and places to sit down for food. Apartments rose here and there; a sprawling complex of offices with all manner of different facilities connected to the industrial complex and also expanded into the city.

The portal facility was off from the city and had multiple automatons on it.

Xue's eyes fell on a similarly armored structure a bit away from the city with heavy runic lines and an automaton force that must have been three or four times more than the portal facility that they were at.

"It's something, isn't it?" Dave paused as well as he saw that they were looking at the city.

Xue could only nod, left speechless by this city.

"He didn't just mine the ice planet—he made a city within it," Adams said in a whisper.

"It doesn't look like there's enough residents to fill the city yet, maybe he's still recruiting?" Edwards asked.

"Or maybe it's a fallback position if something happens to Emerilia," Sato said.

"It's incredible. Even with everything that's happening, you've been able to carve out a place to live here," Xue said.

"Well, this isn't anything compared to Terra, only about a sixth the size and with twenty-four times less usable space. But here we have room to expand easily, unlike Terra, which is a pain in the ass to mine out and then form into a livable area." Dave looked out over the city.

This isn't much. I know from what people have been saying that Terra is supposed to be a massive facility on Emerilia, but then I never really thought it would live up to what they were saying.

After a few moments, Malsour cleared his throat. "Shall we proceed to the testing facilities?"

"I'm game. Xue?" Dave asked.

"Certainly." Captain Xue regained his composure.

"Sola, Draculs, if you want to go back to whatever you were doing, that's fine," Dave said.

A man in a black cloak and similar features to Malsour clapped his hands and grinned.

"Gravity coding, here I come." With a run and a leap, wings tore out of his back. His body elongated and turned scaly, forming into a massive Dragon.

The other humans also changed and flew away—some toward the offices, others toward the city proper.

"Damn Dragons showing off," Sola complained under her breath. "See you later, Dave."

"See ya, Sola. Let me know if you need any help with the mining," Dave said.

"I'll let you know. Malsour, if you've got any free time, I'd be interested on your input into the processing asteroids and refining asteroid plans," Sola said.

"Once I'm done here, I'll find you." Malsour smiled.

"Later!" Sola threw out a metal plate under her feet that connected to the floor and rushed off.

Xue was left in shock at what he'd seen. His security detail also looked at the Dragons, who were now landing in the city.

"Never seen a Dragon before, huh? You'll get used to it." Dave chuckled, sharing a look with an amused Malsour.

"Uh, no," Xue said.

"Don't worry—we'll try to be gentle." Malsour's eyes turned into vertical irises as he smiled.

"You're a Dragon too?" Xue asked. It took him a moment in order to make sure that his voice wasn't trembling.

"Yes, I am—since the day I was born. Don't worry, you'll get used to it," Malsour said.

"In here, we have people from all manner of races from mer people to Beast Kin, demons, humans, dwarves, and elves of every variety. The kinds of races that were made on Emerilia at first only grew with time. There are hundreds of races and sub-races, with thousands of creatures littered all over the place. Which can be a real pain in the ass when you go adventuring and you run into fifteen types of creatures you don't recognize," Dave grumbled.

Malsour chuckled a bit as they walked toward the city.

Xue and the rest of the security detail were left in shock as they continued after the duo, looking over the city as people walked past them with interest in their eyes as they talked to their peers.

However, even as they were talking, Xue couldn't pick up what they were saying, even with his amplification cranked all the way up.

"Why is it that we can't hear anyone talking?" Xue asked.

"Most of them are using the private chat feature. The Jukal can't hack it and well, we told them about the Jukal and all the measures that we use on Emerilia to stay under their radar. They started to adapt over some of the ideas we had and now they use them in their everyday lives. Think of it as conditioning. If they do it here, then they're bound to use it in places where the Jukal's network would pick them up and they can listen in," Dave said.

The more Xue learned about the people within the Nal system and the things that they were doing, the more he felt as though he were losing his grip with reality.

"Growing lab?" Dave looked to Malsour.

"That works. I'll message them." Malsour opened his interface. A few moments later, his mouth moved but no noise came out. Xue wasn't able to truly focus on his lips to read what he was saying.

"Dragons, real life Dragons," Adams said.

"To build all of this... We underestimated them again. Who knows how long it will be before they're able to mobilize a fleet? Emerilia is surrounded by enemy forces and they are waging a massive battle on the surface, but still they have all of this behind the scenes. If they were to pull out even a tenth of the strength that they had hidden here, they could turn the battles on Emerilia on their heads," Edwards said.

"Look at the citadels—are they not turning the world on its head with those?" Sato asked.

Chapter 16: Inventions and Progress

Dave and Malsour had taken Xue through the different parts of the city and showed off their normal apartments, which were a shock to them. It seemed that they were living rather cramped back wherever they came from.

The growing towers and areas were an eye-opener for them. They had been experimenting with making their crops grow faster but here they were used to not only create food, but also supply organic materials needed for experiments and to convert a mix of chemicals into breathable atmosphere that was pumped out into Ice City.

They'd gone through the refinery and looked upon the massive mines that were constantly harvesting materials from the ice planet.

Now, for the last part of their trip, they were paying a visit to the automaton workshop.

Dave was excited to take a look. It was his hope to work here; and help in making automatons that were better than what they could get from the Aleph and were purposely built to help in the creation of the warships and other projects, as well as the mining and refining.

They entered the workshop of the automaton group. Machines were all over the place and a number of them were in assembly stages or, for the Aleph creations, were actually disassembled. There were piles of metal ingots, various smithy workstations, soul gem constructs and tables all over the place.

"Dave!" Dwarven Master Smith Quino called out.

"Hey, Quino. Where's Kol at?" Dave asked.

"He's hammering out a central support member for our newest project—well, spreading it out, I guess, with his skill," Quino said.

"I thought that he was supposed to go back to the smithy in Terra?" Dave asked.

"Jesal is covering for him, though she's demanding more time over here because of it." Quino grinned.

"I give you lot one place to play around and you all jump on it." Dave sighed as the corner of his lips raised in a smile.

"You brat! You're in here all the time!" Quino said, also with a smile on his face.

"Hey, I built the damn thing," Dave complained.

"This must be Xue and his people from the *Sprite*?" Quino pointed to Xue and his armored people.

"Yep. Captain Xue, meet dwarven master smith and member of the Council of Anvil and Fire, Mister Quino." Dave waved to Quino.

"Calling me mister—only my father's called mister. You're making me sound old," Quino said in a disgruntled voice.

"You're nearly two hundred years old!" Dave said.

"Exactly—in the prime of my life! Nice to meet you, Captain Xue and armored dudes." Quino waved to Xue and the others. "They got runes on their armor?"

"Yes, they've got runes on their armor," Dave said in a defeated voice.

Quino rubbed his hands in excitement.

"And you're not to start asking them about how they made them inside the armor panels." Dave waved his finger at Quino.

Quino's face fell. Watching him, one wouldn't think that he was a two-hundred-year-old dwarf but rather a mischievous kid getting told off by his mother.

"Though you can show them around and let me know what you've been up to. Just got free from portal development with Ela-Dorn. Hopefully the first portal will work—take a week till it's complete but if it works then we can put that into the big ones," Dave said.

"Come to join the dark side, eh? You just want some of my fine aged dwarven whiskey!" Quino said.

"Now that you mention it, that doesn't sound bad." Dave tapped his chin thoughtfully.

"Quino, tour?" Malsour said in stilted words.

"Right, oh scaly arse from above! Welcome to my workshop."

"Our workshop!" Kol yelled out from a back room that had been converted into a smithy.

"*OUR* workshop," Quino amended, giving that back room a dirty look. "Here, our main idea is to take the various automatons that are used throughout the bases part of the Pandora's Box Initiative and improve upon them or to make more types that are able to speed up the process of building the various projects that we have underway." Quino's attitude turned to that of a teacher instead of his normally childish behavior.

"We have worked with the miners and the excavators to improve them from their base designs. But now we're looking at creating various automatons for specific jobs.

"We've got haulers to move items to and from storage chests across places that have a gravity and those that don't. We've also got welders that can fuse metals together, speeding up the process of building large metallic structures. This is good for the creation of superstructures as well as the building of armored panels. There are extruding automatons—these have soul gem limbs that allow them to work in smaller places, work with soul gem constructs as well as create different tools with their soul gem limbs.

"The manipulation type automatons are good for more diverse jobs. They're a medium-size build and can do most jobs, at a slower pace but they can be everywhere." As Quino talked, he pointed at different tables and areas that held parts and semi-assembled automatons.

"When I was looking through the battleship, I found that there were a number of issues. For the third one, I was wondering if we would have these automatons ready. If we do, then I want to see if we can group people together and do a ground-up build—see where these issues are coming from. From that, we can update the other battleships and then leave it up to Jeeves to work on the remaining ships," Dave said.

"We've got the basic ideas down, but the factories needed to assemble these, it might take a few months. If we're willing to use more of the automatons and repair bots, then we can cut that down to a week or two," Quino said.

"Sounds good to me." Dave had been hoping that Jeeves would have been able to make the ships all by himself. Looking through the battleship's coding when he was working with it and studying it with his Touch of the Land.

Even if they allowed the other ships to be made at the same time, it wouldn't be a great loss. With the combination of soul gem constructs and the new automatons adapting the older versions of the battleships to whatever they came up with would at most take a few days.

Kol came out of the workshop that he was in, with what looked like a spine with overlapping plates midway up it in his hands. He put it on a table. The heat still came off it as the runes on the table quickly pulled the heat from what he'd been forging.

It had been formed with silver and ebony metal fused together, as well as a number of trace minerals and metals. Kol had gained a great interest in searching out new permutations of metals and materials to improve his smithing. With his smithing art Blind Man's Touch, he was able to easily find a resonance with the metal that he was using and to greater understand what every manner and mixture of material would create.

"What's that?" Dave looked at the metal contraption.

"This is the backbone of the new automatons. They're too inflexible and based off using just metal to create them. I took some inspiration from our own bodies. This spinal column is hollowed out and will have a soul gem construct grown inside. With a certain mixture of soul gem and various materials, it is possible to turn it into a flexible material, much like ligaments instead of simply a hard one." Kol smiled. "It can also be as strong as steel."

Dave had a look of shock on his face.

"To have flexible soul gems, and at that strength, the number of things that we could use that for—we could save a massive amount of time, allowing them to follow paths that the regular sheet-like soul gem constructs wouldn't be able to." Malsour sounded lost but his brain quickly caught on as his eyes filled with excitement. If they had this kind of information and ability before, they wouldn't have needed to sink the roots of the metal into the ground underneath the citadels. The soul gem could have used its malleable state to instead grow outward instead of from on top of the metallic superstructure.

"It will also make creating these automatons a lot faster. With the right magical coding, we can grow out different arms and various tools from this spine unit. We've been looking at having different machines for different uses and it's a good idea, but with this, it could have presets, directly replacing the repair bots. It could carry items, weld them, work with magical coding—acting as an extension of Jeeves," Kol said.

"I am currently running simulations and I believe that the time savings of this automaton with current rough models and with a three percent variation, we could save twelve percent production time. With increased data and greater use, in time, I believe that this number will increase," Jeeves said from above.

"That's incredible—bring a build time of ten days down to nine. The resource costs would simply be this base spine unit and the metal plating. The soul gem constructs, now that we've got the factories up and running at full blast, aren't an issue. We've got plenty of power and the mines in the ice planet are yielding high fuel numbers." Dave talked it over, thinking on it.

"You never said that you were working on this." Quino looked over the construct.

"Well, right now, it's really rough. I don't know enough about magical coding or soul gems workings, only about altering their material characteristics. I melded the two together and it seems like it would be possible." Kol shrugged.

"The interior of this isn't bad, could use some refinement, but I don't see too many issues with it," Quino said, a grin appearing as he looked to Dave. "Well, looks like we'll be able to do that build faster and sooner than you thought!"

"It'll take a few days to get this unit grown and test it out, but afterward we should be able to make the various parts pretty easily," Kol said.

"Okay, well, let us know if you need anything. This could be a massive boost to our production," Malsour said.

Captain Xue cleared his throat. The group had forgotten about Xue and his security detail.

"Ah, sorry about that. Well, these two have a lot to work on so we're off to look at Jeeves's processing plants. You probably won't find this as fun, but I know Edwards will and it will also mean delayed reaction times on your fire programs if you're using AI and other computer programs in order to use your weapons and other systems within your craft." Dave smiled.

***

"What can you tell us about the situation within the system Nal?" one of the Deq'ual system councillors asked Sato, who sat in front of the entire council.

Council Leader Wong sat in the center of the council members, also looking down upon Sato.

"Captain Xue and his protection detail were shown around the asteroid base and the location known as Ice City within the Nal system. They have now returned to their craft safe and unharmed. They were watched the entire time by Mirrors of Communication to make sure that there were no issues. We were able to learn of a great variety of technologies that Edwards and his people are working on to develop and understand to a greater degree. We hope to be able to bring this information and these creations to the rest of the people within the Deq'ual system," Sato said.

"What were their military capabilities?" another councillor asked, sounding a bit bored with what Sato had already stated.

"We know that the people within Nal have advanced stealth technology, born from the magical coding system that we ourselves use. They also have sensor units that are better than our own. We do not know of their weapon capabilities nor do we know fully what their power plant situation, armor or other shielding is like. We do know that they currently have three large ships under construction. They refer to them as destroyers. We do not know their capabilities at this time but it is thought that they are built to enter and exit atmosphere. They have a variety of weapons. They have two more massive ships that are also under construction.

"They are referred to as battleships. They appear to be more heavily armed and armored. They also either have an incredibly powerful ability to do small jumps in-system, or they are able to stealth themselves, easily avoiding our sensors. Both of these ship types do not have any what we would call normal drive systems. They do seem to have the ability to move in space but we have not yet seen this," Sato said.

"What kind of threat do you think that they present?" a new councillor asked.

Sato couldn't stop himself from frowning. "It is my opinion that they are not a threat to us. They have no information of where we are or what our true capabilities are. They have allowed us to see within their base that they are keeping a secret from the rest of the universe. Ice City is not only a location that they use to innovate and work on new technologies that will aide them in throwing off the Jukal. It is the home of the majority of the people who work on the Pandora's Box Initiative. They accepted us, not only to see what their abilities are but to see their families. They have shown again and again their trust in us and have given us information that has allowed us to greatly advance our own capabilities and strengths."

"Commander, there is no need to be defensive. We simply need to know if they are a threat or if they are someone who can help us attain our goals," another councillor said.

Sato kept his words down as he heard the tone of the councillor. It didn't sound as if they cared about the trust displayed—only the threat of the people in Nal and what they could get out of them.

The second councillor to talk spoke up again. "Would they be willing to give us their plans on their ships?"

Although the councillor didn't outwardly display it and the question seemed innocent, Sato had been in these circles enough by now to see the greed in the councillors' eyes and the way that a number of them leaned forward.

With the boost in how the military was doing things and the conditions within Deq'ual had been improved, the councillors had gained more power and they liked to have the people on their side.

"I do not believe that they will and that it might strain relationships between our two groups if we were to ask them," Sato said in a voice devoid of emotion.

The second councillor seemed to have a thoughtful look on his face as Council Leader Wong spoke up.

"If it was up to you, what would you do, considering this recent development?" Wong asked.

"I believe that this is a good opportunity to create an outpost within the Nal system near the asteroid base. We have been talking about plans to create a forward-operating base to be used if and when we begin our offensive against the Jukal and to also act as a place to send out stealth craft from. There is no population in the Nal system other than the people from Emerilia. It is perfect to create a base. It would also allow us to strengthen ties with the people of Emerilia and we could start to trade resources and items," Sato said.

"What kind of items?" the third councillor asked.

"Growing beds, automatons, items that would make our people's lives easier while also increasing our production, both in speed and quality," Sato said.

Before the tech that Edwards had been using to make ships and the shipyards, the council would have fought tooth and nail to build any warships. Now, with the extra resources and people being excited that they were actually doing something, they were happy to continue with making more ships. Changing the plans and upgrading them, however, that was being controlled by the Deq'ual leadership.

One of the councillors made to speak. Sato, reading their body language, quickly spoke.

"I believe it is of *military importance* that we place an outpost within the system Nal."

A few of the councillors' faces went darker for a few moments.

Sato had clearly seen that the councillor who had made to speak was looking to take a break from this meeting in order to talk to her allies. If they had enough time, then they would wrap it all up in red tape until Sato essentially gave them control of it. Once he stated that the military thought it was important, because the military had the people on their side, it became much harder to slow the process and wrest control to themselves and thus take the credit for everything while placing the blame on the military for anything that went wrong.

Sato saw a look of approval on Wong's face.

"I believe that we should then put this to a vote, whether or not to fund a mission to create an outpost in the Nal system. It will be responsible for creating a safe harbor for our forces away from the Deq'ual system as well as building a stronger relationship with the people of Emerilia." Wong looked to the council.

The council quickly voted. Wong read the results when it was all said and done. She looked up at Sato with a blank expression, hiding her emotions.

"Very well, Commander Sato. You are given permission to create an outpost within the Nal system. I expect a plan of action in front of this council within the next few days," Wong said.

"Yes, Council Leader." Sato nodded slightly.

"Very well. Are there any more questions? Otherwise, I believe it would be best to address the people of the Deq'ual system and tell them that we are not the only known spacefaring human group that we know of and that we have made allies in the Nal system," Wong said. Her words mobilized the councillors.

Even though it was the military that had done it, they would use it to bring themselves into a better light with the people.

Sato didn't care as he had gained the approval he needed in order to create his outpost.

Chapter 17: Weapons of War

"They've shaped up faster than I had hoped," Lox said. He and Deia stood on top of Citadel One. Behind them, the artillery crews were hard at work, moving around rounds. They were just using training rounds that would let off flares of light where they would strike, not harming anyone but allowing the crews to work on their accuracy.

The aerial forces were moving constantly, making it hard for the defenders to peg them with their training weapons as well. They were erratic and almost suicidal at times but it flowed. Their communication skills had been good to start within their own units but now they were working with multiple units. They had trained and trained until they could communicate throughout the aerial forces, ground forces, and citadel forces to coordinate their actions.

The five Dragons were like heavy bombers being protected by the lighter aerial forces. The aerial forces fought off the biggest attacks from the defending citadel while the Dragons unleashed illuminating spells that showed where they would hit.

Mages and ranged fighters from the citadel added in their own fire, working with the artillery and the ground forces to suppress the defending citadel.

From the skies, the citadel's forces had dropped in a dense stream. They had filled the sky with platforms and those wearing drop packs. Through training, their ability to trust their gear and focus on what they needed to do instead of what might happen had taken over.

Here and there, the defenders would knock out those coming from the citadel but Deia had faith that they would quickly rectify these issues, evolving their battle plans.

The speed at which they dropped out was much faster, not allowing the defenders to pick them off at leisure. And they were even quicker to move into formation; groups would land close together, quickly assembling into their units and advancing upon the defenders.

The dwarven shield units as well as the various skirmishing, ranged, and mounted units that they brought with them charged toward the enemy as soon as they formed up like an unending swarm. Anything that had a ranged ability worked to suppress the defending citadel and give these forces the cover and time they needed in order to close with the enemy.

"Feels like a lifetime ago that we were training together in the Kufo'tel forest, with me teaching you lot the basics of scouting," Deia said, a fond smile on her face.

Lox snorted. "Fat lot of good that did. I remember Deli ripping the loudest fart on the first scouting excursion we went on!"

"Scared the deer we were stalking right off!" Deia laughed and shook her head, her smile dimming.

"What's on your mind, lass?" Lox asked, seeing Deia's expression.

"Just, you know, a number of us won't make it back from all of this. We're not only fighting the event, the gods are also stirring and the Jukal await us. If we're to survive, we're going to have to show our true strength at some time, and doing that will mean that the Jukal will descend upon us with all they have." Deia looked at those forces assaulting and defending Citadel Two. "How many must die for us to get our freedom?"

They stood there in silence, looking down upon those they had worked with for five weeks to train and make them capable of fighting from the flying citadels.

"Too many," Lox said, his soft voice in contrast to his build. His eyes held sadness in them as he took in the glorious sight of those fighting.

They captured that moment in time, not because they loved to see people fighting and training, but because no matter the training that they gave them, some would live, some would die, but here and now they were alive and they were giving their all to survive—to win.

Even in the sadness of the moment, they wore proud smiles. Proud in the strength of those who had come together to fight for their families, their loved ones and for the people on either side of them.

In one week, their first battle would come—the end to their training and the start of the campaign to bring Emerilia back under the control of the people who called it home.

***

"Hey, Jung Lee." Dave entered the secured laboratory that was buried deep under Ice City.

"Dave." Jung Lee greeted him with a smile, reaching out his hand which Dave clasped, the two of them turning to face what Jung Lee was working on.

He had worked with the flying citadels for a bit but he had found that his skills were put to better use elsewhere. He had come to Ice City, lending his hand to the growing facilities as well as the alchemists. He worked on both of their projects but his main project within Ice City was working with the weapons, armaments, shields and armor that were supposed to stop them, of the Pandora's Box Initiative.

The area that they were in wasn't that large but it had multiple heavily armored and Mana shielded rooms with some of the most complex stealth runes and even self-destruction magical coding around it. The entire facility was powered by an isolated fusion power plant and could be completely shut off from the rest of Ice City.

Down here, Jung Lee experimented with bringing life and working on his various maladies and healing potions, and he also worked on weapons of mass destruction. It seemed like the two were vastly opposite but the more Jung Lee worked on them, the more they became similar.

"How have things been down here?" Dave asked.

Jung Lee spent a lot of time out and about Ice City; he talked to a few people and seemed to just take in the atmosphere and enjoy being around other people. He also liked to have his own privacy and disappeared underground to these weapon development facilities. Only a handful of people worked down here.

"I have finally been able to complete the two-stage grand working that I have been working on." Jung Lee smiled.

"Oh? How were you able to separate the two spell formations?"

"As you know, we have been imprinting the rather unstable and compact soul gem constructs with a magically coded imprinter. Once the imprint or spell formation has taken effect on the soul gem construct, we pump it with power, causing the spell formation's effect to create a much larger effect than it would originally. Simply imprinting two of the spell formations onto the same unstable soul gem construct—well, that's why we had to remake the third testing laboratory," Jung Lee said.

"Now we've tried making shells with both of them in it and then on impact they would activate. However, we found that the energies annihilated one another so that their strength was just a portion of what it would normally be. We've tried to imprint two different spell formations onto the same grand working. They should have not had any effect on one another, but, the soul gem construct was so distorted that they ignited one another and turned a grand working machine into slag."

"Yeah, it's like we're working with damn nitroglycerin—great stuff but just a little too much jostling and you're turned into flying mince," Dave said.

"Quite. So I've been working with soul gem permutations, specifically, I have created a soul gem construct but the highly unstable and compressed sections are now separated by a sheet of properly formed soul gem. I tried this first and it took more time but it blew itself up after a few minutes.

"So, I coded in some fail-safes and the round is still stable after a few weeks. It is nearly ten times more powerful than two other grand workings. It consumes the power of both the spell formations that is used to amplify their effects. I have taken the good sheet of soul gem and coded it to take power from special containers. The containers keep the round's containment powered. Then, once it hits, the first grand working goes off and then the second mutually amplifies the effect," Jung Lee said with an excited look.

"Damn, that's incredible! Now we've got the round working—what combinations are you thinking of?"

"Well, we can use Light spells to break through shield and armor, followed by Earth magic that kills people from the inside, or Dark magic that would ignite once inside an enemy ship and warp the ship from the inside. Or we can use ground penetrators: they use Air or Light to break into a facility then the second part summons creatures from other realms; they attack from the inside, causing havoc. A boarding action, as I believe you call it, but since we are not using people but energy constructs, we can attack again and again," Jung Lee said.

"We could mix the light penetrator with a fusion bomb grand working, get it inside and then break them apart."

"Indeed. We can use this for all of the cannons. With the missiles, while we could do it, the needs for storage would be complicated and if they were to become unstable, then we don't want to be on top of thousands of missiles. Although they are useful, if they are broken we need to have power draws in place ready to consume the released power before it can activate the spell formations. If these grand workings are broken, they could rip a hole in the side of our own ships," Jung Lee said.

"Okay, well, that would be some serious coding, but I have a few ideas on that. I've been thinking of updating my outfit anyway so I'll be looking into drawing in more power and ambient energy," Dave said.

"What kind of ambient energy?" Jung Lee's eyes flashed.

"Whatever I can get my hands on, probably." Dave laughed.

Jung Lee was, however, silent, caught in thought. "If we were able to make a two-stage grand working, but then add in some additional coding to the stable section, we could make the first a light penetrator grand working; the second grand working would create as much damage as possible. Then the coding in the stable section draws in the ambient power from the light, the ship and everything else, using it to power the second grand working, make it a self-repairing code and it would increase the effect of its attack multiple times!"

"Would be a lot to figure out, though I can pass on what I figure out while I'm working on the new outfit," Dave said.

"New outfit? I thought that your armor was fine?"

"It's good, but it could be better and we're going up against some pretty big heavy hitters. I want to have the strongest weapons possible," Dave said.

"What are you thinking?" Jung Lee asked, unable to hide his interest. Dave was not known as a person who would make something less than amazing.

"Well, seeing as I'm taking on the role of a mage, I should get some mages robes, right?" Dave grinned. "How are the interceptor modules?"

There were three main weapon systems for the warships. The first and primary was the cannons. After them, there were the heavy missiles, followed by the interceptor modules. These were not technically weapons but rather a countermeasure. They worked off the close in weapons systems from Earth—basically a system that spat out a large amount of items to destroy incoming rounds and attacks.

"We're still working on it. It's not so simple now that we've integrated the spell disruption ability." Jung Lee sighed and sat back in his chair.

"What about the main system?"

"You want to see it?" Jung Lee asked.

"Sure," Dave said, excited.

"This way." Jung Lee got out of his seat. The air seemed to part for him, his every movement one of grace. He had come to integrate himself more and more with his Free Affinity spirits, gaining a deeper understanding of their elements and ways in which to use them.

His training had also come to change the aura around him and his very movements. He looked graceful but his movements contained power in them; he seemed calm but ready to leap out in a moment. It created an aura that demanded respect from those around him.

They exited the workshop where Jung Lee had been working on alchemy potions and headed deeper into the weapons facilities.

"I didn't see Jekoni. Where is he?" Dave asked.

"He's the one working on the interceptor modules. I simply don't have the understanding for magic that he has. He's been poring over it as soon as we got here and hasn't left other than to find information from others," Jung Lee said.

Jekoni didn't need to eat or sleep, and over the years, as he had been kept within the dwarven mountains, he had further increased his already vast knowledge of magic. Something that took him weeks to work on would shock most people from Emerilia. Even Dave looking at it all was left in shock at his ideas and plans.

They entered a room where there were a variety of tables along the walls and a range extending to the right. On the only desk in the room, there was what looked like a massive Gatling gun. But this one was covered in runic lining and hooked up to a soul gem interface behind it.

Jekoni looked up from where he was tinkering on rounds that were off to the side of the interceptor unit. "Dave, Jung Lee!" Jekoni said in greeting. Even his hat perked up, the tip of it waving at them in excitement.

"Hello, Jekoni, Hat," Dave said.

The hat jumped off Jekoni's head and landed on Dave's, bopping around in excitement.

"Seems that I haven't been taking him out nearly enough," Jekoni said.

Dave blinked a few times; it felt as if he had just leveled up his Intelligence by a massive amount. His mind seemed to open as ideas moved through it. "I didn't know that Hat was this powerful."

"He's useful at times." Jekoni smiled. "So what brings you two here? Want to check out the interceptor modules?"

"That was our plan. Dave came down here in order to check out how we've progressed," Jung Lee said.

"Well, good and bad. I've nailed down what form the interceptor is going to be in. After going through the information on weapons that the humans had and their ability to defend against the Jukal weaponry, these Gatling gun prototypes have proved that they can fire rapidly and with the right adjustments be incredibly accurate. As you know, the Jukal's main weapon systems are their massive laser cannons, their fighter wings, and their missiles.

"The interceptor is good to deal with the missiles. However, dealing with the cannons—unless we want to have that energy smashing into our shields constantly—we need to break it. From the information we were able to gather with the sensor units on the *Datskun* watching the generations of Jukal ships moving through Emerilia and hovering behind the second moon, we know that they have refined these cannons with magical runing. So we really need to deal with them first.

"So, we need to insert something that can disturb spells. There are two ways to break a spell. One—understand the spell formation and rip it apart, or two—insert so much energy into it as fast as possible in order to overload the caster's ability to control the Mana and it all backfires. Now, we don't know what kind of resets these cannons will have, so the second option will make it easier as we've got to just throw in wild Mana that will surge the cannons. How much Mana we'll need to make it backfire—well, that depends on their systems. I don't like the solution as we've got to concentrate our interceptors on the spell beam for long enough to destroy it. If if we break the spell formation, it's much harder. We need to adjust each of the rounds ourselves, or we can automate it. I'm stuck on trying to figure out a way to automate it and make it fast enough to imprint it onto the interceptor's soul gem rounds without stopping. These rounds are going to need to change from one type of round to another in order to break different beams and spells they launch," Jekoni contemplated, stroking his face, while Hat moved from side to side, looking at Dave and Jung Lee like an excited puppy and waving to them adorably, the contrast of the two made Dave shake his head, hiding his smile under his hand.

"We're trying to make the one weapon system do too much—have the interceptor system have a Gatling gun and then a Mana-based projection weapon. The Mana weapon will target spells; the Gatling gun physical weaponry. The Mana projection will only target one single rune, the power consumption rune, destroying or altering it. Destroying it will take more power, but altering it—if it is carved into the magical circles, then it will be impossible. We can only use the projection against people if we wanted to do the second way. Instead, we attack that single power consumption rune and we burn that thing out, melt it so that it's useless. They'll have to replace it or their weapon will be dead," Dave said.

"How could we target it?" Jekoni asked.

"Well, we make the projector able to change." Dave smiled. "We have magical coding plates built into it, ready to change from rune to rune. Only when the projection senses that it is affecting the spell formation will it stay and deal with it. We're going to need to give it some decent processing power but then we've got good things coming from the group dealing with AI and their processing centers. We can use that to change through the nearly one hundred runes that control power. Then they will smoke the little bastard out and the Jukal are down their main cannons."

"That would be impressive. The Jukal's laser cannons can be regarded as their strongest weapons, capable of burning away shields with the sheer power output that they channel directly into the shield's power couplings," Jekoni said.

"Looks like someone has been reading up on the materials," Dave praised.

"Well, as the tests are running, there's plenty of time to read a few books with the help of Hat," Jekoni said.

Hat straightened up proudly on Dave's head.

Dave thought on the armor that he was building. Information and ideas started to flood his mind as he felt power from Hat channeling into his head.

"Do you mind if I borrow Hat for a bit?" Dave asked, stunned by how Hat had been able to increase his Intelligence, allowing him to easily see through some problems that he had been thinking on.

"Sure. It won't be too hard to work on the disruptor," Jekoni said.

"Good. In that case, I have some armor I need to work on!" Dave quickly left the workshop. He saw a free room and headed into it, opening up windows and altering the designs that he had created on his interface.

It looked like a cloak with a hood. Runic lines covered the cloak on the inside and out; gray lines cut against the black cloth. Inside, Mithril plates were formed to the body, creating close-fitting armor. They, too, had runic lines that reached up to spread out to the cloak. Other lines covered the white body, gray lines on the pure white and textured Mithril.

On the model's hips were the two conjuration rods, modified with bands on them that could be flicked with a finger. There were multiple pouches along his belt and on his wrists, there were two large bracers. They had multiple bands that could be rotated into different formations. Runic lines covered them.

The armor was sleek and powerful. The white armor and midnight black coat created a striking difference, while the gray lines seemed to speak of barely controlled and ferocious power.

In the weapons facility, there was everything one might need in order to build anything. Dave pressed a preset on his toggle bar. His clothing changed to his working gear, including an enchanted dwarven smithing apron. His conjuration rods turned to two different sized hammers. He reached down to his pouches as he found a table; he pulled out different materials that had gathered for his project.

Ingots of Mithril, silver, and ebony were stacked neatly. Two different soul gem constructs were placed to the side: one a solid state original; the other the flexible version that Kol had created.

Then he pulled out a roll of cloth. It shimmered slightly, drawing the eyes to the dark material. Dave put this down with almost reverence.

As Mithril was the strongest metal on Emerilia, Dragon scale was the strongest cloth. It was lightweight and breathable but when hit by magic or by force, it would create ripples, expending the force outward. It could also be made to form a shape. Unlike cloaks that would wrap around people as they were fighting, a Dragon-scale the cloak seemed to have almost sentient ways as it moved out of the way of people's arms and feet.

Hat bent forward to look at the cloth.

Dave stopped, thinking of Hat and the cloth—they were actually very similar.

"Ah, you must be made from Dragon-scale cloth," Dave said out loud.

Hat bounced slightly in agreement.

"Well, then, I will have to put this to use!" Dave said. The cloth was nearly as expensive as Mithril. It could only be made by special weavers of the Per'ush Islands and mage's college and one needed to create special tools in order to form it. This created a powerful but extremely expensive material.

Dave pulled out plans for the Dragon-scale clothing as well as the various plates and pieces of the armor that would go against his skin. He would use the Dragon-scale cloth to back his Mithril plates as well as for his cloak. The amount in his arms would make many supreme experts on Emerilia fight bitterly for even a few square feet.

Dave laid out the materials. He looked over them and then pressed his hand against the table. He connected to the soul gem construct of the facility. In the corner of the room, a smithy appeared, identical to the smithy he used in Terra.

There were anvils and working tables, as well as multiple tools to form, heat, and cool metals. Runic lines carrying power appeared in the corner of the table. Dave guided them to the flexible soul gem construct.

He then pressed his hand to the flexible version, closing his eyes as he put in heat exchanging magical coding, then gave it his plans for the armor so that it would grow into the form he desired.

It gathered power and started to create a cuirass as well as the pauldrons, greaves, upper arm and lower leg outlines. With time, these outlines started to become more solid as the soul gem grew faster.

Dave gathered up the Mithril, ebony, and silver and moved to the smithy. He prepared the Mithril and put it into the furnace. The heat was so intense Dave had to increase his Mana barrier's power as he placed the Mithril inside. He quickly followed with the ebony and silver.

From a pouch, he pulled out different metals and materials, putting them onto the metal so that they would melt in and serve to alter the materials to better suit Dave's needs.

Flames and waves of heat washed over his Mana barrier. He pulled on goggles over his face. Heat blasted at him as he stood there, his attention wholly focused on the materials within the forge's heat.

As the metals changed states, he started to add in different materials or work them in different ways. All of this was to alter them. Just adding a few flakes of another material as they were being smelted wasn't enough to change them. With the soul gem-created forge, Dave was able to section off the forge to get different heats for the different metals, allowing him to alter and change them.

All of his knowledge came from Kol's own playing around with various metals and combining it with Earth's knowledge of metal smelting processes.

As the metals were finished, Dave used tongs to pull them from the forge and into cooling areas, where the magical coding pulled the heat from the metal to cool them rapidly. Dave kept them all close, even as they went off to the side.

Finally, all of the different types of ebony and silver had been completed. Dave hadn't succeeded with the altering of the metals each time and it had taken him two days to get all of them sorted out. Using his soul smithing art and his Touch of the Land as well as Kol's information, he was quickly able to assess which metals had reached the state he desired and those that hadn't. The Mithril, which had been under the greatest heat for the entire time, looked as if it was no longer as solid as before but still that criss-crossing pattern was revealed.

Dave took off all of his rings and his librarian necklace, replacing them with rings that would enhance his Willpower as well as his Endurance and smithing skill. Dave looked over his workplace before he looked into the fires once again. He had adjusted to the heat, now letting it hit him in violent waves. He smiled slightly at the Mithril that sat untouched in the center of the forge.

Jung Lee, had been watching for a number of hours, smiled as Dave put his hands into the furnace. Mithril seemed to form on his hands and gray Mana pooled from his hands. Runic lines across Dave's body lit up with mana, grey runic lines appeared on his bare skin, a smoke drifting off from them. His eyes glowed with a similar light. His hair was wild and his body bent in fatigue but each movement was done with precision wholly focused on what lay in front of him.

Dave submerged his consciousness into the Mithril. He poured Willpower into those bonds, breaking them with his strength. As soon as they were broken, it was as if a dam had broken. The Mithril moved like putty under Dave's hands, growing into various shapes. Dave moved from one piece to another: in his hands, an ingot would turn into a bracer; another two would turn into armor plates for the groin. Five ingots spread outward, becoming one back plate.

As Dave's eyes glowed and he stared down upon the Mithril, his one hand created a connection between him and the Mithril. His other hand would pull out different materials from his pouch, adding them to the Mithril, altering their chemistry.

Dave rolled and turned the Mithril before expanding it outward into the shapes that it would form. In the forge, pieces were placed down, creating the outline of a suit of armor.

Dave wiped his brow, drinking from a potion to restore Stamina and also another to buff his Endurance and Willpower. Dave was tired from forming that sheer amount of Mithril. When he had first become a master smith, he had passed out from making just two simple breast plates.

Now these breast plates had lines carved into them, waiting for the soul gem construct as well as carvings in the back of them for parts that were to be added.

Dave put down the potion bottle, slightly panting. His face was covered in soot. Time had no meaning for him as he let out a deep breath. He placed different metals into the forge, heating them up once again.

He placed his right hand on the Mithril armor and the left on the metals he had added back into the forge. "Merge." Dave's low and rough voice rumbled with power as the newly added metals obeyed.

They combined together into various magically coded components, simplified down to runic lines. A number of them were hollow inside, awaiting the soul gem construct.

In front of Dave, multiple pieces floated up into the air. The different metals would turn from amorphous blobs into components that made up different sheets or sections.

Once all the components were finished, they came together perfectly.

The forge glowed as the Mithril plates floated upright in the air. The smaller components came together, interlinking with the larger parts and inserting themselves into the Mithril armor.

There were tens of thousands of parts and magical runes, thousands of components and hundreds of systems—all of them combined together, perfectly made for one another as they created one whole. The armor was connected and compiled.

The last of the pieces were coming together when the inflexible soul gem construct shot toward Dave, passing over his shoulder and stopping inside the chest of the armor. It spread outwards a nucleus in the center of it all.

It grabbed onto the different parts, flowing through the recesses that had been made for it and sealing over the components that lay under the armor.

The armor plates stopped being sections and started to become a whole. Dave beckoned with his hand; the armor floated out of the furnace as the soul gem construct worked its way through the interior of the armor. The armor glowed from inside with the power of the soul gem construct. From the ceiling and floor, Dave commanded the room's soul gem construct to reach out toward the armor, supporting it and powering the soul gem within.

On the table, the flexible soul gem construct had completed its work.

With a wave, Dave raised up the flexible soul gem construct. It was shaped like the armor. However, its form followed the runic lines of the armor; it didn't work to cover it like the inflexible armor did. It had connection points that would allow Dave to freely move his limbs while keeping the armor linked all the time. With the first and second generation Abscondita armor, Dave had needed to use bolts and pivots in order to connect the various pieces of armor that he wore.

The flexible soul gem construct was much larger than the armor, encompassing it before shrinking down in size to match perfectly with the runic lines that ran across the body of the armor, connecting to the legs and running down the leg bracers.

Dave paid special attention to the bracers and their multiple rotating bracelets. They carried small runic lines that would allow him much greater control over his armor, only needing him to move a bracelet instead of needing to conjure and destroy runes within his armor.

On the shoulders of his armor, the flexible soul gem spread out behind the armor, like tree roots, creating an overlay for the cloak.

Dave had a tired expression on his face. His body was covered in sweat and grime and his mind was becoming fuzzy.

He made a grabbing motion. The Dragon-scale cloth appeared in his hand. Dave's soul smithing art didn't just work with the Mithril. He was also able to break the bonds of the Dragon-scale cloth. The cloth seemed to burst apart, covering everything in the room.

After some time Dave's vision cleared as he looked upon his armor.

The cloak fluttered in the air slightly, the cloth pervaded by soul gem runic lines that extended over the shoulders and down the length of the armor to its shoes. Lines ran from the neck to the ankles and down the shoulders to the Dragon-scale gloves with Mithril-reinforced knuckles.

The Dragon-scale cloth lay as the base; covered by soul gem construct, components integrated with the Mithril armor and soul gem construct were completely hidden.

The flexible soul gem constructs were gray where they created runic lines but at the joints, they were wholly integrated with the Dragon-scale cloth, making them one single material.

Dave pulled out the hood that Bob had given him so long ago. It flew from his hand and connected to the back of the armor. Threads of the soul gem construct weaved into the material of the hood, forming runic lines across it.

Dave looked at his armor.

With every piece, among the materials, he had added his own blood and worked it with his Willpower, wholly saturating it with his power.

Dave sat down heavily on a chair, simply staring up at the armor that was suspended in midair, soul gem construct connecting to it.

"I'll call it Lux," Dave said, his voice rough as he looked ready to collapse.

He looked at the armor until he fell asleep, ignoring the notifications on the side of his screen.

Chapter 18: To War's Edge

Deia was sitting in Ice City, playing with Koi as she looked out over the city from her balcony.

Dave had been sequestered in the weapons facilities when she'd first arrived. Jung Lee had told her that he was working on a new set of armor.

Deia had left him to his work and instead spent her time with Koi and the other children of the Dracul family, her family.

Her father, who was also in Ice City, working at the refinery, was also with her.

"So you've been having fun here?" Deia fed Koi as her father Mal fed his son, her brother, Desmond. For Elves it wasn't odd having a brother or sister that was hundreds of years different in age.

"It's been so much more than I ever thought it would be," Mal admitted, an excited gleam in his eye as he looked out over the city. "There's so many brilliant ideas here and I've actually increased in strength in leaps and bounds with all that I've learned here. Water and his people work with the various mining projects, with the ice asteroids, to the ice planet. They've really turned into chemistry savants and have been working with me and the dwarven master smiths to make different compounds that might help us as well as create water and sewage systems that work for the entire city. All of the Dracul family members have been pitching in all over the place. Here they can freely reveal their Dragon form and unleash their power. With their strength, we've been able to make things that should take years in mere weeks." Mal let out a laugh, shaking his head in disbelief. That look of excitement only grew stronger.

Deia smiled, seeing that similar look in Dave's eyes when he was stuck in his work or started talking about it. Seeing that passion that both of them held for their work, Deia could only smile at their clear happiness.

"How goes the training?" Mal turned to Deia. Seeing Desmond was making a mess of his food, Mal sorted that out.

"Training is nearly done." Deia's smile turned solemn. "In three days, we will begin our counterattack."

"So soon?" Mal let out a deep breath as he finished cleaning Desmond up.

"Yeah. I wish we had more time, but at this point they're as ready as they're going to be. We've worked together to develop tactics and they're used to the different ways of the flying citadels. Tomorrow we'll raise the flying citadels and move them to the Xelur's portal in the Densaou Ring of Fire near Egas Nation," Deia said.

"Look after yourself." Mal gave Deia a deep look.

"Don't worry, Dad. I'll be okay," Deia said.

"It's hard for a father to send his daughter off to war." Mal looked much older than his outward appearance.

Deia placed her hand on his and squeezed it. "I've got Dave and all of Party Zero. We look after one another."

"I know, but still..." Mal had a sad and forced smile on his face as he looked to Deia.

"I heard that you had some guests," Deia said, changing the subject.

"Yes, humans who escaped humanity's destruction and are hiding out somewhere. They have a stealth ship sitting out near the asteroid base, putting out observation platforms to watch over the system. There's even talk of them establishing an outpost in the system, which might allow us to share ideas and get closer to them," Mal said, forcing himself out of his dreary thoughts.

"Dave talked about them but I never thought that we might meet them here," Deia said.

"It seems that everything is coming together at an alarming pace," Mal agreed. "We're just rolling with it. Hopefully it all turns out well, but right now we're just riding a wave of production and innovation. We've got more people coming over every day and we're even going to start reviving people from the Earth simulation in the near future. Air has been around a lot, talking to Bob. She brought a number of people with her who are to ease the players' transition from the simulation into reality."

"That is going to be one hell of an undertaking," Deia said. Koi had finished eating, so Deia put her over her shoulder, to burp her.

"Yeah." Mal nodded. "They're going to have millions of people to deal with. Jeeves is working with them to make up an AI that can help with the transition—there's simply too many people to deal with individually. In the meantime, we've got to expand Ice City and all of our facilities in order to accommodate them."

Deia focused on dealing with Koi as they lapsed into silence.

"All that you've been able to do here—even I had no idea of the extent that Dave, Malsour, Bob, and Steve had pushed the boundaries," Deia said suddenly.

"Your fiancé is an impressive man," Mal said with approval.

Deia blushed, looking at Koi, who was now closing her eyes, a sleepy and content look on her face.

"That he is," Deia said quietly, a proud smile on her face.

***

"Oi! You want to keep it down!" Jekoni yelled as he entered the room that Dave was in, snoring his head off.

Dave woke with a snort and looked around blearily as Hat moved to Jekoni, who floated at the doorway into the room, looking at the armor that Dave had made with wide eyes.

"Hey," Dave said sleepily, rubbing at the big white circles around his eyes caused by the goggles he'd worn while working. The rest of his face and clothes were covered in a layer of black soot.

"Lux," Jekoni said, his voice almost reverent as he glided toward the armor that was still suspended in the middle of the room.

Jekoni passed Dave, looking at the armor, his face slack.

Dave groaned at the blinking notifications that were annoying him. He opened the notification panel, waking up as he went through the descending list.

Quest Completed: Dwarven Master Smith Level 9

You must craft 4 Weapons of Power, 30 weapons of SS quality, or 250 of S Quality with your Smithing Art (Currently 4/4, 0/30, 0/250)

Rewards:

Unlock Level 10 Quest

+10 to all stats

900,000 Experience

Class: Dwarven Master Smith

Status: Level 9

Effects:
Allowed access to all Dwarven Mountains and smithies.
Allowed to take on smithing apprentices.
+90 to all stats
Access to special quests.

Quest: Dwarven Master Smith Level 10

You must craft 5 Weapons of Power , 50 weapons of SS quality, or 500 of S Quality with your Smithing Art (Currently 4/5, 0/30, 0/250)

Rewards:

Unlock Level 11 Quest

Stat Increase

Level 255

You have reached Level 262; you have **35** stat points to use.

Dave opened up his character sheet, placing twenty-five into his Willpower to recover some of that he had used on the armor, placing the remaining ten into his Intelligence stat.

Character Sheet

Name:	David Grahslagg	Gender:	Male
Level:	262	Class:	Dwarven Master Smith, Friend of the Grey God, Bleeder, Librarian, Aleph Engineer, Weapons Master, Champion Slayer, Skill Creator, Mine Manager, Master of Space and Time, Master of Gravitational Anomalies
Race:	Human/ Dwarf	Alignment:	Chaotic Good

Unspent points: 0

Health:	52,060	Regen:	25.32 /s
Mana:	16,630	Regen:	62.45 /s
Stamina:	5,770	Regen:	53.15 /s
Vitality:	5206	Endurance:	1,266
Intelligence:	1,663	Willpower:	1,249
Strength:	577	Agility:	1,063

"Nice," Dave said, a pleased smile on his face. As he looked up at the Lux armor, a prompt appeared in front of him.

Lux Armor

Forged by Dave Grahslagg, this armor that was once hidden is now revealed.

Quality: Weapon of Power

Defense: 32,514+ (Mana Barrier with enough power)

Abilities: Mana Barrier

Mana Shield

Orb control

Control hub for linked devices

Power hub for linked spells/devices

Storage devices

Mana bolt projectors

Heat exchanger

Cold exchanger

Automated Mana Siphon

Automated Soul Siphon

Automated Self-Repair

Automated Self Heal

Increased Agility and Strength (base 15%)

Grows in strength with user

Manipulation possible (Associated values liable to change due to creator's changes and level of charge)

Teleportation ability (group and individual)

Armor Link (Users can share their power and link capabilities. If one armor is fully charged, then it will feed power to the other to charge it.)

Charge: 3,450,845/10,000,000 (Linked Armor 32,514,383/ 36,000,000)

Durability 51,574/51,574

 Active Skill: Soul Manipulation

 Level: Master Level 5

Effect: Tools you make to manipulate souls and their energy is 95% stronger. Able to use soul energy to fuel spells. 30% increase to soul energies reserves (can only be used for spells; does not act as extra Willpower points).

Cost: Dependent on creation.

Active Skill: Soul Smith

Level: Expert Level 9

Effect: 81% less soul energy necessary for crafting with soul smith.

Cost: Dependent on creation.

Active Skill: Builder

Level: Master Level 8

Effect: Speed and efficiency is doubled. Creations material cost is reduced by 40%.

Required: Tools

Active Skill: Smithing
   Level: Master Level 8
   Effect: 99% improved quality of smithing creation. 40% chance to imbue metal with innate skill. Able to analyze items made of stone, iron, steel, silver, malachite, gold, ebony, and Mithril, aluminum, titanium.

Dave laughed out loud, punching his hand into the air, and nearly dropped from the seat he'd passed out in. A smile split his face as he was filled with a sense of pride and joy in his work.

He was tired, hungry, and he was still regenerating the energy that he had expended on the armor. However, he couldn't refrain from expressing his excitement. Laughing and whooping loudly, he quickly gathered Jung Lee's attention, who had been carefully working on different projects within his workshop.

He entered the workshop that Dave had taken over to work on his project. A smile blossomed on his face at Dave's euphoric look at the armor.

"Jung Lee!" Dave said, sensing Jung Lee at the door.

"It seems that you've finished your work," Jung Lee said, happy for his friend and also astonished by the armor that was held in the air.

Jung Lee didn't know much about armor, using only simple clothes himself. When he looked upon the armor in the air, there was a powerful aura to it. As if it looked upon the world like some all-powerful god, deeming which people it thought worthy of its time.

"Yes, I finished it last night but I fell asleep," Dave said.

"Was snoring loud enough to wake up people at the asteroid base," Jekoni said, finally withdrawing his gaze from the armor.

Dave scratched his head awkwardly. "Thank you for letting Hat help me. He was a great help in completing this."

Jekoni smiled as Hat stood up straight proudly.

"While you were working on this, I made you something," Jekoni said. From his hand, a soul gem construct appeared and moved toward Dave. It didn't hold any light in it but looked like a glass ring with different striations on the inside.

Dave took it into his hand and examined it.

Ring

Created by Arch Mage Jekoni so Dave would stop stealing his Hat.

Quality: Magical Artifact

Abilities:

Increase user's Intelligence, Endurance, and Willpower by 35%

Legendary ability: Overclock. The user can increase their Intelligence, Willpower, and Endurance by 55% for ten minutes; can be used once per day and will most likely lead to user collapsing from mental fatigue.

He let out a cool breath as he looked at the ring. "Jekoni, there was no need to do this."

"You're a man with a lot on your shoulders and you constantly give to others. I thought it was about time that someone gave something back to you." Jekoni smiled.

"Well, thank you." Dave took off a ring on his hand and then put on the glass one. It turned black as night but those striations turned white, making them an eye-catching piece.

Dave closed his eyes, feeling as if the world—no, the universe—was within his grasp.

He opened his eyes. The feeling of power that had come with wearing Jekoni's hat came back in a portion. It wasn't as strong of an effect as Hat had been, but with Dave's base stats, he had entered a whole new realm of power.

"We have three days before the assault on the Xelur castles at the Densaou Ring begins," Jung Lee said.

Dave took a deep breath and frowned slightly. He'd lost four full days to creating this armor.

"Deia has come to Ice City and the forces on the flying citadels are stocking supplies and readying themselves for the move. Tomorrow they will begin their advance toward the portal," Jung Lee continued.

"Well then, I'd best take a shower." Dave held out his hand. The soul gem construct around the armor released and retracted as the armor moved toward Dave. He was already connected to the armor and added it to his hot bar. The armor disappeared into his bag of holding, ready to be worn if he changed his outfit.

"See you in a bit." Dave teleported from the weapons facility to his apartment. It was impossible to teleport into the weapons facility but Dave could use the coding to allow him to leave.

He quickly showered and cleaned up before equipping the new armor. Power surged through Dave to new levels. It was intoxicating.

Even without calling on his Mana, the runic lines he'd made inside his body glowed. His eyes glowed gray while gray vapor wafted out from his eyes and the runic lines.

As the lines appeared, he felt even more strength flood his body.

He looked up at the mirror. His face was obscured by the hood. The runic lines on his face and his gray eyes were visible. They lined up perfectly with the runic lines of his armor and hood.

His white Mithril armor plates gave off an aura of strength, the runic lines a sense of power, and the Mithril a noble aura.

"That looks bad ass." Looking like a god of destruction, Dave admired the fit of his armor and tossed his cloak behind him.

He ran through the apartment, to see how much his cloak would pick up, and jumped around a bit. Realizing how it must look, he slowly stopped, looking around to see whether anyone had seen his actions.

Finding himself still alone, he cleared his throat and walked out the door of his apartment.

Wonder what Deia's expression will be seeing this? Dave tapped his chin in thought as he walked through the halls.

People stared at him with odd looks. He looked like a god of destruction, but his pose made it seem as if he were debating what he was having for dinner later that night. It made more than one person frown in confusion at the scene.

Dave quickly located Deia across Ice City. His heart warmed as he saw her with Koi while talking to her father, who was looking after Desmond.

Dave disappeared, his steps not pausing as he appeared outside of the balcony and stepped onto it.

Deia readied herself; a sword appeared in her hand as Mal circulated his Mana, both of them putting themselves in front of their children.

"Nice threads, right?" Dave reached up and pulled his hood down, revealing his face.

"Dave!" Deia said, her voice filled with outrage as she pouted at him.

"Was worth the look on both your faces." Dave smiled.

"I take back what I said about your husband being smart." Oson'Mal relaxed his circulating Mana.

Koi started to cry, being jolted awake from her post-feeding nap.

"Oh honey, everything's okay. Daddy's here." Dave moved to Koi, who Deia was now trying to soothe.

Deia passed Koi over to her father. Her eyes thinned, reminding him that Dave had caused his daughter's cries.

He smiled sheepishly, taking Koi and comforting her.

"So now we know what you've been up to the last couple of days," Oson'Mal said once Koi's crying had come down in volume under Dave's comforting words and actions.

"Yeah. It took a bit longer than I thought and a lot more energy than I was expecting. I call it Lux," Dave said.

"Lux?" Deia asked.

"As Abscondita meant hidden or shadows in Latin, Lux meant light or bright, something that was to be shown, not hidden. We have been hiding our abilities, our strength, and trump cards for too long. With this armor and our coming actions, we are telling the rest of Emerilia and the universe that we will not take it anymore. We will show them our true strength," Dave said. His voice was level and called forth the fighting spirit within him as well as Deia and Oson'Mal.

"And we'll show them some of that strength when we destroy the Xelur forces in the Densaou Ring of Fire and push them back into their portal," Deia said with finality.

Dave and Deia shared a look, understanding each other completely.

***

Lox and Gurren stood on the battlements of Citadel One.

"Looks like it's happening," Steve said beside them. "Think it's going to be magenta?"

"Why, oh why, do you ever open your mouth?" Gurren shook his head.

Steve just grinned as the citadel started to shake. A rumbling noise came from the walls and the ground. One by one, the citadels around Goblin Mountain also started to shake and rumble.

The walls shifted slightly as in different parts they changed from polished stone to polished metal. The stone structure of the citadel changed, the rock making shifting noises as its inner structure was changed from stone to metal. The gray stone was replaced with silver-gray steel.

All around, the walls were increasing in strength; new magical circles started to cover the different layers of the castle. The farther inward, the higher the buffs were.

The walls glowed with magical inscriptions, the power held within making those within the citadels feel their scalps tingling.

The citadels kept their original structure of the main castle and the two outer walls but now all of the walls and the castle had been turned from stone and armored areas into a fully metal construct, with the armored areas improving in thickness and better cover.

The magical circles pulled in power from the surrounding areas, overlaying the magical coding that had been integrated into the castle and adding their effects to those that had already existed with the runic lines that ran over the walls and the grounds.

Even as the stone turned to metal, the soul gem construct that had been interwoven into the walls and ground of the citadel was left undisturbed, as if the citadel knew that it was a strengthening measure and didn't wish to break it or force it from the walls.

"Well, that's better than I hoped. I thought that it might not work at all or that it would change in a way that we would need to change out tactics for dropping," Lox said, relieved.

"Armor upgrade, nice," Steve said.

"Well, now onto the second part of today—moving time," Gurren said.

Lox transmitted orders to the citadel group leaders.

The citadel group leaders were in command of eight citadels. The citadel wings were four of them and citadel pairs was just two. Each had a different commander who was also in command of their own citadel.

"Understood, Mister Lox. We will check our castles and be prepared to fly within fifteen minutes. With the stone changing to metal, our weight has increased but thankfully our balance hasn't been altered," the citadel group leader for the Goblin Mountain citadel group transmitted.

"Good. I'll let you get to it then." Lox ended the party chat and then opened another to Party Zero's private party chat.

"Anna, how's it going over there?" Lox asked.

"We're on the move. Crossing over Heval right now. We'll be there in three and a half days, though with the flight, the captains are pretty sure that they can speed it up," Anna said. She was with the Gudalo citadel group near Kogar.

"Not a lot going on, and they know what they're doing over here. We'll move to your citadels soon enough," Suzy said. Induca and Lu Lu were also with Anna. Induca had been assisting with training while Suzy worked with Florence to get the citadels stocked with all the supplies that they needed. The Kogar citadel group didn't have drop capabilities but they had ranged fire power and could support the Goblin Mountain citadel group at range.

"How did the upgrade go?" Induca asked.

"Everything went well. We got an armor upgrade instead of the citadel expanding. The captains are changing their lift plans but we'll be moving soon," Lox said.

"See you there," Anna said.

Lox muted the party chat and looked out at the citadels. Only Citadel One was floating, serving as a test for the citadel upgrade.

"Brace for lift!" the captain of Citadel Two of Goblin Mountain citadel group called out. Their voice linked to the commander channel for the Goblin Mountain citadel group chat.

Gravity runes lit up as a number of people held onto grab bars that had been added into the citadel for extra safety.

"Lifting in five, four, three, two, one." The flight officer's countdown ended. Citadel Two shook as it freed itself from the ground; dirt and debris fell from it as it ascended into the sky.

Lox looked around. In that early morning light, citadel after citadel rose from the ground, their soul gem islands that they were rooted into revealing themselves as they rose randomly. They held their breaths, looking at the powerful sight of those citadels rising from the ground—behemoths rising from the depths, ready to fight those that had disturbed them.

"Move into triangular flight formation," the Goblin Mountain group leader called out once all of the citadels had reached their holding height.

The citadels' move created a triangle in the air, ready to defend from attacks in any direction.

"Move out! Destination—Xelur portal at Densaou Ring of Fire!" the citadel group leader said.

The flying citadels pushed forward. The creatures hiding in the wilderness of Ashal looked up at those citadels with fear in their eyes, sensing the bloodlust and fighting intent of the thousands who had been training for months for this moment.

"Check gear and all of the drop mechanisms," the citadel group leader called out.

Lox smiled to himself.

"Looks like we're not needed anymore," Gurren said, a proud look in his eyes.

"Seems that way," Lox said softly.

They had trained these people as best as they could, working with those who would drop on platforms and with their packs. Their knowledge with the Devastator armor and its ability to fly put them in a good position to talk to the dwarves who would be dropping and get them used to dropping and getting into battle.

Now they stood on the top of Citadel One as they surged forward. Within those citadels, the different groups checked their equipment. The flying citadel would take two days to reach the Xelur. This wasn't their top speed, but it would allow everyone to get used to flying and also allow them time to adjust any plans they had instead of just rushing into battle.

"Move out, aerial scouts," the group leader said.

Aerial forces that had been waiting in the main castle's towers now jumped into the slip streams and launched into the air. The various aerial forces spread out to create a net around the flying citadel formation to catch anyone that might try to attack the citadels.

The automatons and their repeaters scanned the sky and the ground.

Dwarven artillery checked their gear with a few crews on duty in case they were needed.

The mages and ranged groups were resting or sitting in waiting areas, ready to move up to the battlements at a moment's notice in order to deal with any potential threats.

They moved through the sky, ready to deal with anything that dared to block their way.

Even the high-leveled creatures of the Ashal wilderness that could fly didn't try to antagonize or attack them, scared that they would fall under the flying citadel's group.

Quickly, they left behind the citadel that had been built outside of Goblin Mountain. Those within the citadel could only look on in awe.

***

"The citadels have begun to move," an aide said into Esa's ear.

A cold smile spread over her face as she looked over the hellish scene that was the Xelur portal. They had been able to hold onto their castles but only just. The Xelur's continuous reinforcements wore on the defenders.

The Xelur held the southern and western castles around the portal, as well as the southern outer castle.

They had all gone through their first citadel upgrade except for the eastern citadel that had changed owners twice, resetting it twice.

The Xelur weren't as simple as they looked. They had brought out powerful arrays and totems that they used to gather ambient energy to increase or restore their power at a high rate, as well as arrays that created Mana barriers and shields around the citadels to protect them from the aerial bombardment as well as the ranged spells and artillery fire.

Even now, shields flared on both sides from impacts of the Xelur's ranged arrays or their personal-ranged soul beams or the Terra Alliance's ranged attacks.

The Xelur seemed to be content with skirmishing every now and then to keep the Terra Alliance off-balance. However, they hadn't showed any more Grand Demon Lords since the Alliance had taken the eastern castle.

Esa hadn't been feeling comfortable as these powerful masters hid, growing their strength and waiting. She knew that they were planning something and had feared that it would come to fruition before the flying citadel groups could support them.

In three days, they would begin their campaign against the Xelur and all of the other portals.

"Deia, Malsour, Dave, Jekoni, and Jung Lee have entered the castle through the ono," another aide said to Esa.

"Very well. Have them come and join me," Esa said.

The feeling of unease over the past couple of weeks was replaced with confidence. She had now gained the power she needed to clear out this Xelur invasion.

Chapter 19: Flying Citadel's Might

Anna felt the slight wind that passed over the citadel. They were moving at a fair speed but runic lines created different barriers to decrease wind resistance and to allow a part of that wind to wash over the citadel.

She looked over the eight flying citadels that crossed over Emerilia. Below them was the sea that separated Opheir and Heval. She could see Opheir in the distance with her vision.

"It's time that we met up with the others," Anna said to Induca and Suzy, who were eating their breakfast on a storage crate of grand working shells for the nearby artillery cannons.

"Okay," Induca said. Suzy put her hand over Induca's and squeezed it. The two of them shared a look and smiled at each other.

Anna pretended to not notice. Her hand moved toward the necklace that Alkao had given her after she had caved in and finally agreed to go out with him. A smile flourished on her face as her stomach dropped. She wanted to just leave this all behind to stand with Alkao, walk around Devil's Crater, to talk, laugh and play around. Her duty and her conscience wouldn't let her leave her friends behind or avoid this duty that she had placed upon herself. Even as she longed for that, she had to fight now. If she didn't, then she wouldn't be able to attain that freedom.

She tucked the necklace into her armor.

Induca stood. A powerful aura came from her as she motivated the Dragon bloodline that ran through her veins. Mana surged around her as her face became solemn. Suzy rose from her seat, pulling out her staff of Hecate and touching it on the ground. Lu Lu flew in from where she had been flying around the citadel, changing her size from the size of a small truck to a housecat as she landed on Suzy's shoulder, her eyes cold as lightning sparked over her body.

The corner of Anna's mouth rose into a cold smile. Her eyes turned white as the air seemed to gather around her, called to her command. She flew over the battlements, dropping from the tower.

Fire curled around Induca as Suzy's Air creations appeared from her bag of holding. The two of them also rose over the walls and dropped.

They reached an impressive velocity before their speed started to slow. They landed on the castle that lay at the bottom of the tower. Here, multiple dwarven artillery cannons, casting platforms, and repeater batteries were located. They walked lightly into the castle and through to the central area that lay underneath the tower.

Anna activated the ono from a control panel. It took but a moment before the ono connected to Terra. They stepped through the ono, into Terra.

"Citadel One Goblin Mountain Group," Anna called out to the teleport pad controllers.

"Dialing Goblin Mountain Group, Citadel One!" the controller confirmed as the event horizon closed. Runes started to move on the ground, changing into a new formation.

It had barely stopped when power surged through the teleport pad's runes. As it reached the central runes, the teleport pad connected to the ono that was their destination.

Anna led them through the ono.

People were moving from their barracks to their ready positions. A tense feeling filled the air; few people talked as they moved.

Anna continued onward, out of the castle. She rose up into the air, propelled toward the walls that surrounded the inner castle.

Induca and Suzy followed.

They looked over the battlements. Instead of the sea, they now saw the foreboding mountains that made up the Densaou Ring of Fire.

There were dark clouds in the sky, even in the early morning sunlight. The clouds reflected the reds of the magma that flowed from the Densaou Ring of Fire and flashed with lightning occasionally.

This was a powerful place.

In the distance, another kind of light illuminated the sky. This was not a light born from nature, but the light and sounds of battle.

The flying citadels were moving in low and fast, the bottom of their soul gem islands just meters above the tree line.

Anna's face was an unemotional mask as she heard the unnatural rolling thunder that was a dwarven artillery barrage, the impacts of soul and Mana fueled spells striking barriers and walls.

The misses left deep craters and gouges in the ground.

There was the sound of whistling wind as Deia, Dave, Malsour, Jung Lee, Jekoni, Steve, Lox, and Gurren all landed on the battlements. They didn't need to say anything as they stepped forward, in line with Anna, Induca, and Suzy.

Lu Lu, sensing the oncoming battle, let out a cry to the heavens.

Other beasts roared, and let out their own war cries.

"Move to attack positions!" the group leader said.

The final safety measures were removed from different weapons as people moved to their ready positions. The citadels that had been acting as a rear guard at the bottom of the triangle now folded outward, lining up with the other two sides of the triangle.

Magical formations and runic lines started to glow as Mana surged through the citadels. In this desolate land, the citadels glowed with clean, pure, and untouched power. The soul gem islands beneath started to glow as their power increased dramatically.

"Raise to drop height!" the group leader commanded.

The citadels rose; as they did, they became visible to the Xelur forces.

Fighting seemed to stop for a moment.

"Ranged weaponry, prepare to fire on your preset targets!" the group leader barked. The distance from the oncoming castles decreased rapidly.

"Citadel One, your target is the southern citadel!" the captain of the citadel yelled.

Artillery cannons were dialed into their targets as aerial forces rushed out of the tower's exits like a swarm of locusts. They turned, creating a cloud around the citadel.

Dragons let out their roars, shaking the sky as they soared above their citadels.

The Xelur, sensing the danger that these citadels represented, quickly changed their targets from the citadels on the ground to those in the sky. Arrays that they had been holding in reserve unleashed their attacks.

They slammed against the flying citadels, burning energy and making the Mana barriers shake as the attacks were blunted.

Grand Demon Lords that had been gathering more energy and preparing for the next Xelur assault now exited the areas they had been resting in. They used their own arrays or worked together. Massive beams tens of meters wide smashed against the citadels, slowing their speed as they took the damage.

The Mana barrier flared up with these impacts but it stayed solid in the face of this onslaught.

Energies clashed, the ripples strong enough to kill those below the level of a thousand. The citadels forged onward, the impacts smashing against the barriers, but they didn't seem to care.

"Fire!" the group leader yelled.

Energy shockwaves appeared around the artillery cannons that were barely audible over the sounds of the Xelur's attack against the barriers.

Hundreds of spells and artillery rounds filled the air like angry fireflies illuminating the sky. Some were caught up in those beams and detonated in the air. Some activated in the air and called down nature's wrath upon the Xelur-controlled citadels.

The Xelur shield flashed into existence, defending against the massive onslaught of energy that was now brought down onto them.

Other spells and rounds ignited on the curved surface of these Xelur shields. The sound of the ranged battle shook the Densaou Ring of Fire. The expended energies excited the volcanoes, causing magma to bubble and shoot outward. The sky darkened with ash and debris that had been thrown up into the sky as the red light of the volcanoes illuminated that hellish scene.

Aerial forces that had swarmed out earlier used the Xelur's attack as cover to get higher, coming over the Xelur citadels. Now they unleashed their own attacks; the sky was filled with Mana bombs and magical attacks.

The Dragon groups worked together, their attacks combining to create attacks that made the Xelur shields buckle.

The citadels were fighting with everything they had. Their battle lit up the sky, an awe-inspiring display of power.

The Terra Alliance citadels on the ground let out a cheer as they fired their own artillery and ranged attacks. Their morale soared to new heights as the three Xelur citadels now came under the attack of thirteen citadels.

The flying citadels continued forward, only now crossing the outer citadels. With every meter they crossed, the power of the Xelur citadel's attacks increased. Their attacks also increased in power.

The Xelur under that barrage could only turtle up, more and more of their attacks turning to defense.

"Rotate citadels!" the group leader called out.

The citadels, like doing some complicated dance, turned their faces. This distributed the attack force of the Xelur over a larger area, allowing the first Mana barrier runic lines time to cool down, charge and repair itself.

Anna looked to Party Zero on either side of her. The wind rushed past them, their eyes alight with the sights of battle, cold looks on their faces, and their hands resting on their various weapons.

She turned to look at the Xelur citadels once again.

The citadel formation continued onward, ranged attacks flashing through the air, igniting upon the Xelur's and Terra Alliance's shields and barriers.

***

Esa looked up at the flying citadels in awe. They were still crossing the sky, passing over the Alliance citadels.

They had split into two groups: one headed for the western inner castle, the other larger group headed for the two southern-controlled citadels.

Kim was coordinating the mages of the ground-based citadels while Josh was in the western outer castle, unable to keep away from the battle and seeing the flying citadels finally in action.

Hope filled Esa's heart.

These citadels had been described as the way that they would win the war. However, it was only now that she was seeing them in action that she agreed with that assessment. She still had to see how capable they were in taking the Xelur citadels but hope had infected her now.

"Reports from the Aleph: their scouts have recognized multiple Grand Demon Lords leaving the portal. It seems that they called for reinforcements," an aide said.

Esa hissed, her face turning ugly. The Aleph automatons could use the size of the Xelur to figure out what class they fell into, but telling their possible level could only be done by someone who was of Emerilia.

"How many?" she demanded.

"Looks like dozens," the aide replied. The room went quiet as others tried to listen in on the new development. The Grand Demon Lords had been a pain in their ass for this entire campaign. Now that so many more of them had appeared, it would only make their lives that much more difficult.

"There's nothing that we can do but endure." Esa looked to those in the command center. "Warn the flying citadels as well as our forces closest to the Xelur portal."

The Flying Citadels glowed with power, lances shot out from the Flying Citadels as Dwarven Artillery fired into the heavens.

Runic lines glowed on the flying Citadels soul gem islands, spell formations appeared in front of the Flying Citadels as spell after spell was formed.

The concentrated fire of the Citadels battered the Xelur reinforcements, without shields or barriers they were washed away in the unending sea of fire.

Light illuminated the area around the portal, the Flying Citadels turning the area around the portals into nothing more than a killing zone.

Esa's eyes went wide as artillery started falling from the skies. This was the Flying Citadels first action, but it could only be called dominating. There was no mercy or pause in their actions.

***

"Moving to drop positions," the captain of Goblin Mountain Citadel One said while the flying Citadels rumbled with artillery cannon fire and spell formations activating.

"Follow me," Deia said. They entered one of the defensive towers, heading down to its base. There an elevator departed, taking a group down with it.

They waited for another elevator to appear. They stepped on it and shot downward.

The elevator was clear around the sides. They passed through the foundations of the citadel that was integrated into the soul gem island beneath it.

They passed through that for a while before passing multiple areas hidden within the island. There were ammunition lockers for the different weapons inside the castle; there were stables for the aerial creatures and those that were ridden into battle. Next were the barracks for the drop forces as well as those on the surface.

Finally, they started passing the drop bays and drop tubes. The island underneath the citadel wasn't symmetrical but rather looked like an upside-down mountain.

The drop tubes and drop bays exited at different points for the most part. Some areas, there were groups no larger than ten warbands waiting to drop. In other places, there were mounted forces and War Clans waiting on platforms, ready to go.

Hidden down here was the true threat of the flying castle.

They stopped at a drop tube.

Mages and fighters from across Emerilia waited silently in lines that led to the drop tubes. There was a red light off to the side.

The leaders were talking to their people, repeating the plan that had been laid out weeks ago.

People glanced to Party Zero. Quickly, the word passed that Party Zero would be joining them in this battle. It gave the nervous and tense drop forces something else to think about and raised their spirits as they ran final checks on their gear.

None of the Party Zero needed drop packs and stood, ready and waiting behind those who were ready.

"Our target is the western castle. We will drop as close as possible under the supporting fire of the citadels, as well as the aerial units. This is going to be one hell of a ride down. Make sure to stick to the way point circles you see unless you've got incoming—in that case, evade as you can! As soon as you're clear of enemy-ranged attacks, continue to follow the way points! Otherwise you might hit someone else on the way down, or you could be separated from everyone else," Deia said, for the benefit of those who hadn't been part of the training group.

"Three minutes out!" the captain yelled out to everyone on the citadel.

"Up!" the drop leader said. Everyone stood from their seats.

"Check the person in front of you!" the drop leader said. Everyone checked the person in front of them, making sure that their gear was secured and that their drop packs were functional. Afterward, they tapped the person in front of them on the head.

"One minute!" the drop leader said. Everyone looked to the red light. The drop doors opened, showing the ground racing below the citadel.

Here and there, spells and attacks would hit the ground, throwing up a plume of dirt and rock shards into the air. The rounds streaked through the air like rockets. Xelur soul beams impacted the Mana barriers, causing them to shake from the hits.

The red light snapped green.

"Go, go, go!" the drop leader yelled over the noise of the attacks and wind.

Before they could think on what they were doing, the first people rushed forward, pencil diving out of the drop doors.

Quickly, the sky filled with people dropping out of the citadel. The lines moved forward quickly. Soon it was Party Zero's turn.

Dave quickly squeezed Deia's hand. He smiled to her before he pulled up his hood.

Deia calmed the jittery feeling in her chest as she stepped forward and jumped through the drop doors. The runes on the side made sure she didn't hit the sides of the soul gem construct before she was spat out the bottom of the drop door.

The sky darkened with the sheer number of people dropping from the citadels. Bay doors had snapped open and the platforms hurled toward the ground. The groups on them had stony faces; the gravity magical coding kept them from feeling the drop as they watched the sky and focused on their target.

Repeaters that had been mounted to the citadel's underside unleashed their bolts. Dwarven artillery cannons that had been placed into swivel mounts inside the soul gem construct fired as well, working to give the drop forces cover.

The Xelur, seeing the descending groups, fired out beams at the drop forces, cutting down people here and there. But they were moving too fast and erratically for them to inflict meaningful casualties.

Deia felt pain in her heart as she saw people she'd trained dying, but she knew it was better than what it could have been.

Blue flames ignited around her, making her look like a meteorite. The white runic lines of the drop packs were visible as the different drop forces weaved through the sky.

Platforms howled through the sky, dropping through corridors created in the individual drop forces' lines. They couldn't dodge very well but they could drop faster than anything else.

The first of the platforms flared its runic lines; the ground illuminated beneath it. It hit the ground the walls falling to the side allowing those on the platform to dismount.

Xelur fired at the newly arrived platforms, trying to kill those who had landed.

Powerful Mana barriers covered the forces as they charged off, forming up into their groups as they jogged forward. The dwarven warbands formed up in blocks of one hundred people, with mages supporting them. Mounted forces landed, the mounts racing off the platforms under the heed of their riders.

More and more platforms came down, those with individual drop packs not far behind.

All manner of creatures swarmed forward, gathering together. The Xelur focused their attacks on the mounted forces. The Mana barriers held for a while but there were simply too many incoming beams.

Xelur soul beams cut through the openings in the Mana barrier. Here and there, riders and their mounts were thrown backward or pierced through. Some were able to blunt the attacks with their own magic and shields as they spread outward, the ground rumbling with the charge of thousands.

It was a force of mounted riders that tore through the ground.

With a yell from within the gates of the Xelur Citadel; Xelur soldiers poured out from the gates in droves. From their hands, the soul beams cut through that darkness, smashing into the remaining barriers or hitting the mounted forces.

The mounted forces weren't without their own attacks. A furious battle of ranged magical attacks was hurled between the two forces.

"Dwarves, ranged!" the dwarven War Clan commander bellowed. From the dwarves on the ground, their creatures that had been riding on their backs now took to the sky, expanding in size. They unleashed their own attacks.

A smoke spell went up in front of the Xelur, blocking them from seeing the advancing mounted forces, who continued to charge forward to get every bit of speed from their mounts as possible.

The Xelur had been saving up their forces for weeks. Now all of those forces were surging out of the citadel, ready to fight. They didn't place the smoke screen in their eyes, blindly shooting out their soul beams.

The repeaters and swivel artillery cannons fired down on the Xelur forces, able to easily see the forces on either side of the smoke screen.

The artillery cannon's shells exploded above the Xelur, killing tens of them with every blast. The repeaters tracked across the Xelur lines, killing many of them.

The Xelur used that power, pulling it into themselves to get stronger faster, throwing up shields and not slowing their pace in the slightest.

Deia didn't land but instead the flames around her flared, reducing her speed and leveling her out. The rest of Party Zero was in a line off her.

From the sides, mages grouped together, creating artillery spells to give the forces up front cover.

The dwarven formations were getting stronger and stronger. As more of them came together, their creatures were in the air above them, unleashing their attacks.

Platforms landed with thuds as drop packs lit with their runic lines, bringing those using them to a halt. A week or two ago, they might have paused but now they had trained for so long that their reactions were automatic, putting away their packs and rushing to meet their groups that were moving forward already.

Aerial forces came out of nowhere, a group of DCA raking the Xelur that were charging forward, protecting a Dragon who came in behind them, unleashing their powerful Affinity flame breath.

Hundreds died in minutes, and the aerial forces raced back up into the sky.

As one, the mounted forces raised spears and totems. From them, dozens of banners snapped in the wind. The men and women on those beasts yelled out their defiance, their mounts unleashing their roars as they rode together.

These banners marked them as riders from different kingdoms, nations, empires and creeds. It was a testament to their families, their ancestors, the people they defended and the ones they were willing to die for.

They were the people of Emerilia. They had been beaten down, their homes attacked and their friends killed. They had held that pain at bay for weeks in order to come together in this moment right now, to show the Xelur, the aggressive species, the creatures and people that had returned from the event of Myths and Legends, the lords and ladies of the Affinities Pantheon, that this was their home, and they would not back down. Not now, not ever.

The first of the Xelur was just making it to the wall of smoke that had been created.

The mounted forces lowered their spears and weapons, readying themselves as they tore through the smoke.

A spear appeared out the other side, still wreathed in smoke, and plunged into the Xelur.

The mounted came out like a tidal wave, clashing with the Xelur. There were Xelur Demons and Demon Lords among the Xelur that had charged outward.

They let out roars, burning their soul energy as they wielded their weapons. The mounted were like an unstoppable wave rushing through the Xelur, but they were not without casualties. Soul beams and weapons cut down their mounts from under them or smashed them off their mount.

The chaos of battle took over as people fought in groups or individually, both sides fighting with everything they had.

Special shells from the swivel artillery cannons as well as those from within the flying citadels made white streaks across the sky. They burst into brilliant light, creating spell formations in the sky. Rampant ambient energy was pulled into these spell formations, stopping it from reaching the Xelur and sending it back toward the flying citadel.

The ground forces, now largely assembled, came together, creating a wall of shields as they passed through the wall of smoke. They stepped out like avenging ghosts, their blades and shields moving as they cut down the Xelur that had survived the mounted forces' attack.

The mounted forces, unable to keep up their momentum, turned away from the Xelur citadel, moving outward.

"Shields!"

Dwarven shields came together with the sound of metal on metal. Their advance was quick as they finished off any Xelur in their path. Healers quickly pulled wounded mounted or beasts to the rear to treat them as they continued forth, not slowing their pace lest they lose their momentum and the initiative.

The Xelur's attacks rang off the barriers that surrounded the dwarven War Clans as they advanced.

"Fire!" archer commanders called out. Arrows filled the sky like angry wasps, cutting down the Xelur charging forth.

As the Xelur died, their energy was ripped from the ground and into the magical formations born from the dwarven artillery cannons' grand working shells. They didn't kill the Xelur but they suppressed their ability to gain any more power.

Mages unleashed their attacks as summoners and necromancers called on their forces, using them to disrupt the Xelur's attempts to gain any form of cohesion as the other forces moved up.

Players joined in on the fray, adding in their own powerful attacks and rushing through the Xelur.

Deia glanced at them. She hadn't worked with any of the players. The Stone Raiders as well as the Fellox Guild worked closely together to make their guild more militaristic. If they messed up, then it would affect their plans.

They, however, allowed players to use the ono to join in on the battle. If they could soften up the Xelur some, then it was worth it.

The people of Emerilia were good at fighting and they were already trained fighting forces. Their coordination was impressive and they didn't care about their levels, gear, or loot as long as they won the battle.

That mindset allowed them to become a fighting force that was capable of fighting off the Xelur. Players were too selfish for the most part to work together on grand-scale things. If it was in small groups, they were good but more than twenty and they started to look at their own gains instead of the good of the group.

A group of five Grand Demon Lords stepped out from one of the gates that the Xelur were rushing out of. They looked over the battlefield, observing the flying citadels above that were pounding on their own defenses as well as the forces that had descended from the flying citadels. Their auras surged as Xelur Demon runes appeared on their bodies, directing the soul energy within their bodies and enhancing their own abilities.

"Kill them!" one of the Xelur Grand Demon Lords yelled, raising a massive sword into the sky. The Grand Demon Lords around him let out battle cries as they started to run forward.

Attacks blossomed all around them, striking the soul shield that they had created. They ran in formation, the one with the sword in the lead; the other two on each side, brandishing their weapons.

The ground around them was torn apart under the force of these attacks. Xelur were thrown backward, unable to defend against these powerful attacks.

"Looks like we've found our first customers." Steve slowly pulled his axe from his back.

Malsour let out a growl as he transformed into his Dragon form. Induca did the same on the other side of him.

Dwarven artillery cannons swiveled on the citadel, tracking the moving Xelur Grand Demon Lords.

Rounds whistled through the sky, smashing against their soul shield but still it didn't go down and the Grand Demon Lords showed no sign of slowing down.

"Blades!" the commander on the ground called.

Suddenly, dozens of powerful auras were unleashed across the battlefield.

Hidden among the ground forces and the mounted that had returned to the back of the formation were those wielding Weapons of Power!

Through the dwarven tournament, a good number of people had been given these Weapons of Power. Through training and coming to know these people more, the War Clan council recommended various people to the Dwarven Council of Anvil and Fire to reward remaining Weapons of Power to.

A Weapon of Power, when matched with the right person, could give them a boost of two to three times their overall combat power. Those who wielded the Weapons of Power, if they were not high levels, were people with hidden strengths or fighting ability that exceeded their level. Many of those who gained Weapons of Power were not the types to simply relax once they had these powerful items.

Instead, they trained to their utmost to use all of the power that they gained from these Weapons of Power. Much like how Gurren and Lox worked tirelessly to improve their own combat ability.

They might not be a match for a Grand Demon Lord by themselves, but together, they were much stronger.

"Let's see if we can't slow them down," Deia said. All around her, spell formations appeared as wings of blue flame grew on her back. She raised her bow, already vibrating from the energy contained within it. Around her bow, spell formations appeared. Her fingers flicked the different notches on her bow's grip.

She pulled back on the bow. All around her, red streams of Fire Mana were drawn in, guided by those spell formations. As she drew back, more appeared around her bow and along the intended path of her arrow. They rotated; their lines looked solid and clear as if made from Fire crystal.

Even the Grand Demon Lords looked up at Deia in shock, a war goddess of Fire. Their eyes went wide as a massive spell formation fell around Party Zero. It was complicated and unfathomable. The power surging through it made them feel fear as they looked to the man in armor. His cloak fluttered behind him as spell formations appeared up his arm and in his hands as he manipulated them.

The black and red Dragons pulled back their heads; power surged from their mouths as spell formations gathered in front of them.

The two black armored-looking golems had their runic lines turned from white to gray; turbulent energy came from between their hands that were cupped together.

The metal man's body glowed with power, spreading into his axe slowly. The condensed power made the air around the axe vibrate.

A woman held her staff up high. Power surged from it as creations spread outward, moving in front of the rest of the party and lining up their attack paths at the Grand Demon Lords. Clearly she looked to be enhancing them all.

A chilling noise could be heard through the battlefield, as many eyes from the Xelur side were drawn to a wolfkin. In front of her, her blade moved; the notes seemed off time with her movements, sounding as if they wanted to rip apart the very fabric of air.

Jung Lee appeared like a wraith his face emotionless as his sword seemed unstoppable. Jekoni floated above him altering and adjusting his power as well as unleashing his own power, the two of them synergistic in their movements and attacks, reading one another perfectly.

Deia released her arrow. With each spell formation it passed through, its power would compound and increase. The spell formation became miniature as it wrapped around the arrow and it turned into a red streak of light.

Gurren and Lox unleashed their attacks, twin gray spears five meters long. They melded together into one attack, their power increasing by a factor of two.

Induca and Malsour unleashed their Affinity breaths. Black and blue flames cut through the sky, following the other attacks.

Steve, Jung Lee, and Anna unleashed their weapon-based attacks.

Behind them all, Suzy, Jekoni, and Dave refined and increased the power of the spell formations held within those different attacks, increasing their power tenfold. Those six attacks turned into flashes of light, cutting through the air.

Deia's attack smashed into the Grand Demon Lord's soul shield. The soul shield was like a shield breaking a wave. The energy released attacked the soul shield crazily. The energy runoff blasted around the shield, tearing up the ground and turning it into burning debris. Xelur that were close by were killed; those within a hundred meters felt the heat of the blast.

Lox and Gurren's arrow came in behind. The Grand Demon Lords poured more energy into their shield and the one holding it up. The arrow struck; the Grand Demon Lord's forward momentum stopped just as Malsour and Induca's attacks landed. Red and black flames hit either side of that shield. It held for a few seconds before breaking, a portion of the energy tossing the Grand Demon Lords aside.

Anna, Steve, and Jung Lee's attacks hit. Two of the attacks hit; the other missed. Those that were struck had deep cuts on their bodies; the others that had those weapon attacks imbued with the Mana of an Affinity felt as if all the air in their bodies had been forcefully ripped from them as they suffered internal injuries due to the air pressure change that came with those weapons.

Those with Weapons of Power didn't hesitate as they charged forward. The Grand Demon Lord group was only a few hundred meters from the front lines of the advancing ground units.

"Move in to help!" Deia called out to the rest of Party Zero. All of them followed her downward.

On the ground, those with Weapons of Power matched their speed, cutting through the Xelur that dared to stand in their way as they cut toward the Grand Demon Lords.

Deia was merciless as she unleashed a hail of arrows on the Xelur blocking those with Weapons of Power.

The rest of Party Zero displayed their own powers at a much lower level than before, clearing out a path for those below.

The Xelur fired up at them but Dave, floating behind them and covered in magical formations, moved the bands on his arm constantly as his hands moved and flickered, changing spell formations that lay at his fingertips. The Mana barrier around them moved as if it were a live organism to redirect the incoming attacks. The orbs around Party Zero kept on moving, making it nearly impossible to hit them easily.

From Dave's hand, a tunnel of spell formations seemed to appear. From his wrist, darts or grenades appeared, turning into gray streaks as they tore through the sky, killing those that targeted his massive Mana barrier and Party Zero inside.

This gave the Grand Demon Lords time to recover from the first attack. Power surged forth once again as they spread out. These were not simple Grand Demon Lords that had only just gained their power. From the way that they moved and looked to one another, they were part of a group and they had trained heavily in fighting.

"Break them apart—don't allow them to coordinate!" Deia said.

"Looks like we have incoming." Dave's voice cut through the party chat. "Players are joining in on the fray!"

Deia was a mix of emotions with having players join in on this fight. If they died, they would come back, but the possibility of them getting in the way was even higher.

"They're moving to assist with suppressing the Grand Demon Lords," Dave said.

Guilds that had joined in on the battle had now finally got themselves sorted out and were adding themselves to the battle, supporting the people of Emerilia who were already engaged with the Xelur. They attacked with their normal abandon—their attacks buffs, heals, and blocks all practiced to perfection.

They might be an unknown but as long as they were under pressure, they were a hellish fighting force, quickly pressuring the Xelur, taking on the larger opponents and bringing down as much destruction as possible.

Once again, the momentum that had been lost with getting into a close combat fight with the Xelur was returned, and the drop forces once again pressed forward.

A cry rose up from the side. A mounted charge rushed through a gap in the line, pushing back the Xelur and tearing through their ranks before quickly peeling away once again. The group of Grand Demon Lords used their weapons, imbuing them with soul energy and cutting through the air with impressive force.

Soul energy stabbed out toward Party Zero and those Weapons of Power users.

Dave's hands flickered as he held them outward. The attacks landed. Dave grunted as the runic lines across his body shone. The barrier that he was projecting became darker and darker from the damage.

Melee types slashed back. Dave's barriers paused the attacks long enough for them to counterattack.

With the sound of breaking glass, the weapon lights broke a wave of power, sending out a shock wave as they continued forward.

Deia drew an arrow. The Fire Mana once again circled her and was funneled into her bow and her arrow.

She released it. A Grand Demon Lord blocked it; a dent appeared in his shield as he was nearly forced back a step. Deia unleashed arrow after arrow, not allowing the Grand Demon Lord time to think, let alone find a way to regain his balance. He took a step back and then another. The arrows rang through the battlefield as energy blew past the shield-bearing Grand Demon Lord.

The others started to unleash their ranged attacks. Anna, Induca, and Malsour were also able to push back Grand Demon Lords or at least make their footing unstable with Dave and Suzy's supporting creations and spells.

Induca and Malsour turned away, raking the Grand Demon Lords but their real aim was the Xelur surrounding them. Their breaths cut through the Xelur, opening up a dead ground around the Grand Demon Lords.

Gurren, Lox, Steve, Jung Lee, and Anna charged forward. Their weapons appeared in their hands as they rushed through the air.

The Grand Demon Lords increased the soul energy that they were channeling into their bodies, their weapons blocking the oncoming attacks.

Deia continued to fire arrows through what seemed like impossible gaps, each of her arrows as strong as a weapon blow and targeted at the Grand Demon Lords' weaknesses. They were massive and powerful, but with being so big, their vulnerabilities were easier to target and see.

Deia glanced over to Dave. Mana threads of all colors were gathering around his hands. A complex weave of spell formations that Deia couldn't come to understand appeared in front of his hands as he moved his fingers, the different bands on his arms moving by their own volition.

The spell formations were dense and powerful between his hands as he spread his hands apart slowly. A small pin appeared from the holding item that had been incorporated into the bracer.

The pin shot off in a ray of silver light.

It hit a Grand Demon Lord's protective soul energy. It exploded, making the Grand Demon Lord cover up from the explosions. Gurren's sword smashed against the Grand Demon Lord's side, only to find the soul energy there. It fluctuated with the strength of the pin's hit and subsequent explosion, followed by Gurren's impressive blow.

Jung Lee was fighting one of the Grand Demon Lords by himself, with the occasional support from Suzy. Steve was also facing one but Lox was bouncing between Steve and Gurren to support them. Anna was facing off against the rest with Suzy and Deia's help.

Dave raised his hands toward the unoccupied Grand Demon Lords that were looking to assist their fellows. He unleashed more of the pins, reducing the stress on Deia, Anna, and Suzy.

The pins hit with incredible speed. However, the Grand Demon Lords were getting smart about it and used their soul energy beams to take down the needles.

A war cry erupted behind Party Zero as those with Weapons of Power charged forth. Spells tore through the battlegrounds, smashing the Grand Demon Lords back as mages entered the fray. The melee types rushed ahead of them, their weapons clashing with the Grand Demon Lords. They weren't able to match the Grand Demon Lords' height of their full power, but they had numbers on their side.

Deia didn't need to call out anything. Arrows streaking from her bow—, over shoulders, under arms and into the Grand Demon Lords that were using their soul energy to the limit in order to fight Party Zero and those wielding Weapons of Power.

Dave and the suppressing shells made it so that they couldn't gain back any energy.

Dave used his darts while Suzy's creations acted as distractions, pulling at the Grand Demon Lords' feet and their arms, and creating blinding flashes in their faces.

Induca and Malsour landed on the ground, using the Affinity breaths to kill any Xelur near the fight.

The Xelur in the citadels started to target them, making them have to shoot off into the sky and come back in at random angles to avoid the powerful energy beams that were hunting them across the sky.

The first of the Demon Lords went under Jung Lee's blade. As soon as their protecting soul energy collapsed, Jung Lee called upon his Affinity spirits. All of them rushed through the Grand Demon Lord, forcefully ripping energy from them as Jung Lee shot forth, his blade moving in a shimmering arc. The Grand Demon Lord looked around for a moment, seemingly disoriented before its eyes went glossy and it collapsed, not understanding that it was dead already. Jung Lee used their falling body to charge forth.

Steve's axe clashed with a Grand Demon Lord's sword. Steve's body started to glow brighter, a look of determination on his face. He swung his axe, every hit punctuated by a word.

"Stop. Being. Such. A. Pain. In. My. Metal. ASS!" Steve bellowed. Each of his hits pushed the Xelur Grand Demon back, a look of shock in their eyes. Steve opened up their defense the hit making them both stumble backwards. "Jung Lee!" Steve yelled out.

Jung Lee came in like a dart under the raised shield as the Grand Demon Lord flailed slightly to regain their balance. Jung Lee's sword was almost ethereal as it cut through the Grand Demon Lord's protective energy and into the side of the Grand Demon Lord.

The Grand Demon Lord let out an enraged roar. With Jung Lee's attack the Grand Demon Lord's soul energy was thrown into chaos, quickly being converted into Mana. The Grand Demon Lord's cries of anger turned into ones of pain as its soul energy surged forth.

"Who needs soul energy when you have Mana!" Jekoni's voice came from within the Grand Demon Lord as all of its soul energy was converted in bare seconds.

Jekoni took control of the soul energy within the Grand Demon Lord, killing their mind and taking possession of its body.

The runes on the Grand Demon Lord changed as the aura of soul energy was changed to that of Mana. The Grand Demon Lord's lifeless eyes recovered as it blinked and looked at its body and hands. "Been awhile since I had a flesh body." Jekoni's voice came from the Grand Demon Lord as it turned toward the other battles.

"Jekoni, what did you do?" Deia asked.

"Oh, possession—just took over this big ole bag of meat. Now all of his energy and his strength is at my disposal. I'm not so good in the melee part of things but I can use this guy to cast spells," Jekoni said.

Jekoni, in the Grand Demon Lord's body, dropped his weapons and started to move his hands; spell formations appeared around him. Lances of ice appeared in the air and shot forth. The Grand Demon Lords tried to escape but the spears followed, forcing them to fight them off as Jekoni was using the full strength of the Grand Demon Lord under his control. Their power combined with his knowledge made him an extremely powerful mage on the battlefield.

The Grand Demon Lords had too many threats to deal with. Lox's sword took out one's knee; Gurren bashed away their shield as Deia's arrow penetrated their soul energy and their body. The flames that made up her arrows burned through the soul energy, making the Grand Demon Lord howl in pain as they were destroyed from the inside, their energy like gasoline to Deia's flames.

A player with an Axe of power separated the Grand Demon Lord's head from its body.

The last opponent was killed with a Weapon of Power in the form of a spear.

The Grand Demon Lord looked stunned as it tried to hold its neck as blood spurted downward. Even with its regeneration abilities, it wasn't able to heal the wound. Several other Weapons of Power users quickly stabbed at the Xelur Grand Demon Lord's weaknesses so that it wouldn't be able to recover.

A massive power beam shot out from the Xelur citadel as the last of the Grand Demon Lords fell.

Dave let out a shout. Orbs appeared from his hands as spell formations surrounded him. The beam smashed into the rapidly forming Mana shield, making it buckle under the power that was charging into it.

The power was enough to tear the ground apart anywhere that wasn't covered by the shield. The runic lines across Dave's body and his clothing surged with power as he held off the attack with his power and that which was saved up in his armor.

"We need to move forward!" Dave yelled, energy parting just feet in front of his hands.

Jung Lee stood beside Dave, pouring his power into the Mana shield and pushing the Xelur beam backward.

Malsour and Induca, circling overhead, saw the attack and unleashed their own at where the beam was coming from. The soul shield shuddered under the impact.

Lu Lu shot back with her own lightning breath, reducing the power of the beam somewhat.

"Use our power!" Lox and Gurren moved up to Dave's other side.

Streams of power came from their armor as the shield strengthened.

"Forward!" Deia yelled.

Party Zero and the Weapons of Power users who had fought beside them against the Grand Demon Lords followed as they pushed forward. More and more of the beams that were coming from the walls changed from hitting the dwarven formation to hitting Party Zero and the Weapons of Power users behind Dave's shield.

They forged forward. Any of the Xelur around the shield were torn apart by the rampant energies of the beam being broken by the shield.

A roar came from the dwarves and various fighters advancing behind them, their fighting spirit surging as they pushed onward. Without the pressure of the beams and seeing their own charge forward, they doubled their efforts and picked up their speed.

Deia looked to Dave, her eyebrows coming together in concern. If Dave couldn't hold this shield, then they would all die under the power of those beams. She could see the toll that it was taking on him but still he continued to move forward step by step, gradually increasing his pace.

"I've figured out a way to disrupt these arrays they're using for the beams. I'm sending it to the citadels— they can smash the arrays apart. Good thing that the Xelur were so generous in using a bunch of different types to display their Magical Circuits!" Dave laughed as Deia and the others looked on in shock.

He had been defending them against the beams while also using the time to come to understand how they worked and figure out a way to shut them all down. Few of them would have the presence of mind to do that in the middle of fighting for their lives.

They walked forward step by step, preparing themselves for what was to come.

"I can get us to the gates. It it will be up to the rest of you to hold off the enemy. I can breach the walls and collapse the main gate, but I'll need five minutes to do so," Dave said.

"We've got you covered!" Lox said.

"We're with you," one of the Weapons of Power users yelled out, the others with looks of determination on their faces. They would do everything in their power in order to help Dave take down that wall. If they could, then their own forces could surge forward with less of the soul arrays attacking them and a way right into the Xelur's citadel. If they were lucky, it might even weaken the Xelur's soul shield, allowing the three flying citadels around the Xelur citadel an opening to fire into the Xelur stronghold.

Deia looked over her party, as well as the Weapons of Power people who had attached themselves to her group. Behind them were the people of Emerilia forces that were smashing through the Xelur forces, as well as various player groups that had entered into the fray. Here and there, a charge was led by the mounted forces to break the Xelur's formations apart.

The three citadels and their drop forces completely surrounded the citadel, not allowing anyone out as all of their fire was focused on suppressing the Xelur.

The citadels were still being hammered by Xelur beams here and there but other than a slight discoloration the citadels were fine. They rotated occasionally in order to spread out the impact and power of the Xelur soul array's effects. They welcomed the damage, offering themselves up as a willing target and taking it on instead of the Drop forces.

All of that fire concentrated on the Xelur stronghold was making it hard for them to stay protected. Their soul shield buckled here and there under the constant pressure. They had nowhere to go and could only use their own soul energy to make sure that they weren't torn apart by the furious energies that rained in from above.

The sky was lit with different spells hammering down on the strong hold as well as the flashes of impacts against various shields or chaotic battles that raged along the front.

Dragons and their protecting aerial forces came down out of the heavens. They poured their attacks down upon the Xelur stronghold and raked the Xelur forces that were surging out of the gates still.

The Xelur forces that had built up within the citadel were on par with the drop forces of all three flying citadels. Here and there,

Grand Demon Lords and a gathering of highly ranked Demon Lords would exit the Xelur citadel, pressuring the citadel's drop forces, making the Weapons of Power and the players reveal their strengths in order to defeat them as the citadels supported them from above.

In some places, these powerful Xelur made it to the dwarven or player lines, turning that area into chaos as the Xelur fought to break the drop forces' lines while they tried to pull down these powerful Xelur.

Deia withdrew her gaze from the battle and concentrated on the gate ahead of them and the walls that were unleashing soul energy beams against Dave's shield, as well as hitting the Terra Alliance's forces.

***

Lox's face was set in grim determination. None could see it as he was within his Devastator armor. Their pace had increased from walking to running. As Dave came to understand the beams better, he was able to mitigate their attacks. More and more attacks had come from the sides, however; the regular Xelur ground forces were adding in their attacks.

"We're only one hundred meters away!" Deia yelled out.

"Induca and I won't be able to support you this close to the wall in our Dragon form. We'll assist the forces moving up behind you," Malsour said over the party chat.

"We're going to need them as soon as we crack open this citadel," Deia replied.

"I will do what I can," Malsour said. Black flames ripped through the sky as metal beams seemed to fall from his wings, killing all of those that lay under him.

A trail of destruction ran from Party Zero to just a few meters in front of the ground forces.

Induca crossed over, thinning out the Xelur forces arrayed against the Terra Alliance.

Those under the shield crossed the remaining one hundred meters quickly. The beams fell away as they were unable to hit the advancing force anymore.

"Ready yourselves!" Deia called out.

"Shield coming down!" Dave called out, sounding drained from working it.

The shield fell. The war cries of those with Weapons of Power surged as they charged ahead. They might have needed to use numbers against the Grand Demon Lords but against the rather weak Xelur soldiers, one of them was able to handle easily half a dozen at one time.

Those with ranged and area of effect attacks used them, clearing out any of the Xelur that remained in their way. More of them continued to pour out from the gate—not in the massive numbers that they had at the start of the battle, but enough that it pressured the group.

Lox and Gurren stood on either side of Dave while Jung Lee took point and Steve watched their backs.

Jung Lee, now combined with the knowledge and abilities of his Affinity spirits, was like a war god. He moved forward as if he were taking a simple jog. Xelur died all along his path, coming nowhere close to reaching his ability or strength. The Xelur tried to escape from the slaughter but there was nowhere for them to go. Jung Lee carved a path to the wall near the gate.

"This will work." Dave pulled out a grand working. Gray Mana appeared around his hand as he punched the wall, creating a crater in it. Jung Lee, Gurren, Lox, and Steve fought off the Xelur that now pressed in on them as Dave inserted the grand working into the wall.

Lox shield bashed one Xelur and sent them flying. As he cut down another, he headbutted a third, blocking a sword blow with his shield. His, sword darted outward, opening up the attacker as he whirled around on his knee. Opening up three Xelur with one strike, he got to his feet, his sword and shield an extension of his body as he slaughtered any that dared to come into his range.

The rest of the party was taking their time to deal with the stronger forces.

"Done! To the wall on the other side of the gate, as far as possible!" Dave said.

Jung Lee led once again, surging forth as they took up the same formation. It was all Lox could do to follow in Jung Lee's wake, reacting to those that found their way into his own path, stopping them from getting close and putting them down ruthlessly.

They got near the entrance of the gate but found themselves unable to push through all of the Xelur.

"Don't move!" Dave yelled. He adjusted the bands on his arm. Magical circles appeared under everyone's feet as they quickly rose into the air, passing over those in the gateway and landing on the other side.

"Nothing like the good up and over trick!" Steve yelled over the sound of battle.

Once again, Jung Lee, Lox, Gurren, and Steve had to clear a path through the Xelur forces.

The rest of the party and the Weapons of Power had created a fighting pit in front of the gates, slowing their progress and also cutting them down before they could reach the drop forces. It was making it hard for the Xelur that were still trying to exit to get anywhere.

Once again, they reached the wall. Dave punched out a hole and placed another grand working.

"They're placed!" Dave said. The others didn't have the time to look behind them as the grand working seemed to expand, reaching out like tree roots to break through the structure of the wall and work their way upward and outward.

Dave stepped up to the line that the other four had made, adding his own sword to the fight. He pulled out his conjuration rods, creating twin swords. They flashed with Light runes down their blades as they sliced through the Xelur that were swarming them. The grand working on either side of the gate grew, expanding until they reached through the wall over the gate and growing until they reached the battlements at the top and stretching to the sides.

Their growth was alarming. Only the drop forces could see it in the distance as those root-like structures continued to grow; their commanders ordered them forward into the fray.

Swords flashed and feet marched in time with the dwarven war drums, like an impossible tide coming in.

Lox fought alongside his brothers, each of them looking out for one another unconsciously, killing those that were eyeing the other. It was a bloody and hellish melee. As Xelur fell before them, they roared out their defiance.

"Move toward the rest of the group!" Lox yelled out.

"I'll clear a path!" Dave yelled. He waved his hand. From his wrist, several grenades appeared shooting off into the ranks of Xelur, exploding in their depths.

They surged forward, the stunned and weakened Xelur that were unable to fight back. Dave threw out more grenades; they appeared in lines in front of him, waiting to be sent off. With barely a thought, they rushed forward and lit up the Xelur lines. Where they had grouped together in strength, voids were made, allowing Lox and his group to surge forward into stunned and injured Xelur, quickly carving a bloody path through the Xelur lines.

Their weapons cleaved a path through the tide of Xelur, fighting for every inch. They

They reached the circle that the rest of the party and Weapons of Power users were in.

In the center were the mages and ranged fighters, with the melee types on the outside, tanks on the front, and the faster and less armored groups in the second rank.

Dave stepped into the middle, moving his arm bands. As he threw out orbs, they floated around the group. A spell formation appeared around Dave, one layer and then another, growing in complexity and power as they moved outward until they touched the outside ring of fighters. The flowing runes glowed with a gray light; smoke came from them on the ground as they pulsed with energy.

Lox felt more power surge through his armor at Dave's buff.

Jung Lee stayed at the second rank while Steve, Lox, and Gurren replaced the injured tanks and those who weren't proper tanks but taking over the role so that the formation didn't come apart.

They were an island within the Xelur forces that broke around them like a sea around a rock.

The mages' hands flashed as attacks poured down on the Xelur. The ranged attackers used their bows; with every arrow, another Xelur dropped. Their speed was incredible as arrow after arrow pierced the air in a matter of seconds.

Jekoni was still using the Grand Demon Lord's body, consuming its stored energy. With a lack of water around the Densaou Ring of Fire, Jekoni was now using blood to substitute, turning them into swords and minions, high-speed projectiles and curses.

Suzy's creations hid on the ground, becoming traps and making the Xelur off-balance as they fought those around the perimeter.

Lox, Anna, Jung Lee, Steve, and Gurren stood shoulder to shoulder, facing the gates that the Xelur were pouring from and where the fighting was the hardest.

Lox yelled inside his armor, pulling power from his armor and using the enhancements of the magical formation Dave had put down. He moved in a flash, his sword cutting down Xelur with every movement. His shield seemed to have an intelligence of its own as it blocked, bashed, and slammed Xelur.

All of them were fighting with everything they had; there was no room for thought, only reaction.

"Jung Lee, right! Gurren, watch that Demon Lord! Steve, pull back!" Deia called out to them, each of her words like commandments from an all-seeing god as they reacted with complete trust in what she said.

"East side, get some healing potions into yourselves! Ranged support, east! We need to hold until the drop forces can get closer. We block off the Xelur here and they can speed up their advance!" Deia yelled out to all those in the formation.

Dave's formation surged with energy. Each Xelur that died had their power torn away and poured into the formation around him charging his soul gems that were being directed into a new spell formation he had created. He changed out the runes and altered the different spell formations. With every second, it became more powerful.

Lox's screen blinked angrily with notifications but he paid them no heed; to think of something else for even a moment would end him. He threw out grenades that Dave had given him; the Xelur thinned out slightly before more surged forth.

"Incoming support!" Deia called out.

Lox threw out more grenades; again hearing an angry howl from above, he glanced back. He couldn't help but laugh madly.

"You got a screw loose?" Steve yelled, kicking a Xelur backward ten feet. He stepped forward, his axe cutting through dozens of Xelur that couldn't hope to reach past his long axe handle.

"I just thought it was a good day for rain!" Lox laughed.

Artillery rounds crossed overhead, falling among the Xelur outside of the gate and trying to attack the group holding out in front.

Explosions threw Xelur and dirt up into the sky, creating ten-meter-wide craters that shook the very ground. Their destructive light illuminated the ranks of Xelur that charged toward the group. Many were tossed forward, losing their footing. The group didn't waste the opportunity, cutting them down.

The group's morale lifted once again. They had been wounded and beaten down and ready to lay down their lives in order for the rest of the drop forces to make it. Now, as that artillery dropped all around them, creating a hellish scene, they cheered. Cold light gathered in their eyes, their expressions a mix of focused fury and hunger.

A wave of power expanded from Dave as a spell formation in his hand collapsed into one entity. The wave had healing properties, healing those within the formation. People stood up straighter, the wounds that they had gathered disappearing and their hope restored once again.

**

"We're ready," the weapons controller of Goblin Mountain Citadel One said.

"Get rid of those damn arrays," the captain and leader of the Goblin Mountain group said.

The weapons controller passed the confirmation to all of the different flying citadels that had converged on the three Xelur citadels.

The flying citadels had positioned themselves so that they were an equal distance from one another and the Xelur citadels that they were attacking. Now, magical formations appeared underneath their soul gem formed islands of the flying Citadels; runic lines tore across the sky, between the different flying citadels, connecting them and creating lines around the Xelur strong holds.

Inside these formations, another magical formation appeared directly above the Xelur citadels.

The power from the surrounding area was pulled inward, as if the spell formation were a black hole. The spell formation became more complicated as more and more rings were added into the center.

The Xelur arrays opened up on the citadels once again, with all of their strength.

The spell formations dropped downward, creating funnels above the Xelur citadels.

Power was channeled through these different layers. A blinding light filled the world as a twisting vortex of Mana appeared at the upper reaches of the spell formation. It turned for a few moments before it was grabbed by the funnel and shot downward, condensing and gaining power with every level it went through. But this wasn't destructive energy.

The vortex of energy came out of the last of the spell formations looking like multiple arrows coming from the sky, each of them guided down toward the Xelur citadel. They hit the shield, being delayed for a few moments before driving through. They weren't targeted at the shields but rather the soul arrays that amplified the soul energy beams.

These streams of light were covered in runes if one was to look closely.

They hit the arrays, causing them to overload with energy. Some exploded, others melted, but it took out the offensive capabilities of the Xelur in a single shot.

Without the pressure of the soul array enhanced Xelur energy beams, the drop forces surged forwards. They were just fifty meters away from the Weapons of Power and Party Zero group.

The captain looked to where the greatest Mana disturbance was happening. A man stood in the center of those turbulent Mana waves, the walls being torn apart by a series of roots that impaled Xelur in their way.

The power was shocking, nearly rivaling the power that had just been used in that disabling attack.

The man in the center of that spell formation raised his hand. The wall and gate in front of him exploded inward. Sections of the wall came apart and landed on the Xelur eager to get into battle.

With the soul array just being broken, the Xelur were in a state of shock. They weren't prepared when a wall exploded inward.

The spell formation that centered around the man rose up into the sky. Multiple spell formations slammed together, creating an increasingly complex spell formation.

The last of the subsidiary spell formations added itself to the overall spell formation, flashing with power once. Its structure glowed from the inside with greater and greater power until a shock wave of gray light propagated forward and sideways from the man. It tore Xelur apart in all three directions, slamming into the soul barrier of the wall, making it shake. Nearly three hundred Xelur not strong enough to resist were either killed or tossed aside with ease.

"Target that gate! Break their soul barrier!" the group commander ordered.

Citadel One, closest to the hole, positioned itself so the majority of its mages, spell formations and Dwarven Artillery could bear on the opening. All of them fired as fast as possible; tens of rounds a second smashed into that gate. The soul energy barrier shook with the powerful impacts that were hitting its weak points.

With the sound of breaking glass, the soul energy barrier collapsed around that new breach where the gate had been.

The players surged forward, unable to keep themselves in check once seeing the Xelur defenses were down. Grand soul gem rounds were changed in, calling down the wrath of the Affinities and summoning creatures from the depths of hell inside the Xelur citadel. Now that they had broken into it, they couldn't allow the Xelur the time to recuperate and sort out their counterattack.

The people of Emerilia, closed off behind the player groups, advanced at a slower pace. They had expected the players to run free so now they were ready to close up the holes in their lines and cut down all of the Xelur that they had left behind.

The aerial forces came down like avenging gods. Without the soul arrays to combine and direct the power of the soul beam attacks, the Xelur were stuck with using their own power and understanding of the soul energy beams to attack the forces in the air.

They weren't as strong nor did they have the reach. Seizing the opportunity, the aerial forces pounced on the flying between artillery shells, they dropped their own spells and other ranged attacks, their efforts quickly destabilizing the Xelur for the ground forces to finish off.

The Xelur were in disarray. The Emerilian mounted forces and the soldier formations pressed ahead, an indomitable war machine bearing down on the Xelur.

The lines reached up to where the Weapons of Power users as well as Party Zero were. The dwarven War Clans broke down into War Bands and charged toward the growing breach.

Inside, soul energy beams flashed and spells tore through the sky as shades from the grand workings attacked Xelur without care of the harm to their bodies and artillery shells and spells left behind craters and destruction.

The citadel's outer wall had been broken down but still the inner wall and the castle with its protruding tower remained in the center of the citadel.

The flying citadel's fire switched from the outer defenses and the dead ground outside of the citadel to the inner defenses of the citadel.

These rounds flew faster and their impacts illuminated the sky. They had been using regular rounds before; now they were pulling out their precious stocks of grand working shells, hoping to keep up the momentum and pressure the Xelur into making mistakes.

"Hold off on our other trump cards. We need to keep those hidden for later battles with stronger opponents. The Xelur might not talk to any other groups now but the people of Emerilia do," the leader of the Goblin Mountain group said, his voice stiff.

He wanted to use the more powerful weapons but to do so would give their future opponents an advantage. He knew that holding onto different trump cards was one of the few ways that he could turn a battle later on. In his heart, he debated whether they would fight a battle worse than the one below him. As much as he hoped not, he wasn't sure and he was under strict orders so he stayed his hand.

Good luck. The Goblin Mountain group leader looked down at those drop forces, his heart tight as he looked over the various screens. Another group of Stone Raiders and people with Weapons of Power also reached an outer wall, putting in a breaching grand working.

It grew rapidly, exploding inward, allowing the group to quickly surge forth.

In a handful of minutes, three more breaches were opened up into the citadel.

Chapter 20: Into the Xelur's Den

After the wave of power that Dave had shot out in every direction, he coughed roughly, the action shaking his body as his aura weakened considerably. The power dimmed around the Weapons of Power users and Party Zero.

Anna looked around, there were no enemies nearby thanks to Dave; Dave was kneeling on the ground, having to support himself with an arm and his body was shaking from the power that he'd unleashed.

Even channeling that much power from his armor's reserves, pulling it into and through his body was enough to make him regret it. However, he'd not only poured it through his body but also poured in his own Mana, making him closer to Mana fatigue but reducing the power that was forced through his body by the armor that he was using.

The wall had exploded inward, throwing the Xelur into disarray and killing dozens that had been hiding behind the gates, standing on the walls or were behind them.

The battlefields seemed as if a god had landed, blowing them all away with their descent. The battlefield froze for a moment before the firepower of the flying citadels increased once again, their attacks hitting the weakness that Dave had exposed. The soul energy shield broke; shining lights of grand working rounds passed through the area that the shield had been.

Anna heard the cheers behind her and felt the ground shaking. The battered mounted forces yelled as they charged forth past the lines of dwarven War Clans that moved out of the way of their charge with fluid-like grace.

They ran down any that were left alive. Aerial forces and Dragons let out their own roars and cries as they raked the Xelur that were attempting to hold back the drop forces.

The dwarven war drums beat faster and harder. The pace of the dwarven War Clans surged forward.

Player groups rushed toward the breaches, unable to hold themselves back.

The Xelur fired back with their soul beams but they were unable to kill the forces approaching wantonly as they could have with the soul arrays.

"Once the mounted make it past us, we'll lead the charge into the walls!" Deia yelled out to the group.

Those with Weapons of Power recovered their condition, taking healing, Mana, and Stamina potions.

"Dave, how are you?" Deia asked on the party chat, her voice filled with concern.

"Just overusing Mana that's not mine, as usual. Looking forward to a time when I can start using my real inventions," Dave said in the party chat, coughing again and taking recovery potions. He drank them greedily, before getting to his feet.

Anna looked at the armor that he wore. The sense of foreboding power that seemed to radiate from it was much more profound than her own sword that he had forged for her. She knew that unlike her sword, Dave's armor and its gear held secrets that few others would be able to see through. This armor was not meant simply for this war—it was meant to end the wars of Emerilia and the wars of humanity and the Jukal. It was not a simple creation.

Anna swigged back recovery potions that Jung Lee had created. Her body surged with power as the Grand Demon Lord that Jekoni had been using collapsed to the ground, Jekoni appearing where it had been standing.

"That's some real heebie-jeebie shit." Steve shuddered as he looked at the Grand Demon Lord's corpse.

"I am the sword that Jung Lee uses. How easy would it be for me to gain access to the body of a person who has had their protective power stripped away by that sword?" Jekoni asked.

"I'm guessing very," Steve said.

"He's not the dumb piece of crystal that he always looks like." Gurren laughed.

"Dammit! They cut open my armor again!" Steve complained, putting a finger through the hole in his armor where a soul energy beam had vaporized the armor and part of his soul gem construct body underneath.

"Not as creepy as a walking, talking piece of crystal that dresses up in pink outfits," Jekoni said under his breath. But it nonetheless reached everyone's ear.

"Props," Gurren said, his voice of deep respect as he held up his massive fist that was nearly as big as Jekoni's spiritual body.

Jekoni tapped the fist with his own, a big smile on his face.

Anna smiled at the antics.

The mounted forces raced past them and toward the open breaches. Malsour swooped overhead, casting a spell as he did, the stone rubble turned into ramps to allow the mounted easy access into the castle without having to slow their charge.

"You lot ready down there?" Induca asked over the party chat.

"'Bout as ready as we're going to get," Dave said, Mana once again circulating around him.

"Ready yourselves!" Deia said as the tail end of the mounted forces could be seen.

They started jogging at first, and then picked up their pace. As the last of the mounted had gone past them, they broke out into an all-out run. They were nearly as fast as the beasts that the mounted forces rode on.

"Half to the right, half to the left!" Deia yelled over the explosions of grand working shells that were now making the soul barrier in the inner sections of the citadel shake and shudder under their massive power.

Anna found herself with Lox, Jung Lee, Dave, and half of those who held Weapons of Power.

They rushed forward. Dave pulled out his conjuration rods and created a bow. The mounted forces were cutting through the Xelur that had been between the outer walls and the inner walls that ringed the castle and the tower in its center.

Dave's arrows cut through the air, taking down the Xelur along the ramparts and hiding in the outer walls of the castle.

"Clear out the walls!" Lox yelled, pointing at the walls before he leapt upward. With a single leap, he made it to the top of the wall.

Others jumped upward, entering the broken sections of the walls and the corridors that ran through the outer walls of the Xelur citadel.

The sounds of battle broke out as the roar of the dwarven War Clans arrived in Anna's ears. The War Clans made their entrance into the breach, spreading outward rapidly, ready to take on the Xelur defenders.

Anna moved forwards her party members at her side, as they cut down all of the Xelur that stood in their way. Their movements together made the most complex teamwork flow as their movements covered one another and served to push along the Xelur outer walls.

Her eyes flashed with a cold glow as she called upon wind and threw one attacker to the side. Her sword unleashed an Air blade in one direction as she reversed its momentum and cut through a Xelur's sword and their chest with one powerful blow that sent them flying backward.

She turned her foot and snapped upward, catching the Xelur that she had tossed to the side in the face and sending them over the wall. They yelled out but their voice came to a brutal halt as they smashed into the ground tens of meters below.

Anna never paused. None of the Xelur in her and Jung Lee's path were their match.

Dave walked behind them, shooting those needles from his bracers; the needles blew thru the Xelur soul barriers and hit the Xelur with amazing energy. Once the needles were inside them, they ignited, converting the soul energy into mana.

Anna was shocked as rampant soul energy ignited. The Xelur turned into a bomb as they destroyed a section of the wall, stunning those that had been nearby to witness the attack but had survived the blast.

Dave was a Dwarven Master Smith, and he had worked for months to create soul gems and other soul capturing spells, to him the Xelur were nothing but amateurs using soul energy.

Dave's attacks killed off Xelur and helped break up the mass of Xelur into smaller groups, making it so that Jung Lee and Anna weren't fighting a wall of Xelur but rather smaller and easier groups to handle. Inside the walls between the inner and outer castle, the dwarven War Clans had already established a shield wall and were advancing even under the attacks from the Xelur on both the inner and outer walls.

Their summoned beasts were a surprise as they hid within the dwarven War Clans' Mana barrier and unleashed their attacks. In the fight up to here, they had increased in power. They had been mere distractions before but with the shared experience, they were quickly gaining in levels and power, making their attacks enough to rival the weakest of the Xelur's soul energy beams. The dwarven War Clans moved forward under the cover of their summoned beasts.

The mounted forces weren't simply charging through the area between the walls.

Anna watched as one with a spear struck out at the inner wall; behind them, another person tossed in a grand working into the crater left by that spear-wielding mounted fighter.

The grand working spread in a familiar spider web. Along the outer and the inner walls, multiple glowing spider webs were created.

Anna felt as more breaches were opened up along the outer walls, the other drop forces surging inward and strengthening the forces inside.

***

Anna wasn't the only one watching as the drop forces surged into the Xelur citadel.

A truly massive Grand Demon Lord, sitting on a massive metal throne inlaid with soul arrays, smashed his fist against the armrest.

Even with those strengthening arrays, the armrest broke under the force.

He was Clan Leader Che of the Grand Xelur Clan Ish'tal. His clan was ranked among the top five of the Xelur world. His people were some of the strongest in known existence. When the portal that his people had been guarding from the other Xelur opened, they had surged forth to claim their position within the soul energy-rich planet Emerilia. They had come to meet with the forces of Emerilia and subdue or eliminate them.

Che remained on Xelur to make sure that no one would think anything was amiss as they worked to establish a foothold in this world. Already another portal that was well known about had been opened and three of the five major clans were warring over it. Their gains within Emerilia had been pitiful as they fought not only one another but the people of Emerilia.

Che had held disdain for them in his heart. He knew that his own clan controlled many more castles on the other side of the portal and they were working on taking more. With their cooperation and under the banner of the Ish'tal clan, they had worked tirelessly to carve out a portion of Emerilia to control. When they had not gained the northern castle but instead lost a handful of Grand Demon Lords that were the backbone of the Ish'tal clan, Che had been furious and ordered the clan to gain strength and prepare themselves for a great offensive.

They had sent more and more of the clan over to Emerilia to fill their ranks and to gain power to increase the chances of the clan's victory.

Then flying citadels had appeared in the sky, able to take the full forces of his three remaining citadels' soul array beams and had weapons capable of greatly weakening his citadel's soul energy shields.

He had sent over the best of the clan's soul arrays and had personally come with the strongest of the elders at his side. They had split up to the different citadels in order to take command of the situation, to push back these Emerilians and take their position within this soul energy-rich land.

He had thought that they would defeat them on the plains around the citadels but instead, the western citadel that he occupied had been breached along its outer walls. More breaches appeared every minute.

Now he watched as the inner wall exploded inward, killing dozens that had been on the wall and raining down debris and rubble on the forces inside. A few had been killed but these were the elites and strongest of the clan. Most of them were able to destroy the shrapnel that rained down on them with their own abilities.

"Useless trash!" Che yelled as he watched from his seat upon the highest tower in the citadel. The soul energy beam arrays had been discarded and only the soul energy barrier was still working, one of the main cruxes of the soul energy barrier that controlled the barriers around the citadel.

With each explosion, the secondary energy shield anchors were destroyed and their shield weakened, as the flying citadels continued to pound on them.

Che's eyes were red with anger as he stared at the outer wall defenses that were being cut down by the Terra Alliance's drop forces.

In his mind, there was no excuse for not destroying these weak creatures. His own body released a powerful aura of soul energy that was incomparable to the Grand Demon Lords that had been sent out onto the plains to break these forces but instead had been cut down by those wielding impressive weapons.

Che's eyes fell to these people, his inner greed filling them. "Target those with strong weapons. Let us see how able they are without their different arms!" Che said.

One of the elders around him transmitted the message.

"For those that kill them, they will be allowed to use the weapons! We will take their strength and turn it into ours!" Che's lips curled upward into a sneer.

Dwarven lines continued to advance but the other groups—the players, the skirmishers—ran through the walls, pitching their own battles against the Xelur.

As the inner walls exploded, mounted forces once again charged inward like a virus infecting the citadel, spreading out in every direction and using their momentum to carry them inward and open up the Xelur. Many of them died as they entered the inner walls. The Xelur in here were a much higher grade than those that had been on the outer walls and had faced them on the plains.

They had much better coordination and reacted in groups.

Behind the mounted Emerilians, through the dust of the breached walls, those with Weapons of Power, players, and others rushed in. Different groups immediately raised their shields and

Mana barriers as they created a solid base from which to fight the Xelur. Others used their speed to close with the Xelur and charge their ranks.

Along the outer and inner walls, people climbed upward, topping the walls and fighting the Xelur on the battlements.

The drop forces did everything in their power to open up the Xelur defenses and hit from every possible angle as more and more breaches opened up along the inner walls.

The Xelur here cut down many who rushed through those breaches, but a number of them, mostly those who had hidden behind their shields and barriers, advanced forward, their attacks pressuring the Xelur.

Che looked down at this all, unable to believe it. Through his mind, he continued to call those of his clan that fell to these Emerilian trash and useless, but in his heart, doubts started to creep in.

"Send out the Grand Demon Lords to deal with the situation." Che's eyes flickered to an explosion along the wall. His face froze as another powerful stream of soul energy destroyed a section of the wall, killing those on the other side.

"How dare they break the ten thousand soul's shielding array!" Che yelled. The array was the strongest that the Ish'tal clan owned, its cost was incalculable. But here and there, the Emerilians were gaining access to the various soul array totems and mercilessly attacking and destroying them. The shield weakened and forced the main totem beside Che to take on the load that the others couldn't handle.

The resources and power that Che had poured into this couldn't be compared. The clan would be ruined if all of these items and forces were laid to waste.

Che let out a cold laugh that made even the other elders take a step backward.

"You come to kill my clan members and to attack *my* citadel—you are truly extraordinary! I will use you to weed out the weak from the strong of my clan and then I will thoroughly destroy you, ripping the souls of you and your clan members out from the roots!" Che declared. Boundless soul energy rushed through his body and his veins. His abyss-black skin lit up with powerful Xelur runes that had been carved into his body. They shone like a beacon in the night as soul energy vapor seemed to coalesce around his body, unleashing a terrifying power.

***

"Seems someone's pissed!" Steve said. He had summoned a shield that covered his entire body. Lox and Gurren were on either side with their own shields, while Deia and Suzy used the cover to call down hell upon the Xelur through their minions and spells.

Behind them, a wall of dwarves was followed by lines of DCA forces. The ranged casters waited behind the breach, unleashing their attacks from a safe distance, covering those of the drop forces without putting themselves in danger and thus making them a distraction for these advancing forces that moved forward under their metal shield turtles.

The sides of the dwarves were already in combat, forcing the Xelur backward and away from the breach. The DCA were split up into three groups. Those providing support for the dwarves moved forward and those that were rushing the walls on either side moved to clear out the Xelur that lay within them. Many of them hadn't moved through the breach but had climbed up the outer walls, opening up the wall and entering the different corridors of the inner wall or making it to the battlements and engaging in fighting there.

The air above the dwarven War Clans was filled with the flashing and dazzling light of hundreds of summoned creatures unleashing their attacks upon the Xelur. They focused on single targets. With each Xelur that fell, they grew in power, taking fire away from their dwarven shield bearer masters and onto themselves, protected by the powerful Mana barriers the dwarves used.

Here and there, shields and barriers failed as both sides hurled incredible power at one another.

The players were a calculating group for the most part, but the people of the Stone Raiders had come to think of themselves as people of Emerilia. They knew that they could come back from death. They changed out their gear and put in the stat points that they had earned and then moved for the walls. The biggest threat to those advancing toward the castle was getting hit in the rear and cut off by the Xelur still on the wall.

The Stone Raiders, DCA, and other drop forces of the Terra Alliance rampaged through the walls, paying special attention to the different soul arrays that powered the soul energy shield.

As they fell, the shield weakened and the citadel's impacts struck harder and harder.

"Hold!" Lox planted his shield into the ground. Steve and Gurren did the same. If they advanced any farther, then their sides would be open to the Xelur. They raised their hands to fire Mana bolts at the Xelur. Beams smashed against the Mana barrier that overlaid their shields, not wishing to use their personal barriers as they needed to conserve energy in order to not run out before the battle had been completed.

The dwarven line moved upward. Those behind Party Zero shifted, creating a gap for Party Zero to insert themselves.

"Prepare to move!" Lox called out, looking at the formation. All three pulled their shields from the ground.

"Forward!" Lox called out. Gurren, Lox, and Steve stood as behemoths among the dwarven line but they kept pace with them as they moved forward.

"Show them the power of the Ish'tal clan!" one of the Xelur yelled out. The Xelur rushed forward, many of them being cut down by the ranged attacks but there was too many of them as they hit the dwarven wall.

Lox felt his blood go cold as Grand Demon Lords that had been hiding now sprung forwards, their bodies alight with soul energy as they engaged the dwarven lines.

The shields of the dwarves were shaken. Those behind the shields cried out in pain from the impact of the hits. They barely had time to react when the Xelur Grand Demon Lords hit again and again with savage energy that broke the dwarven shield wall.

Lox looked to Deia. The Dwarves were his people; seeing them being cut up by the Xelur Grand Demon Lords had his heart burning with rage.

The flames around Deia turned into a raging torrent but none of the heat escaped as her bow disappeared from her hands and they went to her swords.

"Stone Raiders to the front!" Deia's call was heard across the citadel.

Stone Raiders among the drop forces, upon hearing Deia's call, knew that she would only call upon them if it was a dire situation and the POEs were being slaughtered indiscriminately. In this case, they knew that their role was to hold back these enemies and give their lives if they must in order to protect their allies and the people of Emerilia.

They surged with power. Those who had been playing it safe surged forward and those who could, burned their Mana and Stamina to finish off their opponents, rushing to Deia's call.

From around the citadel, they converged on Deia. Those with Weapons of Power followed them as they entered the inner wall of the citadel.

"Leave none of them standing!" Deia yelled,

Lox and Gurren let out roars, their shields opening up. Steve tossed his shield back and away, pulling out his war axe as he rushed forward. From behind them, Suzy slammed her staff into the ground. Creations made formed from cores of all six affinities. Ten of the formed creations rushed to follow the rest of her party.

"Stone Raiders!" one called out. The entire guild took up the call as they rushed forward through the dwarven lines that were in shambles, engaging the forces that were tearing into the dwarven shield bearers.

Deia charged forward into the lines. Lox caught a glimpse of her. Any Xelur that came within five feet of her was cut down mercilessly. Her hair looked like flames as it danced behind her; flames moved along her blades and formed into plates of fiery armor.

Her most powerful weapon was never the bow, but her two swords. Lox focused on his own fight. He pushed his power to the maximum, as he tore through the Xelur as if they were nothing but weeds. All of the training made his reactions as fluid as they were brutal.

None that lay in his path were spared.

Steve and Gurren ran beside him. Steve's normally relaxed face was now solemn, his eyes cold. Steve's axe moved in a golden blur of speed and power; with each movement of his axe, Xelur were felled.

A Grand Demon Lord that was among the dwarves, being attacked by the summoned creatures as the dwarves tried to injure him badly enough he couldn't recover, looked back as he felt three powerful auras closing in on him. He laughed and jumped to engage them.

Steve, Lox, and Gurren jumped into the sky. White runes appeared on their bodies as they cut through the air.

The Grand Demon Lord swept down at Steve. Lox and Gurren's speeds increased, their swords coming out like gray ghosts.

The Grand Demon Lord had a look of surprise on his face as he could only lower his arms in order to cover his sides that Lox and Gurren were aiming for. He let out a roar as Lox and Gurren's blades dug deeply into his arms.

"Shut up!" Steve yelled. Power surged through his body. His axe made the very wind shriek as it passed. Lox and Gurren's attacks had made the Grand Demon Lord lower his war hammer so it was just below his chin. Steve suddenly appeared beside the Grand Demon Lord's head. He was in the air so the Grand Demon Lord couldn't do anything to move as Steve's axe flashed across, smashing through the Grand Demon Lord's disrupted soul energy barrier and into his head.

Lox and Gurren landed like two warriors of legend as they landed among the Xelur in front of the dwarves who had been ruthlessly attacked by the Grand Demon Lord.

"Pull the wounded back! Reform the line!" the dwarven leader called out. As the dwarves who had been fighting on the edge of life and death just moments ago listened to these commands, the shield wall reformed. Wounded were pulled back. Stone Raider healers quickly used Health potions to stabilize the wounded as well as potions to knock them out and send them back out of the fighting toward the platforms that were still dropping and rising into the sky, carrying out wounded with every trip.

Steve landed his axe, taking down three Xelur as the Grand Demon landed lifelessly among the ranks of the Xelur. Shocked looks stared at the trio.

Lox and Gurren had trained to the extremes in order to be worthy of the armor that Dave had gifted them. After being able to do nothing but be punching bags for the Grand Demon Lords at the northern castle, they'd worked to raise their strength to where they could suppress a Demon Lord completely and even possibly kill them.

"I see another one!" Lox called out. He didn't feel satisfaction in having killed a Grand Demon Lord; instead, he had moved past it and was already looking for others that had broken the dwarves' lines.

"Let's go!" Gurren said. They cut a path through the Xelur. The dwarves they had saved surged forward, filling the gap left behind them and letting out roars of their own. Their eyes were red with anger and loss at their friends and the knowledge that they had only been saved by the actions of the trio who had come out of nowhere.

Even in their anger, their actions were only more refined, their training taking that anger and turning them into a hellish wall of shield and sword.

***

Jung Lee, Anna, and Dave heard Deia's call. Anna unleashed a series of Air blades that killed anything fifteen feet in front of her as she ran and jumped from the wall and headed toward where Deia was. Dave was already surging ahead, with Jung Lee quickly catching up.

They passed the inner wall, unleashing attacks from above and cutting down the Xelur that were engaged in fighting the different Terra Alliance drop forces that had made it onto the battlements.

All across the Citadel, Stone Raiders as well as the more powerful among the drop forces rushed to Deia's call, knowing that it would only be called if there were incomparably powerful and strong enemies that the forces within the inner walls had found.

Jung Lee could feel the raging torrent of energy that Dave was giving off. Jung Lee's eyes thinned as they crossed the inner wall to look upon the chaos of battle below.

The dwarven lines had been smashed apart in several places and all of the breaches were under attack by the Xelur, who had revealed a great number of Grand Demon Lords.

"We need support! For that, we need to destroy the soul array barrier!" Dave called out on the party chat.

A way point appeared on their maps, highlighting the top of the tower in the castle.

"We take that out and the flying citadels can give us support!" Dave yelled.

"Very well. On our way," Malsour said through the party chat.

Dave, Anna, and Jung Lee fell toward the ground. Their impacts cleared a space for them among the Xelur. They faced outward, their backs facing one another.

Dave held up both his hands. Mana bolts shot out of them, throwing the Xelur backward with each blast.

Jung Lee came out of his crouch. His sword created a gray ribbon in the air, killing those within ten meters. He rushed forward; bodies fell around him as he moved with impossible grace. His , actions seemed feeble and almost lazy, as they focused on looking beautiful instead of being actually used to fight. These thoughts were instantly erased, with every movement of his sword, Xelur were killed as if they were nothing but rotten wood. He moved through those Xelur with a look of apathy on his face, as if his actions didn't touch him.

Using his affinity amplified senses, he could feel that Anna and Dave were no longer holding back. Anna's blade, let out piercing howls that would make one's heart tremble in fear. Her movements were even faster than Jung Lee's. Her sword and body was covered in Air energy, allowing her to break through the air resistance that pooled around her and tried to slow her actions.

"Grand Demon Lord this way!" Jung Lee said as his senses picked one up. He stabbed forward with his blade, clearing a path toward where he felt the energy coming from.

The other two changed their movements so that they followed him.

Around Dave, grenades appeared. He had only used ten or so before at one time, but now there were nearly a hundred. Dave's attacks filled the air with gray smoke and arcane energy discharged from his Mana bolts. His grenades rushed outward, exploding and widening the path that Jung Lee had made from a meter to nearly five. The rippling grenade explosions tore apart the Xelur.

Anna and Jung Lee could only kill those that were within a certain range of them and were limited in the number and speed that they could kill. Dave's creations and abilities were made to kill people at any distance and were effective at any of those ranges.

"Welcome the rain!" Dave yelled out. Pins fell from the sky, like shining raindrops; they were summoned within the soul shield so they couldn't be stopped by it.

Many of them were stopped by the Xelur soul energy, but a few penetrated their tough hide. The runes on them discharged power into the Xelur. Their, soul energy turned chaotic; many sustained heavy injuries while the weaker among them that couldn't regain control of their soul energy exploded as their energy ran rampant.

The rain of pins spread over a one-hundred-meter wide area, but its effects were immediately apparent; tens of Xelur were killed either by the pins or by their allies soul energy turning into mana and exploding.

"Move!" Dave yelled.

Jung Lee's sword cut down Xelur as he rushed forward. Now able to see the Grand Demon Lord ahead, Anna moved to his other side. The two of them automatically adjusted to each other's fighting styles and opened a wider path. Dave followed behind, chugging a Mana recovery potion.

A roar shook the heavens and the ground.

From above, fifteen Dragons led by Malsour passed through the citadel's soul energy shield that now only covered the inner walls of the citadel and was fluctuating wildly.

Xelur soul energy beams attacked the Dragons. Grand Demon Lords made to attack but the Dragons had come in from nowhere. They unleashed their attacks, not on the ground but on the tower of the castle.

The stone exploded outward with the force of the Dragons' attack.

They split into two, attacking the sides of the tower that were already greatly weakened.

An enraged shout came from the top of the tower as five Grand Demon Lords jumped from the tower and unleashed their attacks upon the Dragons. Their soul energy-filled attacks cut through the air and landed on the Dragons. Their Mana barriers were broken through but only three sustained any injuries against their scales.

Malsour let out a cry as his scales revealed a bloody line.

"Watch out, one of them up there is extremely powerful," Malsour said even as the Dragons rushed out of the now distorted soul energy shield.

The tower tilted and then dropped. On top of the tower, a massive totem with glowing runes could be seen. As it shifted, the soul energy shield showed holes where grand working shells made it through, landing on the tower and the castle, opening up the defenses of these structures.

The tower dropped onto a section of the castle, breaking apart and crushing that section of the castle. Dust spread out from where it landed, making it hard to see on the battlefield.

A cheer rose up from the drop forces as the shield completely collapsed. The flying citadel's fire was now unimpeded as it smashed apart the castle. The forces that had been on the walls firing their energy beams down onto the advancing drop forces were now laid bare before the flying citadel's guns.

The five Xelur that had attacked the Dragons now dropped down into the cloud of dust, hidden from view.

Rounds were changed from the purely destructive rounds to the various summoning rounds.

Domes of darkness started to cover the castle. Xelur yelled out as grand soul gem rounds smashed upon the ground, releasing energy pools from which different Affinity spirits and energy constructs were called from, attacking the Xelur with abandon.

The battlefield became even more chaotic, neither side willing to back down, knowing that to pause was to invite death in.

Jung Lee and Anna focused on the Grand Demon Lord ahead. It didn't have time to turn from the DCA it was fighting when Jung Lee rushed forward. His sword cut the Grand Demon Lord's back. Jekoni, who had been within the blade, managing its strength, surged outward, killing off the Grand Demon Lord and making him his own.

Blood gathered around him, creating a whirlwind of blades that shot out at the Xelur, killing dozens as they looked in shock at their Grand Demon Lord that had turned on them.

Jung Lee's power could be rated near the top of Emerilia; when combining his strength with the Affinity spirits, he was a force to be reckoned with.

Jekoni wasn't as strong as Jung Lee, but his knowledge of the arcane, magic, and Mana was much more deep and profound. A creature like the Xelur, which were filled with raw energy that could be converted into Mana, were just asking to be dominated and their power used by Jekoni.

The Stone Raiders gave their lives in order to buy the strongest among them and the people of Emerilia time to react. They, sold their lives dearly, using all the tricks that they knew in order to delay the Xelur Grand Demon Lords.

Those with Weapons of Power moved in groups, engaging the Xelur Grand Demon Lords, wearing them down before landing the final blow that felled the Grand Demon Lords to their knees.

The drop forces roared with anger and power, unleashing their rage as they fought forward. In groups here and there and lines in other places, the Xelur citadel was truly a place of chaos.

Explosions illuminated the sky as beings of energy moved like a swarm, clearing out the area around where their grand working rounds had struck and carved through the Xelur, unfeeling and unflinching as they were attacked again and again by the panicked Xelur.

Jung Lee spared a glance for Dave and Anna. Anna fought like a demoness, her armor covered in blood as air moved around her with deadly grace unleashed upon the Xelur that came within her reach.

Dave was like a war god overlooking the battlefield. With a flick of his fingers, grenades or pins flew out; with a gesture, a shield would snap into existence, covering their allies and stopping a soul energy-powered beam that was coming at them. Attacks flashed at him but he didn't seem to pay them heed.

Xelur rushed toward him in a group. He pulled out a sword but Jung Lee rushed forward, his sword dancing among them.

Dave was good with the sword, but he couldn't approach Jung Lee's mastery, nor did his strengths lie there.

He returned to being the omnipotent war god. While Jung Lee could kill dozens in as many seconds, Dave could kill ten times that number as he used not only his own skills but enhanced them with his creations.

Jung Lee moved forward and called upon his Affinity spirits. They rushed out from Jung Lee and appeared in the air around Dave.

He might be powerful offensively but his defense was lacking as with each attack his shields would have that much less power to draw from.

Jung Lee knew that Dave had pushed his boundaries again and again.

"Time to see what I'm capable of." Jung Lee felt a calmness settle over him. His movements increased in speed but to Jung Lee, it felt as if he was in harmony with the world. His sword moved as if it were no longer a part of his body but a divine beast that he was merely attached to.

To those watching, they would have seen Jung Lee's movements seem blurred as he walked forward with steady steps, their scalps tingling at the slight smile on his lips as Xelur were cut away.

No one, not even Deia, had the ability to fight in this manner. Even with her two swords unleashed, she was only barely stronger than Anna, but Jung Lee's power was in a whole other realm compared to them.

There was always someone stronger, and always someone to look up to.

***

Dwayne looked at the reports coming from the Xelur portal in the Densaou Ring of Fire. He then looked out of his citadel and at the growing earth works that the Jakan had laid down. His expression became dark. With every day, there were more Jakan and they were dug in like a tick.

"Hey, Dwayne, I thought that you might want a hand in negotiations," Josh said over a party chat.

"What are you up to?" Dwayne asked, a smile unconsciously forming on his face.

"Well, I was thinking that eight flying citadels might be a way to get the Jakan to rethink their strategies and see if we might be able to turn them into mercenaries," Josh said.

"Mercenaries?" Dwayne asked.

"We give them the opportunity to fight others that are looking to take this place. We give them transportation and supplies; they go off and destroy them. We reward them with land—kind of how the Nalheim were dealt with," Josh said.

"They fight for honor—what makes you think that they're willing to fight beside us?" Dwayne asked.

"We're fighting on multiple sides. How can we be the stronger force? Also, there are people saying that they are gods and are trying to control Emerilia—it defames their god. We get them to get engaged with the Earth and the Dark Lord— paint Water, Fire, and Air as defenders and fighting avatars. I'd bet that they'd go for it. Also, I have been told that we might not need to deal with these negotiations—we might have some help," Josh said mysteriously.

"Who?" Dwayne frowned, unsure of who might be able to sway the Jakan's hearts.

"Well, warrior avatars, of course," Josh said lightly, leaving Dwayne all the more confused.

Chapter 21: Clan Leader Ish'tal Che

Esa watched the battle that was going on at the western and two southern Xelur-controlled citadels. The fighting was fierce and the lines that the different sides had started out with had dissolved into a wild melee.

The Terra Alliance had the upper hand now as the last soul energy shield at the western citadel collapsed. The other citadels had been using weaker soul arrays in order to keep up their soul energy shield.

The citadels concentrated their fire on the towers and the castle, large grand workings at work as they suppressed the Xelur in those strongholds and toppled the towers onto the castles below.

Esa's eyes flickered to the western citadel's view. Her eyes narrowed as she saw a blur reach out and grab the falling soul shield array from the rubble and pull it into the depths of the citadel. "What the hell are they doing?" Esa pondered.

A new flash filled her vision on a different screen. This one was watching the area between Dwayne's controlled citadels at the Jakan portal.

Flames and water seemed to come together right beside each other before revealing two people: one woman in her prime as well as an elderly and sage-looking man with a long beard. They wore red and blue clothes.

Esa's eyes went wide as she looked upon the Lady of Fire and the Lord of Water.

Silence fell over the command center as all eyes were fixated on two of the Affinities Pantheon members.

They were the undoubted strongest existences on Emerilia and here they were, standing in midair and looking down upon the Jakan, their expressions unreadable.

They glided down toward the Jakan as if not worried in the least by the weapons that the Jakan raised in their direction nor the rushed movements as the Jakan came to full readiness.

Josh said that he had a trump card when talking to the Jakan but Esa had never thought that he would call on two gods to negotiate with the Jakan.

This was well beyond her expectations.

***

Deia paused in her movements; the three Xelur she had sliced through fell to the ground. She had been fighting with her ranged attacks and her bow for so long, keeping back from the battle in order to better command Party Zero or to protect herself when she had been pregnant. She'd been assured that she could escape no matter what but still she stayed in a support role, protected by the others, not willing to risk Koi.

Now Koi was safely in Ice City and there was little use in trying to coordinate Party Zero and the forces within the western Xelur citadel.

She'd pulled out her blades and freely joined the melee; she'd cut through a swathe of Xelur. Now she felt a great energy coming from within the ruins of the citadel's castle.

The rest of Party Zero and the stronger members of the drop forces all looked at the center of the castle, confusion in their eyes.

Whatever it was, it felt as if it were dangerous.

"Party Zero on me!" Deia yelled and moved forward. Her blades, wreathed in blue sheets, cut through a Xelur's sword and then cut them in two. The blue flames condensed around her blades to create physical sheets of flame.

They easily cut through everything in her path. As she moved, flames appeared behind her, looking like Dragons. Their bodies were attached to Deia by a thread of fire but they attacked as if they had their own intelligence, killing any that came near Deia as she forged ahead.

The rest of Party Zero carved a path toward her and the castle that was still being hammered by the flying citadel's grand workings, turning into energy pools for energy-based beings to attack the Xelur and boost the drop forces' combat strength or smashing into the castle, destroying entire sections of the castle and turning them into rubble.

Around the castle, there was an open area where the Xelur had been killed already.

Deia led Party Zero forward.

"I'll clear us a path." Anna rose upward into the sky, a goddess ascending as her eyes flashed with cold white light. Air currents built around her, forming into her Air titan. It was much faster than when she had used this form before and also stronger.

She turned and slashed at the castle. A blade of wind five meters tall and one across slashed into the castle, blowing away walls, debris, Xelur, and anything that lay in its path. It extended through the castle and into the main area that had been underneath the main tower.

Anna unleashed three more attacks. Her attacks left deep grooves in the ground and opened up a path to the center of the castle.

"One battering ram coming up!" Steve charged down the path that Anna had created. Rocks hit him as he charged forward, putting his axe on his back and summoning a shield on his arms. He smashed through everything that lay in his way, making the gap big enough for others to follow.

Gurren, Lox, Jung Lee, and Jekoni in his massive Xelur Grand Demon Lord body all charged forward. Deia followed them, with Suzy right behind her and Anna condensing her Air titan so that it only doubled her size. The circulating air was powerful enough to tear apart anything that came near Anna as she rushed forward.

Steve smashed through the damaged walls and into the central area that had been under the main tower.

"Such impudence!" A voice that made Deia's eyes widen and her body feel as if it had been dunked in cold water reached her ears.

An old multicolored soul energy beam lit up ahead of Steve. It easily pierced Steve's shield, and pierced his chest, a hole right through him.

Gurren and Lox raised their shields and their barriers to full strength. They were right behind Steve and even as they stopped the beam that had gone through Steve, their summoned shields were destroyed and their Mana barriers fluctuated wildly as they were tossed in opposite directions from the strength of the single attack.

The rest of Party Zero rushed into the open area and Deia could finally see their opponents.

There were four Xelur Grand Demon Lords standing in front of a Grand Demon Lord with a raised hand. Their auras and the power rolling off them couldn't be compared to the strength of the Xelur Grand Demon Lords that were fighting outside the castle.

The Grand Demon Lord that had shot Steve, Lox, and Gurren looked over them all with clear disgust in his eyes. "Kill them," he said flippantly before he turned back toward the main soul array that controlled the soul energy shield that had covered the western citadel.

"Yes, Clan Leader!" the other four replied, their eyes focused on Party Zero.

Debris fell from the castle above and rocks had formed a small hill in the center of the area where the tower had been located.

The remains of the tower had served to create a blockage that they couldn't see the sky through.

The soul energy shield array lit up the room, as did a few torches that were strewn around the room. The only other light was provided by Party Zero's Mana, weaponry, and the Xelur Grand Demon Lord's runes that had been carved into their bodies.

They rushed forward; their muscles rippled, supplied with powerful soul energy.

Jung Lee's six Affinity spirits rushed outward, condensing into one creature and then imposing themselves on Jung Lee as his aura surged wildly. He let out a cry and charged forward.

Lox and Gurren picked themselves up and rushed ahead, roaring with anger. Their armor's runes turned a glowing gray, almost silver, as gray vapor trails were left behind by these glowing runes and their summoned weapons.

Dave rose up into the air. Pins and grenades appeared around him as gray streams reached out from his body to the others in Party Zero, strength filling them.

He let out a yell as the Xelur Grand Demon Lords unleashed their soul energy beams. Within his domain, Dave was like a god, as he distorted and broke the Grand Demon Lords' soul beams. He sank slightly, his body being taxed to the limit even as he threw out grenades and pins that rushed at the Grand Demon Lords.

Suzy summoned her six Affinity creations that rose up into the air and unleashed attacks from every Affinity upon the Grand Demon Lords, smashing against their shields, adding to Dave's own attacks and suppressing them. The core of her staff floated above the staff as she used her powerful Summoner's Bastille in order to call upon more summoned creatures.

From around Jekoni, blood rivers split into four streams. Each hammered the Xelur Grand Demon Lords' shields with deep and powerful impacts.

Anna's titan exploded outward, expanding to its normal size. She rushed forward; with each attack, her sword left behind white sword lights that hit the Grand Demon Lords' shields. One-meter long grooves were left where their shields hadn't blocked the attacks that came in a blur.

Deia pulled from her deep reserves. Her armor became thicker and a deeper red color. She looked to the Grand Demon Lords, her eyes alight with power. Her body tensed and then exploded forward as she ignited the air underneath her feet.

She used a movement technique she had come up with herself. Using her own flames to explode around her, it allowed her a greater movement ability which she could move in any direction without needing to push off with her hands or feet.

From behind her, a dozen flame-formed Dragons appeared, their roars reaching the heavens.

Lu Lu added in her own screeches. Her lightning bolts came from the sky and hit a Xelur Grand Demon Lord's shield.

Deia was reminded of that time so long ago at Boran-al's Citadel when she'd gone up against the undead Xelur Demon Lord. The same fear and uncertainty filled her, as did the knowledge that she had to fight.

The Xelur Grand Demon Lords erupted with power, pushing off the attacks for but a moment before they charged forward. Weapons appeared in their hands as they rushed to meet their attackers. Jung Lee, Deia, Anna, Gurren, and Lox directly clashed with them, their movements becoming blurry to others as the sound of weapons smashing against one another filled the room.

Jung Lee was able to suppress the Grand Demon Lord, making Deia look at him in alarm as she and Anna were only able to bring their opponents to a standstill. Attacks smashed back and forth; the air around them turned into a series of shock waves each time their weapons met.

Gurren and Lox worked together, as if they were one body with two heads. The Grand Demon Lord they were fighting reeled from the attacks, unable to fight both of them at the same time. Their combat ability was less than Deia's and Anna's but not by much; combined together, they surpassed both of them and were able to wound the Grand Demon Lord.

Suzy's creations rushed forward to help Gurren, Lox, and Jung Lee. If these Grand Demon Lords could be defeated, then Deia and Anna could get the support that they needed to defeat their opponents.

Dave stood on the ground. The runes across his armor and his body were faded compared to before. Each of his actions was carefully thought- out as pins rotated around him, with spell formations circling them. They were ready to be shot out at any time to deter the Grand Demon Lords and take pressure off Party Zero.

There was no support coming from the outside world as all of the drop forces were engaged with the Xelur in a vicious life-or-death battle.

Deia could feel the aura from the clan leader and the soul array in front of him changing as he continued to move his hands and chant out something. The central totem of the soul shield array fluctuated.

Jung Lee let out a shout, disappearing from where he stood and appearing on the other side of the Xelur Demon he was fighting. Dave's pins had opened up the Xelur; before the Xelur had time to react, Jung Lee was on the other side of him, with blood on his blade.

The Xelur Grand Demon Lord let out a cry as he bled from his thigh. The Xelur's burned soul energy as the vicious wound repaired itself quickly.

Jung Lee dashed in again.

The Xelur was enraged, lashing out at Jung Lee, this ant that had dared to attack him.

Jung Lee seemed almost serene in that moment, as if he wasn't caught up within a battle. His attacks were quick, precise, and powerful. The Grand Demon Lord finished healing his leg but his attacks increased in power. Even as he took on more wounds, none of them were life threatening as he would turn his body to alter the path of Jung Lee's blade at the last moment.

Now Jung Lee and the Xelur Grand Demon Lord were on par for strength and viciousness.

Deia's blade clashed with the broad axe of her opponent; she took a few steps back but her blade left a deep cut in the axe head. With a series of explosions, she darted to the side and then past the Xelur at great speed. Her sword lashed out, impacting the Xelur's protective soul energy.

The Xelur didn't have time to react to the attack physically but his protective soul energy surged, rebuffing Deia's attack. The Xelur had a look of shock on their face as they realized how much soul energy they had burned through in order to stop Deia's attack from connecting with their head. A look of seriousness passed over their face as they attacked. Their attacks were tighter and faster, with a speed that was at odds with their size.

Deia used her explosion movement technique to get out of the range of the Xelur Grand Demon Lord's attacks and dish out a few of her own from range.

Soul-burning black flames rushed from her hands, sticking to the Grand Demon Lord. With a cold look on her face, Deia rushed back in as the Grand Demon Lord fought to try to extinguish the flames that were slowly but steadily eating through his soul energy protection.

Deia's attacks left them no more time to care about the black flames. Her twin swords lashed out again and again. The speed of her attacks and the threat of the black flames that grew up each of her blades made the Grand Demon Lord retreat, a hint of fear in their eyes.

The five Dragons that Deia had pulled into her body in order to utilize that Fire Mana now reappeared—no longer red, but black. They looked at the Grand Demon Lord with hungry eyes before rushing around Deia.

There were too many of them for the Grand Demon Lord to block as the Dragons attacked from every angle, covering him in angry black soul energy-consuming flames.

As normal flames need fuel like wood to burn and a supply of oxygen to combust while producing carbon dioxide, Deia's flames needed Fire Mana to combust, with soul energy as their fuel and the product being wild Mana.

As the Xelur Grand Demon Lord's protective soul energy was being converted by these flames, the wild Mana shot off in different directions. As it interacted with Mana or physical objects, it could be assimilated or it could have a reaction. The Xelur Grand Demon Lord, filled with soul energy that was trying to rebuff the Mana attack, had a bad reaction with it, causing small explosions all around them. As their soul energy protection continued to get weaker and weaker, the Xelur Grand Demon Lord looked at the woman covered in blue armor with her swords covered in black flames fear and a sense of despair filling them.

They had never heard of something that could consume soul energy with such destructive and rapid effects that left them feeling scared to the point of panic.

**

"Well, looks like I'm holey now!" Steve sounded rather displeased as he picked himself up, his body recovering from the hit that had not only torn a hole through him but disrupted his inner workings.

He could only lean his big body against a rock and focus the energy within his body to fix the various runic lines and coding that had been destroyed or corrupted by the clan leader's attack. He looked to the rest of Party Zero, who were caught up in a heated clash with the Grand Demon Lords that the clan leader had sent out.

They moved faster than someone under the Level 100 would be able to possibly follow. For them, they would merely see moving shadows and the clash of blades. Steve saw everything: how Jung Lee was using his skill with the sword to fight on par with the Grand Demon Lord that was using all of his energy without care to increase his strength and speed.

Dave's pins as well as Jekoni's threads of blood darted in to open up the Grand Demon Lord to Jung Lee's attacks.

Deia's opponent was wreathed in black flames that continued to eat at their soul energy protection. If they were to lose that protection for even half a second, then those flames would make it inside the Grand Demon Lord's body and start to consume the soul energy stored within their body. The results could be imagined.

Anna, in her Air titan form, fought the Grand Demon Lord in front of her. Both of them used every bit of their strength and skill to try to find a way to put the other at a disadvantage.

Anna might be at a lower level than Jung Lee but her knowledge over the Air Affinity was higher than the mages who lived on the Per'ush Islands. While Jung Lee had been held in the Six Affinities Temple for centuries, Anna had been fighting people and creatures all across Emerilia for centuries not counting before she'd gone into hibernation. Her fighting skills had reached a much higher level and her level of comprehension and her Air titan's abilities allowed her to fight on par with the Grand Demon Lord.

Gurren and Lox were like rabid dogs in their attacks. They were fast and vicious. Their swords rushed outward and changed lengths, keeping the Grand Demon Lord off-balance. Their shields were like a metal wall, stopping all attacks and working to throw open the Grand Demon Lord's defense.

Suzy's six Affinity creations worked with them, suppressing the Grand Demon Lord that could only roar out in rage as numerous injuries covered their body and their clothes were in shreds with the continuous attacks. Already their strength was half of what it had been as they were unable to lash out with their full strength as Party Zero dominated them.

Steve's gaze was drawn to the clan leader that was still moving his hands and chanting in a low voice, altering the totem in front of him. Its energy had already receded but it seemed as if it were being stored up inside.

Steve felt danger well up from deep within him. With a grunt, he flopped on his front and started to crawl toward the clan leader. "Making me scuff up my armor—you know how long it's going to take to buff that out?" Steve muttered under his breath as he continued to pull himself along the outside of where the battle was happening, lest he be caught up in the powerful arcane and physical shock waves that were emitted with every blow inflicted by both sides.

"Getting too old for this shit." Steve continued to mutter complaints as he dragged himself along.

There was a powerful roar from the side. Gurren and Lox's opponent raised up his hand; a wave of soul energy threw them back as its power receded. It was as if it no longer had any soul energy but a cruel look flashed in its eyes as it moved like a streak of light, hitting Lox. Gurren's blade was there; the Grand Demon Lord continued to hack at Gurren as Lox was pushed back a few steps before he recovered from the blow and rushed forward.

The Grand Demon Lord had used some trick to increase his speed by nearly two times; now Gurren and Lox were on the defense.

Suzy's creations rushed in, once again pressuring the Grand Demon Lord.

Like a beast being annoyed by flies, the Grand Demon Lord lashed out in anger. Being swarmed, it took multiple attacks but they weren't all that strong.

Steve's analytical runes and his eyesight were sharp. "He took down his protective energy in order to attack with all of his speed. Each of those attacks might only be light compared to before, but without that layer of protection, they're actually hitting the Xelur Demon Lord instead of just reducing its soul energy protection," Steve said, his eyes not missing a thing.

"Use the draining runes!" Dave yelled out to Lox and Gurren. Gurren took a hit on his shield, using the momentum to retreat as his sword disappeared and a new one was summoned with different runes. Lox's sword also changed as they lurched forward.

Dave had passed to them the coding that he was using for his pins. With their armor, they simply needed to accept the coding and resummon their swords with it, and they would be carved with the different runes.

The Grand Demon Lord smashed Suzy's creations away. They started to repair themselves as streams of Mana surged into their bodies. Their Endurance was high and their power was good but it couldn't be compared to the power, strength, and abilities that Gurren and Lox could display.

The Grand Demon Lord's eyes lit up as it looked at Suzy and rushed forward.

Lu Lu came out of nowhere and unleashed her most powerful lightning attack that created a stream of blinding light across everyone's eyes.

Steve remained unaffected as he saw the lightning strike the Grand Demon Lord. He had dodged at the last moment, taking the hit on his shoulder and part of his neck instead of in his face. A burn appeared on his body as he shuddered; the lightning made half of his body convulse in shock and pain.

Gurren and Lox caught up with the stunned Grand Demon Lord. Lox's sword was dodged but Gurren's landed.

The Grand Demon Lord let out a cry of pain as blood and a multicolored stream of soul energy was ripped from the Grand Demon Lord, surging up Gurren's sword and into his armor.

Steve laughed. The coding not only opened up the Grand Demon Lord and pulled their soul energy from them, it actually pulled it into Gurren and Lox's bodies.

The creations also caught up, once again pinning the Grand Demon Lord as they clashed and focused on holding the Grand Demon Lord there as Gurren and Lox worked to deplete his strength.

The Grand Demon Lord focused on Lox and Gurren, but he was only one person. There was no way that he could stay vigilant of both their attacks the entire time. He yelled out in pain and again more wounds appeared on his body as Gurren and Lox clashed with the Grand Demon Lord, becoming more and more bold.

Two pins, creating silver lines, hit the Grand Demon Lord. Lox and Gurren, who had been both attacking, adjusted their attacks. Gurren's sword stabbed the Grand Demon Lord in the back as Lox took a hit on his shield. A crater appeared under his feet; his sword darted out and stabbed into the Grand Demon Lord's leg.

Lox rolled away, using the side of the crater to jump to the side as he summoned a new sword. Gurren left his sword in as well, not destroying the conjuration as the two swords were like holes in a dam.

Soul energy spewed forth from the Grand Demon Lord as he cried out in pain. Their Health points dropped quickly. It pulled out the swords; the energy stopped flowing from him at such a speed. The composed Demon Lord was now in a haggard state.

"Die!" Lox yelled out, charging forward. Gurren yelled out his war cry as once again they rushed in. The creations followed them.

The Grand Demon Lord yelled out in anger, punching themselves in the chest.

"Watch out!" Steve yelled.

Gurren and Lox retreated at Steve's words. The air around the Grand Demon Lord seemed to be sucked in toward it before an explosion rippled outward.

Sections of the castle came down from the ceiling as Gurren and Lox were shot backward and smashed through walls of the castle. Sections of the ceiling came down; the fighters had to move and dodge to get away from the attacks.

Jung Lee forced his opponent backward under a large section of the roof that was caving in. They defended against the falling debris as Jung Lee rushed past, leaving a savage cut on the Grand Demon Lord's stomach.

The Free Affinity spirits in his body rushed into the Grand Demon Lord. They separated, becoming six different spirits instead of the combined and balanced spirit that Jung Lee fought with.

The Grand Demon Lord yelled out as blood spewed from one side; on the other, he burned. Roots grew out of his leg; the other turned to rock and broke off. The Grand Demon Lord collapsed as the ravaging energies of the six Affinities tore his body apart from the inside.

With a flick of his hand, all of the six Affinity spirits jumped from the Grand Demon Lord's body and shot toward Jung Lee, entering his body as he rushed toward Deia and the Grand Demon Lord that she was fighting. Gurren pulled himself out of the wall that he had broken through. His, armor broke down more of the wall as he got to his feet.

Steve let out a sigh of relief as Gurren raised his hand. Screens appeared in front of him as he moved through his notifications, increasing his power.

Raising one's power in Emerilia had large drawbacks: they would increase in power, but if it was Vitality, Endurance, and Willpower, those respective attributes would increase but their points would only increase in regeneration—their bars wouldn't just suddenly fill up.

However, when increasing Intelligence and Strength, the person would have a large increase but it would be more taxing on the person and it would be easier for them to fall into Mana and Stamina fatigue.

While Gurren's power surged now, later he would need more time to get used to his abilities and he had a short time in which he could use this new strength without causing more issues to himself and increasing his recovery time.

Suzy's creations rushed the Grand Demon Lord that Anna was fighting. Giving her an opening, her sword rushed forward. The Grand Demon Lord raised their scimitar just a few moments too late. Anna's sword made of Air rushed ahead, pushing the Grand Demon Lord's sword out and away. The blade of air cut through the Grand Demon Lord's protective soul energy and pierced their chest.

The blade only went halfway through the Grand Demon Lord but the power released into the Grand Demon Lord made all of their power explode outward in every direction.

Anna's sword of Air fell apart into ribbons. The Grand Demon Lord fell forward. Its knees thumped on the ground, making it shake from its weight as soul energy poured out from the wound in its chest. Its

Its weapon dropped from his hand onto the ground before they, too, toppled over sideways.

Jung Lee and Deia were able to fight the last Grand Demon Lord together. It condensed all of its soul energy into a dazzling armor over its body.

Anna rushed forward; all of Party Zero attacked the Grand Demon Lord. Pins and grenades rained down on it while the melee types came in from every direction, their attacks cutting that soul energy armor.

It hit a number of Suzy's slower moving creations away, breaking them apart—only to have them recover themselves after a few minutes. Steve had a look of concern on his face as he looked at Suzy's pale face. Using Summoner's Bastille for so long and using so many of her most powerful creations took a heavy toll on her.

Steve continued crawling as he had, regaining some strength in his body as his body was restored rune by rune.

Party Zero were all low on Mana and they had used an incredible amount of Stamina to get to this stage. They tried to conserve their energy as much as possible as they whittled down the last Grand Demon Lord.

There was a black and blue flash as Deia threw her sword. It cut through the air with the sound of an explosion. It landed in the middle of the Grand Demon Lord's back. Black flames from the sword grew rapidly on the inside of the Grand Demon Lord.

It bellowed out in pain but there was no mercy in the eyes of Party Zero as the soul energy within its body started to become wild Mana, speeding up the rate at which its body fell apart. The sword Deia had thrown at it was destroyed under the power of the wild Mana.

Dave threw out one of his conjuration rods. Deia caught it as it turned into a sword identical to the one she'd impaled the Grand Demon Lord with.

Party Zero was tired and hurting but they consumed their Stamina and Mana potions to recover what they had lost. They faced the clan leader. Around the shield array, a number of Xelur runes floated in the air, revolving around it and changing with every passing second.

The clan leader looked from the shield array. The power that rolled off from its body was as strong as three of the Xelur Grand Demon Lords that they had just fought.

None of Party Zero dared to look down on them.

With a roar of complete anger, the Grand Demon Lord raised his hands.

Steve's eyes went wide as he felt the soul energy that was focused in the palm of the clan leader's hands. Soul energy was already ten times more powerful than Mana but this amount made Steve yell out in panic.

"Run!"

Even as he said it, he saw that it was too late.

Dave's hands moved as orbs created a shield in front of Party Zero. From his hands, more orbs continued to fall from his wrists and charge forward.

A soul energy beam that turned the world into a stream of glowing violent colors shot out from the clan leader's hands. A trench was dug in the ground as the castle shook with power with just the passing of the soul energy beam.

It hit the hastily erected orb shield, lasting for less than a second before it smashed through. Dave grunted as more orbs he'd thrown out created another shield; more and more orbs followed them, creating more shields to block the beam, breaking it.

Around the shield, the soul energy cut deep grooves into the ground and hit the already ruined castle.

It caused the remaining section of the castle to blow outward. This beam attack was ten or twenty times more powerful than Anna's slashing attacks to gain entrance to this area underneath the tower.

The castle was blown open; the soul energy beam lost power a few hundred meters out as Dave's shield broke it. The continuous stream of power, cutting deeper into the ground, increased the opening in the side of the castle and destroyed any of the debris that fell from the ceiling.

Shield after shield failed. Dave's hands moved as spell formations appeared in front of him; more and more orbs came from his hands to create rows of shields that were destroyed under the power of this soul energy beam that was no less powerful than the ones that had been used to target the flying citadels.

The beam died away. Sections of the castle came down as the clan leader pulled a massive sword from his back.

Dave's entire body seemed to radiate exhaustion. Orbs still moved in the air, ready to create more shields at a moment's notice.

Steve couldn't see Dave's face as his shoulders moved, as if he were panting.

Steve gritted his teeth. Rocks pinged off his body as he continued forward toward the soul array.

"Still not dead yet? Very well. It seems that you are worthy to be my opponents. My name is Che, leader of the clan Ish'tal. Let's see what you Emerilians are made of!" With these words, a crater appeared under Che's foot. None of his soul energy leaked outward as he rushed Party Zero.

Jung Lee rushed to meet Che. Even with the six Affinity spirits, his attack was smashed to the side, his feet leaving deep grooves in the ground.

Deia cut out with her blades, the black flame Dragons behind her lashing out. Che destroyed the Dragons. His massive blade moved as fast as Deia's two blades, sending her in another direction. The soul energy-consuming flames tore at his soul energy protection but it didn't stick as he made an annoyed sound and it was expelled.

He made to attack Deia, who had annoyed him with her flames, when Anna's titan form appeared next to him.

Che dodged the first few attacks, regaining his footing and fighting back. Lox and Gurren joined the fight. Che cut Gurren's armor's shoulders and forced him back. Jung Lee raced in and replaced them.

Once again, Suzy called upon her power as more of her creations rose to meet Che. They were smashed constantly but Che had to split his attention to deal with them even as he sent them back, trailing Mana that repeatedly tried to rebuild them time after time.

Jung Lee pressured Che, only to be rebuffed, and Che lashed out with the momentum of defending against Jung Lee's attack to smash against Anna's titan. Screeching, noises filled the inside of the castle as Deia charged in. Anna recovered her titan body while Deia's swords were blocked by Che.

Their speed and coordination had reached the apex as they sensed as soon as the other was in danger and targeted areas that would allow the others openings.

Dave was recovering as fast as possible, drinking Mana potions and holding back his attacks. His movements made it look as if he were almost drunk from the repeated Mana consumption and fatigue the entire day.

Suzy's creations, Lu Lu's lightning, Deia's flaming swords, Anna's Air titan, Lox, Gurren, and Jung Lee's gray smoking swords: all of them flashed through the air, hitting Che again and again. They battered him into a position where he could only react; to be able to keep them all off at once showed just how powerful his techniques and abilities had reached.

With each hit, a section of the castle was torn apart and a crater deepened around Che, creating a sort of arena in the midst of the castle.

Steve continued to crawl. Feeling danger from the Xelur runes he saw moving around the soul array, his mind was running analytics on it against his knowledge. The magical coding that was being repaired made any assessment sluggish.

"It seems you Emerilians are stronger than I thought!" Che yelled out. Power surged from him, creating a shock wave of soul energy. He lashed out at Party Zero. His sword slashed at Deia. She was able to shift the angle of the sword but it was too strong and powerful; a deep line streaked across her collarbone. Her Abscondita armor stopped the blow from actually hitting her, but the kinetic energy tossed her back as Jung Lee dodged away from a vicious kick. Lox blocked a fist with his shield that dented inward before dissolving; a new one was conjured just a moment later as Che's blade hit Anna's titan once again. That screeching noise as the Air blades of the Air titan met up with the sword made everyone's ears flinch in pain.

Jekoni called upon his sea of blood once again and attacked Che from several directions.

He jumped free of his encirclement and slapped the blood-formed snakes away, breaking their spell constructs. He was breathing heavy as he and Party Zero stared at one another.

A cold smile passed over his face as he looked at them. "You might've killed my elders and destroyed my citadels here, but you have only invited your own death!" Che laughed and jumped into the air, facing toward the portal at the center of the citadels.

"Down!" Malsour's voice echoed through the heavens as a spell formation appeared above Che.

Che was thrown down to the ground as the gravity greatly increased on him. He smashed into the ground. A crater formed around him, the strength of Malsour's spell formation too strong to allow Che to move.

Steve saw that the runes had finally stopped moving around the soul array. All of his processes were focused on figuring out what it meant.

"Looks like you've been learning something from my gravity manipulation," Dave said in a tired tone as Malsour glided in. His claws rested on a part of the castle that hadn't collapsed. His weight made part of what he was standing on crumble away; he had to adjust his claws to remain upright.

"Seems that you're all all right," Malsour said in a conversational tone as a four-meter-long metal spear with runes carved on it dropped from the heavens. It passed through the gravity spell formation, multiplying its speed.

Che let out an enraged howl, actually able to raise himself, moving slightly.

Malsour frowned and increased the power of the spell formation as the created spear smashed into Che's stomach instead of heart. The blow wasn't what damaged him the most but the runes along the pillar that pulled that energy and sent it to the Stone Raiders' soul gems that they kept on them.

Che, with blood running from the corner of his mouth, coughed wetly as the gravity rune was released, the spear still in his gut. "Seems that today I will not be leaving, but then, neither will you," Che said with some madness in his eyes.

"It's a bomb!" Steve yelled out. Fear ran through him as he saw the lack of time that he had in order to do anything.

The soul array exploded outward, expelling all of its energy in one blast that tore apart its very structure.

Jekoni, who was closest to the soul array, turned and let out a yell.

Jung Lee's sword flashed brightly with power.

Jekoni's Grand Demon Lord body was destroyed, all of its energy barely able to restrain the energy of the soul array's explosion.

Shields smashed into the explosion, containing it and driving it upward, but these shields continued to be destroyed.

Jekoni glanced back at Party Zero as that power raged against the shields.

Steve saw the small, kind smile on the edge of Jekoni's lips.

An imaginary staff appeared in his hands as his hat stood proud on his head. His mage's cloak fluttered as magical runes making up his spectral body glowed with power.

Steve watched in awe as Jekoni embodied the archmage of legend.

The shields failed and the power surged outward again.

Dave collapsed on the ground. His body had gone past Mana fatigue.

Jekoni let out an angered yell, his body submerged into that vortex of soul energy.

Steve could see Jekoni, his robes whipping around him as massive powerful spell formations appeared around him. The energy was focused upward and away from Party Zero.

Steve knew that Jekoni couldn't stop all of that energy. His analytical mind was over overclocked, giving him the cold hard facts of what was happening in front of him.

Lox and Gurren charged forward and Steve hurled himself forward. The three of them entered that energy beam, their armor and, in Steve's case, body, acting as massive magical conduits to change the direction of the power.

Suzy, Deia, Jung Lee, and Anna rushed forward.

The raging air threw all of them back but Anna's titan reduced in size and power as the soul array's energy climbed once again as the stored energy was continuously broken through.

Steve saw Anna pushing forward, his eyes filled with fear. As much as they had joked around and dodged their relationship, Steve knew that without Anna he would not exist. She hadn't been forceful but at moments he had felt that almost motherly feeling coming from her.

Anna saw his face and smiled. She entered the soul energy beam that was shooting hundreds of meters into the sky.

As soon as she stepped into that energy, it rushed through her body. The spell formations Jekoni had made with Steve, Lox, and Gurren's assistance allowed the power to surge upward.

The rest of Party Zero struggled forward. Even Dave, when he regained his consciousness, hauled himself to his feet. His hood fell down, showing his pale face and the grim look of determination underneath.

They stepped into that beam of energy, firming up their control and directing it upward. Each of them stepped forward without pause or regret on their features. With all of them, the power started to become more manageable.

Their bodies glowed with power, their eyes shimmering with power. All of them worked together to share the burden. Jekoni, who had stepped into it first, had taken the brunt of the soul energy.

"Seems I will be going ahead first. Look after my mage's guild and college and see that Emerilia survives. These few months have been some of the best in my life." Jekoni smiled at them all, his face at peace as his body faded away. The control over the soul array surged, relieving the pressure from the rest of Party Zero.

Lox and Gurren's armor overloaded from the energy and ejected them out of the beam. They rolled on the ground, their energy drained.

Steve stepped forward. With each step, the power running through his circuits was more powerful and savage. He eliminated any of the extra circuitry just to route the power until he got to the center. His armor was being ripped off as his soul gem construct body was battered and wrecked by the energies that assaulted him.

He stood in the center of the formation and placed his hand on the soul array, directing the power through his body and reducing the stresses on the others.

He felt a hand in his already badly damaged hands. He looked over, finding Anna with a metallic look in her eyes.

She had been created from the merger of a wolfkin body and the monitoring AI of Emerilia that Bob had created. He saw in those eyes that she understood what was going to happen.

The soul array couldn't be contained by all of them, but if the two of them were to use all of their energies, then the others could survive.

Emotions that Steve didn't know were there moved within him.

"Look after them." Anna's voice passed through the destructive energies of the soul array. With that, her head snapped upward; the beam condensed and shot upward, reaching to a height level with the citadels.

Magical Circuits aligned around the citadels and suppressing grand working spells worked, tearing apart that beam of energy.

All eyes were focused on that beam of energy and the members of Party Zero who stood within that beam of destructive energy, the energy enough to make those looking at it tremble with fear.

Steve's mind was slowly being erased away as his Magical Circuits were destroyed. The central power directing magical code within his body became larger and stronger to try to contain the massive amount of power that ran through him.

His body shut down, his eyes on Anna as her hand reached up to the necklace she wore as soul energy started to tear at the very fabric of her body. A small but sad smile was on her lips as she held that necklace.

Chapter 22: Victories and Losses

The Lady of Fire and her brother the Lord of Water descended from the sky like the gods that they were supposed to be.

The Jakan, thinking that it was an attack, used their ranged attacks against the two of them. The ranged attacks slammed into a barrier of water and fire that appeared only as the different attacks landed.

"Well, they certainly like to fight," Water said, not sounding too pleased. He had been called from the ice planet, where he'd been able to use his powers to the limit and without the ability to fall back on his divine wells. He'd not only worked at his full power but his knowledge had been greatly increased as he came to understand the different things that the Pandora's Box Initiative was working on.

His eyes held a cold light to them as he looked at the Jakan. He didn't care for them; , if they could become allies, then Water was ready to show his powers. With the information he had come to know and understand, he knew the threat that the Jukal were. These Jakan were just taking up time and resources that could be put to better use with the Pandora's Box Initiative.

All of the petty fighting within the Pantheon seemed to be ridiculous now that his eyes were open. He knew that no matter what, the others in the Affinities Pantheon wouldn't give up their struggles, no matter what evidence that he, Fire, or Air brought to the table. Their rivalries and their anger were too great to be swayed anymore.

Water and Fire floated over the Jakan's defenses. Their strongest attacks did not affect them in the slightest as they floated over the citadel's walls and headed over the inner walls toward the central castle.

"You must be the commander of the Jakan forces. We've come to discuss your future campaigns." Fire walked into the command center. The Jakan all looked at the two of them with slack jaws.

"I think by now you should understand that with your weapons and abilities, it would be extremely hard for you to kill us?" Water asked in an annoyed tone.

"Sorry about him—he's a bit grumpy that he got taken away from his various tests." Fire smiled and took a seat. "Never thought that you would get so wrapped up in theories and testing."

"What can I say? Your people at the mage's college opened my eyes," Water said, a slight smile on his lips. He wouldn't be able to express the joy he had come to find with working with magic and the excitement of working on new magical theories that had been opened up to him by Fire's mage's college.

"Who are you?" the Jakan commander demanded, his voice becoming more firm.

"I am Water, and she is Fire." Water pulled out a book and started to read it.

"The so-called *gods* of this planet," the commander spat.

"Some people say that. I personally don't— just a gal with the ability to burn your little citadel down and I'm getting mighty pissed off with all of you people attacking us. I swear, there's no honor in this world anymore. People just ganging up on one group, saying that they want a fair fight but instead suppressing us in every direction and calling it fair." Fire shook her head.

Water shot a disgusted look at the Jakan, who were taking on ugly expressions. Water went back to his book. Even as he frowned, inside he felt a smile coming on.

The Jakan were a race that thought of fighting as a holy thing, complete with rituals and conditions. If these conditions were not met, then it would not be a battle that their god believed in.

Emerilia was being attacked on every side by multiple people, not allowing them to bring their most powerful forces to bear. This wouldn't make it an honorable battle, but if Fire could plant the idea for them to fight these other enemies and that they, Emerilia, and their people would stay out of the fight—or at least the Terra Alliance would—then they would be able to deal with two birds with but one stone.

***

Air and her people had spent a large amount of time trying to look over all the possible contingencies that they would need to deal with when the players started to wake up in Ice City.

Now all of them were looking at what was being called an implantation laboratory. It was the first of its kind, with a total of seven cloning laboratories that were working nonstop to create the bodies of the players who were within the server farms at the north and south poles of Emerilia.

Bob was at the controls, looking over the whole procedure. With this, they would be destroying the player's brain in order to code it to the cloned body. At the same time, Jeeves's program would insert an AI-controlled program that would replace them within their Earth simulation in order to make sure that the simulation's AI wouldn't be able to detect anything amiss.

The runes around the player's body glowed, Mana thick in the air as everyone's eyes were on the player.

Bob's eyes were fixed on a series of complicated-looking medical screens.

After a few hours, the glow around the body dimmed. Bob's eyes moved from screen to screen. Silence fell over the room as different people checked out different status screens.

"We did it!" Bob yelled, a smile on his face. "We're going to have to wait for them to wake up to see just what everything is like for them and to check their condition. Though all of the readings I'm getting show that they're healthy and good to go!"

It was like a dam had burst as everyone cheered and yelled out in excitement.

Air smiled and looked to Venfik. He nodded to her; halfway through the motion, he suddenly stopped and frowned as he looked over to Bob.

Air also looked over, seeing Bob's face turn from joy to sorrow in a moment. The look on his face pulled at Air's heartstrings.

***

The Lady of Light sat up from her chair and looked to Khanundra.

Her hall was more bright and refined than ever with the power of all Markolm coming in and more people joining in, giving their devotions to the Lady of Light that protected them from the war that was happening across Emerilia.

Many of them had turned fanatical with the turn of events, something that Light had grown and worked on.

"Khanundra, go retrieve them," Light said. With a wave of her hand, Khanundra disappeared from the hall as Light looked to Daeundra.

"Seal Markolm. Only the followers must be allowed in. The Legions of Light have returned." A cold light flashed in Light's eyes as a cruel smile formed on her face.

Daeundra disappeared in a flash.

Light used her pool to look at the location where she had felt a large outpouring of energy and devotions to her. She looked at the air above Heval where formations of angels appeared one after another. The air filled with their golden armor and weapons as they looked at Emerilia.

Their cold faces seemed to deem everything as trash within their eyes. As Khanundra appeared, they all kneeled. Those who appeared afterward also dropped to a knee in mid-air, their wings flapping behind them to keep them aloft but on a lower level than Khanundra.

She issued orders. The Legions of Light, formed from Light's own angels, formed together, waiting until no more formations appeared in midair.

Khanundra turned and shot off across the sky. A flood of golden light followed her.

"The time for my rise and the destruction of the Pantheon has come," Light said, a pleased smile on her face.

Emerilia will be continued in The Pantheon Moves.

As a self published author I live for reviews! If you've enjoyed Emerilia, please leave a review!

Hope you have a great Day! ☺

Want a bigger map of Emerilia and the continents? Check out **http://theeternalwriter.deviantart.com/**

You can check out my other books, what I'm working on and upcoming releases through the following means:

Website: **http://michaelchatfield.com/**

Twitter: **@chatfieldsbooks**[1]

Facebook: **Michael Chatfield**[2]

Goodreads: **Goodreads.com/michaelchatfield**[3]

Thanks again for reading! ☺

Interested in more LitRPG? Check out **https://www.facebook.com/groups/LitRPGsociety/**

Continue on for Character Sheet!

---

1.   https://twitter.com/chatfieldsbooks

2.   https://www.facebook.com/michaelchatfieldsbooks/?ref=hl

3.   https://www.goodreads.com/author/show/14055550.Michael_Chatfield

In Alphabetical order
Ankol

Dwarf
  Dwarven Master Smith. Smithing Art: Metal Spinner. Lives in Grorart Mountain.

Boran-Al

Lich

One of the Dark Lord's Champions. Works directly under the Dark Lord. Creates Creatures of Power and carry's out the Dark Lord's orders. His Citadel was destroyed.

Alastair Montgoa

Arch Lich aka former Lord Vailyn. Gave up his fellow Aleph to have everlasting life; used the centuries to build strength and knowledge

Barry

Dwarf

  Dwarven Master Smith. Smithing Art-Unknown. Wandering
smith.

Cassie

Elf/Human Halfling

Holy warrior. Leader of the Golden Sabres. In a relationship with Josh Giles.

Dark Lord

God

    Embodiment of the Dark affinity. Created Demons. Normally an ally with the Earth Lord. Always looking a way to tip the power balance of Emerilia in his favor.

Dasano

Dwarf

    Dwarven Master Smith. Smithing Art: Metal Press. Lives in Grorart Mountain.

Akatol Dracul

Dragon

   Water Mage. Was the second Dragon, Denur's husband. Went mad and started a genocide, disappeared.

Denur Dracul

Dragon

Fire Mage Hailed as 'Mother of Dragons'. First of her race, a creature of power created by the Lady of Fire. Seen as her daughter. Sister to Oson' Deia.

Gelimah Dracul

Dragon
  Dark Mage. Brother to Induca, Louna and Malsour

Fornau Dracul

Dragon

Earth Mage. Quindar's mate Malsour and Induca's grand-nephew.

Induca Dracul

Dragon

Fire Mage. One of the youngest from the first generation of Dragons. Sister to Malsour, daughter of Denur, aunt to Quindar, great aunt to Fornau. Member of the Stone Raiders and Party Zero.

Kinal Dracul

Dragon

Louna Dracul

Dragon
    Induca, Gelimah and Malsour's sister.

Malsour Dracul

Dragon

Dark Mage. One of the oldest Dragons in existence, first born of Denur. Deia and Induca's Guardian, Stone Raider and Party Zero member. Brother to Induca. Great Uncle to Fornau Dracul and Uncle to Quindar Dracul.

Quindar Dracul

Dragon
    Wind Mage, wife to Fornau, Niece to Induca and Malsour.

Wokui Dracul

Dragon
> Water Mage

Xednai Dracul

Dragon

One of the first Dragons, had several Dragons. Her son is Fornau.

Gorpal Dunsk

Dwarf

Dwarven Master Smith, lives in Aldamire Mountain, created 3 Weapons of Power - Mace of Fury, Tower Shield, Boots of Smash. Smithing Art: Paint Copy

Earth Lord

God
   Embodiment of the Dark affinity. Created Earth Sprites.

Edmur

Dwarf

Dwarven Master Smith. Had been in the Dwarven War Bands as a Shield Bearer. Former pupil of Quino's Brother to Endur. Smithing Art: Metal's Song

Edwards

Human. Military scientist within the Deq'ual System. Friend of
Sato's

Edwin

Beast Kin. Beast Kin representative on ruling council.

Endur

Dwarf

Dwarven Master Smith. Had been in the Dwarven War Bands as a Shield Bearer. Former pupil of Quino's, brother to Edmur, lives in Zolu Mountain. Smithing Art Hammer Blows

Esa

Human

Melee fighter. Member of Mikal and Jule's party. Fought at Boranl-Al's Citadel.

Member of the Stone Raiders. Going out with Jules. Works under Dwayne as a fighter. Being trained for a leadership position under Dwayne.

Lord Esamael

Human.
    Lord of Emaren within the Gudalo Kingdom.

Ela-Gal

High Elf.

Warrior living in Aleph, married to Ela'Dorn. Persectued by high elves as heretic.

Ela-Dorn

Orc.

Researcher and professor at Aleph College. Aleph Council •
Member. Married to Ela-Gal

Fend

Dwarf
  Lord Under the Mithsia Mountains.

Geswald

Human.
 Trader's Guild Chapter head in Emaren.

David Grahslagg

Dwarf/Human Halfling, in-game character of Austin Zane. Dwarven Master Smith, Resident of Cliff Hill, member of Party Zero and the Stone Raider's Guild. Other names: Austin Zane

Josh Giles

Human

Rogue. Leader of the Stone Raiders. Was a investment broker on Earth, became an E-head. In a relationship with Cassie from the Golden Sabres.

Gimel

Human
   Warrior.
   Fellox Guild Master.

Gorrund

Dwarf

Dwarven Master Smith in Benvari Mountain with Jesal, teaching four apprentices. Smithing Art: Blood Bender.

Goula

Demon
    On the Ruling council for Devil's Crater.

Gurren

Dwarf

Shield bearer, member of Dwarven War Band under Lox's command, sent to guide people to Cliff-Hill. Friend of David Grahslagg, Kol's Grandson. Member of the Stone Raiders.

Helick

Dwarf
  Dwarven Master Smith.

Kim Isdola

Human
    Cleric/alchemist. Lieutenant in Stone Raiders.

Ishox

Demon
  On the Ruling council for Devil's Crater.

Arch-Mage Jekoni

Human/item

Soul bound to Staff of Growing, over 2,000 years old; missing legs. Held within Dwarven Vaults with other Weapons of power.

Jeeves

AI

Made by Bob to assist the Dwarven Master Smiths.

Jeremy

Human
  Fellox Guild member.

Jesal

Dwarf

Dwarven Master Smith, Dave's master smith trainer. Smithing art: Nature's Guide

Jules

Human

Healer. Member of Mikal and Esa's party. Fought at Boranl-Al's Citadel.

Member of the Stone Raiders. Used to be an army medic, E-head without legs IRL. Going out with Esa. Works under Lucy as support, leads the healers of the Stone Raiders.

Joko

Dwarf

Shield bearer, member of Dwarven War Band under Lox's command, sent to guide people to Cliff-Hill. Friend and trainer of David Grahslagg.

Deceased.

Anna'Kal

Wolf Beast Kin/Administrator AI24681

Air mage. Originally a program meant to assist Lo'kal with the running of Emerilia. Anna was uploaded to a Player body and inserted into Emerilia. She became emotionally attached with her charges. When the Beast Kin people were wiped out from Emerilia she went into cold storage, waiting for her father to awake her when a chance came to fight against the prison they had created.

Member of the Stone Raiders and Party Zero. Daughter of Bob.

Lo'kal

Jukal

Scientist, created Emerilia. Awarded the position of the Gray God, maintains Emerilia, its people and Players. Other names: Bob, Bobby McMahnon, The Balancer, Gray God.

Kino

Demon
  On the Ruling Council for Devil's Crater.

Kol

Dwarf

Dwarven Master Smith. Gurren's grandfather. Resides in Cliff-Hill. Taught Dave how to Smith. Runs his Smithies. Smithing art: Blind Man's Touch

Lady of Air

Goddess

Embodiment of the affinity Air. Known for causing mischief. Her Champions act as spies and information brokers, tilting the balance of Emerilia.

Lady of Fire

Goddess

Created Dragons, Mages Guild and College. Gave gift of 'knowledge' to the people of Emerilia. Mother to Deia, Lover of Oson'Mal and best friend with Bob.

Other Names: Ignil

Lady of Light

Goddess

Sent Players to kill/capture Dragons to make her own Creatures of Power. Created the race known as Angels. Large rivalry with the Dark Lord.

Lena

Demon
   On the Ruling Council of Devil's Crater. Wife to Vrexu.

Lovan

Dwarf
  Mithsia Mountain War Clan leader

Lox

Dwarf

Shield bearer. Was the commander of the War Band sent to guide people to Cliff-Hill. Friend of David Grahslagg. Member of the Stone Raiders.

Suzy Markell

Human (IRL)

High Elf (Emerilia)

Austin Zane's secretary and best friend. David Grahslagg's best friend and assistant with running Cliff Hill Smithy and Factory. Summoning Mage. Steven's contractor, member of Party Zero and the Stone Raiders.

Max

Dwarf

Shield bearer, member of Dwarven War Band under Lox's command, sent to guide people to Cliff-Hill. Friend of David Grahslagg.

Deceased.

Meda

Dwarf/Elf

Aleph Council member. Deals with the food within Aleph cities and facilities

Melanie

Human
    Arch Mage Alamos' Wife.

Melhoun

Water snake made by the Water Lord.
   Sealed away.

Mikal

Human

Rogue. Jules and Esa's party member. Member of the Stone Raiders. Friends with Party Zero.

Oson'Deia

Elf/Demi God Halfling

Elven Ranger and Fire Mage. Daughter of Oson'Mal and Lady Fire of the Affinity Pantheon. Resident of Cliff Hill and member of the Stone Raider's Guild, Leader of Party Zero.

Other names: Ouluv'Deia

Penelope

Human
    Fellox Guild member.

Pete

Human
  Geswald's secretary.

Queen Farun

High Elf
   Queen of Raolor.

Queen Mendari Selhi

Human
    Queen of Selhi.

Quino

Dwarf

Dwarven Master Smith, lives in Zolu Mountain. Trained the brothers Endur and Edmur. Smithing Art: Internal cutting.

Rola

Dwarf

Dwarven Master Smith. Smithing Art Puppeteer. Lives in Aldamire Mountain.

Sato/Communications officer Sato

Human

Lives in De'qual system.

Communications Officer, becomes Vice commander of
Deq'ual military forces. Grandfather original settler.

Emperor Talis

Human.

Ruler of the Xeugrera Empire, located in the Ashal Continent.

Tounk

Dwarf

Shield bearer, member of Dwarven War Band under Lox's command, sent to guide people to Cliff-Hill. Friend of David Grahslagg.

Deceased.
Demon Prince Alkao/Alkao Travezar

Aerial Demon

Melee fighter. Commander of the Third Demon Horde and leader of Xerzit lands. Oldest of the five remaining Demon Prince's of Devil's Crater.

Dwayne Trebault

Human

Melee fighter. Lieutenant in Stone Raiders. Leads and trains the melee fighters in the Stone Raiders.

Venfik

Elf
  Lady Air's advisor.

Lucy Vernia

Wood Elf/Human

Lieutenant in Stone Raiders. Spy master, deals with supporting the Stone Raiders and paperwork.

Vrexu

Demon

One of the seven Demon Princes. General in the Devil's Crater Army. Married to Lena, the youngest of the five remaining Demon Princes.

Water Lord

God

Embodiment of the Water Affinity. Created the Mer-People and water creatures. Created the Water Serpent Melhoun. Rival to the Lady of Fire.

Austin Zane

CEO of Rock Breaker's Corporation. Engineer specializing in space vehicles. Background in Astro physics. Other names: David Grahslagg

Wis'Zel

Wood Elf

Bard. Works for David Grahslagg, managing his Ceramics factories in Cliff Hill.